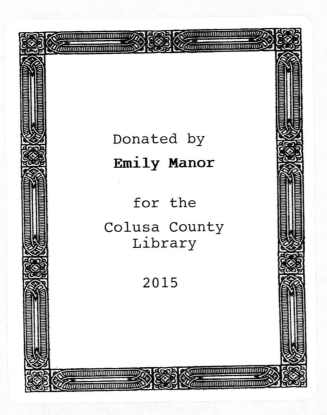

Donated by
**Emily Manor**

for the
Colusa County
Library

2015

# CHILD OF MINE

## BOOKS BY DAVID LEWIS

Child Of Mine*
Sanctuary*
Coming Home
Saving Alice
*with Beverly Lewis

## BOOKS BY BEVERLY LEWIS

**Home To Hickory Hollow**
The Fiddler
The Bridesmaid
The Guardian
The Secret Keeper
The Last Bride

**The Rose Trilogy**
The Thorn
The Judgment
The Mercy

**Abram's Daughters**
The Covenant
The Betrayal
The Sacrifice
The Prodigal
The Revelation

The Beverly Lewis Amish Heritage Cookbook

**www.beverlylewis.com**

# DAVID & BEVERLY
# LEWIS

## CHILD OF MINE

DOUBLEDAY LARGE PRINT HOME LIBRARY EDITION

BETHANYHOUSE
a division of Baker Publishing Group
Minneapolis, Minnesota

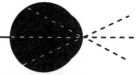

**This Large Print Book carries the
Seal of Approval of N.A.V.H.**

To our dear Shari Bieber

# Chapter 1

Kelly Maines sat nervously on a bench at the edge of the playground, wearing dark aviators and pretending to be obsessed with her cell phone. Last night she'd slept in an unfamiliar bed in a ratty hotel, and this morning she'd dressed in a blond wig and a stylish knit maternity dress. Burgundy was not a good color for Kelly, but it was an important color for today.

Ten yards away eight-year-old Sydney Moore was full of **joie de vivre**. The petite girl wore a set of red hairpins to match her top and designer blue jeans. She ricocheted about the playground with a dozen other squealing kids—sliding and swinging, scaling the plastic boulder, and teetering on the totter.

**She's beautiful**, thought Kelly, observing

the exuberant little brunette. From the very minute Sydney had arrived at the park, Kelly had been studying her intently. She noted the way the child sometimes clomped about after zipping down the slide, the charming way she ran with hands out-stretched, overly cautious, how she jumped like a jumping bean on the padded wood chips, giggling all the while. Sydney's brown hair glistened in the sunlight, com-plemented by the tanned hue of her skin and heightened further by her expressive brown eyes. And those **freckles**, the ador-able spots around her cheeks and forehead.

**Like mine at that age**, Kelly mused.

Despite the gloomy weather report, it was a glorious spring afternoon in Malibu, California, with sunlight flickering through filmy clouds. The playground at the edge of the bluff overlooking Zuma Beach, not far from Sydney's Juan Cabrillo Elementary School, was lined with lush California trees—exotic for a lifelong Ohioan—and the salty air felt fresh. The remaining land-scape looked dry and scrubby, unre-deemed by a scattering of blue and yellow wild flowers near the park's perimeter.

Kelly checked her phone: four-twenty. According to Ernie's reports, Sydney's adoptive mother ruled by a strict routine, rarely allowing her daughter more than thirty minutes at any one location. Since they'd already been here for nearly twenty, Kelly figured that time was running out.

She anticipated her first move, shivering as visions of what could go wrong flipped through her imagination like a row of dominoes. It had been nearly four weeks since her last encounter, a mere month, though long enough to feel rusty.

Deborah Moore, a round-faced blonde, looked nothing like Sydney. She wore strappy sandals and a flowery blue sundress and was sitting on the park bench a few yards from Kelly, focused on her own cell phone. Born to the upper crust, Deborah Sills had married Jeffrey Moore, a young man destined to join his father, William, who headed up a billion-dollar exporting firm out of Los Angeles. A family of three, they employed a full-time staff of five for their eight-million-dollar Malibu Beach estate overlooking Zuma Beach and the ocean beyond.

Due to their exorbitant wealth, Deborah and Sydney never left their home without the security services of Bruce Stiles, a muscle-bound thug in tight-fitting jeans, a purple silk shirt, and a leather jacket. Hidden behind his own dark designer sunglasses, he was presently sitting across the park pretending disinterest, though he couldn't have been more obvious. Perhaps that was his intention. **Intimidation.** If so, it was working.

Feigning difficulty, Kelly pushed herself up with one arm, supporting her stomach with the other. She headed to Deborah's bench, shaded by a palm tree, and grabbed the back of the wooden slats, exhaling with an exaggerated sigh. "Whew, it's warm in the sun."

Deborah barely noticed her.

"Mind if I share the bench?" Kelly asked, sitting down.

Deborah flashed an obliging smile while Kelly arched her face into the sunlight. Should she say something more? Already,

Kelly felt Bruce's eyes on her, decoding her mannerisms and scrutinizing her behavior for tells.

A few minutes passed before Deborah looked her way and then did a double take. "I **love** that color."

Kelly smiled. **I know you do.** She smoothed her skirt. "Me too."

"Are you close to your due date?"

"Any moment." Kelly grimaced suddenly, touching her rounded belly.

Deborah slipped her phone into her purse and studied Kelly with newfound interest.

**Gotcha**, Kelly thought.

She glanced toward Sydney across the playground. "Was it difficult for you?"

Deborah shrugged, apparently unwilling to admit she'd never given birth.

"The way I feel today," Kelly replied, "this might be my first **and** my last."

Deborah only smiled, and for the next few minutes they talked about raising babies. All the while, Kelly pretended not to notice Bruce's edging closer and closer. If she gave any hint of recognizing his function in Deborah's life, he'd surely become even more suspicious of her.

Despite her rising anxiety, Kelly proceeded with her plan, skillfully leading Deborah through her carefully prepared trap door: Kelly's one-time supposed profession as a magician's assistant. As hokey as that might have seemed, it always worked.

Perhaps Kelly resembled most people's image of a magician's assistant. Or maybe the juxtaposition of a very pregnant woman as a once skimpily clad assistant was too bizarre not to be believed.

"What was that like?" Deborah asked, clearly amused.

"Actually, I got tired of being sawed in half."

Deborah laughed.

"At least I learned some magic myself," Kelly replied. "Card tricks, how to make quarters disappear—you know, that sort of thing."

When Deborah's eyebrows rose, Kelly made a show of digging through her purse.

"Wait. I have one," Deborah said,

reaching into her own purse, her eyes rapt with anticipation. She picked out a quarter and gave it to Kelly.

Bruce's lips froze in a scowl. He stepped a few yards closer. Any nearer and he would be breathing down their collective necks. Kelly could imagine his wolflike eyes behind the shades, glaring at her, ready to pounce at the first sign of trouble.

Kelly maneuvered the quarter between her fingers, back and forth, back and forth—a trick that had taken six months to learn. Then...voila! She promptly made it disappear. She held up her hands, twisting them in the sun, showing her palms and the back of her hand.

Deborah's eyes grew wider. "Nice."

Next, Kelly reached behind Deborah's ear and produced the quarter—to her amazement. Kelly offered the coin to Deborah, who refused. "My little girl would **love** this trick."

Deborah called to her daughter, standing in the shadow of the boulder, sharing conspiratorial whispers with her friends.

"Coming, Mom!"

By now, Bruce had dropped all pretense and was standing two feet away. He leaned over and whispered in Deborah's ear, undoubtedly concerned about the strange woman.

Kelly noticed his muscular biceps as they strained against his leather jacket and could even smell his musky alpha-male cologne from where she sat. She could see a slight bulge under his arm. Apparently Ernie was right—Bruce never left home without his Glock.

Seemingly annoyed, Deborah waved him off. Reluctantly, Bruce took a few steps back but continued his iron stare in Kelly's direction.

Deborah rolled her eyes and explained quietly. "That's our bodyguard, Bruce— such a pain. But my husband insists."

Kelly pretended to observe Bruce for the first time, giving him the once-over. "I don't blame your husband," she whispered back. "It's a dangerous world."

"True, that," Deborah agreed.

Meanwhile, little Sydney remained side-tracked, apparently unable to separate from her friends.

"We're going home, sweetie," Deborah called again, and Kelly held her breath, frustrated. Had she come so close only to miss her chance?

After a few quick exchanges, Sydney finally came running over. "Sorry, Mom! Taylor had a big secret."

Kelly couldn't help but smile, remembering her own happy childhood.

"You've got to see this magic trick," Deborah said, nodding toward Kelly. "This is Mrs...." She hesitated.

"Michaels," Kelly lied, holding out her hand to shake Sydney's.

"Nice to meet you," Sydney replied, giving Kelly a polite smile and shaking her hand. She sat next to her mother, between her and Kelly, and leaned her cheek against Deborah's shoulder while looking at Kelly.

Talking softly, Kelly did the trick, moving the quarter about her fingers. Sydney inched closer, eyes wide. When the quarter finally disappeared, only to reappear behind her mother's ear, Sydney burst into laughter and clapped her hands. "Do it again!"

**Do it again**, the universal childhood refrain, and how sweet it was! Kelly repeated the trick and Sydney clapped louder. This time, at the moment the quarter disappeared, she grabbed Kelly's hands, excitedly turning them over and back again. "Where'd it go?"

Sydney's unexpected touch was like an electric current. Kelly worried her stunned reaction might give her away. Forcing composure into her movements and voice, she breathed deeply, and when Kelly removed the quarter from Sydney's ear, the little girl giggled with delight.

"Want to see another one?" she asked, catching Deborah's eyes to confirm permission. Deborah nodded eagerly.

Clearly displeased, Bruce fidgeted. Kelly switched to the most important trick, the **coup de grace**, the cotton-swab-on-the-inside-of-the-mouth trick, although what she was about to put into Sydney's mouth didn't look like a cotton swab—it resembled a red lollipop.

Kelly removed it from her purse, ripped off the plastic wrapping, and before Bruce could object—though he'd raised his hand—she offered the red sucker to Sydney, who popped it into her mouth.

**Too late**, Kelly thought. **Snooze and you lose, Bruce.**

Kelly asked Sydney to remove the sucker, passing her hand across it, and voila! It was suddenly **blue**. Deborah and Sydney oohed and aahed.

Kelly handed it back to Sydney, who promptly put it into her mouth again. The trick had gone off without a hitch. It wasn't the same sucker, of course. Kelly had palmed the red one, hustling it out of view.

"And to think we almost didn't come to the park today," Deborah murmured.

"I know it!" Sydney exclaimed, touching Kelly's arm again, her little girl scent warming Kelly's heart. "Do another trick!"

How Kelly would have loved to stay longer, hours for that matter, but she wouldn't push her luck, not with Bruce sweating bullets beside them—and packing real ones.

When Kelly pretended to experience a spasm of pain in her "pregnant" tummy, Deborah looked concerned. "You really should be at home resting."

Kelly commented about being so excited about motherhood she sometimes spent hours just watching other children.

"Oh, you'll get your fill, believe me," Deborah laughed, ruffling Sydney's hair.

After further niceties, they exchanged good-byes, and no one was the wiser. Bruce certainly seemed to breathe easier.

"Perhaps we'll see you again," Deborah said, waving as Sydney skipped sideways.

Kelly waved back. "I'm sure you will." She risked a nod at Bruce, whose expression remained deadpan and distrustful. I'll be back, she thought. **And you won't be any happier to see me.**

Kelly waddled her way to the car, collapsed into the front seat, and closed her eyes. Young Sydney's face hovered in her imagination.

**At long last**, she thought, ignoring eight years of dead ends and dozens of lollipop tricks, followed by an equal number of negative lab results.

Kelly fired up the rental car, ignoring Bruce's lingering gaze and her own sneaky temptation to flash him a bright **gotcha** smile.

**He suspects**, she thought. **Later, he'll kick himself.**

Instead of driving east on the Pacific Coast Highway back to her cheap Malibu hotel, she made a beeline for the nearest FedEx facility. At the first traffic light, she removed her uncomfortable pregnancy padding and tossed it into the backseat.

When she arrived at the FedEx parking lot, she parked and turned off the ignition. She placed the red sucker-like swab into the proper canister, put the entire kit into a lab-appropriate package, and headed for the lobby.

A young man with blue streaks in his blond hair took her package, applied a label, and set it aside to be mailed to the lab in Akron, Ohio. Then he printed her receipt and pointed to a long assortment of digits. "Here's your tracking number."

**My tracking number**, she thought,

grinning at the irony. The clerk noticed her amusement and gave her a cordial smile in return. She fought back tears on the drive back to the hotel. "Mission accomplished," she told herself.

Despite the lull of ocean waves, she slept fitfully.

Kelly checked out of the hotel the next morning and drove the short distance to LAX. There, she took the midmorning commercial flight to Atlanta, then on to Akron, Ohio.

On the plane she sat next to a white-haired woman in a pretty black-and-white polka-dot dress, who introduced herself as "Doris, from Minnesota," and pulled out of her purse a batch of pictures. She showed off her five grandchildren—all brunettes, as fate would have it.

"You remind me of my daughter," Doris said. "She's thin, like you. Too thin, really."

Kelly smiled.

Enduring another thirty minutes of benign small-town conversation, if only to appease the woman, Kelly nibbled on the standard flight fare of pretzels, washed down with a cup of orange juice.

"Would you like my pretzels, too?" Doris asked. "I have more snacks in my purse, if you'd like."

Kelly thanked her politely but was glad when the doting woman nodded off to sleep.

Kelly closed her own eyes as images of darling little Sydney emerged. Slipping deeper into her reverie, Kelly prayed silently, grateful that things had gone so well. Relishing the breeze from the small air nozzle above her, Kelly was barely aware of the passing landscape thirty thousand feet below.

**Could it finally be her?** Kelly thought before dozing off.

# Chapter 1

**What's taking her so long?** Jack Livingston wondered. It was just after nine that evening and already fifteen minutes had ticked by since he'd sent Nattie up to get ready for bed. Typically, she would have come bounding down in a matter of minutes, taking as little time as possible for fear she might get trapped into the fearsome "sinkhole of bedtime."

Jack tossed his flight charts onto the coffee table and sighed. Leaning his head back on the sofa, he closed his eyes and focused on the patter of rain outside, letting his work concerns wash away. He heard the muted sound of a car muffler outside, growing quieter as it receded, and in the kitchen the fridge buzzed softly.

Nattie had occupied herself with a book earlier, while he'd studied the charts, mapping out their next big adventure—this one to coastal Maine. Someday, he hoped to fly her through the Rocky Mountains. The last time they'd flown together, he'd even let her talk on the Common Traffic Advisory Frequency, or CTAF, raising a chuckle from fellow pilots. "You keep yer uncle in line, little one!"

**"I'm trying!"** she'd radioed back, catching Jack's eye and giggling.

Jack was about to check on Nattie when his cell phone rang. He rose from the sofa and snatched it from the end table. He greeted his sister, San, whose given name was Sandra—though she had been known to give him a withering stink-eye if he dared to call her that. "Well, you won't believe it, brother dearest."

Jack could see Nattie's closed bedroom door from where he stood. "Just a sec." He covered the receiver. "Nattie?"

He waited a moment and heard a muffled reply, "I'm okay."

Meanwhile, San had been barreling

forward with details of her terrible day. While she chattered, Jack wandered to the tall window and observed the heavy cloud cover darkening the sky. The stars and the full moon were no longer visible. **Another stormy night in Wooster, Ohio.**

Across the side yard, recently married Diane Farley, her strawberry blond hair cut short, stood next to her new husband, Craig, in the kitchen washing dishes. Sometimes, like today when Laura had to leave a few hours early, Diane would watch Nattie for him. Diane and Craig spotted him and waved.

"Distracted, aren't we?" San muttered into the phone.

"Greeting my neighbors," Jack said.

"How're they doing, by the way?"

"Terrific," he replied, ignoring the insinuation in her tone: **"You sure missed the boat with her, didn't you?"**

Sparing him further grief, San asked about Nattie. Jack filled her in. The fact was, nothing much had changed since they'd talked last. San went silent for a moment. "So, tomorrow's the school meeting?"

"The final one for the year," Jack confirmed and wandered into the kitchen. He opened the fridge and looked inside. Remnants from Laura Mast's Amish feast—chicken, flavored with garlic— filled his senses. His mouth watered, but he closed the door.

"What's Laura think about all of this?" San asked.

Jack was surprised she would solicit their nanny's opinion. "She thinks Nattie will grow out of it."

"Laura said that?"

"Not in so many words."

San paused. "Okay, change of topic, Jack-O'-Lantern. Someone asked about you today. Anita Goodrich. You and Nattie met her last summer at my office picnic. Remember?"

**Faintly**, Jack thought.

"She's pretty. And funny. And she likes kids. Nattie hung all over her."

He nodded as if San could see him and noticed that Laura had forgotten to start the dishwasher. "I'm sure Anita is very nice," Jack replied, meaning it. With his free hand he opened the washer, finding the dispenser loaded with soap and ready to go. **That's strange.**

Jack pressed Cancel, waited a moment, then pushed the series of buttons. This time when he closed the door, the dishwasher began its soft humming, followed by the swishing of water.

**Don't die on me**, he thought. He'd just replaced the furnace last fall, and two months ago the transmission in his pickup had gone out.

"So why not ask her out?" San suggested.

Call Waiting was beeping in his ear, cutting out San's words. It was Laura. **Didn't she just leave the house?** So this had to be important, but San was still making her case for Anita, and before he could excuse himself from his sister's vise grip, he heard the final **beep beep beep**.

**I'll call her back**, he decided.

"I've got Anita's number if you want it," San pressed him. Jack flicked off the kitchen light, then went to the living room and turned off the lamp. In the darkness, the now steady rain sounded ominous.

"Don't you think it's about time you got back in the dating scene?" she quipped, then added, "Before you're a certifiable old man."

He chuckled, then glanced upstairs to the sliver of light beneath Nattie's door. "I'd better check on Nattie-bug. Love you, sis."

"Take care of my darling," San said, sounding mildly peeved at his brush-off. "And call me after the school meeting, okay?"

Jack promised and hung up, but instead of rushing upstairs, he returned to the fridge, grimacing at San's determination to get him married. While pouring some orange juice, his thoughts returned to Nattie, but he resisted the urge to hover more than he already was, recalling San's frequent refrain, **"Give the kid some breathing room, Jack!"**

He noticed Nattie's latest list of favorite foods, taped to the outside of the refrigerator, written in red marker:

TOP FIVE SUMMER FOODS:

1) Pop-Tarts—(Big Shocker! ) ☺
2) Anything Amish, but only if Laura makes it, otherwise not so much.
3) Ice cream, especially cookies and cream
4) Spaghetti (Did I spell it right?)
5) Green beans—Ha, Ha! (You know I'm kidding, right?)

He smiled at number two but seriously doubted Amish food was Nattie's second favorite. Certainly not before ice cream. Placing Laura's cooking at number two and posting it on the fridge was Nattie's way of telling Laura, **"I love you."**

Jack glanced up again at Nattie's closed door. Relax, he told himself, heading for the stairs. **She's fine.**

But that wasn't true, was it? As far as Jack was concerned, Miss Natalie Livingston—known to one and all as Nattie—hadn't been fine in a very long time.

Just after nine-thirty that night, Kelly Maines tried to start her finicky fifteen-year-old Toyota Corolla and marveled when it actually turned over. She eased the car out of the corrugated metal car shelter, the motor ticking like a time bomb. Turning on the windshield wipers, she headed for the convenience store where she worked, ten miles from the tiny walk-up apartment she rented in town.

Joe Callen, the general manager, graciously allowed Kelly to set her own hours, sometimes as few as ten a week, depending on her circumstances, whether she was in town or out, or whether she was busy trolling for money, a task that was becoming more difficult as the years passed. Without her friends Chet and Eloise, she would have gone broke years ago.

While she needed little money to exist, just enough to pay rent and keep the fridge minimally stocked, she needed a lot of money to pay the bills that mattered most: airline tickets, hotel bills, and of course, Ernie's investigating fee, well deserved but expensive nonetheless.

Kelly arrived at work ten minutes early, wearing her convenience-store uniform, with enough time to psyche herself up for a shift that was becoming more and more daunting. The work wasn't difficult, but getting to sleep afterward often was.

While waiting in her car on the dimly lit side of the building designated for employees, she listened to the local Christian station. She detected the scent of hickory smoke from the steak place across the street and jumped at the sudden clang of the metal Dumpster behind her. She jerked around to catch her co-worker Len's bright grin as he waved to her while heading back in the rear door. Attempting to calm her nerves, she drummed her fingers on the steering wheel, focusing on the imminent test results from her excursion to California.

She mustn't let herself get too excited, but it was nearly impossible not to imagine **what if**.

Tense at the thought, she plugged her phone into the cheap cassette tape adapter and switched to her own music mix, then opened her wallet and stared at Emily's baby picture, taken nearly nine years ago. She hummed along with an older worship tune.

The memories rushed in. Music had a way of doing that, taking her back to that pretty pink-and-white nursery where she'd soothed her newborn baby in the wee hours, sometimes gently moving about the room to the beat, whispering along with the words, imparting her own love of Jesus to her infant. How she'd lovingly dreamed of their future as mother and daughter, a future that once seemed so bright with possibility.

With five minutes until the start of her shift, Kelly cut the music and prayed silently, finding it impossible not to think back to her visit to Malibu and the encounter with adorable Sydney, her latest prospect.

She finished her prayer and opened the car door, then headed up the shimmering sidewalk to begin work for the night. The gentle rain misted her face, but she paused long enough to take in the convenience store sign, bright red against the darkened sky, a harsh reminder of what her life had become.

It won't be forever, she promised herself, whispering the prayer she'd been praying for more than eight years. **Please keep her safe.**

# Chapter 3

Jack knocked on Nattie's door. "Sweet pea?"

A tiny voice answered, "Okay, ready."

Jack pushed the door open and entered Nattie's world of cool green walls, accented with a flowery wallpaper border, purple foot-prints, and posters of Ariel, Belle, Rapunzel, and Nemo. In the right corner a large net housed her stuffed animals above her dresser.

**"Hasn't she outgrown these yet?"** San had recently asked.

**"Let her be a kid,"** he'd told her. **"For as long as she needs."**

Wearing her pink-patterned nightgown, Nattie was sitting cross-legged on the bed, arms folded, her face splotchy. She looked up at him with her big brown eyes, her fine chestnut brown hair swirling around her shoulders. The overhead light cast a halo-like sheen on it, and Jack noticed a tear on her cheek. Wiping it away quickly, Nattie forced a smile, eyes glistening. "Sorry I took so long."

"You okay, sweetie?"

She made a face. "I just got carried away."

**"Carried away."** One of Laura's trademark expressions, a response to just about anything out of the ordinary, like when Nattie went back for seconds at American Buffet, or if she wore mismatched socks, or came home exhausted at the end of a few hours at the park. **"Oh my, didn't you get carried away?"**

Jack sat beside her, tousling her hair. "Whatcha thinking about?"

She shook her head, scrunching closer to him and leaning against his arm. "I'm just sleepy."

**Already?** Jack glanced at her Hello Kitty clock. It was only nine-thirty, and summer break had just begun. He asked if she wanted a story, and she agreed, with little enthusiasm.

He began to weave yet another tale about the handsome young prince who flew his plane into a black hole in the sky.

"Which plane?"

"Marvin," he replied. It was Nattie's nickname for their Cessna 182 Turbo.

He told her the story, adding a few new flourishes just to keep things interesting. This time, the fairy princess had long red hair and wore a golden gown and a diamond-studded crown.

The phone rumbled in his pocket. Most likely it was Laura. He'd forgotten to call her back. "Just a sec," he mouthed to Nattie.

"Who is it?" she mouthed back.

Jack kissed the top of her head and headed toward the hallway, then closed the door behind him. He walked toward the master bedroom, apologizing to Laura for having missed her call.

"I just wanted to check in 'bout Nattie." She sounded worried.

Jack caught her up to speed. "She seems fine. At least for now."

"Something happened at the park," she added. "Thought you'd want to know."

"Uncle Jack?" Nattie called from her room.

"**Ach**, I'm interrupting," Laura said, hearing Nattie's voice. "This can wait till tomorrow."

He wondered about that, since she'd called twice. They exchanged good-byes and Jack hurried back to Nattie, where she was engrossed with her fluffy animals.

"Okay. Time for prayer."

"Nice try," Nattie replied. "I have questions."

"I'm impervious to questions. I eat them for breakfast. Fire away."

Nattie smiled at that, taking a deep breath. She pushed a few strands of hair behind her ear, and finally she blurted it out. "Do you think I look like Laura?" She extended her neck, twisting her head from left to right.

Jack made an exaggerated effort of studying her face. "Hmm. Maybe a little."

Nattie came unglued. "So she **could** be my mother!"

"Huh?"

"I don't mean she is, but she looks like she could be, right?"

"Well..."

"So, if you married her, everything would seem normal."

"Whoa there, sweet pea."

Nattie was just getting started. "When people meet us, they wouldn't ask if I'm adopted. Instead, they'd say things like, 'Wow! She has her mother's eyes. And her nose. And even her fingers.' Don't you think so?"

"Her fingers?"

"Be serious!" Nattie exclaimed. "I mean, you like Laura, right? She works really hard here. And she's pretty cool for a grown-up, not old like some of my schoolteachers. She already knows my favorite foods." She paused, then added, lowering her voice, "And you can't say she's not pretty, Uncle Jack."

He tried to rein in this galloping horse. "Well, sure, but—"

"And that's without makeup," Nattie added.

"I think you're forgetting a few important things," he said. "Laura wears Plain clothes—a white head covering, long aprons, and clunky square black shoes." He paused, studying her face. "That's big, honey. Huge."

Nattie shrugged. "She's just Amish, silly. Besides, what would be so different? She's over here all the time, and she acts like a mom, and you guys act like you're married."

Jack frowned. "Honey, people don't just marry other people. They go on dates first."

Nattie inhaled, which seemed more like reloading. "So ask her out on a date!"

No matter what he said, Nattie would play **paint Uncle Jack in the corner** until he gave in. So he went for a truce. "What do I have to say to get you to go to sleep?"

Nattie smiled with mischief. "Just say yes."

He could almost hear San's voice: **"You are so wrapped around her finger, brother dear."**

"Sweetie?" He leaned in and kissed her

cheek, wishing he could pull some kind of string and give her everything she wanted. "Is this why you were sad before… because of Laura?"

Nattie blinked.

"Laura's not going anywhere, okay? I don't have to marry her just to make sure she doesn't escape."

Nattie giggled at first, then narrowed her eyes. She was only eight, but old enough to know life held few guarantees.

"Laura loves you very much," he assured her.

Nattie nodded and crossed her pink-clad legs. "Did **she** say that?"

"Laura doesn't have to. I have eyes in my head."

"You have two—two that I know about, and probably more I don't."

"And I love you, too, you know. More than spaghetti, even."

Nattie brightened. "You must love me a lot."

Staring at her, he bit his lip, holding his emotions in check.

Seeing this, Nattie wiped her cheek and

then, reaching up, smudged the moisture onto his cheek. "Here. Have one of mine. It'll make you feel better."

"Thanks."

"I have more, you know." She looked serious.

At last Nattie folded her hands, closed her eyes, and began to pray for her friends at school, for help finding her lost library book, which was the first he'd heard of it, and for world peace, or as Nattie put it, "For everyone to just get along." She continued with a few words of concern for her birth mother, for her adoptive mother who was already in heaven, and waxed on, praying for her "wonderful-good" nanny, Laura.

When she opened her eyes, Jack kissed her cheek again and stood up, ready to leave her to the company of Bear Bear, Cheetah the cat, and Grover the dog. Not to mention a hundred other surrogate brothers and sisters, aunts and uncles, all brilliantly disguised as stuffed animals. Most important, all of them had mothers.

Nattie reached behind her and handed

over Felicia, the stuffed unicorn. "This one's yours for tonight."

Affectionately, Jack examined the blue horse with a horn in her forehead.

"She has secret powers," Nattie explained. "You never know when that might come in handy."

**Indeed**, he thought. "Thank you." Straddling the unicorn on his shoulder, he stood by the door, poised at the light switch. "G'night, sweet pea."

"Uncle Jack?"

"Yes?"

"I love you more than spaghetti, too."

# Chapter 4

In the dim light of his room, Jack pulled on a well-worn T-shirt and his striped pajama pants. Rain was falling harder now, hammering the roof. Lightning flashed across the sleepy middle-class neighborhood, and sheets of rain flickered in the glow of the streetlight. The storm was moving closer. No sooner had he thought this than another flash of lightning illuminated the windows. He counted two seconds before the thunder cracked.

**Oh boy.** The evening was about to be extended. Waiting, he sat in the leather chair near the dresser and tightened the belt on his robe. He stared at the picture of his father standing in front of his single-engine plane, the same one Jack had flown in as a boy. Other photos of his dad were on display downstairs in his office and another at his airfield office. The only photo he owned of his mother, a photo he rarely displayed, was stored away in the darkness of his bottom drawer.

As expected, there was the squeak of a door, the padding of feet across the hallway, and the soft tapping of Nattie's fingernails against his door.

"Uncle Jack?" She peeked in, her eyes pleading as she held on to Bear Bear for dear life. Grinning, Jack motioned for her, and she ran to him, leaping onto his lap. "I don't like storms."

"And you don't like sleeping, either."

She nuzzled her face into his neck, curling herself into his arms.

"What am I going to do with you, sweet pea?"

"Well, you could feed me." Her lowered tone had an almost mock desperation, as if she hadn't eaten in days.

He laughed. "To the lions, I'm thinking."

"No…to the ice cream!"

He carried her downstairs, where they scarfed up bowls of mint chocolate chip on the family room sectional, huddled beneath tan blankets, watching **The Little Mermaid** for the umpteenth time.

When Nattie fell asleep at last, he reached for the remote and clicked off the DVD, then reached up to turn off the lamp. He sat silently, aware of the soft rise and fall of Nattie's breathing, stroking her hair and listening to the endless rain as it turned into light hail.

Nattie opened her eyes sleepily and smiled. "It's raining ice cubes, Uncle Jack." He chuckled, pushing away a strand of hair and kissing her forehead. That quickly, she was out again.

He considered carrying her upstairs but decided to wait until the cacophony of roof chatter had subsided.

Jack thought of his brother, Danny, and sister-in-law, Darla, gone for nearly five years. A car accident had taken their lives, a mere three miles from where Jack now lived. He would never forget where he'd been when he first received the gut-wrenching call—Wichita, Kansas, finishing up a flight lesson.

He had just landed his small plane and was going through some final items with a flight student when he'd noticed a voice message on his cell phone from Laura Mast, his niece's Amish nanny at the time, a woman he'd never met.

Promptly, he returned the call, and she had answered, unable to conceal her sobs. Within the hour, Jack had refueled the plane, charted a direct course, and was flying to Wooster, Ohio. Laura was waiting for him at his brother's house, sitting on a couch in full Amish attire, cuddling four-year-old Natalie, stunned and distraught, barely able to comprehend the meaning of such a horrific loss.

After the funeral, the will was read, and he could still recall the looks on their faces when it was revealed that he, not his twenty-two-year-old sister, San, nor Darla's parents, had been named as Nattie's legal guardian.

Silence filled the room as the family absorbed the news. **Unbelievable.** Nattie's adoptive parents, Daniel and Darla, had selected Daniel's irresponsible brother to care for Nattie. Jack, the aviation rat, who'd run off to parts unknown to escape his family.

**"You have the right to refuse,"** the attorney had advised him over the top of his half-glasses, apparently reading Jack's own stunned expression. **San is the natural choice**, Jack had thought at the time. **Everyone knows it.**

But that wasn't exactly true. San had just graduated from college with a degree in graphic design and had big plans for her life. Anyone acquainted with San also knew that her future couldn't possibly include wiping runny noses and organizing playdates. Destined for the Big Apple, San intended to conquer the world of fashion one high heel at a time, though at the funeral, she wore shock and grief like a shroud, seemingly unable to absorb the loss. But didn't they all?

While Jack had been given a few days to consider being little Natalie's father figure, a decision had to be made soon. If he didn't step up and if San declined, as surely she would, what then? Darla's parents, most likely, would be appointed. From the way they'd sat so eagerly in the lawyer's office, they were obviously rather anxious to get their hands on Nattie.

**So let them**, he'd thought.

When he arrived at his deceased brother's place, he found Laura wearing a long gray dress and black apron, holding Natalie on her lap. The child looked so sad and vulnerable, observing this stranger with something akin to reverence. **The long lost uncle**, he thought. **Who never had the decency to visit.**

**How can I possibly take this on?** he'd asked himself. **How will I even keep her safe?** He scoffed at the thought. He could barely keep **himself** safe.

"I have to make a decision," he told Laura, expecting her to register disbelief that he was even considering the guardianship. Instead, she looked at Natalie and back at Jack. "What's to decide?"

He moved to sit with them. Natalie sniffed, rubbed her nose, and looked up at him expectantly, as if worried that she wouldn't pass muster, worried that he wouldn't pick her. It broke his heart. She couldn't possibly be that aware, could she?

"I'm clueless," he said to Laura, smiling at Natalie. He touched her little hand, and she grabbed his finger. She giggled suddenly and squeezed harder. **"I got you now,"** she seemed to be saying. **"You're mine!"**

"I'll help ya," Laura offered, and the look on her guileless face underscored her promise. He felt strangely moved. Of all the adults associated with Natalie, this young Amishwoman was seemingly the only one who believed in him.

He looked fondly at his niece. Natalie was so prettily dressed and smelled of something soft and flowery. Soon Jack realized his notions of refusal had quickly flown out the window.

He reached for Nattie, and she hugged him back, unafraid. **I'll take care of you, little princess.** But before Jack gave his official consent, he exacted a promise from the sister he hadn't spoken to in years. A **big** promise.

**"Stick around for at least one year,"** he'd asked San. **"I need all the help I can get."** To her credit, San had already lasted more than four.

Presently, he ran his fingers through Nattie's wispy hair, musing over what Laura would say tomorrow and worried about the meeting at Nattie's school, as well.

It was after midnight when the thunder and lightning fizzled. He carried his little darling upstairs and nestled her in with her beloved stuffed animals, then reached for Laura's homemade Double Nine Patch quilt, one of Nattie's most prized possessions, and tucked it beneath her chin. Sleepily, she sighed and turned over. He also tucked Bear Bear into her empty grasp and kissed Nattie's cheek.

"Tickles," she whispered, half asleep, cuddling her critter, her eyes fluttering.

"G'night, princess," Jack whispered, closing the door to within inches of the doorframe.

He made his way through the house, checking the locks and inspecting the screen on the security alarm: **System Armed.** Upstairs again, he settled into his room for the night. With Felicia the unicorn facing him from the foot of the bed, Jack stared at the popcorn ceiling. Distant lightning periodically flashed, casting light against the walls.

Considering Nattie's prayer, he wondered if Nattie's birth mother ever thought about her. Did she lie awake at night, imagining what Nattie might look like, if she was happy, what her life might have been if she'd kept her? And sometimes he actually considered what she looked like, and if her personality was anything like Nattie's.

But mainly, he felt sorry for her. Children weren't just a dime a dozen.

When he thought of his life before Nattie, he shuddered, remembering those first fragile months of his guardianship, captured by her big eyes, thinking he was going to save her. Believing he could stand between her and the typical sorrows of life, yet realizing how silly that seemed. And naïve.

If anything, she'd saved **him**.

Kelly spent the first full hour of her night shift stocking the shelves. Everything from beans and soups to dog food, while Hailey, her goth-punk co-worker, waited on customers, ringing up candy bars, lottery tickets, coffin nails, and cash transactions for gas.

Later, while Hailey took her break, Kelly manned the front counter. Around eleven-forty, during a lull, a carful of women pulled into number twelve, and one of them popped out to pump the gas. Even from thirty feet away, Kelly recognized her former friend, Melody Hunter.

Not anymore. **Melody Cunningham now.** Her married name.

Kelly swallowed, her nerves unhinging as she remembered: Mel and Kel, best friends forever since middle school and all through high school, including four years at Ohio State. Kelly had completed a degree in marketing with a minor in accounting, while Melody finished with a bachelor's degree in history. When they'd returned home after graduation, Mel and Kel continued their friendship and married their guys within weeks of each other. Their babies were born within the same month.

Kelly steeled herself as Melody came in, wearing jeans, a **Jesus Heals Broken Hearts** T-shirt, and white sandals. Momentarily distracted with her wallet, Melody headed for the cooler in the back of the store without glancing at Kelly.

Aware of the smell of stale coffee and motor oil, Kelly heard the **thwump** of the cooler door. Quickly Melody appeared, carrying a six-pack of cola to the register. She took one look at Kelly, and her eyes bugged out. "Kel? Oh, my goodness, I didn't recognize you!"

Kelly greeted her warmly, **too** warmly, her throat tight.

"So how've you been?" Melody asked, reaching up to touch her flaxen hair. Her tone seemed genuine, and despite the passage of six years and the addition of five pounds or so, Melody looked the same.

Kelly replied politely, if not robotically, nodding toward the car still parked at the pump.

Melody rolled her eyes. "Girls' night out. Hubbies are home with the kids, and we spend most of our time obsessing about what we should be trying to forget!"

Kelly forced a laugh. Melody's exuberance reminded her of the old days, her friend's throw-caution-to-the-wind attitude, tempered only by Kelly's measured, sometimes brooding nature.

"How are you **really**?" Melody asked, edging closer, and before Kelly could answer, Melody placed her hand over Kelly's, a gesture that unnerved her.

Melody lowered her voice to a reverential whisper. "Did you find her, Kel?"

"No," Kelly said abruptly, pulling her hand away. "Not yet."

Melody looked embarrassed and saddened. "Oh, honey, I'm so sorry." She stepped back, sniffing softly. An awkward silence fell over them as Kelly rang up the purchase for her once dear friend, who'd tirelessly campaigned on Kelly's behalf, praying with her, sometimes for hours at the church, who'd once told her, **"We'll find her together."**

And then, for some inexplicable reason, Kelly began pushing her away, refusing Melody's calls and ignoring her texts, until they'd stopped coming altogether.

She felt queasy now, her breath shortening.

Melody grabbed her cola. "I'm real sorry we lost touch, Kelly. I mean it."

Kelly gave her a smile, another shrug, a way of saying, **"Things happen."**

"We should get together," Melody suggested. "For all the old times…" It was what old friends said, a polite way of parting, Kelly thought, just before they raced back to their new lives.

Melody paused a moment longer as her eyes took in the dingy convenience store, the kind of work that was well beneath Kelly's ability. She seemed to evaluate Kelly's haggard appearance, the faded blouse, the dark circles under her eyes that makeup couldn't hide.

"Are you okay, Kelly?" she asked, and it was the sincerity that tugged at Kelly's heart. She steeled herself against it. **Is my gaunt appearance that disturbing?**

"I'm holding up," Kelly replied, wishing Melody out the door. She was relieved when the car horn beeped.

Distracted by her friends, Melody waved her cell phone, but there were tears in her eyes.

**Don't feel sorry for me**, Kelly thought.

"Same number, Kel?"

She was confused at first, then realized Melody was confirming her phone number.

"No," Kelly lied.

"Well, mine is."

One last glance, a quick wave. "'Bye, Kelly," and Melody was gone. Gone to her life of child-raising, girls' nights out, and a loving husband. A life apparently unblemished by sorrow. A painful reminder of two lives taking different turns.

**My fault**, Kelly thought when she was alone again, leaning against the counter, remembering the past. And that pitying look in Melody's eyes, as if Kelly had gone off the deep end. Now, as much as she'd wanted Melody to leave, she missed her terribly. Even more, she missed what might have been and what never could be.

**My baby girl's almost nine**, Kelly thought, having ticked off every second of Emily's life. In reality, she'd raced the clock for years, knowing the longer it took, the harder it would be.

**I don't care how thin I must look**, she told herself. **Not if it means finding Emily.** And she wondered if Melody thought she was crazy for still searching for her daughter all this time—not that it mattered what Melody thought. Because even if the line of people who still believed in her dream was getting shorter, she still had enough hope and faith to make up for all the doubt in the world.

# Chapter 5

Jack awakened to the sound of his neighbor's motorcycle revving to life. He groaned and turned over, covering his head with his pillow. A few tormented moments later, Craig Farley's passion growled down the street until it became a distant whine.

Last night's storm had passed, but the wind remained, buffeting the house with the gravelly sound of twigs and leaves. Despite that, the morning sun flickered through the tall trees surrounding the house. It lit up his bedroom curtains with fiery yellow and scattered shadows across the opposite wall.

Jack opened one eye and peered at the clock. Six-twenty. Turning onto his back, he mentally rehearsed the day's schedule.

Taking the wind into consideration, he might have to cancel his training flight at ten o'clock with Todd Creighton, the mayor's son, a gangly high school student with a need for speed. Depending on the crosswind component, a wind over twenty knots could be tricky stuff for a newbie, even for someone like Todd, who showed up at the airfield in his daddy's old GT Mustang, a rumbling contraption of sleek metal and wicked curves.

As the owner of Higher Ground, which employed a team of Certified Flight Instructors, or CFIs, Jack set his own hours—sometimes as little as five to ten hours a week, especially in the summer when school break allowed more time with Nattie.

Jack shed the covers and swayed into the bathroom. Moments later, he emerged, saw the bed, fought the urge and failed, landing prone again. **Just a few more minutes**, he promised himself.

He heard sounds from the kitchen below—a clattering of utensils and plates, the soft thump of the refrigerator door mingled with spurts of Nattie's muffled laughter, and the scent of pancakes and eggs filtering up. In the background, he could detect the sounds of music eman-ating from the local contemporary Christian station.

Sitting up in bed, Jack reached for the lamp, then picked up his devotional and found a short two-page biographical story on George Mueller, the nineteenth-century minister who'd funded and managed orphanages purely by faith and prayer, never asking for a cent.

Mueller had spent the night in prayer, asking for provisions, but when dawn broke the darkness, there still was no food in the pantry. Unwilling to give in to discouragement, Mueller seated the orphans around the empty table and must have considered that his grand experiment in faith might fail. Undaunted, he asked everyone to bow their heads, and pro-ceeded to thank God for providing. Moments later, there was a knock on the door. Needless to say, the orphans ate well that day.

Jack closed his eyes and whispered his prayers, asking for direction and wisdom, and thanking God for the answers in advance. He prayed for Nattie, for Laura and San, and he asked for understanding regarding Nattie's current troubles, finishing with the usual, **Whatever happens, don't let me fail Nattie**.

Just as he finished his prayer, he heard a soft tapping at the door.

"Sweet pea?" he answered.

Her hair frizzy and somewhat scattered, Nattie peeked in, wearing her green robe and froggy slippers. "Breakfast is served." Pushing in with her elbow, Nattie carried a tray of pancakes, eggs, and half a banana to his bedside.

He sat up straighter, pushing himself up from the mattress. "Whoa, what's the occasion?"

"You stayed up too late, so I thought—" Nattie stopped suddenly, reconsidering. "Actually, it was **Laura's** idea. She thought you might be too tired to come downstairs."

Jack searched the plate for silverware.

"Laura's?"

Nattie followed his gaze. "Hold on!" She scampered away, leaving Jack to wonder about her latest scheme. Moments later, breathless, she was back with silverware and a glass of pulpy orange juice. She placed them on his tray in an exacting fashion, fully determined to achieve the proper presentation.

"You'll have to tell Laura how much I appreciate her thoughtfulness."

Heading for the door, his little green amphibian brightened. "I will! I will **definitely** tell her that." She turned back again. "Oh, and I almost forgot. Laura's fixing your coffee. It's dripping into the thingy. I'll bring it up when it's done."

She dashed away again, leaving Jack to pick through his food. The late-night ice cream hadn't set well, and after taking a few obligatory bites of breakfast, he decided to hold off awhile, taking a few deep breaths. **I'm not twenty anymore.**

Nattie eventually returned with the coffee, placed it on his tray, sniffed it once, and said, "Ick." And then she was gone.

He sipped it in silence, then slipped on his argyle robe, one of the many clothing articles San had threatened to burn. He wandered into the hallway and peered down to the open room below, squinting against the sunlight streaming through high windows along the opposite wall.

Below, Nattie was sitting at the kitchen counter, elbows on the long bar, palms under her chin, accompanied by a furry creature on either side. Laura, wearing a plum-colored dress and matching apron, gave her a cheerful expression and moved about the kitchen with her domestic duties. She placed two strips of bacon in the skillet. They sizzled and spattered, the scent reaching him instantly. Nattie's favorite breakfast food, next to Pop-Tarts.

He observed for a moment longer, watching as Nattie chattered animatedly, gesturing with her hands, once accidently brushing away her list-making paper, sending it over the counter's edge. Laura bent and retrieved it, and Nattie continued her conversation. Every few words, Laura would turn and respond, nodding, smiling, or frowning with surprise.

The scene warmed his heart. Laura didn't just listen to Nattie, and she never patronized her; she participated in Nattie's world, down to the smallest details. She even knew the names and personalities of Nattie's stuffed animals, all one hundred of them and counting. And she could recite, nearly verbatim, every one of Nattie's lists, no matter the topic.

Shortly after his brother and wife had adopted Natalie, they had placed an ad for a part-time nanny-housekeeper on their church bulletin board. Days later, Laura showed up on their doorstep.

"And, get this, she **drives**," Danny had told Jack during one of their rare phone conversations. "Never heard of an Amishwoman with wheels, have you?"

At the time, Jack hadn't, although he now knew of a few Plain groups that allowed car ownership, including Laura's Beachy Amish cousins with whom she lived in Apple Creek, southeast of Wooster.

According to Danny, Laura had been raised and baptized into a conservative church in Lancaster County until she was excommunicated.

"What happened?" Jack had inquired, but Danny didn't know, and he didn't seem to care. Laura was wonderful with Nattie, and that's all that mattered. All that mattered to Jack, as well. So here they were, these many years later, and Jack still knew little about the young woman who ran their lives so efficiently and kept Nattie on the straight and narrow.

Unfortunately, Laura's unexplained Old Order Amish past exasperated San, who was a magnet for mysteries, a moth-to-the-flame for drama, and as Danny had often said, **"Our sister likes to poke the bear, if for no reason other than to hear the bear growl."**

"She may be shunned, but she's still Amish. It's not like she's plunged into the world," San had argued.

"**Beachy** Amish," Jack corrected.

"**Whatever.**" San rolled her eyes. "So why hasn't she repented?" **I'm glad she hasn't**, Jack thought, otherwise they'd have lost her to her former community by now. It was selfish, certainly, but Laura's unresolved issues were their gain, and yes, none of it seemed to hang together, but who cared? He couldn't imagine their life without Laura. And it didn't take a genius to figure out the Amish were known to shun for the strangest reasons, like wearing a hat with a too-narrow brim, or owning a cell phone, or opening a forbidden Facebook account.

Whatever her secrets, Laura kept them to herself, and if she hadn't consistently behaved in contrast to someone shun-able, they wouldn't have wondered. The mere word shun seemed reserved for rebels, not for someone as gentle and submissive as Laura Mast.

Jack was still leaning over the upstairs railing when Laura looked up. "Hullo. **Wie geht's?**" she asked.

He complimented her on breakfast, and she beamed her thanks. Nattie wheeled around. "Uncle Jack! Laura's taking me to the park."

He pretended to be chagrined. "Again?"

"Yes!" Nattie squealed. "Again and again

and again, until I'm old and gray like you."

Jack cinched his robe tighter and joined them downstairs for his second cup of coffee. Busy with her latest list, Nattie gestured to the stool beside her. "Belly up, Uncle Jack."

Laura was now scrubbing the stove top, occasionally wiping the perspiration from her forehead, then stepping back and putting her hands on her hips, as if appraising her progress.

Nattie announced, "Laura's wearing purple today. I think she looks good in purple, don't you, Uncle Jack?"

Jack whispered in Nattie's ear. "Don't start."

"Just sayin'."

Laura looked down, studying her own clothing. "**Ach**, the color ain't too bright, is it?"

"Not at all," Jack replied, eyeing Nattie.

"It's breathtaking," Nattie said. "And **zimmlich**—pretty." Laura said something to Nattie in **Deitsch**, which was lost on Jack. Nattie replied quickly, and he smiled, amused that his little girl and her nanny shared their own private language.

In a few minutes, Laura left to gather the laundry from upstairs. Shortly, she returned to review the grocery list. "Any special requests?"

Nattie spoke up. "We're out of Pop-Tarts."

"I'm afraid three a day is **not** a balanced diet," Laura replied.

Nattie looked horrified.

"You heard her," Jack said, sipping his coffee.

"But I like Tarts."

Laura placed the list on the counter. "Well, I think we're all set, then." She strolled out to the family room. Nattie took this moment to offer another unsolicited suggestion. "I was just thinking about your date, Uncle Jack. You could take Laura out to lunch, you know."

**Our date?** Jack whispered a quick, "Drop it, young lady, and mind your p's and q's if you ever want to eat another Tart for as long as you live."

Sitting up straight, Nattie pursed her lips, taking a deep breath and blowing the dejected air between her lips. They traded glances again. He raised his eyebrows, and she sniffed defiantly.

"Young lady…"

"I was just breathing," she huffed. "I can **breathe**, can't I?" Jack took another sip, then reached over, grabbed Nattie's tiny piglet creature, and slowly walked it over all the way to Nattie's finished cereal bowl. "Please don't eat me, Mrs. Farmer," he beseeched her in a high-pitched pig squeal.

Nattie giggled, and all was well. Well enough to share with him her summer activities list:

1) Riding bikes
2) Swimming at the pool
3) Watching hummers with Laura
4) Going to DQ
5) Playing at the park—(it's number 5 'cause I'm basically nine)

"Ambitious list," Jack said, reading on through number fifteen, pretending to study it, and noting the placement of watching hummingbirds before going to Dairy Queen or playing at the park.

"That's your copy," Nattie said.

"I don't see piano practice listed."

Nattie frowned. "It's **summer**."

Jack chuckled. He pointed to number nine's sleepover request.

"And I don't remember Hannah. I have to meet all of your peeps' parents first. Remember? And if I don't approve, all bets are off."

Grinning, Nattie saluted respectfully. "Aye, aye, captain!"

After folding last night's movie blanket and straightening the family room, Laura came over and put her hand on Nattie's shoulder. "It's gonna be rather hot today, honey-girl."

Nattie replied in Pennsylvania Dutch.

"A good day for shorts," Jack seconded, mentioning the dearth of nectar for their hummingbirds.

**"Jah, gut."** Laura promptly added white sugar to the list. When he finished his coffee, Laura swiped his cup and carried it to the dishwasher.

Returning upstairs, Jack showered and dressed in jeans and a T-shirt. Afterward, he settled in for an hour of work in his office, located at the far corner of the house, where an entire wall was dedicated to aviation history: trinkets, flight DVDs, aircraft posters, and a single wooden shelf holding several models.

Set against the wide window overlooking the tree-dominated yard, Jack's oak desk was piled with bills, statements, and receipts. An aviator Snoopy mug—a gift from San—sat at his right hand, where tendrils of steam curled from his third cup of the day, his limit.

He worked for a while in silence, studying the latest monthly P&L report for his business, Higher Ground Aviation, Inc. Some of the numbers were lower than he'd anticipated.

When he heard the knock at his office door, he looked up. "It's open," he said.

Laura's head appeared around the door. Smiling demurely, she went to sit in the chair nearest the door, the typical routine when they reviewed her plans for the week. She brushed back a loose hair and bumped her **Kapp** slightly off-kilter.

"I forgot to mention, Cousin Peter dropped me off today." She met Jack's gaze. "My car's on the fritz again."

Jack waved off the imminent request. "I can always drive you, Laura. Besides, Nattie loves to visit the country." **Amish country.**

Laura seemed relieved but a little embarrassed. He mentioned the two o'clock meeting at school to discuss Nattie's progress, and Laura nodded to confirm this. She looked at her notes. "So, it's the grocery store, Bill's Hardware, and Walmart." She bit her lip. "Oh, and how much do you want to spend on flowers this year?" she asked, referring to the annuals that graced the perimeter of the house each summer.

"I'll leave that up to you, Laura."

"**Denki.** I mean, thanks." She blushed.

After all these years, he still found her shyness endearing.

"Something else I've been thinking about." She began to describe her ideas for a terraced garden out front. "It's time to replace the one I made some years back."

"Sounds great," Jack said. "Do whatever you'd like."

Laura twisted in her chair and peeked around the door, no doubt looking for Nattie, then reached up to close the door, signaling the start of their private discussion.

Leaning forward, Jack filled her in on his chat with Nattie last night, leaving out Nattie's obsession with playing match-maker. When he finished, Laura covered her face with her hands for a moment. "I daresay this all got started at the park," she said, beginning her "sad tale."

Apparently the place had been crammed with Nattie's classmates and their mothers. Things were going along just fine, according to Laura, until Nattie began calling her Mom. Not wanting to embarrass Nattie, Laura had played along, but during the walk home Laura felt the need to explain tactfully that while she was flattered, she wasn't really Nattie's mother. Therefore, it wasn't appropriate for her to accept such an honored title.

Nattie took it well at first, but as the afternoon progressed she became rather dejected. Laura tried to talk to her before she left, but Nattie shrugged it off.

"I don't think it bothered her as much as you think," Jack offered.

"I hope not." Laura adjusted her head covering, and the way she did it made him think of Nattie's bold statement, **"And you can't say she's not pretty."**

In the past, Laura's appearance—her dress, her lack of makeup— had been an occasional topic of dinnertime talk, especially the times San visited. Still unmarried at twenty-nine, Laura Mast had adopted the Beachy Amish tradition of wearing long plain dresses in a variety of colors, her honey-colored hair parted down the middle and pulled severely back in a bun beneath her white formal cup-shaped prayer veiling. Her **Kapp**, Laura called it, seemed to be a metaphor for her restrained life, as if the freeness of movement was strictly forbidden.

In spite of her plain appearance, it was impossible to disguise Laura's soft feminine lines, the allure of her haunting, if beautiful, brown eyes. There was also that inexplicable something that seemed to whirl about her, especially when she smiled, like sunshine breaking through clouds.

Laura brightened suddenly, getting up and moving toward his aviation wall, to Jack's custom-made shelf. "Oh…I believe I've missed this."

He followed her gaze proudly, not surprised she hadn't seen it before, as he'd only recently purchased the autographed model of the Bell X-1, signed by Chuck Yeager. The X-1 was best known for being the first aircraft to exceed the speed of sound in controlled, level flight.

Studying it closely, her hands clasped as if in prayer, Laura seemed enamored with the addition. He filled her in on the history behind the acquisition, pointing to the empty spot next to it, a place reserved for something—anything— signed by Wilbur Wright.

Laura whistled softly. "What sort of

autograph?"

"I saw his signed pilot's license for sale. That would be nice, but too expensive. I can't justify it."

Laura stepped back, surveying the entire wall. "It's amazing, ya know, how man ever learned to fly, really."

Jack smiled, amused with her fascination. As far as he knew, she'd never set foot in a plane, and he felt a twinge of guilt. Although flying was a no-no for the Amish, he'd never thought to ask her.

Just then Nattie burst in the door. "What's everybody looking at?" she asked, then groaned. "Oh, just the airplane stuff." She folded her arms and raised her eyebrows. "Are we going shopping or not? I'm popping out of my skin here."

Jack chuckled and Laura dutifully followed Nattie out the door. Moments later, Nattie was back to blow a kiss; he caught it on his cheek and blew one back. Giggling, she twiddled her fingers good-bye, and then was gone.

## Chapter 6

When her shift was over, Kelly called a quick good-bye to Hailey and drove back to her small apartment, a remodeled attic above Agnes Brown's creaky house, which smelled of eucalyptus from the vaporizer her landlady constantly ran.

Alone, Kelly enjoyed a long, steamy shower, washing away the memory of the night shift and of Melody's sudden reappearance. Later, at the bedroom end of the studio apartment, Kelly put on a white knee-length T-shirt, pulled the blinds optimistically, and hurried to bed. She reached for her room-darkening mask and jerked the covers over her head, and though she rarely eked out more than four hours of sleep at a time, she had high hopes for today. **Five's a bonus**, she thought.

But as usual, Kelly struggled to fall asleep, lying awake for hours, until she finally succumbed out of pure exhaustion. At just after one o'clock her cell phone rang, which she'd forgotten to silence. Frustrated and dog-tired, she ignored it, letting the call go to voice mail.

Minutes later, annoyed by curiosity, she flipped up her mask and checked the message. **The lab results must be in**, she realized, feeling a rush of anticipation. Quickly, she called back and reached Cara, one of the clerks she'd gotten to know over the years. "Do you mind scanning it in and emailing it to me, pretty please?"

Cara agreed but said it might be an hour. "We're getting slammed here."

Bleary-eyed, Kelly changed her mind. "You know what? I'll be right over." She hung up and sat on the edge of the bed, her spirits buoyed. **This is it!** Her trip to Malibu a mere three days ago was about to pay off.

Kelly wandered out to the mini-kitchen, drank some stale coffee, and discovered something bagel-ish. Spreading on cream cheese from the fridge and taking a bite, she promised to improve her diet tomorrow. She hurried back to her room, dressed, and headed out to her Toyota. Thankfully, the testing center was only ten minutes away. She started the car and gripped the steering wheel, resisting the urge to fist pump.

**Hold steady**, Kel, she told herself.

When she arrived at the testing center, Cara was at the front counter fielding calls. The cheap seats were filled with an assortment of folks seeking to satisfy occupational requirements, submit to drug testing, or discover their own personal nutritional profiles.

Cradling the phone in her neck, Cara reached behind her, removed an envelope, and held it out to Kelly. It was a simple business envelope with **Lab Tests** printed on the lower right hand corner, identified by Cara's own handwriting: **Kelly Maines**.

Kelly's stomach filled with butterflies. Back in the car, she placed the envelope on the passenger seat and drove to a nearby park. **Somewhere quiet.**

She chose a spot near a row of bushes, aware of the afternoon sun streaming through her windows. She kept the car running with the air-conditioner on full blast. Turning off the radio, Kelly sat in silence for a moment, collecting herself. **Here it is**, she thought. **But I have to open it.**

She smiled, took a breath, and cued up some music. An old tune by Sixpence whispered beneath the whirring sound of the fan. A brisk wind buffeted her car, slightly rocking it. **This bucket of bolts could blow away.**

**Do it.** At last, she opened the envelope, removed the folded DNA Maternity Evaluation Report, and began reading. Ignoring the body of the report, which defined the genetic system and the chromosome location, Kelly skipped down to the conclusion. The words at the end hit her like a punch in the gut, sucking the air out of her.

**Kelly Maines is excluded as the biological mother of Sydney Moore.**

She breathed in, faltering, then exhaled, all the while squeezing the steering wheel until her knuckles turned white. If the wind wasn't bad enough, a swirling cloud crept across the sky, hiding the sun, shrouding the entire park with a dismal shadow.

**Excluded.**

No match. Sydney Moore was not her daughter, after all.

Old defensive routines kicked in, years of dealing with bad news. "Didn't I suspect it might be negative?" she told herself. "It's okay." But she'd staked everything on this one. This report was supposed to redeem eight years of fruitless effort.

**I still believe**, she prayed softly. **All things are possible.** She closed her eyes as tears slipped through, falling down her cheeks. **It's okay**, she assured herself again.

She reached for her cell phone and called Ernie, her private investigator. When he answered, she blurted out, "No luck, Ernie. We're still in business."

Ernie sighed audibly.

"She looked so much like me. She really

did, Ernie. More than the others, you know? She had my eyes. My hair. My **freckles**…" Her words trailed off into a frustrated sigh as Ernie seemed to digest this.

"How're you holding up?"

She swiped at a rogue tear but sniffed defiantly. "Ready to hit the ground running."

"I mean, are you sleeping, kiddo?"

"Enough," Kelly replied, exaggerating. She hadn't slept enough in years.

Silence spooled out.

"I can do this, Ernie."

"Okay. Then I've got one more lead for you."

She nodded, feeling relieved. **Another prospect.** They were officially back on the train they'd ridden for eight exasperating years.

She'd first met Ernie Meyers at her church. He was a former policeman whose brother, she would later learn, had once worked for the CIA. For all she knew, Ernie had worked for the government, as well, although he'd never admitted to it, and she wouldn't have asked.

Semiretired, Ernie offered to work for her **"around the edges, at cost."** Cost, however, wasn't cheap—to the tune of thousands each month.

In the early years, Kelly went door to door, unafraid and unashamed, pleading for contributions and showing the news clippings for proof. She spoke at churches, talking about keeping the faith in spite of life's challenges, and passing the plate. Sometimes she even stood on street corners with nothing more than a sign: **Help Me Find Baby Emily**.

Buoyed by prayer and encouraged by her church family, there were times when hope and courage streamed through her soul like the mighty Niagara Falls. **Today is the day I might find her!**

Eventually, she even set up a nonprofit organization, promoting it through her website, Finding My Emily, where she also itemized her expenses online, down to the penny, assuring her contributors that nothing they gave her was applied to personal expenses.

Over time, she'd raised a quarter of a million dollars, but it was nearly all gone now. And lately, contributions had leveled off. The economy was rough and too many years had passed since Emily had been taken, and with the passage of time, fewer people believed in, or contributed toward, Kelly's goal.

Fortunately, several years ago an older couple, Chet and Eloise Stilson, charitable and compassionate millionaires, had taken her under their collective wings. Without them, Kelly would have gone broke, and yet, despite Chet and Eloise's ongoing generosity, overall funds were dwindling.

"I'll need some time to qualify her," Ernie said, referring to the lead. "You're gonna like this one if it pans out, but I don't want to send you on a wild goose chase."

"I can wait."

"And...I hate to mention this, but I've only got a few hundred bucks left on retainer."

Kelly paused. "Uh, I don't have a lot at the moment, but I can give you what I have."

"That's fine, honey. I owe you some free time."

"No, you don't—"

"Shh," he whispered, like a crotchety but loving grandfather.

"I'm not quitting on you just because the money's short. I'll work slower if I have to, but I won't pull out till you say the word."

"Thanks, Ernie. You've been—" She stopped, moved by his generosity. "I don't know what I'd do without you."

"We're gonna find her, Kelly," he growled. "I promise you that."

Kelly returned home, pausing in the doorway and blinking at her familiar surroundings. Eager to access her website for possible leads, her only contribution to Ernie's efforts, she needed to keep working, if only to minimize her disappointment. She'd long harbored the belief that someone could email her out of the blue: **Hey, we saw someone who HAS to be your kid.**

**It could happen**, she thought.

Years before, she'd joined a number of support groups, one local and a few online. The people behind the groups taught you how to cope, how to go from day to day without collapsing, and how to let go. But that was the one trick she hadn't learned—letting go. She refused to become comfortable with loss. And she didn't need friends who helped her cope. She wanted her daughter back.

**Job one,** she reminded herself, **get more money.** But she couldn't bear to ask Chet and Eloise for more. As it was, they deserved an accounting of the money she'd already spent.

Kelly headed to the kitchen and poured some soda over ice, something to soothe her stomach. Praying for wisdom, she trudged to the computer, touched the mouse, and brought up the screen saver: Emily at one month old, cooing at the camera. For a few minutes Kelly indulged herself, savoring more photos: Emily at six weeks, wearing her cuddly pink sleeper; Emily reaching for the colorful **Little Mermaid** crib mobile, and Kelly's favorite, baby Emily and Kelly cheek to cheek.

Another photo of Emily was taken that long-ago October, twenty-four hours before the worst day of Kelly's life. She'd awakened in the predawn hours, trying her best to remember—**had Emily cried at all last night?** No, she hadn't. Her precious baby hadn't cried once that night. And why was that?

Pushing the horrid memories into the farthest corner of her mind, Kelly clicked over to her website, intending to read a few of the old posts, anything encouraging. Instead, she found a recent message, posted for everyone to see: **You're a fraud, Ms. Maines. I gave you two hundred bucks two years ago, and you're STILL dredging for contributions? I want a refund!**

The writer gave his name and email, but no address, so she swallowed her frustration and answered him directly. **I apologize. I haven't found Emily as quickly as I'd hoped. I will return your money. Thank you for your prayers**

**through the years.**

Accessing her online banking records from two years prior, Kelly located his address on the copy of the check. She removed her small file box from the cabinet, found the nonprofit checkbook, and wrote a check for the amount. Just as deliberately, she addressed the envelope and carried it out to the mailbox.

She stood in the heat of the glaring sun, thankful when a subtle cool breeze whispered against her cheek. She heard the **clack-clack-clack-clack** on the sidewalk across the street, and spotted a red-shirted boy balancing precariously on his silver skateboard. From behind her, she heard a soft **meow**, and turned to see Felix, the landlady's calico cat, padding toward her. Smiling, she crouched to pet Felix as he nudged against her leg and purred profusely. "You must be hungry, little one."

The meowing continued, so Kelly scooped up the cat and hurried upstairs to pour some water and Meow Mix. Felix was already sipping from the bowl before

Kelly placed it on the ground.

Watching Agnes's cat drink, Kelly felt sorry for the little rascal, not only because of the unfortunate name, bless his heart, but because Felix's owner was rarely home to feed him. Then, thinking of the last people on earth who still believed in her, Kelly punched in their phone number. Chet Stilson answered on the second ring.

"Are you guys busy?" she asked.

Chet hesitated for a moment. "Uh…we were just talking about you," he replied. "You up for one of Eloise's medley soups?"

"I'm starving," she replied, glancing at her cell phone clock.

They agreed to meet at three o'clock, and Kelly hung up, kneeling down to stroke Felix.

**It takes a lot to ruffle Chet's feathers**, Kelly thought, **recalling his hesitance. Something's up….**

# Chapter 7

Originally from Austin, Texas, the Stilsons lived in an upscale neighborhood in the northwest section of Akron, nestled at the edge of a forest.

Kelly had always enjoyed the drive along scenic Yellow Creek Road and the turn into Chet and Eloise's long private lane. She stopped for a moment to check the mirror and decided she looked too pale. Pinching her cheeks, she sighed. **Little help that did**, she thought as she continued on for the quarter mile, following the gravel road. The red and white rosebushes and the occasional statue decoration offered her solace.

When she arrived at the house, a tall white-haired man in ranch attire, sporting a well-groomed mustache and bushy eyebrows, met her at the door and gave her a bear hug. She breathed in his Texan musk, what he jokingly called toilet water. "How's my favorite detective?" he said with a grin, his tanned face grooved with wrinkles. His cowboy hat was missing today. Chet without the hat was hardly Chet at all.

She gave him an appreciative smile and followed him through the two-story entryway and into the great room with its cathedral ceiling, lofty windows, long drapes, and graceful arches, in keeping with the Mediterranean style of the house.

Due to a childhood accident—a broken leg that had never properly healed—Chet strutted like a feisty ranch hand, not unlike the quintessential movie cowboy John Wayne. Kelly hid a grin as Chet shuffled across the room with a somewhat awkward yet decidedly rugged swagger.

Chocolate-covered strawberries and mixed nuts awaited them in the sun-drenched alcove adjacent to the kitchen, where Eloise, a rather petite woman in a flowing white sundress, had just closed the refrigerator and turned to smile at them, holding a pitcher. "Sweet tea, anyone?"

Eloise reminded Kelly of anyone's favorite grandmother, peppery gray brown hair and granny glasses, tender with her words. Easy to love.

"Sure," Kelly said. "Thank you."

Kelly and Chet were seated at a marble table overlooking the nearby lake, and while they snacked, Kelly waited for the ball to drop. Something was off-kilter; she could sense it in Eloise's faltering expression.

"Are you sleeping, honey?" Eloise asked softly, still moving about the grand kitchen.

Remembering Ernie's similar concern, Kelly smiled. "When I can."

Eloise nodded, but the worry in her eyes remained. "Eating enough?"

"Some..."

Eloise served the hearty chicken and vegetable soup, ladling each portion into delicate two-handled white soup bowls.

Nerves on edge, Kelly crumbled a few crackers and stirred them into the steamy broth, then ate slowly, careful not to clink loudly.

Eloise asked Kelly if she'd like a sandwich, but Kelly politely demurred. "The soup is delicious and plenty for me, thanks."

At one point, Chet chuckled at his wife's overly attentive manner, and she smiled in return. They talked about the church where they'd originally met, where Kelly rarely found time to attend, and they also discussed Kelly's dwindling funds, the slowing of recent contributions. She felt embarrassed, not expecting them to continue their support. They'd already done too much for her, but the fact remained that she **needed** their financial help.

Chet wiped his mouth with his napkin and, after meeting Eloise's gaze, fixed Kelly with his Texas **let's get down to business** look. Chet's rough manners, a refined version of Ernie's own gruff nature, belied his quick mind. Chet had made millions from shrewd investments, real estate holdings, and smart partnerships, and he and Eloise, both in their late sixties, were in the "giving back" stage of their lives.

"Recently, I had a long conversation with Ernie Meyers," Chet began, reaching for a toothpick.

Kelly gripped her glass, heavy in her hands. She could imagine it slipping through her fingers, breaking into a thousand jagged pieces. "I think I've got a handle on why we haven't been successful," Chet said, pausing until Kelly met his gaze. "God is not blessing our efforts, and for good reason."

"Oh, Chet!" Eloise exclaimed, then quickly lowered her voice.

"We agreed you wouldn't be so **direct**."

"That's okay," Kelly replied softly, setting her slippery glass down. "I want to hear this."

Chet leaned forward, folding his callused hands. "Ernie reluctantly shared some things. My guess is he really didn't want us to know." He glanced at Eloise again, requesting approval with his eyes.

Kelly held her breath. Ernie, clever as a fox, would have tiptoed carefully, aware that Chet was funding a lion's share of the search.

"Fact is, you've been extracting DNA unethically, Kelly." Chet's toothpick dangled from his lips at an odd angle, and she knew from her time with the Stilsons that this particular habit annoyed Eloise no end.

"Is it true?" Eloise looked at Kelly, her eyes moist. "You're taking it without permission?"

Kelly swallowed hard. "Only when I have to." **Which is always**, she thought.

"I'm not surprised," Chet clarified, his eyes softening. "But I am disappointed."

"I didn't know what else to do," Kelly said. "I wanted you to have something to show for your money, and I—" She stopped. **I wanted to find my daughter.**

Kelly felt as if the room were closing in on her. Her mouth went dry, and the tears welled up. Eloise reached over and patted Kelly's arm.

"Will you excuse me, please?" Kelly asked, rising, and being the gentleman he was, Chet stood with her, nodding, concern etched in his brusque expression.

Kelly hurried down the hall, Chet's words

haunting her as she closed the bathroom door and stared in the mirror. The circles under her eyes had become darker by the week, and yes, she was as thin as a rail, but only because it was so hard to put on weight, not because she wasn't trying. **I feel fine**, she thought. **Just a little tired.**

Kelly ran some cool water into the seashell basin and splashed the water on her face, drying her cheeks with a towel. Brushing her fingers through her lifeless hair proved futile. She forced a smile and said it out loud: "I feel **fine**."

But she also felt exasperated and embarrassed, as if she'd been caught stealing candy at the grocery store. And she feared that Chet and Eloise regretted hitching their wagon to a falling star.

**I had no choice**, she told herself, but she respected Chet and couldn't help wondering if he was right. **Is God displeased with me?**

When she returned, Chet's toothpick had disappeared. Kelly sat down, determined to take her medicine, to let them have their say.

Chet tapped the table with his knuckles. "Bottom line: We need to take the royal way, honey. We can't expect God to reward dishonesty."

She nodded, but the implications of changing tactics hit her hard. Getting parents to simply hand over DNA samples had proven to be time-consuming and nearly impossible.

Chet continued. "I also want you to know, I plan to give Ernie another ten grand."

"Oh, Chet...**thank you**," Kelly said, looking at Eloise. Tears came to her eyes again. These days, it took months to gather ten thousand dollars from her feeble fund-raising.

Eloise nodded. "Honey, we're committed to seeing this through."

"But you have to promise," Chet warned, "no more fraudulent testing."

She caught the **"no nonsense"** look in Chet's eyes and waited for him to say, **"No more stalking."** If he did, how could she possibly agree to that? How was she supposed to find Emily if she didn't actually **look** for her?

Kelly folded her hands and felt the room whirl about her. She was beyond over-whelmed, not only by their continued generosity, but by the giant wall that Chet had just placed in her path.

He extended his big hand. "Do we have a deal?"

Kelly shook on it.

They bowed their heads, holding hands as they had dozens of times before while Chet prayed aloud, his deep voice boom-ing. "Our gracious heavenly Father, we come humbly today to thank You for Your many blessings...."

Later, in the entryway, she reached for Chet, and he hugged her back tightly, gripping her arms, admonishing her. "You're wasting away to nothing, Kelly-girl."

"Goodness, Chet," Eloise muttered.

"I'll try to eat more," Kelly promised.

Chet frowned. "We worry about you. You're the daughter we never had, Kelly. You know that, don't you?"

Kelly managed a smile. "I love you guys." She hugged Chet again and kissed

Eloise's cheek.

Kelly walked the stonework steps that led to her car, and when she looked back at them, Chet and Eloise were still standing at the threshold, waving. She waved back, grateful for their generosity, sustained by their love, and encouraged by their faith.

Even so, her promise to Chet had put a chink in her methods. And that wasn't the worst of it. Despite his objection to her testing methods, Chet didn't have a clue what Ernie did to gather his leads. Kelly didn't fully grasp it, either, but Ernie's high-tech surveillance process, a process he'd farmed out to other "associates," surely involved invasive and unethical, if not illegal, intelligence work. If Chet knew the full scope of their methods, would he have pulled the financial plug long before now?

**On the other hand**, she thought, beginning her convenient rationalization, **I don't know for sure, do I?**

Kelly put her car into gear and sped down the lane, gravel rattling beneath the car. **Now what do I do?** she thought, not surprised that Ernie hadn't been more forthcoming with Chet.

She'd learned from years of association that, despite his devout faith, Ernie harbored a different perspective, one that she also shared. According to Ecclesiastes, there was a time for everything, including war. Truly, finding her daughter was like a war—she used every method available, including desperate measures, camouflage, and outright deception, not to mention brazen faith and foolish hope.

Dear Chet could be rather long-winded at times, but Kelly soaked it up. **"Whenever things are bleak, missy, consider it an opportunity. Anyone can believe in the light of day, but few persist under the shroud of darkness. Never forget, faith is a light that's best seen in the dark."**

Kelly smiled at the memory, her heart beating harder as she thought about Ernie's latest lead. **"You're gonna like this one,"** he'd said by phone. Bless his heart. Ernie was her other rock, and roadblocks or not, there was always another lead, another reason to hope, and another chance for a miracle.

She rolled down her window, reveling in the afternoon sun.

"I do believe," she whispered. "And I want to do this right. Help me follow Your path—the royal way—to Emily."

For the rest of the way home, Kelly's prayers mingled with the wind as she asked for divine direction, for the opening of doors and windows, for the tiniest break. For anything, even a crumb.

"Someday You'll say yes," she whispered. "I know You will."

Jack stood in the school hallway, surrounded by wall displays of students' art, announcements, and photos of classroom activities. He surfed the web on his tablet, reading the news, waiting for his appointment with Nattie's teachers.

That morning, after confirming the imminent return of favorable wind conditions, he'd left Nattie in Laura's care and drove his Ford pickup to Wayne County Airport, northeast of Wooster. There, he did his own preflight of the older Cessna 172, examining the flight surfaces, filling the plane with gas, and topping off the oil. He'd arrived early for a reason—it had been a while since he'd taken to the skies, and aside from Nattie, flying was still his greatest love.

His soft-spoken father, a man given to few words, had introduced him to flying, and it hadn't taken long to adopt his father's passion as his own, creating a steel bond between them.

If asked now why he enjoyed flying, Jack would merely say, **"I fly because I can't imagine not flying."** For him, it was a way of seeing things, a way of renewing his perspective, providing a sense of control, not only over the skies but over his life. And, too often, as his father could attest, it provided the temporary escape from the troubles of the world, if not the stress of their turbulent home.

Jack's FBO—Fixed Base Operation— was located in a small corner of what served as the airport terminal for the area of Wooster. Todd had shown up on time, keen on soloing. He had forty-seven hours under his belt and had mastered stalls, slow flight, turns around a point, and a dozen other maneuvers but still struggled with two-point landings. Todd had a tendency to force the nose downward, the wrong thing to do if you didn't like bouncy landings, not to mention broken nose gears.

**"We're going to work the pattern,"** Jack had told him, which involved a succession of takeoffs and landings—touch-and-goes. Informed of their lesson plans, Todd's initial fervor began to fade. Like most flight enthusiasts, he wanted to fly solo, sail the ocean without an anchor. To his credit, Todd made the best of it, and by the end of the two-hour instruction, exhausted, glistening with sweat, Todd had made significant improvement with what aviators often called **controlled crashing**.

Presently, Jack waited to meet with Nattie's third-grade teacher, Mrs. Stacy Fenton, a woman in her midfifties, her brown hair marked a few conspicuous silvery threads. Miss Karen Jones, the school counselor, a woman about Jack's age, was also scheduled to meet with them.

Leaning against the wall and wearing khakis and a plaid shirt, Jack pulled out his phone and scrolled through his text messages. A young-looking couple emerged from the classroom, and the husband nodded toward Jack. The wife scrunched her face, then smiled as if to say, **"Not as bad as it could have been."**

Stacy Fenton waved him in, and Jack sat across from her desk. "A very long day," she stated apologetically. "Karen will join us momentarily." She excused herself to make a phone call.

While he waited, Jack recalled Nattie's first day in grade school—how happy she'd been, so ready to learn. Practically delirious. She thought herself a big girl, climbing the scholastic ladder. At six, she was reading at a fourth-grade level, eager to show off her literary prowess to anyone who'd give her the time.

Alerted by the clicking sound of high heels, Jack looked up to spot the counselor, Karen, looking down at him, sporting an encouraging grin. He'd had a limited amount of contact with her, and although Karen seemed pleasant enough, Nattie always pulled a face when the counselor's name came up.

Blond with dark-framed glasses, Karen smoothed her gray tailored skirt and took the chair next to him. Wearing a cream-colored blouse and smart heels, she looked fashionably correct, as San might have said.

According to San, Jack hadn't lived a fashionably correct day in his life, a declaration Nattie softened to, **"That's okay, Uncle Jack, you're a work in progress."**

The outgoing counselor seemed more animated than he'd remembered, discussing her latest read, a collection of short stories by F. Scott Fitzgerald, the ill-fated author of **The Great Gatsby**. "Do you read any fiction?" she asked.

"Mysteries, mostly."

"Well, then," she said, sounding very much like one of his former elementary teachers, "we've got our own little mystery right here, don't we?"

Before long, Stacy returned, and after

more small talk, she met Karen's eyes, and they seemed to share a knowing smile.

"Before we begin, I'd like to extend my congratulations," Karen announced. "I think it will make a big difference to our situation."

Jack was confused.

Nattie's teacher again exchanged glances with the counselor, who added, "Oh dear. I'm afraid we've stepped in it."

Stacy Fenton frowned. "You **are** getting married, aren't you, Mr. Livingston?"

Jack chuckled. The women weren't remotely amused, and he shouldn't have been, either. Truly, this had **Nattie** written all over it. Karen showed him one of Nattie's latest drawings, a picture of Jack, Laura Mast, and Nattie—each one dressed in Amish attire. Grinning like a bandit, Jack had his arm around Laura, with Nattie squished in between them, beaming streaks of yellow light, artistically envisioned in the preferred medium of most primary students: rainbow-hued crayons.

Stacy seemed flustered, her face reddening. Karen leaned forward, asserting her authority as the school counselor. "Maybe we shouldn't be too very surprised," she said. "This particular drawing points to what we've been discussing...."

"Indubitably," Stacy added midstream and with a straight face.

**Indubitably**, Jack thought, one of Nattie's favorite words. For a solid week, she'd answered **indubitably** to nearly every question, until he'd kindly requested her to cease and desist. **"You're driving your nanny crazy."** Cheerfully, Nattie replaced it with **no duh**, a much hipper option.

"Nattie's obsession with, well... **mothers**," Karen finished sharply.

That was the purpose of the meeting in a nutshell. He recalled six months prior, when Nattie wanted to talk about her adoptive mother, Darla, for the first time, followed later by questions about her birth mother: **"Do you think she's looking for me, Uncle Jack?"** At the time, he'd thought, **Isn't she too young for this?**

Karen Jones reviewed her notes. "Natalie's work at school hasn't suffered. If anything, she's become overly focused on her tests, as if they're a reflection of her personal worth." She handed over Natalie's latest report card—top marks in every subject. "But her social interactions haven't improved much at all in the past few months," Karen continued. "**Aggressive** is perhaps too strong a word, but at times Nattie can be overly controlling. And...she'll cry for seemingly no reason."

Jack grimaced. A year ago, Nattie's second-grade teacher had informed him that the other students competed for Nattie's attention. **"They look to her for approval,"** she'd said. **"Nattie's confidence is infectious."**

**And now tears?** He recalled her one-time encounter with a bully as a case in point. While other kids might have cowered in the corner, Nattie had faced the problem head on. Do or die. Had her confidence disappeared with her current obsession over a mother?

"She seems happy, most of the time," Jack offered somewhat feebly.

"Most troubled kids do," Karen replied. "But they act out in small ways, giving us little clues." Karen fixed him with a curious gaze. "How is Nattie at home?"

Jack described his daughter's numerous questions about Darla, as well as Nattie's birth mother. "Nattie also makes many lists. Is this normal?" He mentioned Nattie's fascination with favorite films but stressed again Laura's important role. "Her nanny provides wonderful support for Nattie."

By the quizzical way the women looked at each other, they obviously disagreed.

"Mr. Livingston"—Karen leaned forward, continuing in a tone that reminded him of an attorney's summation—"it's my professional opinion, after everything we've uncovered, that your nanny, this Laura Mast, only aggravates your daughter's desire for a mother. It must be terribly frustrating, if not a little frightening."

**Frightening?**

Karen continued. "We find ourselves concerned about what will happen to Nattie when this Amishwoman seeks employment elsewhere."

Jack sighed. "I can't imagine she will."

Karen looked skeptical.

He mentioned his sister's role in Nattie's life, and they acknowledged that San provided essential maternal support for her young niece. Jack asked for further suggestions, but when Karen suggested counseling again, he cringed. He didn't trust counselors, with their half-baked theories and arrogant Ivy League demeanor. Fact was, he didn't trust anyone with his daughter.

Jack noticed the time.

Stacy must have caught him looking at his watch and promptly inserted Nattie's picture into a folder and gave it to him. They rose and escorted him to the door, where Stacy Fenton shook his hand, then headed down the hallway.

Karen Jones lingered behind to offer her business card. "If you're interested in private counseling for Nattie, I'm available during the summer. I can also give you a referral, if you wish."

Jack stared at the card, remembering she'd given him the same one a few months before. "Won't Nattie outgrow this?" he asked.

Karen paused before launching off into her assessment of the special risks attendant to raising an adopted child. "Adoptees often start their lives feeling cast off by their first mothers. They feel rejected in the womb. In Natalie's case, she grew close to Darla and Danny, only to lose them, too. So in a way, she's lost everything. Obviously, at this stage of her development, she's afraid of losing more, and it's affecting every part of her life." She paused to breathe. "Nattie's desperate for permanence."

Karen gestured to the folder under Jack's arm, the one containing Nattie's drawing, and gave him a heartening smile. "I've worked with many troubled kids," she said. "And I'm convinced that children will find a way to tell you what they need... if we can find a way to listen."

Jack considered this. He'd been listening to everything, everyone, and racking his brain for solutions.

Karen retrieved the card from him. "Here, let me jot down my home phone number, just in case." She wrote it above the school number and handed it back. "I hope this helps. Call me, Jack, whenever, whatever, just to talk, or if you need help making any decisions regarding Natalie."

In the parking lot, Jack opened the glove compartment, checking for his camera, which he'd used to chronicle Nattie's past year, knowing he'd want it at the park, where he was heading. Before starting the ignition, he removed Nattie's crayon drawing from the folder and studied it.

**"Children will find a way to tell you what they need."**

Sighing, he started the car, backed out of the parking spot, and exited to the street.

His cell phone rang, as if on cue. "Where are you, Jack?" It was San.

"Heading to the park."

"I'll meet you," she said, her tone subdued.

"What's up?"

"I'll tell you when I get there," San said and hung up. **No more drama**, Jack thought. **Please.**

# Chapter 8

Light crept through the blinds in her bedroom and she pushed away the sheet. **Something's wrong.** Getting up, Kelly yanked on her robe and staggered across the hall to the small nursery, peering into Emily's crib.

She froze, panicked, then rushed down the steps to the kitchen and into the living room. Heart throbbing, she dashed back to the nursery and saw that Emily's diaper bag was missing, as was her crib blanket. Hysterical now, Kelly could scarcely think.

Turning to the white wicker bureau, she began to pull out one drawer after another—all empty—her hands shaking wildly.

And then it came to her.

**Bobby. No! Please, God, no!**

Kelly flew back downstairs to the front door and saw that it was clearly unlocked, even though she'd locked it before going to bed.

Grabbing her cell phone from the kitchen counter, she called out to God for help, then dialed 9-1-1 with shaking fingers, sobbing out her fears when the dispatcher answered.

Moments later Kelly was outside, standing on the edge of the curb, looking up and down the street as if she could somehow snatch back her missing infant.

**He must have taken her**, she knew then with certainty, the horror of it washing over her.

The distant wail of a siren began to grow in the distance as she punched in the phone number for her estranged husband and waited. One ring...two rings...and then his dreaded words, **"She fetched a pretty penny, Kel."**

Kelly jerked awake, drenched with sweat and still fully dressed after her outing to Chet and Eloise's house. Looking down, she found Emily's infant booties clutched in her hand. **I should have known better than to take them out.** Kelly breathed in their aroma, then gently placed the booties back in her bureau drawer.

Still trying to shake off the last vestiges of the nightmare, Kelly wasn't remotely hungry, though suppertime had long since passed. She turned on her radio and straightened up the bed, fluffing the comforter back into position and humming along with Michelle Tumes's "Healing Waters."

In the kitchen, she straightened the dining area and placed her laptop on the sofa nearby, relieved to have another four hours until her night shift began.

Hearing light scratching at the door, Kelly turned to find Felix meowing, posturing for an evening meal. "Is Mommy gone again?"

Felix meowed to the affirmative.

"C'mon, little munchkin," Kelly cooed, picking up the calico kitty. "Let's get you fixed up."

While Felix lapped up the water and

Meow Mix, Kelly vacuumed the floor. She tried to keep the place spic and span, especially since Agnes was giving her a drastically reduced deal on rent. Since the landlady made few demands and seemed to appreciate having her around, Kelly didn't mind the stark studio apartment. Overall, it was a fair arrangement. **Pay little; get little.**

At the kitchen counter, she shuffled through papers and came across a photo of adorable Sydney Moore. Slumping into the chair, Kelly stared at the picture and remembered the hope she'd felt when Ernie first sent it.

Kelly shuddered and tore the picture into pieces. **Old news.** Felix nudged her leg and she stroked his neck. **But I'm still in the game**, she told herself, thinking of Ernie's new lead and taking Felix in her arms, cuddling him close, wondering where Agnes had gone. **Probably playing bingo in the church basement again.**

She considered driving to the coffee shop just down the street and ordering something inexpensive, if only to be around others. Maybe a doughnut?

**Too sugary**, she thought.

Then recalling Eloise's concern about her not eating, Kelly set the cat down gently and marched to the fridge. She peered inside and spotted a carton of strawberry yogurt, normally her favorite, and felt her stomach roil. Instead, she reached for the half loaf of bread and popped a slice into her old toaster, the one she'd picked up at a garage sale for less than the cost of a cup of coffee at Starbucks.

When the toast popped out, she buttered it and took a bite. It wasn't very tasty, but she forced it down with half a glass of milk. **I'm trying**, she thought, remembering the concern in Melody's eyes, too.

**Mel and Kel forever.** Kelly hadn't forgotten their slogan. They'd even had it embroidered on matching T-shirts, personalized with a photo of the two of them, cheek to cheek and not a care in the world.

From the cupboard, Kelly removed the worn photo album of her high school and college years, as well as her early years with Emily. In the meantime, Felix had made himself right at home, lounging on the sofa, just staring back at her.

Kelly smiled. "At least someone's happy."

The cat's eyes drooped, now half-mast. **Of course I'm happy. Why do you ask?**

Kelly perused the scrapbook pages again. Several photos graced the album — Kelly with Melody, nine-year-olds dressed as characters from **The Wizard of Oz**, raring to go trick-or-treating. Kelly had been the good witch; Melody had chosen Dorothy. There was also a shot with their prom dates: Kelly with Bobby Maines and Melody with her own husband-to-be, Trey Cunningham. And a final one: the college graduation photo, complete with bright blue caps and gowns. The picture included their parents in front of the girls' dorm, only weeks away from Kelly's and Melody's weddings.

Even now, she was tempted to text Melody.

**"Same number, Kel?"** Melody had asked.

**It's been six years**, Kelly thought. Six

lousy years since she'd pushed Melody away. To her friend's credit, Melody hadn't much cared for Bobby, even before he took Emily.

Robert "Bobby" Maines had been heartbreakingly charming back in the day. Kelly's mom spotted him first, at church, impressed with such a "polite young man." Determined that her daughter marry and have the same happily-ever-after she'd known with her own husband before his untimely death, she'd practically pushed Kelly into his arms.

**Dear Bobby.** Tall and truly good-looking, his dark eyes could penetrate your heart. Bobby Maines was a back-slapping natural salesman, played varsity football, and was senior class president. The day he turned eighteen, Bobby landed an entry-level job at their local car dealership. Although head over her heels in love, Kelly was determined to finish college. And Bobby promised to wait for her.

While waiting, he made loads of money, startlingly so. Far more than she could've made just out of college. Looking back, there were times when Kelly was puzzled by his ultra-nice approach—his too-smiley demeanor, his upbeat spin on everything, and the surprising flow of money. It worried her at first, then outright annoyed her. Something was dreadfully amiss.

But Kelly was in love and blind. So she married Bobby, despite the warning bells. Their wedded bliss lasted nearly a year before his true colors became apparent, particularly his secret addictions and his paranoid jealousy. Their marriage began to spiral downward.

On top of everything, Bobby wouldn't consider the possibility of having children, wanting Kelly all to himself and claiming kids were just a money drain. When she'd unintentionally gotten pregnant, he became irate and insisted she abort. Kelly refused, signaling the beginning of the end. Eventually Bobby's drug and alcohol usage caused him to lose his job, and he became abusive. By the time little Emily was born, Kelly and Bobby had been separated for six months.

Then, one day after a bitter argument,

Bobby did the unthinkable.

Days later, the police found him in New York City, sprawled on a hotel bed, dead from an overdose. Baby Emily was nowhere to be found. Scant but sufficient evidence pointed to the unbelievable truth: Bobby had sold their infant daughter to a baby broker for the very drugs that had taken his life. And with his death, the trail to Emily's whereabouts died, as well.

**If only I realized what he was capable of**, Kelly thought, now aware of a strange tingling in her arms and legs. Familiar with the first clutches of despair, she brushed away tears, mentally tying a rope to her faith and holding on.

Kelly entered the bathroom and showered, hoping to pull herself together before leaving for work. Dressed and ready to head out, she made it as far as the car before the tears fell again. She tossed her cell phone onto the passenger seat and yanked the door shut, gripping the steering wheel, breathing deeply. Crossing her arms, she shivered in the glow of a brilliant pink dusk. It felt like a sign, one more nudge that God hadn't forgotten her.

When she felt calmer, Kelly dabbed at her eyes and started the car. She considered calling her mom, but their recent conversation hadn't been pleasant. The time before that her mother hadn't minced words: **"You've made a shambles of your life, Kelly, all for a daughter you may never see again."**

**"How can you say such a thing?"**

Mom had been silent for a moment, then added, more softly, **"What kind of life would she be coming home to if you found her, honey?"**

The question still haunted her, and feeling as she did today, Kelly certainly didn't want to risk another lecture.

**So now what?** she thought, feeling lonely.

**Contact Melody.**

And before she could second-guess it to death, she sent a text to Mel's old number: **Can we get together sometime?**

Her cell twirped, signaling the reception of a new text. Melody: **I'm so glad you**

**texted me, Kel! Yes! Just name the place and when.**

Beyond grateful, Kelly broke into a smile.

Jack spotted Nattie near the park swings, Laura perched primly on the adjacent swing, face to the sun. Nattie's skinny legs pummeled the air, and her hair swept close to the ground as she leaned backward on the upswing.

Waving, Jack caught Laura's attention. Then, scanning the area, he noticed her large blue sewing bag on a nearby bench and went to sit, observing from this vantage point. Meanwhile, he was compelled to snap a few nonposed shots.

It was late afternoon, the temperature warmer than was forecast, and not a cloud in sight. The park was filled with summer-delirious children, while the footpath at the perimeter held a few diehard runners and dog walkers.

When Nattie tired of swinging, Laura whispered to her and Nattie twisted excitedly, spotting Jack at the bench, waving fiercely before she scampered away to the slide.

Seemingly out of breath, Laura came over and sat next to him. "They weren't kidding. It's awful muggy out, ain't?" She smiled, adjusted her prim **Kapp**, and removed a crochet hook from deep in the bag. Quickly, she began to make the familiar loopy chains, glancing up every few moments to check on Nattie.

Jack talked casually of their summer plans, chuckling about Nattie's most recent activities list, which was sure to undergo revisions as the weeks progressed.

"Ice cream's high up there, no matter the subject, **jah?**" Laura said, laughing. She asked about the school meeting, and Jack gave her the gist of it, leaving out the discussion of Laura's role in Nattie's life. He paused, considering Nattie's family drawing, curious how Laura might respond to it.

At an unexpected **whoop**, the attention flew to Nattie, their antennae ever on the alert.

Nattie stopped, saw them eyeing her,

put her hands on her hips, and gave them a scolding look: **"What?"**

Laura waved and Jack smiled.

Nattie was an intuitive child. She had a talented way of perceiving situations, sensing emotions, putting two and two together. And like any bright eight-year-old, she had her share of harebrained notions, including the most exuberant flights of fantasy, but she also had a knack for coming up with the most insightful reflections.

"So...I guess Nattie's graduated to matchmaking," Jack ventured.

Laura looked at him and bit her lip. "Hard not to notice. In a way, I'm flattered that she's ever so fond of me." She laughed softly, continuing to crochet. "But it worries me."

"Perhaps she'll grow out of it." Their answer for everything, like whistling in the dark.

"**Jah**, maybe so," Laura murmured.

They sat silently for a moment. Now and then, Nattie would pause long enough to grin at Laura, eliciting a warm smile back from her. It was comforting to Jack the way Nattie gauged her place, her behavior, her **correctness**, by confirming it with her sweet-spirited nanny.

It fueled his faith in Nattie's future. His little girl would do well to model Laura's respect for hard work, her polite demeanor, and gentle humility. **And faith in God**, he mused.

Jack was startled by a commanding thud on his shoulder. "Well, lookee here," San declared behind him. His sister scooted around the bench, wearing off-white capris, a sleeveless lime green top, and designer tennis shoes.

True to form, Laura was already getting up. "Excuse me. I'll leave you two alone."

He was about to object, but San was all over it. "Thanks, Laura."

Watching Laura cross the playground toward Nattie, San sat where Laura had been and folded her arms. Her smile vanished into an expression of dismay. "How is she not hot in that outfit?"

Jack cleared his throat.

San sighed loudly, taking the hint.

"So what's up, dear sister of mine?" Jack asked, breaking the stillness.

"The sun, moon...and the stars," San replied, her eyes narrowing when Nattie ran from the sandbox and practically leapt into Laura's arms.

Looking down, San became preoccupied with her shoes, twisting one foot to the left, then to the right. Her short brunette hair was glossy and thick, her eyebrows sharply plucked and finely detailed, her soft complexion creamy white, her brown eyes intense, her facial features thin, which seemed somewhat Italian to Jack with her somewhat prominent nose—not large, more regal—despite their family's decidedly Scottish background. After all, their great-grandfather had emigrated from Glasgow.

Mimicking her movements, Jack extended his own Nikes for comparative examination. Laughing, San rolled her eyes.

"What?"

"Shoes are ground zero for fashion, Jack. You need a wife, if for no other reason than to coordinate your wardrobe."

Jack wiggled his foot. "But I just broke these in."

"They **look** broken." San waved her hand reproachfully. "Tell me this, was Nattie with you when you bought them?"

"She was five."

"You bought those **three** years ago?"

"At least."

San frowned. "Did you get Laura's opinion?"

Jack shook his head, smirking at the image of Laura approving his shoes, and San harrumphed. "It's rather disturbing when an Amish nanny has better fashion sense than her **English** boss!"

"Maybe I should marry her, then," Jack laughed.

San's face fell. "Don't even joke about a thing like that, Jack. It's bad enough that she's got Nattie speaking that guttural German dialect or whatever."

"San," Jack warned. "You promised—"

"Okay, okay. I'm sorry." She sighed and changed the subject, deftly transitioning to the school meeting.

Jack confirmed what they already knew:

Nattie's diminishing social skills, and her fixation with lists, movies, and stuffed animals, but he kept the drawing under his hat, unwilling to give San further ammunition. His manner must have seemed evasive to his drama-sniffing sister.

"Do I have to call Karen Jones myself?" San asked.

**Karen?** He must have visibly flinched.

San leaned back. "I met her through my friend Misha's sister, whose friend Jenny knows her through her neighbor Sally."

Jack shook his head. San made most extroverts look like wallflowers. She put the **net** into networking. And yet, in spite of her social skills in the adult arena, and despite her devotion to Nattie, San had only a modicum of tolerance for children in general. **"I've got Mom's voice in my head,"** she'd once said. **"I'd probably strangle my own kid."**

True enough. Having acquired their mother's tongue, San had a first-class temper and little patience for those who tested it. Woe to the child—or **man**—who crossed San's path. Notwithstanding, in her eyes, Nattie could do no wrong.

Nattie spotted her auntie and jumped off the monkey bars, splattering dust and wood chips, as she came running—an awkward out-of-control sprint. She burst into San's arms. "Auntie Santa!"

San kissed her cheek and held on to Nattie's hands as she leaned back. "Where have you been all my life, kiddo?"

"Waiting for you!" Nattie squealed, gesturing dramatically toward San's outfit. She stretched her arms to the sky, as if San had scored a touchdown. "You look simply mah-velous, Auntie San! You're the fashion queen of Wooster. I wanna look just like you when I grow up."

San and Nattie high-fived.

Modestly, Laura stayed where she was, near the swings, shielding her eyes, a study in all things simple.

"I owe you a shopping trip, don't I?" San asked, seemingly thrilled that at least someone in her immediate family appreciated her talents.

Nattie applauded the prospect. Then,

as quickly as she'd come, Nattie darted away, joining Laura again.

San clasped her hands over one knee. "Well, are you ready for my terrible news, Jack?"

He clenched his jaw.

"The magazine finally offered me the promotion, and they want me in-house this time."

"Ugh."

"I'm moving, bro!" San exclaimed with her usual flourish. "Flying the coop and spreading my wings, so excited I'm ready to sing! Yes, Jack, I'm taking a jet plane to New York!"

Jack groaned. Although he had been expecting it, he'd hoped to be wrong. "Excuse me if I don't break into song."

"I know, I know. I'm gonna miss Nattie terribly. And my church friends." She sniffed and gave him a mischievous squint. "And **you**…maybe a little."

He smiled. "I guess New York isn't that far away."

"Hey, I'll be back a couple times a month. Okay?"

He nodded, and they discussed further details of her move and when it might happen: September, a good three months away.

"I told my boss I couldn't leave until Labor Day weekend," San continued, "since Nattie will be starting school the next week."

Jack frowned, then remembered the school district was starting late this year… something to do with construction on a media center.

"I'm replacing Cassie as lead graphic designer. She's moving up to **Paris**." San said, shaping the word with a tone of dismay. Paris was San's lifetime goal.

Jack chuckled. "The fashion capital of the world. Too bad you're stuck with New York."

"Someday, Jack. All in good time, you'll see." She turned and peered at him through her dark sunglasses. "So…have you given any further thought to Anita? I want to leave you in good hands—that is, **female** hands."

Jack waved off the notion: Nattie and

San, the two matchmakers in his life.

San folded her arms. "Lord, help my obstreperous brother."

They both went silent, watching Nattie zip down the slide, whooping it up as she did so, and for the moment, the little princess looked fully and completely happy, apparently without a care in the world.

**Another loss for her**, Jack realized, remembering the counselor's litany of Nattie's misfortunes. In light of San's imminent departure, and despite the growing concern on seemingly everyone's part over Nattie's nanny, Jack was especially grateful for Laura's presence in their lives.

# Chapter 9

Jack and Laura lingered at the park after San's departure, until mothers began to gather up their children. Close to five o'clock, when bored at last from having repeatedly scaled the fake boulders, Nattie made her way back to them. Jack was catching up on the national news on his smartphone while Laura had resumed her crocheting.

Without batting an eye, Nattie requested a visit to her favorite burger dive, twenty minutes away. Jack turned to Laura. "Would you like to join us?"

Nattie contributed by fluttering her eye lashes, pleading silently with Laura, who graciously agreed.

They climbed into the front bench seat of Jack's pickup, and Nattie wiggled in between Jack and Laura. And similar to her very telling drawing, she beamed rays of happiness, chattering all the way, telling one story after another. At the drive-through, Nattie ordered chicken nuggets and a large chocolate shake.

"Better not get too used to that," Jack warned with a wink. "This is the summer of green salads."

"Instead of **purple** salads?" Nattie giggled, glancing at Laura. "Junk food's okay once in a while. Even Laura says so."

Laura elbowed Nattie. "Don't throw me under the bus, **Lieb**."

"Just sayin'."

Jack ordered something with fish and turned his attention to Laura.

"Nothing for me," Laura replied. **"Denki."**

Immediately, Nattie shook her head and launched into a stream of **Deitsch**, and Laura chattered back. Sighing, Laura peered up at the menu board. "Well... maybe just—"

"Nuggets?" Nattie suggested. "There's all kinds of sauces, you know—barbeque, honey mustard, chili, ranch, chipotle, and the best of all, chocolate malt!"

"Chocolate malt?" Jack muttered.

Laura was laughing softly, eyes twinkling. "Nuggets sound awful **gut**, actually."

Nattie cheered, urging her uncle to ask for a sampling of every sauce flavor. When their order came, they headed for the highway leading to Apple Creek. Shortly before the road turned into Main Street, and just past a long line of picturesque farms, was the road leading to Laura's cousins' white clapboard house.

Nattie continued to daintily eat her nuggets, urging Laura to experiment with the sauces, making a game of it, voting on which flavor was best and second best, etc.

When Laura tried Nattie's favorite milkshake sauce, she murmured approvingly. "Not so bad."

"Your turn," Nattie told Jack, holding out a nugget just dipped in chocolate malt.

Jack opened his mouth, chewed reluctantly, and had to concur. It wasn't the worst thing. Actually...it was almost good.

"Told you," Nattie exclaimed as she and

Laura high-fived and shared another **Deitsch** aside.

**Maybe it's time I learned their language**, he thought, turning into the driveway at the familiar black mailbox with **Peter & Lomie Troyer** in tall white letters. They followed the dusty road to the rambling farmhouse nestled near a grove of trees. The white clapboard house with its welcoming front porch was surrounded by flower beds—pansies of all colors, snapdragons, and red and white petunias—no doubt Laura's handi-work. On the opposite side of the road stood the barn and pony stable, next to Laura's repaired car, which her cousin must have retrieved.

Jack opened the door of his truck to catch a breeze. Nattie hopped out and headed for the new Shetland ponies, chattering to Laura all the way to the barn.

Jack found Nattie and Laura whispering together inside the stable, the twin baby ponies nudging their soft noses into Nattie's open palms. "Where's their mother?" Nattie asked in a hush.

Jack glanced at Laura, who gave him a

sympathetic look.

"She's out in the field," Laura whispered, "but look how well they are doin' on their own, **jah**?"

On the drive back to Wooster, Nattie was unusually quiet—missing Laura, Jack assumed—while he considered various ways to broach the subject of her curious drawing.

"What're we doing tonight?" Nattie asked, crossing her legs and patting out a rhythm on her knees.

Jack reached over and put his hand on her shoulder. It was time to talk. "So...I went to that school meeting today," he began.

"To see my teacher."

"And your counselor."

She grimaced. "Did they ask about me?"

Jack chuckled. "Funniest thing," he continued, turning off the highway, "they congratulated me on my upcoming nuptials." She turned to Jack, brow furrowed. "What's a nuptial?"

"Well, it's marriage."

"Oh." Nattie squeezed her eyes shut,

her expression twisting as if dreading what was to come. She pointed off to the right. "I think my friend's cousin Madison lives out here somewhere. But her dad doesn't. Not anymore." She sniffed, and Jack went on, gently prying her back to the topic at hand.

"Anyway, your teachers had the strangest notion that I was getting married to Laura."

Nattie pooched her lips.

"Any idea how they might have come to that conclusion?"

"Well...kinda."

"I think you have some explaining to do, young lady."

"It's not as bad as you think."

"Well...it sounds pretty bad."

"I know, I know," she said, and he could almost see the wheels turning while she devised her excuse.

A few moments ticked by as they turned onto the street leading to theirs. Nattie pointed again. "My music teacher, Mrs. Adler, lives over there—"

"Nattie..."

"I'm thinking," she said, sighing softly. "I guess I was only following what Jesus said to do."

"Come again?"

"Remember what Pastor Al said last week? Jesus said that when we pray we're supposed to believe that we've already received whatever we're asking for."

"Hmm."

"I figured I was supposed to act like I'd already received it, and since I was praying you'd marry Laura, it made per- fect sense." Nattie sat there glowing, seemingly thrilled with her airtight defense.

"You are quite the clever girl."

She nodded. "I get that a lot."

Jack thought back to the story he'd recently read about George Mueller, clear- ly a man who lived by faith, and considered how he would explain to an eight-year-old at what point faith became presumption. **When it becomes manipulative**, he figured. "That's not how God rolls, honey."

"Okay. So I won't do it again," Nattie promised, using her favorite get-out-of- jail pass phrase, the one she'd long ago determined could end any discussion of bad behavior.

"You won't, eh?"

With both hands, Nattie held up two uncrossed fingers, like two peace signs, promising without conditions.

Jack sighed. **Okay**, he thought. **Fair enough.**

He recalled overhearing a conversation Nattie had initiated with Laura about prayer, and Laura had given her a thoughtful answer: **"God can give us what we ask for, but He can't just give us character. Character is what we give God. Character is forged by faith and persistence and doing the right thing."**

"Am I out of the doghouse yet?" Nattie asked.

"Yes," Jack muttered, touching her head.

"Good," she said. "I don't like the doghouse. It's dark and it smells funny." She giggled at her own remark, and Jack couldn't help grinning right along with her.

Later that evening, Nattie and the neighborhood kids pedaled their bikes up and down the block **"to see if anything interesting is going on."** Then, around the time the sunlight diminished, Jack and Nattie covered the dining table with plastic and settled in for a relaxed hour of clay modeling.

Accompanied by the **Tangled** soundtrack, Jack molded his own version of Aladdin's Cave of Wonders while Nattie worked on her vision of Rapunzel's tower. He finished early, received a glance of approval, and silently watched as Nattie, tongue firmly planted against her mouth, added her own touches to the tower's turret.

When she finished her masterwork, they sat back and admired it. Jack dismissed what San might have said: **"Isn't she too old for this?"** He didn't care. Nattie was happiest when doing her art. He certainly wasn't going to push her into older stuff just because San wanted her niece to grow up.

At bedtime, Nattie summoned more questions about her birth mom: "Does she miss me? Would she recognize me?"

He did his best to answer, but in the end, Nattie cried. Her face melted, and her lip quivered, and she sniffed loudly. He held her until the sobbing passed, and when she prayed, she gripped his hand tightly.

In light of this, he didn't mention San's impending leaving. One cry a night was one too many for both of them.

Before he switched off the light, Nattie exchanged Felicia the Unicorn for Whiskers, her stubby kitty with the magnificent blue eyes and a concealed motor that rumbled softly. "Whiskers doesn't say much," Nattie sniffed. "But she purrs. And sometimes that's all you need. Ain't so?"

Downstairs, Jack watched the local news while working through some figures. He leaned back to relax but considered Nattie's drawing again. Something about it still nagged at him.

During the commercial he went to his office and removed it from the folder, noting again the bright yellow lines depicting the joy on Nattie's face.

**"Children will tell you what they need,"** the counselor had said.

In thick crayon letters, Nattie had written below, **Dad and Mom...and me**. He'd been so distracted by the Mom part that he'd totally missed the **Dad** part.

In the early days after his brother and sister-in-law's passing, little Nattie had been inconsolable, crying for her mama and daddy. While Laura was of profound comfort to her, he'd been reluctant to change anything in Nattie's life that would upset her further. Not wanting to step into his brother's shoes prematurely, he'd remained Uncle Jack. **Is it time to change that?**

He trudged upstairs again and paused at Nattie's door, wondering if she'd fallen asleep.

"Fee-fi-fo-fair!" he heard from inside. "I can hear you out there!"

Jack cracked the door and flipped on the light. Nattie's eyes squished to a squint. Grinning, she shielded her face from the overhead light, peering up at him.

"Since you're still awake," Jack began, sitting at the edge of Nattie's bed, "maybe we could talk."

Nattie sat up, brushing her hair out of her eyes, undoubtedly eager for the welcome diversion from the chore of sleeping. "I do like talking when I'm not in trouble." She made a face. "Wait a minute—**am** I in trouble again?"

"You're never in trouble, sweet pea."

"Okay. Let's go with that." Nattie propped her elbows on her knees, knuckles to her chin.

"I've been thinking about something, honey."

Nattie frowned thoughtfully, matching his own serious expression.

"You know how much I loved your dad—my big brother, Danny. Well, when you became my little girl, I wanted to keep his memory alive for you. Didn't think it was right to take his place."

"I only kinda remember my dad."

"And that's partly why I think it's time...." He hesitated, as Nattie's eyes drilled a hole in his face. Surrounded by vivid Disney posters, he swallowed hard, aware of Princess Ariel's eyes on him.

As usual, Nattie was two steps ahead of

him, her face suddenly bright. "So...what if I called **you** Dad?"

"That's what I was thinking, actually."

"Deal," Nattie said, extending her hand for Jack to shake, which they did. Proper and legal. He kissed her cheek, and she frowned. "So now I have to go to sleep?"

"Yes, goof."

"Aren't we going to celebrate?"

"How?"

She gave him a look of exasperation. "As if!"

"How 'bout a cookie instead?"

She agreed on the condition that the cookie be accompanied by ice cream, because to Nattie nothing was truly celebratory without the cold stuff.

When Nattie was tucked in for the second time, Jack headed back downstairs to turn off the lights.

He had just settled into his corner of the tan sectional when his cell phone rang. It was Diane, his next-door neighbor.

"Didn't mean to call so late, but I saw your light still on."

He set her mind at ease. "It's fine." He

listened as she explained the reason for her call: Craig and Diane's upcoming anniversary.

"Congratulations," he said, happy for them, surprised at how quickly a full year had passed.

"Which is why I'm calling," she continued. "I have a special request, but please feel free to say no."

She certainly had his attention.

"I just bought my husband a new dirt bike!"

"No kidding," Jack said, hard-pressed to conceal the awe in his voice.

Diane lowered her voice to a conspiratorial whisper. "And I need to hide it."

**Oh boy**, Jack thought.

After listening with growing fascination and, frankly, more than a little envy, they said good-bye just as he caught a flicker of movement in the hallway upstairs.

"Hey, Dad!" Nattie called down.

For a moment, he was taken aback. **Oh yeah**, that's me. "What's up, sweetie?"

"Nothing," she said, grinning. "Just checking to see if it worked."

# Chapter 10

Having gotten a miraculous five hours of sleep, Kelly was thrilled to hear from Ernie Meyers the following Wednesday after-noon. His thick gravelly voice rumbled over the phone, and she could almost smell his trademark Old Spice. She'd been up for an hour or so, twirling her hair and reading computer posts. Hearing his voice, she felt psyched. "Got something for me?"

"Ready to rock and roll?" He sounded a bit more hoarse than usual and admitted to struggling with a lingering case of bronchitis. "But I gotta make a livin', so here I be, sucking on throat lozenges and popping aspirin."

"You shouldn't push it," she cautioned.

"It takes more than a nasty bug to do

me in." He coughed and she heard the sound of shuffling papers.

Kelly went to the sink for some water, her anticipation building.

"So," Ernie began, "I forgot to mention… this one's in-state."

Kelly nearly dropped her glass. **"How in-state?"**

"Forty minutes to the southwest, tiny place called Wooster."

She knew the town well. In fact, she'd gone there with Bobby on weekends when they were first married.

"You could whisk down there in your free time. Check it out. Work your magic." Ernie paused, then chuckled wryly. "Oh, that's right. I forgot. We're ditching our tool kit of tricks."

Kelly could only focus on one thought: **Forty minutes away?** How many times had she longed for…no, **prayed** for something this close? She looked at the wall clock, just above the corkboard she used for reminders. She could be in Wooster before six. Easy. Maybe even earlier.

"Girl's name is Natalie Livingston," Ernie said.

**Natalie.**

"Cute little thing, too," Ernie continued. "Smart cookie. They call her Nattie for short."

Kelly stood near the open window overlooking the tree-lined neighborhood. Bright sunlight twinkled off the glass. She could hear kids shrieking and dogs barking, a car door slamming and a husband and wife having a pleasant conversation. There she stood with her heart in her throat. "Does this child look like me, Ernie?"

"There's a strong resemblance," he replied. "Especially with our aged-progression of Emily." He began coughing harder now until he had to cover the receiver. When he finally came on again, he apologized. "There's something you need to know, Kelly. This little girl's adoptive parents, Danny and Darla Livingston, were killed in a car crash four years after her adoption."

Kelly shuddered. **Poor kid.** Then she

realized: **Maybe** my **kid.**

"Nattie's guardian is her uncle, Jack Livingston. He never married, but he does employ an Amish nanny."

"No mother?"

"Nope."

Another long pause. Kelly listened to the soft whirring of the ceiling fan, an attempt to cool the place without turning on the AC, trying to save money on the utility bill.

"Wooster," she said finally. **Incredible.** "Charming little town," Ernie said.

Kelly asked politely about his wife, Penny, and in turn, Ernie asked about Kelly's mom.

"She's busy as ever," Kelly replied. "Still belongs to about twenty different social clubs."

Ernie made a grunt but didn't speak.

She had to smile. Ernie called things as he saw them, but if he couldn't say anything nice, he usually said nothing.

"I think my mom still blames herself," Kelly added in her mother's defense.

"What? For introducing you to that sociopath?"

Yeah, she thought. **Sociopath pretty much covers it.**

"I have to take the blame too, Ernie," she admitted. "And I've made so many mistakes since."

"You did what any mother would have done under similar circumstances," Ernie assured her. "You did your best."

Kelly was encouraged by his loyalty. She thought of Wooster again, eager to drive there. At the kitchen counter Kelly fumbled with her faux leather purse, removing a pen and lined notepad.

"Okay. I'm ready for the address whenever you are."

She wrote it down quickly, and before hanging up, she encouraged Ernie to take it easy. "You really should be in bed," she urged.

"Get some rest. You need it."

He seemed to dismiss her concern. "I'll attach Natalie's photo to an email right away." He heaved and coughed raggedly, sounding worse by the minute.

She thanked him, heart racing. Disconnecting, Kelly stared at the address with a renewed sense of optimism. **Every failure brings me closer**, she thought. **Thank you, Lord.**

While she couldn't manipulate a chance meeting this time—having promised Chet and Eloise not to "steal" another girl's DNA—there were even greater difficulties with a direct approach.

Pursing her lips, she imagined ringing the bell, picturing Nattie's uncle at the door, and giving him the spiel: **"Nearly nine years ago, my baby daughter was taken from me and sold into the black adoption market. I have reason to suspect your Nattie might be my own precious Emily."**

But such a bold approach had never worked in the past. In fact, Kelly had wasted years having doors slammed in her face, enduring months of legal wrangling before adoptive parents coughed up court-ordered DNA testing—the reason she'd eventually changed her methods.

**You know where my little girl is, Lord. Guide me there.** Smiling, she grabbed her car keys and dashed out the door.

Laura was grating cheese for their evening meal when Jack walked in with the mail, a collection of the usual junk and little else.

Her face was flushed, glowing with perspiration. "Nattie's out playing in the backyard with Marina, that nice little girl from down the block," she told him.

**Ah, friend number four on the current list**, he recalled with a smile.

"By the way, how do you like the terraced garden, Jack?" she asked, eyes bright.

Distracted with the mail, he hadn't even noticed and felt chagrined. "I'll take a look right now." Promptly, he headed for the front door to inspect Laura's handiwork. There, he surveyed the perfectly spaced rows of pink petunias; deep purple pansies blooming along the perimeter; red, purple, and pink starry-shaped asters; and the narrow silver-gray leaves of snow-in-summer filling in the borders.

**This took a lot of work**, he thought, marveling at Laura's accomplishment, and in a single day, too.

Moments later, Nattie came running from the back of the house to the front porch with Marina in tow, her blond hair flying, blue eyes streaked with tears.

"Marina's got a sliver," Nattie said calmly, exerting her confident leadership. Marina nodded, dramatically holding her right hand up, gripping it tightly with her left.

Nattie handed Jack a pair of tweezers like a nurse supplying a scalpel to the surgeon. "I told Marina you're the expert on slivers." Nattie shrugged, smiling. "Laura says so, too."

Sitting on his haunches, Jack met Marina's worried gaze. "I am the sliver extractor. And don't you forget it."

Marina swallowed hopefully, blinking up her courage.

Just then Laura called for Nattie to come inside, and Nattie left Jack in charge of Marina's "surgery."

Gently positioning Marina to take best advantage of the sunlight, Jack gripped the tweezers and examined the wound. "It might hurt just a little, but it'll be over quick, I promise."

"Don't dig!" Marina exclaimed, her arms trembling.

"I won't, sweetie." Holding Marina's finger, Jack took a closer look but was distracted by an older model gray Toyota Corolla with darkly tinted windows pulling up in front of their spinster neighbor's house, a few doors away. Mrs. Madison was a disagreeable soul who kept to herself, who turned off her porch light on Halloween, and who was known to lecture skateboarders from her front lawn.

Jack turned back to the task at hand—saving Marina from the giant wooden plank in her finger. "Hold still now," he murmured while Marina held her breath, her cheeks puffing out. Jack took aim, and in one fell swoop removed the sliver.

"Ta-da!" he exclaimed, holding up the offending speck.

Marina's mouth fell open. She examined the sliver, then her finger, and broke into a wide smile, smothering Jack with a hug. "Thank you, Mr. Livingston!"

Dramatically, Marina held up her arm and marched back into the house, yelling, "Nattie! Nattie! Your uncle—I mean **dad**—is a genius!"

Jack smiled. Fewer joys on earth exceeded the rescuing of a damsel in distress.

He could hear Nattie from the kitchen. "I told you!" Followed by Laura's, "Hold still, young lady." He wondered why Nattie was being asked to hold still, although it might explain why Nattie hadn't hung around to observe his supposed life-saving procedure.

Casually, he glanced down the street again before heading inside, noting that the driver still had yet to emerge from the Toyota. Making a mental note to check on it later, he headed back inside the house.

Kelly felt heartsick as she watched the obviously caring man with the blond girl on the front steps. **Something's wrong, though.** She checked her email only to find that Ernie hadn't sent the picture of Natalie Livingston yet.

Instead of getting out of the car, Kelly screwed the telephoto lens onto her expensive Olympus camera. Comfortably hidden behind the tinted glass, she honed in on the front porch, getting a closer look and snapping a couple of shots. Again, she was moved by the exceptionally tender scene but frustrated by what appeared to be another wild-goose chase.

When the child hugged her dad and ran inside the house, it only confirmed Kelly's fears. Blue-eyed and blond, with an angular face, sharp chin, and a slightly pointy nose, the girl nicknamed Nattie looked nothing like Kelly or her late husband.

**"Strong resemblance,"** Ernie had adamantly said.

**Big mistake,** she thought, **unless it's the wrong address. Could that be?**

She rechecked the email again. Still no photo. This wasn't like Ernie. He'd promised to send it immediately. Then again, Ernie hadn't been himself, struggling with bronchitis and a vicious cough.

She paused for a moment, reconsidering what she'd just observed. At her first meeting with Ernie, he'd placed two rows of photos in front of her on the table. He had explained that the top row contained photos of five parents, and below them, eight photos of their birth children, unmatched, scattered randomly. "**See if you can match 'em up,**" he'd said.

After a few tries, she'd managed to get 50 percent right. Some of the matches were obvious, but some weren't. Some kids strongly resembled their parents, and some clearly did not.

"**That's what we're dealing with,**" Ernie had said. "**Your kid might look like you...or she might not. We have to be prepared for either possibility.**"

Yet all of the children shared some resemblance to their parents. Even if Kelly couldn't line them up perfectly, there weren't any matchups that screamed "**There's no way this kid is related to these parents!**"

Frustrated, Kelly dialed his number and was greeted by the cheerful voice of Ernie's office secretary. Cindy was a kindly, industrious woman in her mid-forties, married with teenagers. She had been a solid friend who had consistently expressed support for Kelly's plight.

**"We're going to find her,"** Cindy had often said, which spurred Kelly onward.

"I told Ernie to go home early," Cindy confirmed, her tone worried. "And I doubt he'll be in tomorrow."

"Poor guy," Kelly responded.

"Antibiotics just aren't doing the trick," Cindy added.

Kelly asked her to confirm the address Ernie had sent earlier, and after putting Kelly on hold, Cindy came back on. "That's the correct address."

**Okay,** Kelly thought. **Right address, wrong girl.**

Nattie Livingston was a complete miss, a rarity for Ernie, but even the best of them had off days.

Cindy cut into her thoughts, "Hey, sweetie. My other line is beeping. Need anything else?"

"Nope. Thanks, Cindy. And tell Ernie I'll keep him in my prayers," Kelly said.

Cindy expressed her appreciation and hung up.

Perturbed but more worried for Ernie, Kelly put her jalopy in gear and left the lovely neighborhood. She was hard-pressed to figure out how Ernie, sick or not, could fail so thoroughly with this latest prospect.

Nattie's little splinter-free friend, Marina, stayed for dinner, and Laura stayed longer than usual. She was wiping off the kitchen counters when Diane Farley came running over in crisp white shorts, a turquoise top, and white sandals. She was frowning. "They're late, Jack," she muttered, clearly displeased. "What're we gonna do?"

Jack motioned her toward the garage and raised the door. He gestured to the space he'd cleared out for the dirt bike, a narrow aisle between his Ford F-250 and his well-worn workbench, stained and smelling of oil and paint and turpentine. It was a space big enough to accommodate Craig Farley's anniversary gift until the grand unveiling.

"You're sure you don't mind?" she asked again. No sooner had she voiced it when the boys from the local motorcycle shop drove up and parked at the end of Jack's driveway. The coveted bike was harnessed on the back of a large flatbed truck.

"Whew." Diane glanced at her watch. "Finally. Craig's due home in thirty minutes."

"They'll have it unloaded long before that," Jack assured her. **Either that or Craig will be jealous of my new ride.** He grinned at the thought.

The bike was a stunning top-of-the-line yellow Honda. Two of the guys, both sporting jeans and long beards, wheeled it into Jack's garage.

"I can't guarantee it'll still be here tomorrow," he joked.

Diane narrowed her eyes. "Whatever," she returned, obviously happier these days, more so than in the terrifying months after her first husband had walked out for good. For **her** good.

As a conscientious neighbor, Jack had tried to pick up the pieces from a handyman perspective, mowing Diane's lawn, shoveling snow, changing the oil in her Ford Taurus—the very one he'd negotiated for her in the first place, driving a hard bargain on her behalf. Naturally, it hadn't been that hard. The car salesman, Jim Meyers, had been one of Jack's former flight students, a certified pilot. Jim gave him the "former teacher" discount.

On occasion, Jack had also driven Diane's troubled daughter, Livy, to school, sometimes picking her up from the principal's office when Diane was stuck at work. He'd also helped search various neighborhoods when Livy wasn't where she'd promised to be.

Considering his involvement in their lives, it would have been only natural that a romance might develop between them. Diane was a lovely woman, inside and out, who attracted more than her fair share of second and third looks. When his sister heard about Jack's near miss, San had hit the roof. **"Are you nuts? Diane's the most eligible woman in Wooster!"**

It had been futile to argue that point with unyielding San. If anyone, she should have understood his skittishness toward the institution of marriage. Both had witnessed firsthand what happened when a marriage went horribly awry.

Fortunately for Diane, she'd met Craig Farley, closing the door forever on any possible romance with Jack, not that he had any regrets.

Swiftly, Diane signed the papers, and the men pulled out in their delivery truck. She leaned over the bike, marveling at her purchase. "Craig's going to hit the ceiling," she said, eyes beaming.

**In a good way**, Jack thought. "You realize you've reset the bar for women everywhere, don't you?"

Diane's eyes danced. "Don't I know it. What woman allows her man to ride a bike, much less buys him one?"

Jack laughed. They confirmed arrangements for springing the bike on her husband. She started to leave, then asked, "Hey, Jack, how's Nattie doing?"

"Can you wait a sec?" he asked and hurried inside to retrieve the folder from his office. Outside again, he gave another glance toward the interior door, checking for little ears, and removed Nattie's artwork. "Take a look at this," he said. "I haven't even shown it to Laura yet."

Diane examined the drawing carefully, whistling softly. A confused look creased her forehead. "So, does this mean you and Laura are getting cozy?"

"Oh no. Not at all."

Diane laughed. "Apparently Nattie has a different take on things?"

"Well, you know Nattie," he said, and Diane handed the picture back. "She has a very active imagination."

"Okay," Diane said, biting her lower lip. "My opinion?"

"Please."

"Imagine you're Nattie and all your friends have moms, and all the young girls you see in movies and TV have moms, and it seems as if everyone in the world has a mother," Diane said. "You'd probably fantasize about it. You'd create a story world with a loving mother who watches over you, who disciplines you, who cries with you, who prays for you—a mother like the one Nattie had and lost."

The steady rumble of an engine interrupted their conversation. Politely,

Diane held up a **hold-on** finger and peered around the corner, presumably to see if Craig had arrived home.

Relieved, she wandered back. "It's really very simple, Jack. Nattie wants a mother of her own. She misses the one she had, and she wonders about the birth mom she's never known."

Jack crossed his arms, leaning against his truck. "And apparently she'd like her mother to be Laura. I get that."

Diane shrugged. "But how can you be surprised? Laura's wonderful with her."

No argument there.

"On the other hand, it could be that Laura just happens to be closest." Diane gestured at him. "And since you obviously can't marry an Amish lady, I'm sure there's a qualified woman who would absolutely jump at the chance to be a mom to your daughter. You might be surprised at the results." Her eyes twinkled. "Who knows, Jack. You might even fall in love."

Jack chuckled. How quickly Diane had progressed from one point to the next.

Diane extended her arms, palms up, as

if arguing a contested point. "Look at Craig and me. He's been perfect for Liv. Her grades have shot up again, she doesn't run away anymore, and she's crazy about her stepdad."

Jack still remembered Livy as a surly preteen. Hard to imagine the transformation. Diane grinned, as if enjoying his predicament. "I think you're simply one marriage vow away from a contented daughter, Jack."

"Between you and San..." Jack muttered good-naturedly.

"Yes, and say hello to your dear sis for me," Diane replied. A sudden wind picked up, sweeping her hair across her face. She cleared the offending strands and waved, heading back to her house while Jack quickly turned to compare his truck to Craig's soon-to-be pride and joy. A dingy comparison, hands down.

Ten minutes after Diane had left, Jack was still in the garage pondering the whole tangled mess created by Nattie's artwork and praying for direction. Advice, unsolicited, seemed to come from everywhere lately, not that he didn't appreciate the input. But in the end, he had to make a decision for the future. According to her teachers, Nattie wanted permanence— and a mommy. And she wanted **Laura** to be that mommy.

Hadn't Jack always given her what she needed?

**What if I did marry Laura?** He smiled at the outlandish notion. Laura would likely turn ashen, staring at him in horror if he even suggested the idea. At the very least, they'd have a pleasant chuckle at his momentary lapse in judgment. At worst, she might even quit her job.

But nothing would alter the obvious: Laura was Amish, and he was not. Anything between them, any possibility of a romance, started and ended there. Just as he couldn't imagine ever becoming Plain, Laura certainly couldn't imagine going fancy.

Yet, in spite of the radical clash in cultures, they did have one thing in common: Nattie. They'd practically raised her together, creating years of treasured memories, even brainstorming solutions to dozens of childhood issues. But mutual love for Nattie wasn't a strong enough reason to marry. **Right?**

He recalled the school counselor's jolting remark: **"What happens to Nattie if Laura leaves?"**

Kids adapt, he figured. Kids were resilient. Part of growing up was dealing with change. Then again, he considered Nattie's imminent loss of her auntie San to New York.

Losing San was one thing; losing the only mother figure Nattie knew was quite another. **Certain events have the power to change us forever**, he thought. If anyone knew this for a fact, he did.

# Chapter 11

Jack was sorting through his garage tools and his thoughts when Laura poked her head out. "I'm almost finished for the day," she said, sitting down on the concrete steps and folding her arms into her full apron. She studied Jack's temporary acquisition. "Awful **perty** bike, isn't it? Can we keep it?" She laughed softly.

Jack smiled. "Don't I wish."

Laura's white tennis shoes peeked out from under her long dress, the shoes at odds with the formality of her otherwise conservative attire. "I thought Craig already had a motorcycle," she added, tilting her head.

Jack pointed to the tires and the suspension, explaining the unique characteristics of a dirt bike.

Laura wrinkled her nose. "Maybe I should get a motorcycle," she said without cracking a smile.

Jack was amused at the image of an Amishwoman zooming along to work, wearing a helmet and leaning into the wind.

"That, of course, would never go over with the People," she said more quickly. "We have our ordinances to uphold." She looked away. "Well, to obey, anyway."

"Any chance your church ordinance would allow you a motorbike?"

They both knew the answer, but it provided some needed humor between them. After more small talk about the Plain tenets of "separation from the world," she offered some further gardening ideas, especially in creating small box gardens in the backyard.

"By the way, Jack," Laura said, "your Nattie was mighty ecstatic that you asked her to call you Dad."

"Long overdue, too. I should've asked her years ago."

"But she was so honored." Laura cleared

her throat. "She really loves you, Jack."

"And I love **her**."

She smiled. "Oh, I nearly forgot to tell ya Nattie's latest list of her top ten favorite friends."

"Are **we** on it?" Jack chuckled.

"Actually, I encouraged Nattie to at least hide the list in her drawer so as not to offend the friends who didn't make it to number one, ya know."

"Good idea."

Then, after a mutual smile for Nattie's ongoing categorization of nearly every-thing, Laura clasped her hands. "Well...I suppose it's that time." She rose and tied her prayer cap loosely beneath her chin. "Have a restful evening, Jack."

He felt a tinge of regret as he watched her wander out to her metallic blue car. He was about to press the garage remote when he heard the telling groan of the starter, again and again, as Laura tried to fire up her car.

He made his way down the driveway, only to see Laura's hands covering her face. "I just spent three hundred dollars on this," she told him when she looked up.

Jack tapped the car and jerked his thumb toward his pickup. "Let's get you home. I'll call the tow truck."

Sighing, yet apparently relieved, Laura locked her car as Jack headed inside to get Nattie to come along. **Wait a minute**, he thought, realizing it made better sense to have Diane keep Nattie next door. After a quick call, their neighbor happily agreed.

When he found Nattie, she was sitting in the guest room where Laura stayed occasionally when Jack was gone overnight. Nattie was giving voice to her stuffed animals, talking in **Deitsch**.

This space across the house from the kitchen had always struck Jack as somewhat bleak, not in the sense of lacking beauty, but scantily furnished. There was an oak double bed and matching dresser with no mirror, a brightly hued rag rug on the floor, and a small square table near the bed. A room Darla had no doubt decorated with her nanny's simple taste in mind.

Nattie looked up, bright-eyed and hopeful. "What's up, doc?"

"I need to take Laura home, sweetie."

Nattie's face fell. "Her car broke **again**?"

"Yep, and you're going over to Diane's till I get back, sweet pea."

"Goody!"

When Nattie waved at Jack across the yard, he quickly headed to get his truck from the garage.

Laura was apologetic. "Sure ya don't mind?"

"Not at all." He tuned the dial to her favorite country music station. A tune by George Strait filled up the silence.

She looked sheepish. "I know you hate that."

"I don't hate it," he said. "I just don't... like it."

Laura smiled and nodded.

They drove through the side streets of their neighborhood, then Jack headed south toward downtown Wooster. Glancing at Laura, Jack couldn't miss seeing her melancholy expression. He recalled something Nattie had once told him privately. **"I think Laura's always a little sad."**

Nattie was perceptive, although most

people would have disagreed with her assessment of Laura, those who didn't know Laura well. Most would have pegged her as rather cheerful. Despite that, even when Jack's and Nattie's lives were humming along, there was a frequent fade to Laura's smile, as if she were merely smiling through the pain.

**She's a shunned woman**, he thought. **Rejected by her family.**

At times he also guessed that Nattie was attempting to bridge the gap, trying to make up for the family Laura had lost back in Lancaster County.

Eventually, the middle-class neighborhoods gave way to pasture-land and fields of corn—the wide, open places. He enjoyed this part of the drive, liked the feeling of expansion, as if it could free his mind somehow. In a sense, it was a parallel to flying, breaking the shackles of earth.

He turned onto the highway. "You've been with us quite a while now, Laura."

"**Jah**, a wonderful-**gut** time, too." She leaned over to tie one of her sneakers. Then she put her hands in her lap decorously.

A moment passed. "Do you ever miss your family?" he ventured. "Back east?"

Zipping down the highway, Jack eased his grip on the steering wheel. "Yes, I mean...the whole thing, growing up in an Old Order community. The few things you've shared with me, you know."

Laura leaned back a little, sighing softly. "Life is ever so much different back home. That's for sure."

"Ever think of returning there?"

Shielding her eyes from the descending sun, she looked at him curiously. "Are ya tryin' to get rid of me, Jack?" She smiled, her gaze unwavering.

"Are you kidding? I'd sign you to a ten-year contract, if that were possible."

Laura squinted, falling silent.

Jack turned his attention back to the road, worried he had upset her.

"**Nee**, I can't go back," she said at last. "Not unless I'm willing to offer a kneeling confession to the church membership."

"Hmm," Jack murmured, unable to understand the mystery of her life and the past she'd left behind. She'd rarely spoken of her excommunication, which seemed to have stained her soul.

"It's really none of my business," he added. "I just—"

"What are you really askin', Jack?" Her tone was tense now and vulnerable; he wished he'd left it alone.

Like Nattie, Laura had a knack for sniffing out the point to his rambling conversations. And before he could reply, she added, "Truth is…someday I **will** go home to Pennsylvania. At times I haven't been so sure of it, really. But when I am, I'll offer my repentance and be welcomed back into the People's **gut** graces." She paused. "For certain, I'll be happy to give up my broken-down car!" Laura laughed softly.

Jack smiled in kind, but his shoulders drooped at her response. That answer, most of all, settled things for him—more than the teacher's meeting and beyond San's haranguing. Even more than the hidden meaning lurking within Nattie's drawing.

"Does that answer your question?" she

asked.

He nodded—only fair, after all. Laura had dedicated eight years to his girl, putting her life on hold to nurture Nattie. He'd accepted Laura's kind generosity with gratitude, but he'd assumed she would always be with them.

"I'm so thankful for you, Laura. I hope you know that. No matter how long you can stay."

Her face dimmed. "Well, ain't that simple, really."

Another mile passed. The junction to her cousins' farm was just ahead.

"I've been thinking of something," Jack said. "Actually, it might sound like a harebrained idea." He stole a glance and she nodded. "That is, I'm actually thinking of dating…you know, to find a wife and a mother for Nattie."

Laura's eyebrows rose. "Oh?"

He pointed to the glove compartment and asked her to open it, knowing she'd understand if she could see Nattie's drawing for herself.

Laura removed the art and set it on her

lap. As she looked closer, a little gasp escaped her. "**Ach**, for goodness' sake."

Jack explained the back story, leaving out the matchmaking details, but included their neighbor Diane's take on it, that Nattie simply wanted a mother—any mother would do.

"But, **I'm** in this picture," Laura said, visibly shocked.

"Yes, however…" Jack began, hoping to alleviate any pressure she might feel. "I guess we have to look deeper than that, anticipating what Nattie really needs, knowing that we can't give her what she thinks she wants." He looked over at Laura. "Does that make sense?"

Laura turned in her seat, straightening her long dress, saying nothing.

"So…crazy idea, huh?" Jack asked.

Laura continued to study the picture. "Do you have someone in mind?"

Jack hardly heard what she'd said, because at that moment a giant semi came barreling down the highway, hugging the middle line, way too close. Jack swerved his vehicle closer to the shoulder, waiting for the semi to pass. Then, with a giant rush of wind, it careered by them, swaying Jack's own sizeable pickup truck.

Jack shook his head, then glanced over at Laura with a sheepish grin. "You know, I was just thinking…if something comes of it, fine. If not, nothing lost."

"That's a **schmaert** plan, I guess. As long as the Lord's will is accomplished, **jah**?"

Jack then asked if she might consider putting in some extra time with Nattie during the evenings. Laura agreed.

He slowed as they came to the next turn. Jack hoped to exchange perhaps a frivolous smile at his idea, but Laura was looking out at the farmland again.

Later, when she did catch his grin, Laura nodded, but her expression seemed a little exaggerated, almost too bright.

**"Are you okay?"** he almost asked but squelched it.

At the end of the long lane, he parked near her cousins' farmhouse. "Here I am, going on about this as if you don't have enough on your plate," he said.

"I don't mind at all. Honestly." Laura reached for the door handle and gave him a quick smile. "I can't thank you enough for the ride, Jack." She stopped then, motionless, seemingly unsure of herself. "Jack?" Tentatively, she began to trace a small crack in the leather with her pointer finger. "I'd like to ask you something...if ya don't mind."

He nodded, waiting.

"Over the years, I believe you've had certain expectations of me, **jah**?"

Of all times, Jack's phone began to chirp. He assumed it was Nattie, but as he peered at the screen he saw that it was one of his flight students scheduled to solo that evening. "Do you mind holding that thought, Laura? I really need to get this." He clicked the Answer button.

But instead of waiting, Laura reached to open the door. "Later," she mouthed to him, sliding out. Holding the handle, she stepped down gingerly onto the gravel road. It was quite a jump from his cab to the ground, but Laura had mastered it.

In the meantime, Jack's student had

inquired about filling the oil to the top line because there had been some disagreement about whether they weren't just blowing oil out the case vent. "So shouldn't we under fill it and save money?" Jim asked.

"Hold on a second, Jim." Jack covered the mouthpiece with his thumb, curiosity pounding his chest. "I'm almost finished here, Laura."

She was poised to shut the heavy door. "Oh, not to worry. It can wait, **jah**," she said politely but firmly.

Getting back to the call, Jack watched Laura walk up the gravel drive to the farmhouse. Then she turned and smiled, looking strangely forlorn.

Finishing up the call, Jack kept his eyes trained on the farmhouse, wishing Laura would return. He shouldn't have taken the call and wished she'd waited. He noticed the sky suddenly growing dark and realized his student would probably have to cancel his solo flight anyway. A thunderstorm was brewing.

Shifting the pickup into reverse, he wondered if, with all his talk of dating, he'd seemed too eager to replace her. Especially after she'd admitted not knowing how much longer she might stay.

He autodialed Laura's cell number, hoping to apologize again for his insensitivity, but the call went directly to voice mail. Jack placed his phone on the passenger seat, recalling the pathetic look on her face, and kicked himself all the way home. "I'll fix things tomorrow," he promised himself and then realized Laura wasn't coming back to work till Saturday. He sighed with frustration.

Halfway home, it began to rain, and when he got to his street, he saw Laura's car and picked up the cell again. After a quick call to his favorite mechanic, arrangements were made to tow Laura's car back to the shop.

"Put it on my bill," Jack told him. "And while you're at it, see if you can find anything else that might go wrong."

Charlie agreed, and Jack left instructions to have him deliver the car to the farm when finished.

In the garage, Jack parked his truck

cautiously next to the yellow dirt bike, which seemed to glow like a neon sign, and hurried over, amid the pelting raindrops, to Diane's. Nattie greeted him with undiluted relief.

"**Finally!** I thought you'd never get back," Nattie said with a blend of humor and indictment.

In the house, Nattie rushed upstairs to brush her teeth while Jack went to his office, pulling out the narrow top drawer. He removed Karen Jones's business card. Turning it around in his fingers, he recalled the meeting. **Wouldn't a psychologist make an ideal mother for Nattie?**

Besides that, Jack liked Karen. She was attractive; she seemed conscientious, insightful, if a little bossy.

**Maybe bossy is good**, he reasoned, picking up the phone.

The rain grew fiercer, lashing at his windows and accompanied by a howling wind. Distracted, Jack got up to close the heavy drapes, hoping to muffle the storm.

Settling back down in his russet leather chair, he rehearsed the necessary words, practicing them aloud. "Hey, Karen, I'd like to take you out to dinner—"

"Dad?"

Jack swiveled around, heart jumping.

"What are you doing?" she asked.

"Oh, just grown-up stuff."

"Wanna watch **Finding Nemo** with me?"

"I thought you'd never ask. Give me a minute."

Nattie scampered off to get things set up, which required her enormous blanket, at least three stuffed animal friends, and two bowls of ice cream—one for each of them. He'd just bought himself at least ten minutes.

In the meantime, Jack ditched the whole decision to review his pitch and simply picked up the phone and dialed Karen.

Right then, the doorbell rang, and he heard San calling, "Yoo-hoo! Anybody home?"

Jack hung up and Nattie dashed past his office. "Auntie San's here," she announced.

In seconds, San peeked in, her hair wet

and matted. "Hey, bro!"

Nattie squeezed in between San and the doorframe, eyes pleading, hands clasped prayerfully together—for what, he wasn't sure—probably to invite his sister to stay around for the movie.

"Perfect timing," Jack said, gesturing for San to pull up a chair.

"Why?" Nattie fidgeted. "What's going on?"

"I need to talk to San...alone, sweetie."

Nattie groaned. "More grown-up stuff?" she muttered. "There's too much of that in this house." With that, she stomped off to the family room.

San closed the door, pulled the chair closer, and settled in. Her designer sunglasses were poised on top of her head, holding back still-dripping hair. "So...you haven't told her yet, I'm guessing?"

Less than a question, more of an insinuation.

"About?"

"New York. Hello?" San impatiently brushed the water droplets off her floor-skimming skirt.

Jack had completely forgotten. "I was searching for the ideal moment."

San rolled her eyes. "Want **me** to do it?"

He leaned forward. "Listen…I've made a decision. And it's big."

"Good for you." San smirked. "Want a star sticker?"

"Be serious." He cleared his throat. "I'm thinking about dating…that is…hoping to marry, well, ultimately."

San scoffed. "Puh-lease. Don't toy with my emotions." She stared at him closer, gauging his expression, her eyebrows furrowing. "Wait a minute. You're **not** kidding."

"Nattie needs a mother."

San grinned. "Will you simply forgo the falling-in-love part?"

Jack opened his mouth to reply, but San was already moving on. "Marriage doesn't have to be as bad as our parents' was, you know." She screwed up her face comically, and a sudden gust blew a splatter of rain against the window.

"Okay, brass tacks, Jack. Fact is I know a lot of eligible women. So thank me. You're in luck."

Setting aside his thoughts of Karen, he decided to play along. "What about Anita? You mentioned...uh...that she'd asked about me some time ago."

San grimaced. "You missed your chance, Jack. She's practically engaged now."

"In what? Two days?"

San grabbed her purse, pulling out her cell phone, scanning her address book. "Here we go, Jack. Some of these women are lovely, but they talk a lot, and some of them are quiet, like you, but not so pretty. Attractive, sure, but not in the physical sense."

Jack tried to keep up. "Any mommy types?"

"Um, before we get too far into this, Mr. Beanstalk, let me reiterate. Whomever you date will want to be romanced. Flowers and sun-drenched walks along the river, not to mention handholding. And, eventually, some kissing."

"Got it."

San blew out another breath. "Wait a minute. Have you told Nattie about **this**?"

Jack shook his head.

San frowned. "I doubt she'll see this as sunshine and kittens for all."

"She'll come around."

"Uh-huh. Right," San said. "And what about Laura? How do you think **she'll** deal with this?"

"What **about** Laura?"

San seemed disturbed with Jack's naiveté, then turned her attention to her phone again. "Okay. So where do we want to start?" She punched the screen. "I have three names, right off the bat."

Jack handed over the school counselor's business card. Accepting it, San examined the printing. She scowled. "This is Karen's." She turned it over, her eyes narrowing. "Hold the phone."

"So Karen's single. She loves kids."

San looked at him as if he'd lost his mind. "She's definitely not your type."

"And Karen's connected with her church, big time. So we're good."

"She is **still** not your type."

Jack pulled out his phone and began punching numbers. He placed the receiver against his ear.

"Please tell me you aren't calling her."

Jack smiled, counting the rings. San leaned back in her chair and sneered at him. He smirked right back.

On the fourth ring, Karen Jones answered, somewhat surprised to hear from him. Jack made polite small talk, saying how much he appreciated her insight at the parent-teacher meeting. As he talked, he kept glancing at San, who simply shook her head with mock disgust. Then he asked Karen if she'd like to have dinner with him.

San rolled her eyes and whispered, "Tell her there will be a written test afterward."

To **his** surprise, Karen was reluctant to accept. Had he misread her signals? Wisely, he backed up and tried a different course. "Perhaps coffee, instead?"

"Sounds nice," Karen said. Then, taking the lead from him, she suggested a time and a place: Thursday, four o'clock in the afternoon, at Starbucks.

Jack said he'd look forward to that, said good-bye, and hung up.

San crossed her arms, gave him a smug

look. "She wasn't too excited about dinner, I take it?"

"A minor blip. Other than that, I handled things swimmingly."

"You're in way over your head, brother dear," San said. "This woman will chew you up and spit you out." She laughed, as though relishing the prospect. "But never fear, Jack." She waved her cell phone in front of him. "I'll be here to pick up the pieces for my obstinate brother."

"Not for long," Jack reminded her.

"Oh yeah. I forgot! I'm moving to Noo Yawk!" San stood up and did a little jig, ending with a dramatic arm flourish.

Jack groaned, playing along. "If Nattie is anything like you when she hits her teens, I'm going to have my hands full."

San's eyebrows rose in agreement. "I've been telling you that, dear Jack. Now, as I recall, Nattie promised me a movie and popcorn and ice cream, and I intend to collect."

Jack laughed. "Did she neglect to mention we're watching **Finding Nemo**?"

San's expression drooped. **"Again?"**

# Chapter 12

At six o'clock the next morning, Kelly gladly passed the reins to Tom and Shelly, two new hires at the convenience shop. Shelly's face was riddled with piercings, a startling contrast to her bubbly demeanor. Clearly she was thrilled to have landed a job.

The day was already warm and humid as Kelly drove into the rising sun. She was famished, ready for a nice hot meal at Miriam's, an old-timey café just a mile or so up the road, known for their omelets and waffles. It was a favorite with the locals, and Melody was waiting for her there.

The plan to meet early would accommodate Kelly's sleep schedule, which worked fine for Melody, who often hit the gym right after dawn anyway. **"Trey said** he'd handle breakfast with the kids," Melody crowed when Kelly called her recently. "He owes me."

Kelly had laughed and felt a tinge of wistfulness, hearing about Mel's married life. Could've been me, she thought. Then again, in retrospect, Bobby had always been a ticking time bomb.

In the parking lot, she glanced into the rearview mirror and tried to rub a little life into her haggard features. With a sigh, she got out of the car and headed for the diner, its storefront striped canopy and picture window reminiscent of a 1940s café. Inside, she spotted Melody sitting on a long vintage bench, wearing a slate gray jogging outfit. Mel rose immediately, and they exchanged hugs.

"I'm so glad to see you," Melody said.

Kelly thanked her for coming, then they followed the hostess toward the back room, the fireplace section. The place was filled with hungry patrons, both the young hip crowd drinking lattes, and older men sporting crew cuts and baseball caps advertising farming equipment—a true melting pot of people and evidence of the restaurant's appeal.

Friendship was the last bastion of old age, or so it seemed from the looks of these coffee drinkers. **I could do worse**, she thought suddenly, and it struck her as rather odd. Until recently, relationships had been the last thing on her mind.

They were seated at a booth toward the back windows in their favorite room— the one bright with sunshine and mellow wood tones, giving an inviting old-world feel. The ambience was relaxing, even welcoming, after a long night working in a room with snacks, drinks, smokes, and, of course, lottery tickets.

Kelly placed her purse next to her and sat down. Melody pushed in across from her in the booth. "Remember the last time we came here?"

Kelly smiled at the memory.

"It was my eighteenth birthday," Melody reminded her.

Kelly whistled. **Light-years ago.**

"So when do you sleep, Kel?"

"Nine to whenever," Kelly replied.

"And...**how** do you sleep?"

Kelly shrugged. "I put on a sleep mask and shut off my phone." **Most of the time.**

Melody's bright eyes turned dim. "I'm really sorry you haven't found her yet. I can't imagine, Kelly."

**Dispatching the elephant in the room**, Kelly thought. **Just dive right in and get it out of the way.**

"It's been a long time," Kelly admitted. "But I'm still plugging away, you know. Knocking at doors. Pursuing leads."

It sounded like a practiced speech, and in fact, it was. She'd been saying the same thing for years to whomever asked. Sometimes she still gave short talks at various church groups, although not so often anymore, and usually to disbelieving faces. **"I still believe I'll find my daughter. It's my job to believe. It's God's job to provide when He sees fit."**

Melody's eyes filled with tears. "You're amazing, Kel. I remember thinking years ago that God allowed this trial because He knew you'd be strong enough to handle it."

Kelly shrugged this away, slightly annoyed, but she knew Melody meant well. Truth was, there were times when she would have given anything to have been spared this suffering. **Who wouldn't?** Then there were other times when she was affected by a strange underlying feeling that things were exactly the way they were supposed to be for a reason, in keeping with the verse **All things work together for good to them that love God, to them who are the called according to his purpose.**

The first time someone said that to her, she'd almost slapped him. **"How can anything good come of this?!"**

**"It's only when you're empty that you can be filled,"** Chet told her often, especially when despair nipped at her heels. Chet had a lot of these platitudes, and yes, sometimes she was tempted to slap him, too.

The waitress stopped by, asking for their drink order—water for Melody, orange juice for Kelly. Waiting, they talked about the old days, old teachers, old friends, and old jokes. Soon enough the waitress wandered by again, delivering their beverages and ready to take their order, but they hadn't even opened the menus. They didn't need to. They ordered the same thing they had always ordered: for Melody, blueberry waffles and a side of eggs over hard. And for Kelly, a vegetarian omelet. She wasn't actually a vegetarian, but she didn't care much for ham, sausage, or bacon. **"Crunchy carcinogens,"** her father had once called them.

When the waitress left again, Kelly leaned forward. "Thanks...for this."

Melody nodded, almost too exuberantly. "I thought you'd forgotten about me."

**I did**, Kelly thought.

Melody put a straw in her water, took a sip, and fixed Kelly with a serious look. "I want to help you again...looking for your daughter."

Kelly was already shaking her head, thinking of Chet and Eloise. "I appreciate that, but I don't do much active fundraising anymore."

"Oh," she said, eyes dimming slightly.

"Do you still have that private detective?"

"Ernie." She smiled. "Yes."

"I liked him," Melody replied. "He reminded me of my grandpa."

Kelly laughed, conjuring up the image. Melody's grandfather Clarence **was** a sour-faced sweetheart. Just like Ernie.

"How's your family?" Kelly asked, and Melody obliged. It felt good to listen to her talk, to get a glimpse into her life again.

**Why'd I let her go?** Kelly wondered.

Melody rambled on about her husband, her father, her mother, her life as a housewife, but she didn't mention her daughter, Carly, until Kelly inquired. Melody hesitated but Kelly insisted.

"Are you sure?"

Kelly smiled. "Absolutely. I want to hear about your life."

So Melody obliged again, and as much as it hurt, Kelly found solace in knowing that someone else's life was intact.

"I hope you know, I never stopped praying for you...for Emily to come home." Melody smiled, dabbing at tears with her napkin. "Thanks," Kelly whispered, swallowing hard. "I need all the prayer I can get."

While they enjoyed their meal, Kelly brought Melody up-to-date on her own life, her distant relationship with her mother—**"mostly my fault"**—her tiny apartment, and her job, the perfect situation for frequent traveling.

Melody wiped her mouth with a napkin and suddenly looked very serious. She was about to speak when Kelly interrupted her. "I'm sorry for what happened between us."

Melody was shaking her head. "I understand, Kel—"

"No. I really believed I was ruining your life with my mess. I mean, you had everything going for you: a loving husband, a new baby daughter."

"If you think my life has been perfect, please don't. I just wish I could have been here for you all these years. And if you'll have me as your friend, I'm here now. Okay?"

"I'd like that."

Together, they had a little cry, both

swiping at their eyes, and then Melody forged ahead. "I wasn't going to say anything..."

Kelly nodded. "I know, I know. People keep telling me I look like I've been through the ringer and back."

"You're just a little thin," Melody said, diplomatically, folding her hands on the table. "Frankly, I was surprised you were still working the night shift."

She'd never been a night person, and sleeping, under the best of circumstances, had never been that easy for her.

"Not everyone can pull it off, Kel. I've read it can really mess up your system." She paused, considering her next words. "I don't want you to get mad at me—"

Kelly patted her arm. "Say what you want. You were my best friend, you know."

"**Am**...your best friend." Melody slid a business card across the table. "My dad always thought you walked on water—remember?"

Studying the card, Kelly smiled at the memory.

"He needs an office manager, someone

who can also act as a receptionist. It's entry level, but the job pays well, and eventually you could move up." Melody placed a piece of paper on the table, a job description.

Glancing at it, Kelly caught a few phrases: **Deliver high-caliber client service and technical support, provide administrative support to CIO, utilize CRM system and Microsoft Office programs, maintain office filing system...**

"I don't know..."

"Trust me." Melody smiled. "I've already talked to Dad, and it took a split second for him to offer this."

Kelly shook her head. "I appreciate it—"

"Don't say no yet. Please, just think about it?"

Kelly agreed but didn't see how changing jobs could possibly work for her situation. They talked a bit more, until Melody insisted on paying.

"I'm calling you, okay? And there's this thing called texting! Remember?"

Kelly laughed. "Got it."

"Think about the job?" Melody asked

again, then hesitated. "I care about you, Kel."

They waved and Melody rushed off toward the parking lot, leaving Kelly suddenly alone again. Digging her car keys out of her purse, Kelly looked at the business card. She recalled Melody's father bantering with her, wanting to hire her out of college, but since Bobby had been making such good money, she'd decided to be a stay-at-home wife. **Is it time to finally put my degree to use?**

Kelly opened the door to her old beater, slammed the door shut, and considered the prospect of another sleepless day.

**Something's got to change**, she realized.

Just as Kelly was settling into bed, Ernie's secretary called, sounding frantic.

"I don't want to alarm you," Cindy began, "but Ernie's been admitted to the hospital for pneumonia."

"That bad?"

Cindy assured her that he was getting excellent care. "I'm closing down the office until he's back," she said. "Without Ernie around, there's not much to do, and I've got some vacation days to burn." She gave Kelly the pertinent hospital information, including room number.

Kelly hung up, worried about the health of her crotchety PI. Silently, she turned her worries into prayer.

Too wound up to sleep, she padded to the kitchen, where she heard a subtle scratching at her door. She smiled. **Feed a cat once, and you'll have to feed 'em for life.**

She opened the door and Felix strolled right in. Kelly poured a bowl with special cat milk and watched the hungry feline lap away, wondering how to fill her time if Ernie's hospital stay was longer than a few days.

**How selfish is that?** Ernie's health was more important than what he could do for her. She looked again at the business card Melody had given her. Melody was right; the third shift was grueling. She was getting less sleep than ever. Despite that, a new job made her nervous. She'd leave behind a flexible boss, as well as flexible hours. But she would still have the weekends. Couldn't she fly all over the U.S. in two days' time?

Still, it felt like quitting.

**I can't**, she thought. Regardless of how ethically challenged Ernie's methods might be, and no matter how out of sorts she was with her crazy shift, Kelly could not throw in the towel.

She sighed and dropped the card in the trash under the sink, and when Felix was finished, she set him outside. Felix meowed his thanks, glanced up at her as if to say, **"I'll be back tomorrow,"** and wandered down the steps.

Kelly returned to bed, sliding beneath the covers and adjusting her room-darkening mask. Melody's offer kept playing over in her mind. **"Please, just think about it?"**

The next afternoon, Kelly went to the hospital, took the elevator to the third floor, and found Ernie's room at the end of the hallway. Passing the nurses' station, she peeked around the corner, knocking softly, and found Penny, Ernie's red-haired wife, dozing in a recliner near the window. Penny opened her eyes and smiled, then glanced at the bed. "Hey, cranky pants, you have a visitor."

Ernie looked much worse than she'd anticipated, with an IV in his arm and an oxygen tube in his nose. His hair looked shabby and he looked pale and thin—thinner than Kelly remembered.

She was stunned and tears sprang to her eyes. Kelly stepped closer to the bed and gave him a **what happened to you?** grin.

Ernie rolled his eyes. "They forced me to come here."

"Well, wonderful."

Ernie practically growled. "I **hate** hospitals. I **hate** doctors, and I hate the **smells** of this blasted place."

Kelly caught Penny's eyes, and they shared a knowing smile.

Sick or not, Ernie remained ornery and unruly.

She pulled up a chair and sat down,

wanting to be a comfort somehow.

"Hey, what happened with that one kid?" Ernie muttered.

"What was her name?"

"Nattie, but we're not going to talk shop. Okay? You need to get well."

He sighed. "Now they're saying somethin's wrong with my plumbing."

Penny whispered, "Bypass."

Kelly felt sorry to hear it. "You better do what they say here, so you can get out. Okay?"

Ernie merely grunted.

They chatted for a few minutes, and Penny showed off recent photos of their four grandkids. Before leaving, Kelly kissed his forehead and Ernie sputtered, "At least something good comes of all this—I get kissed by a pretty girl."

Kelly patted his chest like a dutiful daughter. She promised to visit later in the week and left Ernie in Penny's care.

Down the hall, she took the elevator and whispered a prayer for poor Ernie. Recalling how decrepit he'd looked, she had to face the facts. Ernie wasn't going home anytime soon.

Pushing open the glass front doors, Kelly hurried to her car and got in. She sat there a moment, feeling helpless, and oddly enough, thinking of Melody's dad once more.

**It's time**, she realized. She texted a message to Melody: **Is that offer still good?**

Minutes later, Melody texted back: **I just now talked to Dad. You can start Monday!**

Kelly smiled away the butterflies in her stomach.

**Thank You.**

Back home, Kelly called her boss and gave her notice, thanking him for his years of generosity. Joe was happy for her. "They don't make 'em like you anymore," he said softly. "If anything changes, or that job don't work out, you let me know, eh?"

Moved by his compliment, Kelly agreed and thanked him again.

On Sunday, Kelly would have the opportunity to attend church for the first time in months. In the meantime, she planned to continue searching the Internet and monitoring her website. **I'll pray more**, she thought. **Without falling asleep!**

Most of those in her support group, the online group she rarely visited, didn't believe in prayer. Sure, the easy prayers: **Help me find my keys, God...help me find a parking spot, help me sleep tonight,** but not the difficult ones: **Heal my cancer, fix our marriage, help me locate my lost baby daughter.**

She went to the bathroom and looked in the mirror. Yes, her cheeks were still pale, her eyes dull, and she looked too thin. **But that'll change**, she realized, **once I get on a regular schedule.**

Eventually no one would say, **"Oh dear, are you eating enough? Would you like a candy bar? You can't find Emily if you don't keep up your strength."**

Pushing aside a hairbrush, Kelly braced her hands on the tile, leaning closer. She studied her complexion in the mirror, mentally trying to filter out the lines around the eyes and mouth.

**Am I pretty?** she asked, thinking of the

Bernstein and Sondheim song "I Feel Pretty." She decided optimistically, **I'll look pretty with a few more pounds and a tad more blush and mascara.**

But pretty for whom, she couldn't imagine. Besides, the idea of dating made her queasy. Pretty for me, then.

Back in the kitchen, Kelly pulled out a piece of paper and made a To-Do list. At the top she wrote, **Find a job**, just for the fun of crossing it off. Next she wrote, **Eat more!**

She thought of her favorite foods and made another list of what to buy at the grocery store. And suddenly, the thought of taking a breather was starting to take traction in her mind. She **needed** a rest, a short reprieve, a momentary pause to regain her health. She could pitch everything if it didn't feel right. She could get right back on the roller coaster if she missed it so much. Melody's dad would understand. Besides, she could always beg Joe for her third shift back.

**It's just a breather**, she told herself again.

# Chapter 13

On Saturday morning, an hour or so before Laura was scheduled to arrive, Jack and Nattie took the truck to the local car wash, a five-stall do-it-yourself operation. The sky was clear, the sun bright, and the wind subtle.

Jack sprayed sudsy water on the tires while Nattie crouched on the opposite side, scrubbing each one with a sponge, her tongue sticking out in concentration. Wearing a red-striped shirt, her blue jeans rolled up past her ankles, Nattie thoroughly enjoyed washing Billy Bob, her name for Jack's blue truck, and she was fascinated with its eventual transformation from dusty and grimy to clean and shiny.

Soaked to the bone, Nattie stood up at last, putting her hands on her hips, appraising her progress. Jack wandered over to inspect and whistled affirmatively. "Better'n I could do."

Nattie beamed. "We should add some bling," she told him. "Lots of chrome, beads, and stuff. Maybe a pinstripe down the side with some glitter."

"But isn't Billy Bob a **boy**?"

"Guys wear earrings, too," Nattie protested. "I've seen 'em."

"Not in my house, they don't. Well...my garage."

Jack mussed her hair and Nattie ducked, giggling. When they finished rinsing and did the final wipe down with specialty towels, they headed home. Nattie leaned on the open window, soaking up the breeze while Jack fretted, unsure how to break the news that Karen Jones, Nattie's school counselor, was coming over for dinner.

The afternoon coffee date with Karen had gone surprisingly well. He'd met her near the front door of Starbucks. She was wearing a pretty white sundress, while he'd managed San-approved attire—

jeans and a button-down shirt. Right away, Karen told him she'd snagged a table in the back.

They'd made small talk in the order line, and initially Jack felt awkward, considering this was his first date in ten years. But once they were settled at the table with a hot chai tea latte for Karen and an espresso for Jack, their conversation progressed smoothly.

Karen sliced her blueberry muffin down the middle and gave half to Jack. Buttering it, she took delicate bites and recited her academic history, how she'd chosen her college. She also casually mentioned having married during her second year, "We were too young to make such a hasty decision," she added. "The marriage lasted scarcely a year."

Holding his espresso like a prop, Jack shared his passion for flying and addressed his brother's fatal accident and Jack's subsequent guardianship of Nattie.

"I officially adopted her a year later," he'd told her, and Karen seemed curious that he, not San, had ended up as the appointed parent.

"I'll tell you all about it over dinner at my house," he said coyly, and Karen smiled suspiciously.

"It's a deal, but you have to dish. I'm a curious woman, and I won't be denied."

"How about Saturday?" Jack suggested, wondering if Karen might think it a little short notice, but she seemed pleased.

She went on to ask if Nattie would be joining them for dinner. Jack demurred and Karen smiled agreeably enough but seemed a tad disappointed. As it was, Nattie still had no clue of his plan to date anyone, let alone her school counselor.

**Nothing like a little procrastination to improve my chances**, he'd thought grimly.

Later that afternoon, Diane had presented Craig with his new set of wheels, and Jack got to witness firsthand a man on the verge of tears. It was a moving experience, not just for Craig, but for Jack, as well. He was going to miss that bike stored in his garage.

Following a supper of soup and sandwiches, he'd called Laura to give her a heads-up about his Saturday evening plans, and she'd agreed to prepare the evening meal. But no word was said about the other night, and she'd seemed eager to get off the phone.

Finally, that night, he'd sprung San's news about moving. Nattie seemed to take it better than expected, especially when he had suggested they might still see her favorite auntie every couple of weeks. San had said as much, but he figured after a period of time San would become too engrossed in her work and new friends. Left to her own devices, Jack and Nattie would be lucky to see San once a month. Hopefully, by then, Nattie would be more accustomed to her aunt's absence.

Of course, they could always visit San on her turf, and Jack floated that idea in the hope of building some excitement for San's move. Nattie had never been to the Big Apple, and Jack knew she'd love it. Madison Avenue, Broadway, and carriage rides through Central Park, for a start.

And today, as Nattie and Jack arrived home from the car wash, Jack spied Laura's old beater on the street. Charlie, his mechanic, had completed the repair work in record time.

In the house, Nattie yelped hello to Laura, who was humming in the laundry room, ironing Jack's work shirts.

Jack stood in the doorway for a moment, impressed by Laura's efficiency as she pushed the iron over the collar, the sleeves, pressing the button holes down the front, all in an even and continuous motion.

He knocked lightly on the doorjamb, hoping not to frighten her, but she jumped anyway. "Whew!" she exclaimed, patting her chest.

"Sorry," he said. "You okay?"

Fanning her face with her hand, she smiled her relief.

"I've been thinking," he said. "You haven't had a raise in years." Still holding the iron, her pretty face flushed, Laura broke into a curious grin. "Well, I have to say that's a **wunnerbaar** way to greet someone."

"Then it's settled," he said, thinking she might yet be inclined to continue their conversation from the other night.

Instead, she thanked him for fixing her car. "You have to let me pay you back."

Jack refused. "Consider it part of your compensation package." Laura laughed. "You're spoiling me."

They went silent for a moment as Jack paused, still curious if Laura would finish Wednesday's conversation, but she only gazed at him.

"I'm afraid I might have hurt your feelings," Jack began, but Laura waved it off.

"Oh, mercy sakes, Jack. I understand."

He felt silly but forged ahead anyway. "And I can't help wondering what you were going to tell me…."

A flash of remembrance crossed Laura's features. "Oh yes…it was silly, really." She set down the iron and clasped her hands. "That is…" She cleared her throat and pinched at her black apron, holding it, then letting it go. "You know how Nattie's been bugging me for years?" She inched back toward the dryer. "I just didn't want to...well, shock you. That is, one of these days, ya never know, I might just show up fancy, if only to give Nattie a fright."

Jack was taken aback, not only by her nervous behavior, but because the notion of Laura Mast dressing like an Englisher was difficult to wrap his brain around. "Well, I'm sure Nattie would get a kick out of it," he finally offered.

Laura wiped at her perspiring face, and Jack took a few steps backward, thumping up against the doorframe. It was a reasonably sized laundry room, with shelves above the washer and dryer, and tile covering the floor, but no window, and for some reason it suddenly seemed miniscule. By the look in her eyes, Laura surely felt it, as well.

She cleared her throat again. "Well, I haven't completely decided. I'm afraid if my cousin Pete saw me leave his Haus without my prayer veiling, he might just pop his suspenders, ya know." She laughed, and Jack joined her, still finding the whole thing rather odd, considering how serious she had seemed after their talk.

Laura bit her lip, suddenly looking tentative. "I'd have to change into my fancy clothes here, ya know. And then dress Plain again before I leave for home."

Jack nodded politely, as if he understood the ins and outs of an Amishwoman's being modern for a day.

Laura leaned forward, bumping the ironing board, and the iron swayed. Quickly, Jack moved to settle the board, and Laura grabbed for the iron. In the process she practically fell into his arms.

"That was close," Jack whispered, gently assisting her as she recovered her balance.

"**Jah**," Laura said, exhaling nervously, brushing at her clothing.

"By the way," she said, "have ya told Nattie yet? About tonight?"

He shook his head, sighing. There seemed to be a never-ending list of things to "break" to Nattie.

Laura offered a faint smile. "The sooner the better, Jack."

**Of course.** He agreed, and after another uncomfortable moment, Laura shrugged, gesturing toward her ironing. He nodded, backing out of the small space, still mulling the implications of Laura's idea to dress modern—fancy, as she'd put it.

He was, however, convinced she had changed her mind about what she'd really wanted to tell him Wednesday night. **But why?**

Jack headed upstairs to change out of his damp clothes and into old jeans and a T-shirt. Next, he trudged back to the garage and decided to organize his tools yet again, if only to unwind. The encounter in the laundry room had left him rattled.

After a while, Nattie joined him and sat on the top step, both palms under her chin, fingers on her cheeks. It was the classic bored-kid posture. Only for Nattie, it was her thinking pose. She mentioned her bike-blinging plans, declaring she wanted her ride to look as cool as Craig's new dirt bike.

"I should paint my bike pink," Nattie announced. "What do you think?"

"Could be ambitious," Jack counseled, positioning two of his best hammers on the pegboard.

She nodded, working her mouth. "Maybe just wax it instead?"

Jack reordered his crescent wrenches according to size and motioned for Nattie to help him hang the screwdrivers.

They worked together and finished the chore. "Perfect," Nattie said and ran inside.

Having missed yet another opportunity to come clean with his dinner plans, Jack hurried inside to wash up. He found Nattie sitting at the kitchen counter watching Laura stand on tiptoes as she sorted through the cabinet for ingredients.

Laura turned to look at him and sighed. "I've misjudged, I daresay. I wasn't prepared for tonight. We need tomato sauce."

"How 'bout the three of us go out for supper instead!" Nattie announced.

Laura closed the cabinet and gave Jack an eyeful, as if to say, **"How long are you going to wait?"**

"Write a short grocery list," Jack suggested, tactfully ignoring Nattie's suggestion. Laura agreed, dictating a list of ingredients while Nattie put pen to paper with trademark fanfare.

Recruiting Nattie for grocery duty, Jack drove to the store, still deep in thought over the very important talk he needed to have with Nattie.

They made their way up and down the grocery aisles, following Laura's list and gathering enough to feed an Italian army.

"So we're having pah-sgettie tonight," Nattie said, giggling and taking off with the cart up the aisle.

When Jack met her on the next aisle, he was encouraged by her jubilant mood. Wasn't now as good a time as any? Besides, they were in a public place; how bad could it be?

"By the way," he said, "Miss Jones is coming for dinner tonight."

Nattie stopped in her tracks. "Say what?"

Jack repeated it, and Nattie became unhinged, logically concluding that a dinner with the school counselor had something to do with **her**. While Jack assured her to the contrary, Nattie remained unconvinced. "Then why is she coming?"

"Because I want to get to know her better, honey." He paused, feeling breathless. "Karen seems nice."

Nattie made a face that looked like **"Are you kidding?"**

"Also, you'll be with Laura at the mall, having fun at the food court," he told her, thinking it would enhance the deal.

"Hold on. I'm not having spaghetti with you guys?" Nattie's face darkened. "**I** should be at the mall with Miss Jones, and **you** should be having dinner with Laura."

Before he could respond, Nattie stomped away, pushing the cart recklessly. Jack groaned, caught up with her, and together they finished their circuitous route around the store. When the list was complete, he noticed a dozen cans of soup in the cart.

He pointed to them. "Nattie—"

"The church pantry—remember?"

**Oh yeah**, he thought, recalling last Sunday's announcements. During the drive home, Nattie seemed overly fascinated with finding just the right station on the radio, turning the dial with exceptional focus.

"It's just a date," he assured her.

Nattie snorted disapprovingly and folded her arms.

Wanting to finish the conversation and hoping to forestall a thunderstorm, Jack pulled into a nearby parking lot and stopped in front of a paint store. Sunlight glistened off the windshields of the cars facing them in the next row. The place was hopping, typical for a Saturday.

He inhaled slowly. "Okay. I should have talked to you earlier, Nattie. Instead of springing it on you."

She looked at him, eyes blinking. "By the way, Dad, what will happen to Laura if you marry Karen?"

Skipping over the **if you marry Karen** part, Jack replied, "Nothing would change, sweetie. Laura stays."

"Things **always** change," Nattie whined.

"Karen won't like Laura. Nobody does. Nobody understands her like me. I'm the only one who has her back."

"Honey—"

"Why can't you just marry **her**?"

Jack pulled back if only to get some distance from Nattie's steely-eyed gaze. A car pulling in behind them tapped its tinny horn. "We've already had this discussion, Nattie."

"I didn't like how it turned out."

"Laura and I are friends...**just** friends," Jack said. "You have to love someone before you marry them."

Turning toward the window, Nattie shook her head. "It's not like Laura hasn't ever dated before, you know. She's had practice."

"I'm not surprised."

"She had a boyfriend once," Nattie muttered. "That's why Laura got shunned."

Jack was taken aback. He'd never heard this part of the story, the real reason, **any** reason for that matter, behind Laura's shunning. "I doubt she was shunned just because she had a boyfriend."

Nattie nodded sharply, as if to say, **"Yeah huh,"** until her expression wilted, her face turning carrot red, her natural response to shame. "But I shouldn't have told you. It's private stuff."

"I won't tell anyone," Jack said.

"You **can't**."

"Listen, Nattie, I've decided to start dating. I'm not sure anything will come of it, but I'm going to trust God and see where He leads."

Nattie flinched. "You're gonna date **other** girls **after** Miss Jones?"

"Possibly."

Nattie looked at him as if he'd lost his mind. "Let me get this straight. **You** are going to go out on dates? You've never even **been** on a date...like **ever**!"

Jack frowned. "Put your seat belt on," he said. "We need to get back."

With exaggerated slow motion, Nattie smoothed her shorts, wiggled into a comfortable position, adjusted her T-shirt, wiped her hair out of her eyes, then finally clicked her seat belt into place.

Backing out, Jack glanced at Nattie,

who grimaced. "I really can't believe you're telling me like...**two** minutes before Miss Jones arrives."

Frustrated, Jack said nothing.

"Why not just marry **Laura**?" Nattie repeated, pursing her lips and going silent for the duration of their trip home.

**That went well**, he thought grimly.

## Chapter 14

From his office, Jack could hear the hum of the oven fan as Laura worked that afternoon to prepare the evening meal for the so-called date with Karen Jones. He'd passed through the kitchen earlier and noticed various chopped ingredients for a salad, which Laura had organized on the cutting board, and the rich scent of bubbling tomato sauce filled the air. It was then he remembered hearing San say something about spaghetti's not being recommended for a first date and wondered if they shouldn't have grilled steaks or salmon outside. But it was too late to rethink this. Besides, he felt fairly confident he could manage not to wear his dinner.

Back in his office, Jack was busy plowing through the aircraft rental figures for the month when he heard a soft padding of feet. Suddenly, clammy arms encircled his neck, and Nattie's silky hair brushed against his neck. "I'm sorry I'm such a girl **and** a kid all rolled into one," she said. "You still love me, Dad?"

Jack grasped her hands, seeing the repentant look in her eyes. "I happen to love you **best** as a girl and a kid," he said, turning in his chair.

Nattie sniffed meekly. "So…we good?"

He wrapped his arms around her. "We're always good, kiddo. Always."

"And…you won't get married without telling me?"

Jack looked into her eyes. Nattie wrinkled her nose suddenly and then sneezed, not once, not twice, but three times, covering her entire face with her little hands. She made a sorry face. "Did I get you?"

Jack pulled a tissue from one of the ever-present tissue boxes Laura kept around the house and Nattie wiped her nose.

He braced her shoulders again. "Okay. Where were we before that explosion?"

They both laughed.

"Listen, Nattie. I won't marry **anyone** unless we talk about it first, okay?"

"Deal."

They shook on it, and Jack ignored the icky-moist splotch that migrated from Nattie's thumb to his palm. **Raising kids is not for the faint of heart**, he thought, grinning.

Seemingly satisfied, Nattie tossed her tissue in the wastebasket and ran off to help Laura in the kitchen. Jack emerged from his sanctuary and began vacuuming the family room.

Later, he and Laura set the table, and the phone rang just as they were finishing. Nattie got the phone upstairs and called for him, "It's Auntie San Fran!"

**My dating coach**, Jack thought with a smile.

Jack got on, but the line had an echo. He turned, glancing toward the upstairs. Nattie was peeking around her door. She hadn't hung up yet.

"Nattie..."

She pulled a face. "How else am I going

to learn stuff!"

As soon as she hung up, San laughed. "I haven't even left yet,and you're already losing control over there." She asked how Nattie had taken the news, and he paused. "She's okay with the dating if that's what you mean."

San began firing questions: "Have you scoured the bathrooms?"

**Yes.**

"What're you planning to wear?" she asked.

"Well, my tan cargos and a Winnie the Pooh T-shirt."

"Very funny," she replied.

When he told her the truth—a pair of broken-in jeans and a sweatshirt—San hit the roof. So he agreed to change into nicer pants and a golf shirt. They discussed further details, proper etiquette for supper, suitable conversation topics, and appropriate behavior until Jack's head began to hurt.

He hung up as quickly as possible and shooed away Nattie, who'd been hanging around, undoubtedly trying to decipher his side of the conversation. She scampered off to change her own attire while Laura continued to monitor the spaghetti sauce.

"Why don't you and Nattie return home before too long?" Jack suggested. "I'd like Nattie to spend a little time with Karen, if that's all right."

There was a whimsical glint in Laura's expression, and they settled on seven-thirty for their return from the mall, an hour after Karen's anticipated arrival.

Jack wandered into the dining room, seeing the candles, unlit but poised for greatness, the table set, the house "redded up," as Laura would say, and all systems go.

Laura hurried Nattie to the door just as Karen pulled into the driveway, fifteen minutes early.

"What now?" Nattie asked, clearly amused.

"Just act normal," Jack said.

"What's that?" Nattie muttered, grinning. Removing her dark sunglasses, Karen came to the door wearing a long soft pink skirt and a sleeveless white blouse. Jack decided immediately that Karen Jones would have easily passed San's muster.

Three sets of eyes met Karen's. Laura and Nattie welcomed her, then tried to slip past as Laura explained sweetly, "We were just headin' out."

Karen frowned, clearly disappointed. "Isn't Nattie staying for supper?"

"Oh, she'll be back later," Jack said, thinking Karen's response rather strange, considering he'd made this clear earlier.

"Are you sure she can't stay?" Karen asked, glancing back and forth between Jack and Nattie.

Nattie took it from there. "Yeah, I want spaghetti, too. I never get spaghetti." She smiled brightly at Karen, flashing her perfect teeth. "You look pretty tonight, Miss Jones."

"Well, aren't you sweet," Karen replied.

Jack found his manners and introduced Nattie's Amish nanny, and Laura flinched a little when Karen offered to shake her hand.

Then, with an amused sparkle in her eyes, Laura gestured toward her car. "Well, yous have a **gut** time, all right? I'll be back tomorrow, then."

Nattie escorted Karen into the great room, and Jack said goodbye to Laura, apologizing for the mix-up. **Really awkward**, he thought. But Laura took it in stride, giving him a few last-minute tips on the spaghetti dinner. Then she gave him a wave good-bye and walked down toward her car.

Standing on the steps, Jack heard the door unlock as she pointed the remote key at the car. Laura turned back again. "Did I forget something?"

Jack shook his head, almost wishing she had.

"You'll be fine tonight...with your date," she said quietly.

He nodded. "Thanks. You're very kind."

Back inside, he and Nattie gave Karen the five-minute tour. The aroma of spaghetti and meatballs wafted throughout the downstairs as Nattie showed off her tower of DVDs, meticulously ordered according to her favorites, in the great room. Shortly thereafter, Jack opened his office to show Karen his aviation wall.

Eventually, they settled into the dining room, with Jack at the head of the table. Karen and Nattie sat on either side of him, across from each other. After the blessing, the meal progressed as planned. Jack recalled Laura's particular instructions for serving the food, and happy conversation proceeded.

Nattie held court and Jack steered the discussion along non-controversial lines. But then halfway through the meal, Karen noticed Nattie hadn't eaten any green beans.

Earlier in the day, Laura had suggested green beans to Jack, since **"Not everyone likes corn or peas, but most folks like cut green beans with plenty of butter."**

**Except Nattie**, Jack had thought at the time.

Presently, however, Karen Jones was leaning forward on her side of the table, coaxing Nattie to "Just try a few beans, honey."

Nattie put on her politest face and shook her head.

"Our tastes can change as we grow older," Karen added.

Nattie nodded exuberantly, overly agreeable. "Well, mine haven't yet."

**Oh boy**, Jack thought.

Nattie wiggled her nose. "I'm cool with just a salad, but thanks." In fact, as a compensation for the lack of beans, nearly half of Nattie's plate was filled with leafy baby greens.

Taking matters into her own hands, Karen did the unthinkable. She dished up a small portion and placed the beans on one side of Nattie's plate. "Why not try a few," she said, winking at Jack. "You might be surprised."

Nattie stared at the offending green things as if they were roaches. She looked over at Jack, horror in her eyes, silently beseeching him: **"Rescue me!"**

"Nattie really doesn't have to eat green beans," Jack intervened. "As long as she's willing to compromise."

Karen raised her eyebrows. "Compromise?"

"Well, sure, by eating salad," he replied.

Karen applied her paper napkin to her lips. "I suppose that's one way to approach it."

Nattie nearly collapsed with relief, and for the next few minutes they ate in silence.

Finally, Karen put her spoon down and steepled her fingers.

Jack took that as his cue. "So…are you ready for dessert?"

"It's strawberry pie," Nattie announced proudly, apparently having recovered from her close call.

"Well, we certainly don't have any objections to sweets, now, do we?" Karen smiled.

Nattie returned the smile, but Jack could tell she was melting under Karen's sarcastic reproach. Jack bit his tongue. **Let it go.**

After dinner they settled into the great room and reviewed the photo album from Nattie's third grade. Later, they played Uno until nine o'clock, when Karen made a move toward the door. Meanwhile, Nattie waited in the living room, nursing aworried look.

At the door, Jack and Karen exchanged appropriate niceties about the evening. Karen inched closer, until she was stroking his arm. She extended her cheek, and if Jack wasn't mistaken, she puffed it out a bit.

After a moment of confusion on his part, Jack kissed her cheek.

"I had a delightful time," Karen said again, reaching up to wrap a silky rainbow scarf around her neck. Jack offered to walk her to her car, but she objected. "No, no. You stay and keep Nattie company. But thanks."

Nattie wandered over and joined Jack at the door. They watched as Karen Jones walked down their steps to the driveway, got into her car, and without further admonishments, lectures, or stink-eyes, drove off into the night.

Jack put his hand on Nattie's shoulder and squeezed. "I'm proud of you, sweet pea."

Nattie looked up at him. "I did okay?"

"Better than that."

Nattie breathed out a long sigh as the two of them, like refugees from a hurricane, huddled in the doorway.

"We survived," Jack said, moving away from the door at last.

"**Now** will you ask Laura out?" Nattie just had to say.

"Please don't start."

"Just askin'."

Together they cleaned up the kitchen, and when they'd finished, Jack sat on one of the counter stools and patted the one next to him. They stared at each other for a moment, faces blank, lulled by the whooshing of the dishwasher.

"I'm exhausted." Nattie yawned. "She wore me out."

Later, when Jack tucked her in, he mentioned how much Karen had enjoyed looking at Nattie's scrapbook.

"She was just trying to impress you."

Jack considered that. "Surely there was something good about the evening."

Nattie creased her eyebrows and pressed her finger on her forehead. "Let me think about that."

Jack tickled her and she squealed. "The strawberry pie was the best part. That's what it was."

"Not the green beans?"

Nattie giggled again as Jack pulled Laura's Amish "quiltie" up to her chin. After their prayers, Jack leaned in to kiss her goodnight, and Nattie widened her eyes dramatically, puffing out her right cheek.

"You caught that, too, I see."

Nattie nodded and Jack kissed her waiting cheek, which deflated suddenly. Nattie chortled. "Wait, Dad, I feel crooked." She puffed up her left cheek just then, and when he kissed it, Nattie's cheek popped like a balloon, complete with sound effects.

"Better?" he asked.

"Better."

**Better indeed**, Jack thought.

Nattie handed him Flounder, and Jack accepted it graciously.

"Flounder doesn't talk any more than Whiskers, but I thought you could use a break tonight."

Jack turned off the light and retired to his room, placing Flounder beside his pillow, wondering what his sister, San, might have up her sleeve for him. He didn't relish the thought of her guffaws once he admitted she was quite right about Miss Karen Jones, bless her heart.

He wandered out to the balcony and gazed downstairs, marveling at this very small step forward, his first date since college. **I actually entertained a woman in my own home.** Small potatoes for other men, perhaps. And despite tonight's disappointment, the whole dating plan somehow didn't seem as daunting anymore.

But he couldn't help reflecting on how Laura might feel about the whole thing, if she felt excluded, or pushed out...or worse, betrayed.

Sunday morning dawned brightly. Jack had just emerged from the shower when he heard the key rattling in the front door and a "Yoo-hoo!" from his sister. He wrapped himself in a robe and shook his damp hair, then stuck his head over the railing. "'Morning, San. Isn't it kind of early, even for you?"

"Hey, you offered to drive," San retorted, kicking off her high heels and heading for the coffee machine. "Besides, church starts in less than two hours, and I've got important things to discuss with you."

**Only San would squeeze in an intervention on the Lord's Day.** Jack chuckled.

Looking in the mirror, he saw how very long his hair had gotten and attempted to create some order to it. He was overdue for a visit to the barber, who was on vacation. Jack lathered up and scraped his face free of offending whiskers, then washed his face with warm water. That done, he slipped on his black dress slacks, twisted on his purple-checked tie with light black stripes—fashion police approved—and headed downstairs to face the firing squad.

She brought him a piping hot mug of java and settled on the couch, wasting no time. "How about I tell **you** how it went with the school counselor last evening?"

Jack opened the curtains and stared out toward the side yard. Craig was on his front porch, leafing through the Sunday paper, his own steaming mug in hand.

"She's intense, right?" San began. "In fact, she's possibly the most like me of anyone you could have picked." She gave a little cackle.

"You're enjoying this a little too much."

Her chortle deepened. "You had to learn the hard way, Jack. Now, are you ready to get real? I mean **really** real?"

"I have a few new names," Jack said, having had plenty of time last night to consider the possibilities.

"So we **still** haven't learned our lesson," San muttered. "Go ahead. Let's get it over with—tell me who you're thinking of asking next."

Jack eased himself into an upholstered chair and recited his own list of eligible and interesting females: Cynthia, red-haired and bubbly; Jennifer, somewhat shy but with a dizzying sense of humor; and Maggie, short hair, five foot two, and a big heart. All from San's church, which he and Nattie had visited quite a few times. He waited for San to be impressed.

"You done?" she asked, clearly hiding a smirk. "And those are just for starters."

"First off, Cynthia's engaged—"

"Fine. She's off the list," he said.

"Jennifer has a boyfriend in Alabama, and besides she doesn't even want kids of her own, so why would she raise yours?"

"Good point. Check."

"And Maggie?" San snorted. "Divorced twice. And she's not even twenty-five yet. How would you like to be number three?"

"Uh...check."

"By the way, very few people know this about her, so keep it under your rapidly thinning hair."

Jack touched his scalp.

"Gotcha." San chortled again. "So let's think out of the box," she said mysteriously, crossing her legs and fluffing her long red skirt. "I'm thinking of...ah yes. Angela Walberg."

Jack took another sip. He hadn't even considered Angela. Long blond hair, very attractive, even model material. She, too, attended San's church. "Okay, you've got my attention."

San laughed. "Uh-huh. That's what I'm talking about. Do I know, or do I know?"

Before he could manage a retort, he heard the bathroom drawer slam shut, and soon Nattie came bounding downstairs, hair brushed and held back by a white headband, sundress twirling around her with each step. She gave her auntie San a quick hug and presented Jack a piece of paper containing her memory verses for Sunday school. She took a quick breath, clutched her hands behind her back, and began reciting from memory. "Create in me a clean heart..." she began, remembering the Psalm perfectly. He and San clapped exuberantly. Proud of her accomplishment, Nattie grabbed the paper from Jack, all smiles, and bounded into the kitchen for breakfast.

Jack hunched in his chair glumly.

"I know what you're thinking," San whispered.

"You remember?"

San cleared her throat. "I try not to. It was just a bad day, Jack." **No, it wasn't**, Jack thought. It was a **typical day**.

His mind flashed back in time, twenty years. They were driving to church for the Christmas Eve service in their Oldsmobile, an oversized rust bucket, his father and mother in the front seat, his father wearing his favorite speckled maroon tie, the one that cleverly disguised food stains, and his mother wearing those gaudy white beads, layers upon layers of fake pearls, like a noose around her neck.

His mother turned in her seat and handed Danny a piece of paper containing a series of Scripture passages relating to the birth of Christ and told him she'd forgotten, but he needed to recite them tonight, by **memory**, in front of the church congregation.

"You're my smartest child," his mother told Danny. "You can do it."

Jack and Sandra must have shuddered, but Danny did his best, whispering the verses over and over again, and by the time they got to church, a mere twenty minutes later, eager-to-please Danny thought he was ready.

Standing in front of the pastor's podium, Danny got through the Isaiah passage without so much as a pause. The Luke section was next, but after reciting **"When Cyrenius was governor of Syria,"** Danny drew a complete blank. He looked out at the audience, hoping for a whispered clue, but only an awkward silence filled the candle-lit sanctuary. Embarrassed and red-faced, he slid the paper out of his pocket and finished the recitation.

Sitting beside Jack, his mother's own cheeks splashed fire engine red, her expression hardening into a fake but socially accommodating smile, her eyes turning to ice.

Afterward, and all the way home, she berated Danny for humiliating her in front of the entire church, while Jack and Sandra sat in stunned silence.

"She wasn't well, you know," San now added softly. "And she was drinking a lot to deal with her pain. She wasn't always like that."

Jack bit his tongue. Maybe not, but that's the only mother he remembered, and he still marveled at how Danny could have emerged from the Livingston family relatively unscathed, eager to forgive, eager to place the best interpretation on others' failings, even their mother's.

Sitting across from San, Jack listened to Nattie rattling about in the kitchen—the clinking of silverware and bowls, and the springy click of the toaster. He sighed and shook off the melancholy. "Okay, back to this dating thing. Surely Angela's seeing someone."

"Nope. She's single," San corrected. "And ready to mingle!"

"Uh...sis? She's a bit out of my league, right?"

San grinned. "She's a woman, Jack. She was **born** out of your league. Thing is, she hasn't been on a date in ages because she intimidates mere mortals such as yourself."

"Um, yikes."

"So I'm thinking she might be just a little lonely about now. Maybe even enough to take your phone call, brother dear."

"Lonely is good." Jack sighed, dying to end the topic and get on the road to church. "Give me her number."

Later that night, one whimper was all it took and he was wide awake. After years of only half sleeping at night, Jack was aware of the smallest sound emanating from his daughter's room.

Hearing the sad moan again, he sat up in bed. Then hearing it louder, he made his way to her door, turned on the hall light, and looked in. Her room smelled of lavender and musty spice. Burrowed into a tight ball, Nattie was murmuring in her sleep.

He moved to sit on the edge of her bed and softly touched her shoulder. Slowly she awakened, obviously confused by her surroundings, peering up at Jack in a daze.

"Bad dream, honey?"

She leaned up to hug him.

"Are you okay?"

She nodded, started to say something,

then let loose with a full-fledged sob. He soothed her gently, until whatever was troubling Nattie seemed to pass. He grabbed a tissue, and she blew her nose.

**So many nightmares for one so small**, he thought, asking her if she needed to use the restroom. Sighing, Nattie threw the covers back and stumbled out of the room. A small shadow of light flickered around the corner, followed by the hum of the fan. Minutes later, she was back, squirming beneath the covers. "Don't go yet," she said as he pulled the quilt to her neckline.

"I won't," he replied. "Do you still remember your dream, honey?"

"I can't tell you—it was **terrible**."

Jack pointed to the chair in the corner of her room. "That's where I'll be until you fall asleep. I won't leave you, Nattie."

"Promise?"

He patted her face, waiting for her to settle some before he turned off the light.

"Can I tell you a secret, Dad?" she whispered.

Jack made a zipping gesture, pulling his

finger across his lips, just as Nattie often did. But she continued to stare at him, as if worried he wouldn't take her seriously.

"What is it, sweetie?"

"Sometimes I play make-believe," she began softly. "And sometimes I pretend that Laura's my birth mom, and that when she saw me, she didn't want to give me up, after all. But the men in white clothes made her, because they had a deal, but she searched the whole country and found me anyway." She stopped to catch her breath. "And then she decided to secretly work for my adoptive parents, so she could be with me forever."

He nodded respectfully.

"Do you think it could be true?"

"No, honey, I don't." Jack felt his eyes water. "I wish I could say it was."

"I can still pretend, though, can't I?"

"Sure," he said. **Sometimes that's all we have.**

He asked her if she wanted to pray, and she did. Afterward, he kissed her again and turned off the hall light. Then he cozied up in the rather uncomfortable chair in the corner of her itty-bitty living space. The bright stars lit her room, casting shadows across her bed coverings as his eyes became adjusted to the darkness.

"I love you, Dad."

"I love you more," he said.

Nattie giggled and her world tilted back to normal. Or so he hoped.

In his own make-believe world, if Jack were to admit it, Nattie was always a happy girl, and she never cried or dreamed upsetting dreams, because he was able to give her everything she needed.

**Just about everything.**

# Chapter 15

At the airfield the following Tuesday afternoon, Jack put Angela's phone number on his desk next to his bottled water and took a deep breath. He was puzzled at his nerves, considering that he, as a seasoned pilot with over ten thousand hours under his belt, could take a spinning plane careening toward earth at blinding speed and swing it to safety without a second thought. Yet the thought of calling a woman like Angela Walberg for a date made his palms sweaty.

Throwing caution to the wind, Jack pressed onward and dialed her number, praying for a red flag if God had other plans for them. When she answered, her voice was tinged with an endearing lyrical inflection, as though expecting his call.

Had San tipped her off?

"Hi," he said, waxing nonpoetic. "I'm San Livingston's brother."

Angela laughed heartily, reminding him of something San had declared. The way to a man's heart was not through the stomach, but by making him feel like he was the funniest man on planet Earth.

"I've known San for five years," Angela informed him after he asked. Then she admitted, "I wouldn't have known you two were related, much less siblings."

"Believe me, we've heard that before."

"Are you **sure** you're brother and sister?"

"Careful, you might get San's hopes up."

Angela seemed pleased with his self-deprecating humor, and at the appropriate lull he ventured in. "I'd like to get to know you better, Angela."

"Well, thanks, Jack. I'd like that, too."

So they agreed to meet for lunch at a restaurant a few blocks from Angela's job as a fashion advisor for an upscale boutique on Main Street.

Jack arrived fifteen minutes early for their

date the next day. Unsure of the proper greeting, Jack was relieved when Angela, wearing a navy blue sleeveless dress, swang in for a quick hug, smelling of apples and flowers.

The hostess led them toward the back of the restaurant, surrounded by exotic paintings and dark wood paneling. The popular place was filled with patrons, assisted by an impressive waitstaff.

It surprised Jack how easily his conversation with Angela picked up where they'd left off on the phone. Talking about her family, work, and faith, Angela described her childhood years in Duluth, Minnesota, and her Norwegian heritage in particular. "I've inherited plenty of stubbornness," she said.

For his part, Jack shared a few flight stories and several Nattie stories. The more they talked, the more it seemed they were uncovering something special. **Maybe even divinely ordained?** Jack thought, uncommonly relaxed.

Angela ordered something light and then leaned back, seemingly comfortable as she looked about the room. When it appeared that she'd spotted someone, she broke into a broad smile and leaned forward to whisper to Jack. "Without looking obvious, notice the couple three tables to our right."

Jack adjusted his napkin and turned slightly, seeing the object of Angela's fascination—a well-dressed brown-haired man, midthirties, sitting across from a younger woman in a pale yellow dress.

"Jeff and Mindy," Angela said. "He's her boss. I've known Mindy for years. But tell me what **you** see."

Angela had certainly piqued his curiosity, but their waitress was walking toward them, carrying their order on a large round tray. Their conversation took different turns, and over the course of a few minutes Jack casually observed the couple—Jeff and Mindy—but saw nothing of a mysterious nature. Angela, however, gave the impression of glee at his bewilderment.

Obviously eager for the revelation, Angela said simply, "It's all in the eyes, Jack."

He took another subtle look but saw nothing.

Angela smiled knowingly. "Mindy's in **love** with her boss and has been for months. She told me so, but I can tell by how she looks at him." She lowered her voice. "But Jeff's clueless, because…"

Just then the waitress interrupted things by coming to refill their water glasses. All the while, Angela's blue eyes twinkled with impatience.

When they were alone again, Angela nodded. "Jeff's totally unaware of Mindy's affection because he's enamored with our waitress, the one who just filled our glasses."

"How do you know **that**?" Jack asked.

Angela shook her head in mock disappointment. "I told you. The eyes!" She clasped her hands in front of her on the table. "I'm a people-watcher, Jack. I should've been a jury consultant."

Later, after finishing her meal of spinach salad and shrimp and noodle soup, Angela studied him for a moment. She mentioned her favorite steak place, adding, "The chef's wife is a friend of mine."

"Is that right?"

"I'll have to introduce you," she continued. "We should go sometime."

An **engraved invitation**, Jack thought, swooping in with, "How about this Friday night?"

Angela beamed at his dating acumen. So another date was set for the weekend. **"Easy-peasy-lemon-squeezy,"** Nattie might have said. But he couldn't help imagining that Angela was watching his eyes for things he didn't even realize he was communicating.

**I've got this dating thing by the tail**, Jack thought while driving home. He remembered San's advice, fortunately not given within Nattie's hearing. "Angela's ready to settle down, so get out your wallet if you're serious, 'cause she's done window shopping."

Laura had quickly agreed to stay late on Friday with Nattie. However, before Jack headed for the garage, Nattie quizzed him with undiluted anxiety. "Angela, **again**?"

"This is what dating looks like, sweetie," Jack replied, sounding even to himself like he'd become an expert. He gave her a long hug good-bye, but Nattie held on, letting go only after he patted the hand that had become super-glued to his neck. He kissed her cheek, but her pout remained—the evening with Karen Jones still fresh in her memory.

"Laura looks really pretty tonight," Nattie said glumly, but Jack didn't bite.

**She'll be happy**, he thought, backing out of the garage in his lumbering Ford, **once she meets Angela Walberg**.

According to their previous agreement, Jack and Angela met in the waiting area of the restaurant. She showed up in an eye-catching red-and-white print dress and white heels. Jack felt quite tailored in his pinstriped gray suit.

After a quick glance at a menu, which Angela had apparently memorized, she pointed to the prime rib and Jack took her suggestion. Their conversation progressed beyond previously established boundaries, during which Angela introduced a few tidbits about her earlier relationships. Jack listened uneasily, scouring her words for clues.

Stretching his rather limited social repertoire, Jack told a few more Nattie stories, including more of their past history. Angela's eyes brightened suddenly. "So you missed out on the diapering years, eh?"

He shrugged. "I guess I did."

"Boy, were you lucky. I was the oldest of four, and let me tell you, I'm not a fan of screaming babies. I don't even think really young kids should be allowed in restaurants."

At this comment, Angela tilted her head toward a far table, indicating a young family of four, including a fussy young child. Jack hadn't even noticed them until now. Angela rolled her eyes, then broke into a soft laugh. "Who in their right mind would bring children to an upscale place like this to eat?"

At the end of their enjoyable dinner, they

lingered in the corner of the plush lobby, making plans to meet again. Jack caught Angela's irresistible gaze and leaned near to kiss her.

Angela brushed her hand along his shoulder, met his eyes in an alluring manner, and said, "So when can I get to know this precocious child of yours whom you and San cannot stop talking about?"

"Nattie can't wait to meet you, either," he told her, hoping he wouldn't be held accountable for the mild exaggeration.

Like most men and women on the brink of coupledom, they texted over the weekend, and when Jack called Sunday night to invite Angela for supper at his place, she said yes immediately. "San says your daughter's nanny is a wonder in the kitchen. I've always wanted to try something authentically Amish."

Jack suggested the following Friday, nearly a week away, but Angela had plans to visit friends in Cleveland. And, as it turned out, their schedules simply didn't mesh during the next week either. Except for tomorrow night. "A Monday night supper—will that work for you?"

"At least it's not Monday night football," Angela laughed. "So, sure."

"Perfect." And it was, Jack told himself. This way he wouldn't be tempted to procrastinate about telling Nattie. **And less time for her to fret or scheme.**

While tucking Nattie in that evening, Jack revealed the plan. She took the news with relative ease. Perhaps it was Angela's special request for Nattie's attendance that made all the difference, not to mention the great interest in Laura's **Amish** cooking. Nattie loved to show Laura off.

"We're going old school tonight," Nattie said, reaching under her covers and handing him Raggedy Ann.

After two Monday morning flights, Jack hightailed it home and dedicated himself to helping Laura with the preparations, as before. She was happy to select several typical Amish offerings, including chow chow, pickled beets, and for the main course: chicken loaf. While Laura worked, she whistled along to her much-loved country radio station.

Doing her part, Nattie took out the garbage and scoured the downstairs bathroom. By four o'clock she was already dressed in a pleated tan skirt and a cheetah-print top, shadowing Laura around the kitchen.

Jack, on the other hand, had no idea what to wear. He came downstairs to model his pants and shirt for Laura, who wrinkled her nose politely. "Perhaps you might call San," she suggested, trying to squelch a grin at his color deficiency.

Jack sighed, dialing his sister's number, then describing the colors over the phone. San was fussier than usual, suggesting a few changes. "I think you might want a tie," she told him while he switched to speaker phone, fumbled around in his closet, and changed into a button-down.

"How long is Laura staying around tonight?" she asked.

Jack hedged. "We haven't worked out the details."

"But she **is** leaving, right?" San pressed,

and then she must have realized the time. "Wait a minute, it's already—"

The doorbell rang, saving him from further interrogation. "Oops, gotta go, San," Jack quipped, disconnecting quickly.

Downstairs, Angela was standing at the threshold, looking exceptionally lovely with her long blond hair loose and wavy. A bold silver and white necklace and matching bracelet harmonized perfectly with her lavender dress. Even Nattie, who'd seen the epitome of fashion with San, seemed impressed, looking up at Jack with amazement. **"You're dating her?"** Nattie's eyes seemed to say.

Jack introduced Angela first to Laura, who greeted their guest graciously, smiling shyly. Then he introduced Angela to Nattie, who put out her hand and actually did a polite little bob as she said, "Pleased to meet you, Angela."

Jack smiled at his daughter's stellar manners and immediately felt more relaxed, despite the fact that he hadn't had time to add a tie per San's instructions.

"Would you like a preview of our Amish

cuisine?" he asked, happy to be the host while Laura completed the finishing touches in the kitchen.

"Pickled beets? I've never even heard of them!"

"They're delicious," Nattie told her.

"I can't wait," Angela exclaimed, rubbing her hands together. Nattie giggled at the gesture. "That's what **I** do!" she said. And the two of them rubbed their hands together, ending in a duet of laughter.

**Already bonding!** Jack thought, contented that the evening was off to a terrific start.

Angela asked to use the restroom, and Jack directed her to the one next to the kitchen before turning to Nattie to model his attire. "How do I look?"

Nattie laughed. "You out-look **me**."

Later, in the dining room, Jack offered a table blessing, and Laura and Nattie glanced at each other and said a short prayer in their private language. Angela seemed to love it, her eyes following Laura after the amen was said by all.

Laura efficiently served the chow chow

and pickled beets as Angela listened to Nattie's tales about her auntie San, one in particular that had occurred at a lakeside cabin not far from here.

"It was Auntie San's one and only attempt to water ski," Nattie told her dramatically, eyes wide, which encouraged Jack. As did Angela's apparent amusement.

Laura brought over a bread basket of hot butter horns, straight from the oven. "There's homemade apple butter or peach jam," she said. "Whatever you'd like."

Jack deferred to Angela, who chose the apple butter, all smiles.

It wasn't long before Nattie asked Angela to recite her favorite movies. Angela was marvelous, glancing toward the ceiling before reciting the kinds of films only a child might appreciate.

Laura carried over the chicken loaf and offered to serve it individually while Angela inquired about her Amish traditions—church every other Sunday, a dress code, and growing up without electricity. Cutting generous portions of the chicken loaf, Laura graciously answered, meeting

Jack's gaze as she moved around the table, likely overly concerned about monopolizing the conversation.

"Do you mind if I ask how long you've been Nattie's nanny?" Angela asked, studying Laura with undisguised curiosity. Laura told her, and Angela's jovial expression faded. "Wow, that's a long time."

"**Jah**," Laura replied proudly, once again glancing at Jack.

"Laura could actually be my Mamma," Nattie announced, then launched into Pennsylvania Dutch. **"Ich lieb dich unauserschprechlich."**

Angela's eyebrows rose and Jack's heart went **thud**.

"I have no idea what you just said," Angela confessed with a smile.

"It means I love you beyond measure—meaning Laura." Then Nattie added another unsolicited morsel. "Nearly **everyone** asks if Laura's married to my dad."

"**Ach**, now, Nattie," Laura said.

Jack struggled to keep his composure.

"And why do you think people say that?" Angela pressed.

Nattie grinned, oblivious to the rising tension. "For one thing, she practically lives here."

Laura squeezed Nattie's shoulder and whispered something in her ear, at which Nattie's expression went cold.

"I'm sorry," his daughter said abruptly.

"That's all right," Angela replied, her expression puzzled.

In fact, the apology only seemed to worsen matters, as the entire room seemed to reverberate with Nattie's over-share. Angela cleared her throat, and Nattie lowered her head to focus on her food. Whatever Laura had whispered had made her completely wilt.

Angela asked if Laura would mind jotting down some of her Amish recipes, and when Jack mentioned one of Nattie's photo albums, Angela responded earnestly, "I'd love to see your pictures."

Nattie nodded politely but without her usual exuberance. Laura met Jack's eyes as she removed the plates, as if to say, **"I'm sorry about this."**

Jack, in turn, focused his smile on

Angela, hoping to make light of Nattie's faux pas. However, Angela's smile had vanished, her face ghostly white, as if she'd just seen an apparition.

**What now?**

The remainder of the evening rolled along without further incident, but Angela's mood never fully recovered. After a spiritless game of dominoes—Nattie won twice—Jack walked Angela to the door, and while she was gracious enough, she wasn't the vivacious woman who'd walked in his house.

Before stepping out, Angela looked around, presumably to thank Laura, but Laura had mysteriously disappeared.

Jack walked with her to her car, and when he opened her door, she extended her hand. "I enjoyed the evening, Jack. Please give my regards to the cook."

He offered a few parting words, but they came out awkward and apologetic. Moments later, Angela backed out of the driveway and was gone.

Jack returned to the house to check on Nattie, now sitting at the couch with

Laura's arm draped around her. It was evident that the two of them had been commiserating.

"I hope you're not mad at me, Dad," Nattie said.

"Of course not," Jack said.

"Can I go and play with Chelsea?" she asked. Chelsea was pal number seven on Nattie's list and lived four houses down. "She called while you were outside."

Nattie agreed to the usual sidewalk safety restrictions, and since it was still light, Jack allowed Nattie to ride her bike, leaving Jack and Laura momentarily alone to mull over the evening.

He helped Laura load the dishwasher, working in awkward silence. Before long he couldn't help it. Holding a dish towel, he leaned against the counter, crossed his arms, and began to chuckle. Laura pressed a few buttons and the dishwasher whirred into life. She stood across from him, regarding him curiously.

"I know, I know. That was a disaster," Jack said. "I might need remedial dating instruction, after all."

"I don't know what came over her, honestly." Laura stared glumly at the floor.

"I wondered the same."

Laura sighed. "The dear child knows better."

It was then that Jack realized Laura was talking about Nattie, while he'd been referring to **Angela**.

Had Laura completely missed Angela's altered mood?

**Surely not.**

Laura must have figured Angela had been frustrated with Nattie, because in the Amish culture, kids were expected to stay silent, to express the utmost respect for their elders, and never speak out of turn.

But Angela wasn't upset with Nattie at all. Jack knew this for certain. Angela was upset by what she **thought** she saw.

Laura sniffed softly. "I think Nattie's been more nervous about your dating than she's let on."

**She's let on quite a bit**, Jack thought.

Laura met his eyes, and they regarded each other for a moment, the kind of gaze that must have unsettled Angela, a natural moment between two people who have a comfortable history with each other.

**And that's all**, Jack noted to himself before replying. "Nattie's worried some-one will come along and replace you, Laura. I've tried to assure her that it won't happen."

Laura didn't respond at first. She seemed peculiarly contemplative, pondering the evening, perhaps.

"What are you thinking?"

Laura shrugged, biting her lip, as if choosing her words carefully. "Jack, I think Nattie's more afraid that you'll find another woman to replace **her**."

Jack suddenly felt deflated. He hadn't considered that. **Replace Nattie?** He groaned inwardly. He tossed the dish towel into the sink and blew out a long breath. "I'm not sure my dating is a good idea anymore."

Laura caught his eyes at that moment, as if judging the seriousness of his intention. Jack extended his arms, smoothing his hands along the tile counter.

"No," he said, fully settled. "Nattie's not

ready."

Moments passed as neither said a word. Finally, Laura grabbed her keys from the counter. "Well, I'd better go."

"Tomorrow?"

She nodded and gave him a gentle wave, and if he wasn't mistaken, she seemed relieved.

Nattie returned from her visit with Chelsea, full of smiles, the evening with Angela in her rearview window.

Waiting for Nattie to get ready for bed, Jack sat in his office, listening to music, unable to forget the pained look in Angela's eyes, as if she'd just witnessed a crime: the lingering gaze between Laura and himself.

A pile of mail lay on his desk, placed there by Laura. He sorted through it, removed one of the very few bills that was not auto-pay, and wrote out the check and sealed the envelope, waiting for Nattie to announce that she was ready to be tucked in.

Their nighttime routine was one of the few constants in her life. No matter how badly the day had gone, at the end of the day, they thanked God for His many blessings, especially for the ones unseen.

In the early days of his guardianship, Jack had purchased a dozen parenting books and had even hired a family counselor for advice. The counselor had suggested a nightly routine, something that would give Nattie stability. Tucking her in became a time when he wanted Nattie to feel safe, where she could speak without repercussions. Of course, Nattie was particularly thrilled to include him in her world of stuffed animals and fairy tales.

Jack also learned that he was supposed to walk the fence between erring on the side of too permissive or too strict. With the passage of time, it was becoming a conundrum, finding the right balance between rules and freedom. He didn't want her to think she was living in a prison, but he wanted her to have the security of boundaries. He also knew that he didn't have to get it perfectly right, as long as Nattie always knew she was loved.

But his aspirations didn't stop there. Yes, he wanted to raise Nattie with clear lines and strong discipline, but he also wanted to transmit to her the message that, as far as he was concerned, she could do no wrong. That she was living a forgiven life.

It was the opposite of how he'd been raised, as if he could do **nothing** right. His mother had a knack for seeing the cloud behind every silver lining, and his father was too weak to stand in her way.

San, of course, told Jack he was obsessing. **"You've put your life on hold for Nattie."**

This was where she was wrong. He hadn't put his life on hold; Nattie was his life.

Still waiting for Nattie's summons, Jack leaned back in his chair and thought about tonight's dinner date with Angela, with its disastrous ending.

**"It's in the eyes,"** Angela had told him at the restaurant.

Had he been missing this all along? Could Laura actually have feelings for him?

No. Of course not.

In spite of Angela's reaction, whatever she thought she saw, she was wrong.

**Badly** wrong.

But still. He couldn't continue dating, not with the slightest possibility of hurting Laura. Or hurting Nattie.

**"She's afraid you'll replace her,"** Laura had said. That, in itself, was reason enough.

**Big mistake**, he thought, squinting his eyes shut. **Big.**

San didn't help matters by calling just then. "Do you have any idea what Angela just told me?"

Jack sighed. "I can guess."

San churned through the next five minutes, blaming him for not exiling Laura to her Amish farm. "You can't let this one get away, Jack. Angela's a keeper."

Jack barely concealed his frustration. "I think she's already gone."

"Jack Livingston!" San's irritation was palpable. "No wonder you're not married. You have to fight for her."

But he couldn't tell San **why** he wouldn't fight for Angela. San would have come undone. As it was, his sudden disinterest rankled the pugnacious go-getter, and she refused to back down. Sometimes, talking to San was like a dog chasing his tail. She continued pounding at him verbally until Nattie walked in the door, showing off her new hummingbird pajamas.

"Gotta go, sis."

In midstream, San ignored him.

"Sis, I'm hanging up now—"

"We're not done, Jack!"

"Later, okay?"

"Jack—"

Click.

**Sorry**, Jack thought. **I'll call her back when she cools down.**

After they prayed together, Nattie asked if Angela was mad at them.

"No," he said. "But it doesn't matter anyway."

"Why?" The hopeful look on Nattie's face melted his heart.

Jack told her what he'd been thinking, that maybe he wasn't ready to date after all, and Nattie sprung out of her bed, hugging him tightly. "I was holding my breath!" she exclaimed.

Jack was unsure where to go from here. The future seemed as hazy and unclear as before. **Nothing's solved.**

With infectious enthusiasm, Nattie dug under her quilt, extracting Dewey the Dolphin and presenting it to him like a reward for his decision. Jack stared at the perennial grin of the seafaring creature and waited for her explanation.

"Dolphins have their own secret language," she said. "But even if you can't understand their words, you can understand their feelings. Kinda like me and Laura."

Jack kissed her forehead. "You two have something very special."

Nattie nodded solemnly. "She's my bestie."

Jack shut off the light, and from inside his little girl's room, Nattie whispered, "You know, sometimes it's hard being a kid."

"Try being a grown-up," he replied.

"No thanks," Nattie muttered. "I can wait." Me **too**, Jack thought.

# Chapter 16

With no urgency to get to the office early, Jack slept in the next morning until Nattie came barging in, wearing jean shorts and a Minnie Mouse T-shirt, her upper lip frosted with a greenish foam. "You do **not** want to go downstairs, Dad."

Jack leaned up, squinting into the new day.

"I'm serious. Stay in here till the coast is clear!"

"Huh?"

Nattie disappeared down the hall without explanation. Jack smiled. Living with Nattie was like a never-ending merry-go-round. He got up, put on his robe, and looked down into the kitchen. Laura was busy at the blender. He spotted the kale leaves and blueberries.

"Oh boy," he muttered.

Laura looked up, gave him a thumbs-up, and pointed to her green concoction, an overly wide smile gracing her face. She pressed a button and the blender began twirling and buzzing. No doubt she'd discovered a new smoothie recipe designed for the overall health and well-being of the Livingston family. **Hopefully, this one has more honey than the last time**, Jack mused, glad that Laura didn't seem ruffled at all from last evening's fiasco.

He wandered down the hall, smiling at Nattie's unusual morning cheerfulness, most likely tied to last night's decision to abandon dating. He knocked on her door. "Nattie-bug?"

"Hark!"

He opened her door, and she was sitting on her bed, staring at some of her artwork. She raised her arms and twiddled her fingers, a Nattie-request for a hug, and he complied.

Nattie was a hug bug. When she was younger, Jack would peek in her room, and sleepy-eyed, she'd grin and extend her arms to the sky, wiggling her fingers, **"Hug me, hug me."** Although Jack hadn't grown up in an affectionate family, he was quickly disabused of that notion. Nattie would have none of it. Due to her own upbringing, even Laura wasn't all that demonstrative, and yet she, too, had succumbed to Nattie's sheer exuberance.

Later that morning, after obliging Laura and consuming a full glass of her healthy concoction, Jack puttered around in the garage. He overheard the unmistakable song of the ice cream truck, a tinkling tin xylophone rendition of "Tones for Cones." Or was that "Sprinkle Twinkle"?

Nattie came scrambling in and held up his wallet, deftly retrieved from his desk inside.

"Hurry!" she said.

"Hey, we have ice cream in the freezer."

Nattie fidgeted. "This is **special** ice cream."

Jack sighed. Ice cream was always creamier on the other side of the fence.

He examined a ten and was about to trade it for a five when Nattie swooped in and removed it from his grasp. "Thanks, Dad!"

"I'll expect some change," he called after her but heard only giggles.

**She seems fine**, he thought, recalling the dinner date last night. **Thank goodness.**

Jack texted Angela later that afternoon, but she didn't respond. He texted again that evening and still no reply.

The following day, he dialed Angela's number, but she never picked up. On the second call, he left a message. "It was wonderful spending time with you, Angela. Have a great week."

San called again, having recovered her temper, and politely encouraged Jack to keep trying with Angela. "Besides, Nattie mustn't have that kind of control," she told him. "**You're** in charge."

"It wasn't Nattie—"

"Well, then you need to talk to Laura, get things straightened out with her."

**Ain't happening**, Jack thought, wary of the prospect of confronting the nanny over the silly notion that Angela supposed Laura had romantic feelings for him.

"Keep in mind that Angela Walberg won't be single forever," San finished, clearly displeased with Jack's lack of courage. "So I'll say farewell for now."

Relieved, Jack said good-bye and hung up.

He wandered out the back door and found Laura sitting out on the porch, gently swinging to the rhythmic squeak of the two-seater. He stood there quietly, taking in the sunset.

Laura looked as wistful as he felt. Occasionally, at the end of her work day, instead of leaving immediately, she would sit and swing, watching Nattie play in the back or simply soaking up the ambience of the tree-lined property.

It was the best setting he could have provided for Nattie, and he was grateful again to his brother for handpicking such an idyllic home. The newer two-story was located on the far edge of the neighborhood, at the end of the block, and framed by their own little grove of maples, oaks, and elms, highlighted by a single flowering dogwood. In the fall, the colors were magnificent.

Laura smiled. "So peaceful tonight, ain't?"

"Would you like something cold to drink?" he asked.

She gave him a playful look. "That's my job."

"Let me," he said, and she acquiesced, suggesting the meadow tea she liked to make. He found some in a pitcher and poured a glass for her over ice. Rummaging in the food saver, he located a lemon, cut a wedge, and pressed it into the rim of her glass.

Back outside, he presented the iced tea.

"Goodness, Jack. I think you've got this dating thing down **perty gut**." Instantly, she turned red. "Sorry, that wasn't—"

Jack waved it off.

"Where's your drink?"

"Not thirsty."

Sitting next to her, Jack enjoyed the lingering scent of the late blooming lilacs from the bushes across the fence, mingling with the smell of freshly mown grass. Behind them came the tinkling of the wind chime hanging from the eaves. A rare tranquil moment.

The scent of lilacs could send him into aromatic heaven, and he mentioned as much to Laura.

"Lilac's my favorite, too." She described her parents' lilac bushes in Lancaster County. As a child, she liked to cut a stem each day for a month, placing the flowers in a vase for her mother. "One of my happiest memories."

Jack was surprised to hear her open up about her childhood. One story led to another, and soon Laura was sharing about the first time a boy had ever given **her** flowers.

"A boy or a beau?" he asked nonchalantly.

Laura went silent at that, and Jack wondered if he'd embarrassed her.

Later, when the stillness became too awkward, he said, "We should plant our own lilac bush."

"I'd **love** that," Laura murmured.

"Is it too late in the season?"

"We could check." Laura pointed to his cell phone there in the space between them.

"Sure, go ahead." He was humored by her interest in technology. **She's practically fancy already.**

The answer immediately showed up on a link. "Not too late, at all," she replied excitedly. "But there won't be any blossoms till next year."

"Let's plant a bush or two tomorrow."

Her enthusiasm took flight. "Tomorrow, it is!"

They sat for another half hour or so, casually chatting. When the sun toppled beyond the trees at the back of his property, they were quiet, unwilling to disturb the moment.

Eventually, Laura said something about getting back to Apple Creek. And ten minutes later, she made good on it. Jack walked her to her car, to make sure the engine would start. If it didn't, he'd have the pleasure of driving her home again.

The motor roared to life, and she waved. After she drove away, he wandered back to the house, noting how very empty the house seemed.

Nattie was in the great room playing her Lego computer game, her eyes twinkling when she saw him. "So...did you have a nice swing?"

Nattie spared him more questions, too busy wielding her controls, guiding her little man through a dangerous forest. He watched for a few minutes, enjoying the beeping musical sounds until Nattie put down her controls and came over to the couch and sat with him.

She put her hand on his arm, her face sympathetic. It would have been almost comical if she hadn't seemed so serious.

"What's your thought bubble?" he asked her.

She searched his face. "Are you sad about Angela?"

"I liked her, but I don't think she's right for us."

Considering this, Nattie bit her lip, then seemed satisfied with his answer. "Wanna play a racing game with me?"

Jack agreed.

"But I have to warn you. I'm out to **win**!" Nattie said, retrieving the second set of controls and handing it to Jack.

"I've never noticed that about you before," he joked.

The next day, Jack helped Laura plant two mature lilac bushes on the south side of the house—carefully removing the root ball from its burlap wrapping. He dug an ample hole, making sure to cut a wide two-foot circle for expansion. Then Laura and he spread topsoil once the bushes were planted.

During the remainder of June, Laura found a number of new gardening projects, enlisting Nattie's help. In the evenings when Jack was home from the airfield, Nattie and Laura gave Jack an account of the day's accomplishments: a flowering vine on a trellis below the porch, a smattering of pink roses on a white arbor, delphiniums, hollyhocks, daisies, peonies, and black-eyed Susans, among others.

The exterior of the house was slowly becoming transformed into a botanical garden.

Later, as the sun fell to the horizon, the three of them often hurried to the back porch for the sunset. Nattie, especially, liked to watch the hummingbirds' antics close to twilight, before they headed for their nests in the grove of trees.

Laura also surprised Nattie with a hummingbird video documentary, which they watched together repeatedly, comparing it with the identification book Jack found at the library. With the help of Jack's camera, Nattie classified the several varieties and, of course, itemized them according to favorites. The green violet-ear, the fastest hummingbird with its shimmering green body and a velvet patch beneath its ears, was her number one. Each time a new hummer appeared in the yard, it became an event of magnificent proportions.

Eventually, nearly half of Jack's office wall was filled with pictures of Nattie's birds, mostly ruby-throated, but sometimes a feisty rufous or a rare calliope. She loved their diving aerobatics but lamented their territorial fighting. **"Why can't they just share?"** she'd ask.

Conveniently, there were occasions when Nattie disappeared to her room, leaving Laura and Jack to occupy the swing and pretend to be ignorant of her rather obvious agenda.

Truth be told, Jack was beginning to savor those quiet moments with Laura, hearing her childhood stories, honored to at last be ushered into her secret world, especially considering her privacy over the years. But it also made him nervous. **Why now?**

The rest of June was slow at Higher Ground, due to days of high winds, low ceilings, and heavy rains, although Jack's company made some bucks flying photographers and other thrill seekers. The Salt Fork State Park, sixty miles to the southeast, never failed to attract a handful of fanatics intent on spotting the elusive Bigfoot, and Jack—definitely a cynic himself—was more than willing to fly them over the woods, if only to enjoy the beauty.

During the beginning of July, the flying weather improved and so did business. In addition to a few quick out-of-state trips and flying the corporate jet for his bigwig clients, Higher Ground fielded a healthy assortment of renters and certification seekers, all of which helped fill out an otherwise uneventful month. When he wasn't flying, Jack spent his free time with Nattie, taking her to the municipal pool, driving through the local Dairy Queen a couple times a week, and taking in family movies at the local cinema.

On the spur of the moment, Jack and Nattie even flew together on short sightseeing trips, but not as often or as far as Jack had anticipated. Nattie's multitude of friends were in and out of the house on a regular basis, hanging out in her room, or in the back-yard tree house, or digging in the dirt at the end of their property. He got whiplash trying to keep track of their names.

Laura had yet to make her "English" debut. Jack figured she'd changed her mind. It certainly wasn't his place to inquire. Most important, she hadn't said another word about leaving for Lancaster County.

They celebrated Nattie's ninth birthday at the local pizza parlor, inviting ten of her BFFs. Jack had acquiesced to her insistence that **four** friends did **not** make a party.

It was a rip-roaring time, and Laura seemed to enjoy it as much as Nattie, both of them ignoring the looks from curious patrons. This was in spite of the proliferation of Ohio Amish culture.

Before the pizza had a chance to arrive, Nattie stood up and gestured to Laura sitting at the table nearby. "This is Laura Mast, my Amish nanny. If you think she dresses funny, get over it, because she's my best friend in the world."

Laura brushed away a tear, clearly moved by Nattie's refusal to be embarrassed of her.

After the introduction, Nattie went to hug Laura. She then waved her arm toward Jack and announced loudly, "And this is my...**dad**. He flies airplanes for a living."

Everyone cheered, and Jack pushed out his chest.

After they were home again, the house was overrun with giggling girls who spread sleeping bags on the floor in the great room, though sleeping was clearly not on their agenda.

Jack looked over the banister and noticed Nattie in the middle of the group, telling a story. One of the girls pointed at Jack and Nattie turned, spotting him upstairs. She waved and went back to her story.

In the past, Jack had used Nattie's sleepovers to instill social behavior: how to get along, how to treat your guests like royalty. More than once he'd forbidden the next week's visit due to Nattie's obnoxious behavior. And she had quickly modified her conduct.

When Jack had reason to believe things were under control for the night, he headed for bed, although he was awakened later by explosive giggling.

He noticed that Nattie must have come up at one point to replace his lion with her elephant, putting it on Jack's pillow. Turning on the lamp, he read her note: **Here's the elephant in your room. Get it?**

Jack grinned sleepily. He doubted she got the **whole elephant in the room** nuance, but it was cute. And heartwarming. She might have been busy with her friends but never too busy to think of ol' dad.

Laura had left about nine that night. **"I think the worst has passed,"** she'd whispered, and he knew what she meant. Nattie seemed to have settled down since the evening with Angela Walberg. She hadn't cried in weeks, and to Jack, it felt as if they were pitching a no-hitter. He was reluctant to address it, as if worried he might jinx the recovery.

The whole notion of growing out of it was making sense. Perhaps Laura was right. Or maybe—**just maybe**—Nattie was holding her breath, not wanting to mess up what she thought was happening between her dad and her nanny.

Either way, their lives seemed to have

reached a peaceful rhythm, and spending time with Laura at day's end continued as a routine. They'd become a happy little family of sorts, and Jack was determined not to disrupt the status quo.

Kelly Maines's summer was looking to be considerably less of a roller coaster than previous ones, when she'd spent the weeks raising money to find Emily and most weekends in a new city, plying her magic tricks for unsuspecting prospects. Instead, she was settling in to her new job, sleeping normal hours, and relishing the camaraderie of office life.

By the middle of June, Ernie had recovered enough from pneumonia to have bypass surgery. On the day of the heart procedure, Kelly, along with Cindy, kept Ernie's wife company in the waiting room.

Four long hours later, Ernie was wheeled out on a gurney. His cardiac surgeon expressed cautious hope for a complete recovery and expressly forbade him from office work for at least a month. From Penny's determined look, Kelly was sure she was going to hold her hubby to it.

In the weeks that followed, Kelly located a nicer apartment with reasonable rent. Unfortunately, while she had enough money for the deposit, she was short on the first month's rent until her new boss caught wind of her plans and insisted on advancing her enough to cover the remainder.

As a going-away gift, Kelly received Felix from her old landlady, Agnes, who declared, "That rascal always liked you better."

Kelly only smiled, thrilled to become Felix's official owner.

Melody, of course, was amused with Kelly's new pet. "Felix. Felix the cat. Really, Kel?"

Kelly laughed. "I'm afraid dear Agnes was a bit name-challenged."

Eager to help, Melody helped her friend move into her new place, which was larger and brighter than her former digs, and Kelly did her magic with dashes of color—blues and soft yellows—doing away with the old blinds to bring in more light. An inexpensive sofa cover also served to freshen the look, as did two new throw pillows and an area rug she found at a discount store. In a corner of her bedroom, she set up Emily's baby crib, a reminder of her mission. Emily was too big for the crib, but she was still coming home.

Next, she proceeded to brighten the place with her favorite inspirational texts. On a bedroom wall, she hung a stenciled Scripture on painted canvas: **According to your faith be it unto you.** In the living room, she hung two more: **Be not afraid, only believe.** And her all-time favorite: **Though he slay me, yet will I trust in him.**

"That verse is so grim," Melody had commented, but Kelly had explained her reasons. "It means that you believe even if you don't think God will answer your prayer. After all, Job was saying that God might allow him to die, but to him it didn't matter. He would still **believe**."

Melody shuddered. "Fine. They're your walls."

Beside the window, the one overlooking a beautiful maple tree, Kelly hung the last one. **If ye had faith as a grain of mustard seed, ye might say unto this sycamine tree, Be thou plucked up by the root, and be thou planted in the sea; and it should obey you.**

To Kelly, this meant that the size of faith didn't matter, but whether your faith was **alive**, like a seed. Plus your faith bore fruit when you buried it in the ground, as if leaving it for dead. **I've buried my hope in the ground**, she thought. **And someday, it'll grow into a huge tree.**

Along with decorating her new place, she loved her new job. Kelly had a knack for numbers and enjoyed working with clients, opening new accounts, managing transfers, and handling paperwork. She especially liked answering the phone and exuding customer love and appreciation. And while she wasn't accustomed to the longer hours—often ten-hour days—she **loved** her new paycheck!

She'd already put on seven pounds and had begun sleeping nearly eight luxurious hours a night. She no longer winced when she looked in the mirror, and her cheeks were rosy again. Her clothes—her **new** ones—actually fit her in all the right places.

Kelly also worked out at the gym with Melody, the two of them often enjoying a smoothie or an iced coffee afterward. It seemed nothing had ever happened to their friendship before. **Almost.**

Kelly got a kick out of inviting Chet and Eloise to lunch after church and tried to pick up the tab. Somehow the check never actually arrived—Chet had already handled it. Despite her vigorous protests, Chet only grinned. "You can get the next one, missy."

"You'll never let me treat you guys, will you?" Kelly muttered good-naturedly.

Chet, toothpick in his mouth, twinkled back at her. Eloise was just as mischievous and shrugged. "What can I say? I married a chivalrous man."

After doing her best to remain patient, Kelly was thrilled when Cindy called at last. "I've been completing some much-needed housekeeping here in the office, in preparation for Ernie's return."

Kelly could hear the shuffling of papers. Cindy added, "Apparently we still have an open file on Natalie Livingston."

"Not anymore," Kelly replied.

"I have a note that Ernie was going to send you the photo, but I can't find a sent file with an attached picture."

"Doesn't matter," Kelly said, remembering the adorable father with his very blond daughter. "Natalie Livingston is no longer a prospect."

Cindy sounded surprised. "Alrighty then. I'll mark it unfounded and file it away."

**Unfounded**, Kelly thought, hanging up and mulling it over. **Like so many others. What will I do when Ernie actually comes back?**

Yet, in spite of the many good things in Kelly's life—her renewed friendship with Melody, her recovering health, and her job satisfaction—Kelly would have traded it all just to have Emily back in her arms.

Sometimes she still cried herself to sleep, wondering if this was what it felt like to give up, worrying that she would regret the choices of the past month.

Many times over the years, she had lain awake at night considering what her little girl was doing, what she looked like, if she liked her teachers, what she might be planning for her birthday, if her new parents loved her, or whether they had they taught her about Jesus.

On the worst nights, her fears took over and she worried that Emily might not be safe, that things might have taken a tragic turn for the worse, that she might not even be alive. Such thoughts only tempted her to despair, which was always just below the surface, nipping at her heels.

**Do not fear**, she'd whisper to herself. **Only believe.**

So she **was** eager for Ernie to return to work. She still had the weekends to check out leads, after all. **This is war**, she reminded herself. **And in war, you do what you have to.** Chet didn't need to know what Ernie did or how his tech friends found Kelly's prospects. After all, **she** didn't even know. What mattered was the final result.

**Finding Emily.**

## Chapter 17

Market day, held each Saturday morning, was one of Wooster's most beloved summer and autumn traditions. This year, it just happened to fall on Jack's birthday, the perfect forum for a celebration.

To Nattie, the weekly farmers' market was like a carnival overflowing with crafts and flowers, fruits and herbal tinctures, bee products and preserves. She loved whirling from booth to booth, sampling the handmade sweets and chatting with the vendors, who in turn fawned over Jack's bright-eyed, brown-haired girl. In fact, with birthdays and market day so high on Nattie's list of favorites, Jack was rather surprised she took Laura's refusal to join them in stride. Jack understood Laura's reasons. Laura had her own life and plenty of responsibilities at her cousin's home. Even without Laura, he was looking forward to spending the day with his number-one girl.

As Jack and Nattie wound their way hand in hand through the crowds, he noted that Nattie had remained remarkably mum about plans for his birthday. Since **mum** wasn't one of Nattie's stronger suits, something big had to be brewing. What his pint-sized daughter had in mind, though, was a complete mystery.

"Be still my heart!" Nattie exclaimed as they came upon a tempting display of chocolates. Truffles and toffee in creative pairings, topped with everything from sea salt to edible flowers, glowed like sculptures beneath glass domes. Nattie screwed up her face and put her hands together in a supplicating manner. "Please, please, please!"

Did she actually think he could refuse her? On his birthday, of all days? They bought a variety box from a cheerful college-aged entrepreneur who recognized a soul sister when she saw one. She permitted Nattie to sample more than any kid should be allowed to, bemused with the seriousness that Nattie brought to chocolate selection until she finally settled on her **ten** favorites.

"You need to stretch these out," Jack cautioned Nattie, handing a twenty dollar bill to the student, who made change from a wooden box.

"One a day!" Nattie promised.

**As if**, Jack thought, imagining all the potential hiding places in Nattie's room. He thanked the young woman and quickly ushered his daughter on to the next booth, featuring a colorful display of hand-crafted kaleidoscopes.

Around eleven-thirty, as they perused a table of organic peaches, apricots, and dragon fruit, they just happened to run into San, wearing a dress-length silk tunic, along with slim pants and strappy sandals.

"Imagine that," Jack said, hugging his sister, "bumping into you."

San's eyes twinkled. "What a coincidence."

Nattie tugged at Jack's arm. "Don't ruin

everything, Dad."

The three of them made their way toward San's favorite handmade soaps and bath items, where she chatted with the vendor and placed a special bulk order for the lavender-hibiscus bubble bath. "It's never too early to think about Christmas gifts, you know," she said, winking at her niece.

It was a few minutes before noon when Nattie handed Jack a vibrantly colored dunce cap, splashed with pink, purple, and yellow polka dots. "You have to wear this now!" she announced with obvious glee.

Jack stared at the offending cone. "In public?"

"**Especially** in public."

Jack put it on, threading the tight elastic band under his chin and modeling it for San and Nattie—not to mention the rest of the market crowd. "I look ridiculous."

"Yes, you do," Nattie said, grinning.

"No worse than any other day of the week," San added with a playful punch.

Nattie was absolutely exuberant. "You're a goof!"

Jack laughed as San took his right arm and Nattie took his left, the three of them marching jauntily up the street, Jack fighting to keep his cone upright.

Leaving the local vendors to box up their goods until next week, they trotted right into his favorite Mexican restaurant, where the friendly Hispanic host, with his jet-black hair and sleek mustache, greeted them as though expecting them. Sure enough, a back booth had been decked out in extravagant birthday decorations, complete with streamers and balloons, and confetti strewn across the table. Lurking beneath were gift boxes wrapped in festive colors and bows.

Removing her sunglasses, San whispered in Jack's ear, "You didn't suspect a thing, did you?"

Nattie seized upon a kazoo and blew it at what she must have thought were appropriate moments until San commandeered the offending noise machine.

"Aww," Nattie whined good-naturedly.

"Thank you," Jack said with a grin at Nattie, who gave him a playful pout.

The waitress, wearing a burgundy apron and floral print dress, came to take their order. Poised with pen and pad in hand, she asked for Jack's order first, which struck him as strange—ladies first, after all—but then again it **was** his birthday, so he read his choice from the menu: "Chicken Burritos. Extra hot," he added, and the waitress bit her lip but wrote his order on her pad. That's when he noticed Nattie staring at him like a volcano ready to blow, her eyes widening by the second, her nose flaring as if she'd taken a whiff of green bean perfume.

"What's so funny?" he asked.

San elbowed him. **"Really?"**

Nattie scrambled to her knees, placed both elbows on the table, her chin resting on her palms, and slid halfway across. **"Really, Dad?"**

"Nattie, honey, that's bad—" He looked up at the waitress to apologize for his family's lack of manners when it occurred to him that their waitress looked awfully familiar.

"Hi, Jack," she said softly. "Happy

birthday."

His mouth dropped open. **Laura?**

Nattie clapped her hands, now hopping up and down on the bench seat, chirping, "We gotcha good, Dad!"

Laura had gone fancy.

**No**, he thought. **It can't be her.**

But it was. Laura handed her apron to their real waitress and settled into the seat beside Nattie, her light brown hair still parted down the middle, but bouncy with soft curls—just seeing her hair was a shock—and her face, unrecognizable with darkened eyelashes, rosy cheeks, and pink glossy lips.

San poked him again. "She cleaned up good, don't you think?"

Laura gave her a grimace, and San continued quickly, meeting Laura's eyes with a sincere smile. "You look beautiful, Laura."

Jack cleared his throat but could only manage a nod. **She left beautiful in the dust.**

Laura blushed, clearly uncomfortable with the attention. "I think I went too far."

She proceeded to recount her steps—how, with San's help, she'd found the dress, spent two hours at the salon, and finished the outfit with a borrowed pair of San's shoes.

Surprised that San actually played a part in this transformation, Jack gave his sister's hand a quick squeeze but couldn't stop staring at Laura. This was the woman who'd spent the past four years in his employ. He wouldn't have recognized her on the street. Actually, he **hadn't** recognized her.

But the new Laura presented a strange contradiction, as well. Her clothing put the spotlight on her, when normally there wasn't a part of Laura's manner that drew attention to herself; she was a behind-the-scenes type, providing support, never asking for validation, quietly indispensable. Despite her plainness, for Laura to walk out of a room was to feel a loss.

"Take a picture, Dad," Nattie announced, slapping the table to get his attention. "It'll last longer."

Jack felt sheepish, but Laura just laughed.

"I think he's completely **ferhoodled**."

During the remainder of the meal, they talked and laughed, while he tried to pretend Laura's new appearance hadn't thoroughly "**ferhoodled**" him.

"So how does it feel to wear English clothes?" San asked Laura.

Laura smiled. "Like a fish out of water."

**Or a girl off the farm**, Jack thought, feeling suddenly guilty. Now that Laura was wearing modern clothes, he realized he'd always felt a little embarrassed of her Amish clothes, and his unconscious pride saddened him.

After their meal and the usual birthday pronouncements and gag cards, Jack opened San's gift, a designer tie, and Nattie's gift, a book of jokes. Laura handed him a humorous Peanuts card with Snoopy as the aviator, as was their custom on birthdays.

When they spilled out of the restaurant, San hugged him goodbye, leaving the three of them to walk down Liberty Street, looking for all the world like three Englishers wandering Wooster.

An hour later, it was time to drive Laura home so she could change back into her Amish garb before her cousins arrived, since Peter and Lomie might not be quite as supportive of her birthday surprise. Jack opened the passenger door and gestured regally. "You may be too fancy to sit in my old truck."

Laura gave him the sweetest smile in return, and Jack hovered near, bracing her arm as she placed her foot on his running board and slid into the cab. He could tell she wasn't used to heels, the way she stepped gingerly, her hands poised in case she tripped, his capable housekeeper rendered delicate and vulnerable.

On the way to the Troyer farm, Nattie remained suspiciously gleeful and secretive. "You didn't get very many gifts this year, Dad," she hinted.

Laura's amusement was evident, and when they turned into her long driveway, she said, "Do ya mind stopping here, Jack?"

Jack     caught     Nattie's     mirth-filled

expression. He pulled to a stop, and Laura seemed nervous as she reached down and pulled a small package out of her bag, then placed it on her lap with decorum, as if proud of what he was about to unwrap.

Beaming over at him, Nattie's hands were fidgeting. She could barely contain herself. "The best present for last!" she exclaimed. "It's mostly from Laura, but kinda from both of us."

Jack smiled back at the two of them, curious now about this first-time gift from Nattie's nanny. Finally, Laura handed it to him, her expression suddenly apologetic and shy. "I hope you like it," she said softly.

Jack took the package and removed the brown paper, revealing a framed document. Holding it up to the sunlight, Jack realized it was a letter, apparently written decades ago, wrinkled, faded, and yellowed but clear enough to catch the signature. **Wilbur Wright.**

He blew out a breath. "Where did you find this?"

"Laura found it!" Nattie exclaimed.

"I remembered you didn't have his

signature," Laura said.

"And...well...I couldn't afford the one you really wanted, but I called a number of reputable autograph stores, one in Aspen, Colorado—the one you told me about, where you took Natalie once."

He stared at the letter, transfixed. "Laura, this must have cost—"

"Less than you think," she answered, leaning over to point at the signature and the date, 1911. "The letter references some lawsuit they were dealing with."

**He died in '12**, Jack thought, nodding. "Yeah, the patent wars."

He read one phrase from the letter, **"At Kitty Hawk, we never would have believed that perfecting controlled flight would only be the beginning of our troubles...."**

Jack set it on his lap, nodding wistfully. "Some people think Wilbur died young because of the stress from defending their patent."

He turned to her, and Laura met his eyes, emotion hovering there, but what, Jack wasn't sure. Nattie's gaze moved back and forth between them, like watching a Ping-Pong game.

Jack sighed. "You shouldn't have done this."

"This'll fill the spot until you get what you really want," Laura replied.

"I like this better," he said, staring at the century-old letter. "The unexpected tragedy of their success." He cleared his throat again, overwhelmed.

"You like it?"

Nattie squealed. "Hel-lo, I think so!"

"I love it," he said.

Laura nodded, seemingly satisfied but self-conscious, too. She rustled through her packages, consolidating them, putting her purse on her lap. It was time to drive the remaining hundred yards or so.

Laura had never given him a birthday gift before—cards, yes, but never a gift. It had been a kind of unspoken rule between them.

**Things are changing**, he thought.

The following Monday, Laura was sched-uled to arrive after lunch, due to a number of appointments in town, including a dental cleaning. Jack was already at his desk, plowing through some accounting tasks—things he could do at home—and anxious to see Laura again.

Jack recalled their conversation in June about Laura's plan to give Nattie a momentary thrill, but after the last few weeks and how far they'd come, he actually thought Laura might be transitioning into a modern woman. Last night he'd even given himself to much puzzled brooding, wondering if it wasn't time to engage Laura in a conversation about a future together. It didn't seem so preposterous anymore, not after his birthday party. The Amish nanny had dressed like an **Englisher**...just for him. What was a red-blooded male to think?

Besides, Natalie wasn't kidding. Laura was beautiful.

How had he missed that?

So when he heard Laura come in and Nattie's happy announcement, "Laura's here!" he headed for the kitchen to greet her, expecting a new outfit, maybe even jeans and a blouse. Jack noticed Nattie settled at the dining room table and turned to see Laura closing the refrigerator. She caught his expression at the same moment he took in her **Amish** attire.

His look of disappointment must have lasted only a moment, a split second at most, but it might as well have lasted an hour considering the effect it seemed to have on Laura. She regarded him with an almost dazed expression.

As a pathetic attempt to save himself, Jack forced a smile, greeting her, "Laura, you're here!"

Even Nattie noticed the exchange, her eyes fixed on him as if observing a train wreck.

"Zero cavities," Laura said, giving him a toothy smile before opening the upper cabinet to check the contents.

Jack slinked back to his office, aware of Nattie's gaze. Ten minutes later, Laura knocked on his office door, asking for a moment. She closed the door and sat in his chair with a list of errands in hand. She noted the placement of her gift on his wall, and he thanked her again.

"Were you surprised to see me today?"

"Not at all," he replied, which wasn't true.

Uncomfortably, Laura looked down at her hands. Somewhere between Saturday and this moment, it seemed as if all the gains they'd made were lost: the feeling of trust between them, the connection, the romance that seemed to dangle in the air about them.

He swallowed the silly speech he'd planned, the one about a possible future between them, not because he'd changed his mind, but because the shy Laura was back, her Amish culture like a wall, as stark and forbidding as before.

**Later**, he told himself.

"Well...I'll be back in a bit," Laura said abruptly, getting up, smoothing her apron.

"Thank you, Laura," he replied, kicking himself for not recalling that she'd only promised to dress fancy once.

She closed the door behind her, leaving him to his thoughts.

A few minutes later, Nattie knocked.

Was he about to receive another grueling interrogation? **Why'd you act so weird?**

Instead, Nattie wanted to know if, since Laura had dressed fancy, she might return the favor and dress Plain.

Jack shuddered at this notion but kept his expression relaxed. "You better talk with Laura about that, make sure it wouldn't seem disrespectful. And you might want to run it by your auntie San, too, just in case."

Nattie's eyebrows shot up at the mention of her aunt. "Oh yeah. Good idea."

# Chapter 18

That Wednesday, late in the morning, Jack's phone beeped and a strange text appeared. He read it, confused by the number at first.

**Just touching base. It's been a while. How are you doing? I've been busy, but that's good, right?**

**Angela.** Long-lost Angela Walberg. Why was she texting him after a month of silence? After ignoring his every attempt to communicate with **her**?

He considered asking San. He also considered texting back with something like, **Glad to hear things are going well**, but decided to delay his reply until the end of the day.

After work, Jack found Nattie at the table writing another list. She looked up at him mournfully, pushing her bangs away from her forehead, meeting his eyes. "Something's wrong with Laura."

Jack frowned. "How do you know?"

Nattie shrugged. "I just do." She returned to her list. "By the way, I changed the feeder."

"Hmm, thanks," Jack said, knowing Nattie was trying to communicate her responsibility in the small things, hoping to parlay this into even greater responsibility, like a black Labrador, which had recently worked its way to the second spot on her retooled want list.

Before she could launch into a new plea, Jack headed out the back door.

Laura was sitting in the swing, rocking gently, staring wistfully toward the trees. Gingerly, Jack let the screen door close without slamming, and she turned to smile at him. "Hi, Jack."

The wind chime echoed her greeting, and the swing's chains squealed slightly with her movements. "The hummers are out today in full force, fighting over Nattie's nectar."

**Laura's fine**, he thought, until he saw the letter in her hand. She observed the focus of his attention and brought the letter to her lap. "My cousin wrote."

Jack reached in and quietly closed the inner door. He joined her at the swing and gestured to the letter, a question in his eyes.

She extended it to him. "It's okay," she said, assuring him.

"Chatty stuff, ya know, nothing personal."

Jack read the return address: Rachel Mast, Lancaster, PA.

"My cousin," she said softly. "At one time my favorite cousin. Would ya like to read it?"

Jack shook his head. "Laura, I don't need—"

"But I want you to."

Still not sure what to make of it, he removed the letter and began to read. **Dearest Laura...**

Some of it was written in **Deitsch**, but it was mostly in English. It was full of family news, various activities, and names he didn't know.

Rachel's letter had ended with a plea.

**I've missed you terribly, Laura. I'm sorry we fell out of touch. We know why you had to leave, but that's water under the bridge, ain't? Please write me. I have so much to tell you, things you can only guess at, if you know what I mean!**

Jack closed the letter and felt his heart constrict.

**We know why you had to leave.**

They were back to this again, his renewed dread that Laura's departure was imminent, something he'd hoped had died a natural death. In light of his newfound worry and her recent gift, the one now hanging on his wall, probably the best gift he'd ever received, he did something he also wouldn't have considered weeks ago. Reaching gingerly, heart thudding in his chest, he covered her right hand with his own and gently squeezed it.

Laura turned to him, her face going pale, confirming again that she was like a skittish butterfly, always on the verge of fluttering away.

"Don't go," he said. It was remarkably selfish, but he was feeling selfish. Nattie couldn't bear to lose her and neither could he. If she returned, even for a visit, she might take the kneeling confession, and they'd lose her forever.

Laura closed her eyes and leaned her head back against the padding. "I'm not going anywhere, Jack."

The growing awkwardness caused him to remove his hand, and she seemed to breathe more freely.

Laura cleared her throat, then frowned. "**Ach**, and I'm certainly not going to write her back."

Jack was surprised by her strong reaction to a seemingly friendly letter. "Aren't you curious, after all these years?"

She shook her head. "Less now than ever before." She turned to him, fresh tears in her eyes and yet smiling. Smiling through the pain of whatever was haunting her. He was sorely tempted to enfold her in his arms but resisted.

Laura took a deep breath. "The letter isn't what it sounds like."

Softly, but with determination in her voice, she told him more about her childhood, the tobacco farm, her brothers and sisters, her parents and her grandparents, her cousins, and especially... Rachel. And not once during the tale did the sad smile leave her face.

"Cousin Rachel and I used to spend hours in the hayloft, talking 'bout our dreams, but eventually we fell out of touch when she acquired a mean streak. She wasn't always like that, not when we were kids. She's two years older than me, and I always looked up to her."

"Maybe this letter is her way of making up," he said.

Laura shook her head. "It's her way of rubbing my nose in everything I've missed." Laura took a breath and dabbed at her eyes with her sleeve. "I was shunned because of Rachel," she said softly. "You see...I was engaged to be married to Jonathan. We'd been sweethearts since our teens. I was good friends with his sister, Rebecca Lynn, who everyone knew would never marry. She was **slow**—a special child—she had a dear place in Jonathan's heart. He looked out for her. We'd all practically grown up at the Lancaster County Market, and Jonathan and I couldn't wait to begin our new lives together." She swallowed. "But we made a terrible mistake...we got the cart before the horse, if you know what I mean."

Jack felt his face flush. It was hard to imagine Laura getting anything before the horse.

"We aren't perfect, Jack." She tucked a few strands back beneath her **Kapp**, then continued on. "Anyway, Cousin Rachel found out—I don't know how—and decided it was her duty to tell my father. Then she proceeded to share it with the entire community."

Jack shuddered.

"I was devastated."

"It's not the first time that kind of thing has happened," Jack said. "You made a mistake. That's all."

"Yes, but...my father is the bishop,

Jack."

**Oh boy**, he thought.

"And he decided to make an example of me to the rest of the community. Couldn't have Bishop Ephraim's daughter sinning so blatantly, under his nose, of all things! He was embarrassed. I had undermined his authority. He was furious with me. His own daughter had tarnished his reputation!"

"Couldn't you two have just married?"

Laura scoffed. "He forbade me to see Jonathan and threatened to shun me if I did. The marriage was off.

"So **I** refused to obey. And I told my father so. Furious with me, he promptly placed me under the **Bann** and announced he would never speak to me again if I defied him." She paused, her eyes bright with emotion. "As an Amishperson, you grow up fearing the shunning, but when it happens to you, it's horrifying."

Jack nodded, wishing now he still held her hand, if only for support.

"I still wanted to marry Jonathan, but he said he couldn't, because it would have meant being put under the **Bann** forever. 'What kind of life would I be offering you?' he asked, but I didn't care. I begged him to take me away, but he wouldn't."

Her face turned stoic. "He finally left, Jack. He broke things off, for my sake, he said. Couldn't bear to come between me and my family, though by then I was totally on the outs with **Dat** and **Mamma**, and my younger siblings. So…after **he** left, I left, too. I went to visit some family near Chambersburg, but they were displeased with my presence, worried I'd be a **Schnickelfritz**—a troublemaker—so after less than a year, I moved out here."

Laura went silent, lost in the past. Then she spoke again, her voice husky with sadness. "My father wrote me later, telling me that Jonathan was lost to me forever, that my fiancé had his own family now, and God's judgment had been delivered."

Jack sighed. "I can't imagine…"

"Neither could I. If my Jonathan was now married, I didn't want to return. I **couldn't**. To this day, I hold **Dat** responsible for denying me the only happiness I ever wanted on this earth, the dearest boy I've ever known." Her voice broke suddenly, and she bit her lip.

Laura shook her head. "That's not very Amish of me, Jack. I **have** forgiven my father. But I can't bring myself to go home. By now, Jonathan is married with a houseful of kids. This letter only reminds me of what I'd be facing." She turned now and met his gaze. "Nattie has been my life, you know. And you've been so good to me, Jack."

"We've tried."

Laura smiled. "You haven't just tried, Jack. You've been like a second family to me, the only family to stick up for me." Her eyes glistened, and his heart twisted in his chest when she slid her hand into his. "Sometimes, I'm just a confused Amishwoman, Jack, but I felt you should finally know."

**Why now?** He opened his mouth to ask but decided against it. Enough had been said already. They sat there for a moment longer, listening to the chime and the buzz of an occasional hummingbird. Finally

Laura removed her hand and simply got up, lingering for a moment with a hand on his shoulder, something she'd never done before.

She paused at the door, her smile cheerful. "Nattie doesn't need to know about my mistakes, **jah**?"

"I won't tell her."

Jack sat in the swing for another few minutes, staring at the trees while Nattie remained occupied inside. He could hear the beeping sound effects and the musical soundtrack to her computer game, repeating over and over again.

**Mournful Laura**, he thought. Not only because of a shunning but from a broken heart. Eventually the noise stopped, and Nattie emerged, popping her head out the door. "What's up, doc?"

"Just thinking."

Nattie hopped on the swing, but she said nothing, sensing Jack's need for quiet. Eventually she squeezed in next to him, leaning her head against his shoulder. Together they watched the humming-birds alighting on the feeder, chasing each other away, beautiful tiny warriors intent on syrupy nectar. The swing continued its gentle, rhythmic squeak as he thought about Rachel's letter. And Laura's story. Why had she told him? And why **now**, when anything romantic between the two of them seemed to be falling apart?

He couldn't imagine her feeling of rejection. Shunned from her family, losing all touch, banned to a shirttail relative in Chambersburg until even they had asked her to leave. She'd spent less than a year there, she'd told him, before traveling west to Ohio.

Yet Laura was still Amish, he mused, after all that. Most folks would have kicked the dust from their feet and gone on with their lives. But not Laura. Not cheerfully sad Laura, observing the customs of the Beachy Amish but Old Order in her heart, and still missing her one true love. **"My Jonathan,"** she'd called him.

Nattie snaked her arm through Jack's. The birds chirped a fitting accompaniment to his tangled melancholy thoughts. He could feel the expansion and contraction of Nattie's breathing, smell the sweet coconut scent of her shampoo.

"I finished my list," she murmured, reaching into her pocket. "Wanna see it?" She unfolded the spiral-torn paper and handed it to him.

**MY WANT LIST** was the title and it comprised the usual suspects: **Cell phone. Dog. Earrings. Clothes.** The last line read, **But if I get a mom, you can forget the rest.**

Jack sighed, and Nattie squirmed in closer. **I'm working on it**, he thought.

After waiting a record amount of time, Nattie finally spoke. "I'm hungry."

**Life goes on.**

San called him the next day with the inevitable admonishment, "Aren't you answering your texts?"

He groaned inwardly, having forgotten to text Angela back. He should have known San was a third party to Angela's latest outreach.

"I've been busy," he replied. "Too busy to text back?"

Jack murmured something unsatisfactory.

San snorted. "I'm coming by tonight," she announced. "I need to talk to you."

That afternoon when he came home, San was already there, playing a computer game with Nattie, who was yelping because San was winning, which in Nattie's world meant cheating.

It gave him pause. How long had she been here? He headed for the backyard, looking for Laura.

"Jack?" San called, but he was already stepping outside. He found Laura tending the garden on the side of the house, kneeling in the dirt, weeding and feeding. She turned away for a moment, reaching to her face with her hand, then turned back and smiled toward him. She was crying.

"Are you okay?"

Her smile widened, betrayed by her glistening eyes. "Of course. Why do you ask?"

He felt his blood boil. He asked Laura about the day's gardening, and she told him, wiping her soiled hands on her apron and leading him around, pointing out her handiwork.

"Has San talked to you?"

She forced another smile. "Sure, but no worries."

When Jack could hold it in no longer, he excused himself and walked back in. San saw him and dropped the controls. "I'm quitting while I'm ahead."

"Auntie San!" Nattie protested, dropping her own controller. "I want a rematch!"

San leaned over and whispered in Nattie's ear, and Nattie nodded obediently, heading upstairs immediately. Noting Nattie's instant compliance, San smiled proudly. "I could teach you the secret to that."

"What did you tell Laura, San?"

She looked surprised. He rarely spoke to her that directly. Without answering, she crooked her pointer finger and led him to the dining room. She sat down as if preparing to give a momentous speech.

He joined her at the table, and San wasted little time. "Angela regrets what happened."

"We had three dates," Jack said. "We barely knew each other. And I've moved on."

Considering this, San took a deep breath. Jack waited for the big announcement and she didn't disappoint. "I told Angela that you and Laura were **not** together, and that there was no **chance** of your being together."

Jack felt his blood pressure rise. "So what did you say to Laura?"

San nodded. "Someone needed to put the cards on the table, and since you weren't going to, I did."

Jack clasped his hands together. "San—"

"She assured me that she won't stand in your way. She even promised to do whatever she can to encourage Angela."

"You have no right," he said.

"But, Jack—"

"You've crossed the line, San."

"I was **trying** to help."

Jack leaned back in his chair, crossing his arms. San leaned over, tapping the table to emphasize her point. "You will never find Nattie a mother as long as Laura is here."

He shook his head, now standing up.

"Where are you going?" she asked.

Jack gestured to the front door. "We're taking this where Nattie and Laura can't possibly hear."

"Maybe they **should** hear," San said, grabbing her purse.

Once Jack closed the door behind him, he continued, both of them standing on the front stoop. San took in the neighborhood, the possible eyes and ears, then muttered, "Yeah, Jack, this is much better."

Jack turned to San, his stomach in knots. "You hurt Laura's feelings. She's out back, crying."

San frowned. "Why would she be crying?"

**Unbelievable**, Jack thought. He leaned against the front railing, preparing to say what he would surely regret later. "Listen to me, San, I don't want Nattie growing up thinking it's okay to say whatever she wants, regardless of how people might feel."

San winced, but her jaw hardened. "I can't help who I am."

"Try."

San's eyes flashed in anger, and then a sudden **aha** crossed her features. "Wait a minute, are you actually in **love** with your Amish nanny?" As if that would have been a blight on his soul.

Jack sighed. "You've been jealous of Laura for years, San, for the place she holds in Nattie's heart."

San shook her head as if she couldn't accept such a preposterous notion and headed toward her car. She turned angrily. "Call me when you come to your senses."

Jack sighed again and hurried inside, only to find Laura standing at the kitchen sink, rinsing her hands, her face pale, eyes red. She looked at him and forced another smile.

"I'm sorry about that," Jack said, trying to console her. "Don't listen to her."

They stood there for a moment longer as the awkward silence spooled out.

Nattie's bedroom door was still closed. She must have gotten engrossed in something. Finally Laura found her voice and softly murmured, "I didn't realize you quit dating Angela because of me. This is my fault, Jack."

"No, it isn't."

She stared at him, meeting his gaze like a lost child. "I need to get home." She slipped past him, and he reached for her, grasping her arm. She stopped for a moment, meeting his eyes. "Let me go, Jack."

"Can we talk about this?" he asked, releasing her.

She shook her head. "Talking won't change anything."

"It might," Jack insisted.

"It mustn't," she said before leaving him alone.

With Ernie now back at work, Kelly dropped by with a welcome-back card and a gluten-free, sugar-free, fat-free cupcake.

Sitting at his desk, Ernie peered

skeptically at her gift.

"It's on your approved dietary list."

"Wonderful," he muttered, opening Kelly's card, reading it.

Kelly sat across from him, noting how fatigued he seemed. At least his spirits seemed bright.

Ernie finished reading and swallowed a grimace. "It's good to still be here." He cleared his throat. "I guess."

"I can second that," Kelly said. "Your work is not finished."

They made small talk for a few minutes before Ernie frowned. "By the way, whatever happened to that kid?"

"We've filed it," Cindy piped up, standing in the doorway.

Ernie turned back to Kelly. "She was the spitting image of you, kiddo."

"Sure, on a very dark day in the middle of a November night."

Ernie frowned. "Let me see that file."

Kelly winced, not eager to prove to Ernie that he'd lost his touch even before he was taken to the hospital. Cindy retrieved the file and placed it on his desk. Ernie picked it up. "Yeah, that Nattie kid in Wooster."

Kelly just sat there, waiting for Ernie to realize his error: Nattie couldn't possibly be her Emily.

"Did you test her?" Ernie growled.

"We're not doing that anymore."

Ernie grunted his disdain. Flipping through the pages, he took a long look at something, shook his head, and handed the file to Kelly. "What am I missing?"

**A lot**, Kelly thought as she took it but nearly gasped when she saw the picture of Natalie Livingston, a young girl with **brunette** hair and **brown** eyes. This was not the girl she'd seen that day.

"I guess I blew it," Kelly muttered. She groaned at her rookie mistake.

"We're still in business," Ernie said, sounding satisfied.

Kelly exchanged chagrined glances with Cindy, feeling a little silly but suddenly invigorated, the old surge of hope coursing through her veins.

Leaving Ernie to his slow reintroduction to the work world and having obtained the number for Jack Livingston's aviation business, Kelly left Ernie's office. She called her boss, Melody's dad, and made the necessary arrangements. Since she was working Saturdays during her training period, she hoped he wouldn't object to a minor schedule modification, especially since she was often at her desk by six-thirty.

According to Cindy's surreptitious phone call to Higher Ground, Jack Livingston would be in the office all day tomorrow, Friday.

"He's a church-going man," Ernie had emphasized before Kelly had left. "With a reputation for honesty. We'll have a better chance with him."

Kelly certainly hoped so.

# Chapter 19

The next afternoon Kelly drove past one farm after another. She arrived forty minutes after she'd left, pulling into the Wayne County Airport at about three-thirty.

Driving along an access road, past a row of airplane hangars and an assortment of aviation businesses, she found Higher Ground, boasting the eager billboard proclaiming **Learn to Fly!** She parked in front and paused for a moment, praying silently, feeling adrift, hoping she wouldn't fall to her old tricks.

**Is it too bold to pray that this smart man would become momentarily stupid?** she thought, smiling to herself and shaking her head, because if Jack Livingston gave any thought to her request, he'd realize they'd radically invaded his privacy just to get this far.

She sighed. **Help me know what to say.**

A single **ding!** announced her entrance, and she was greeted by a younger man standing behind the long counter. Mick Roberts, according to his name tag, was perhaps five-eight, of stocky build and with a shaved head, his right arm tattooed with the trademark eagle, globe, and anchor of the U.S. Marines.

There was another man seated in a small corner office, punching away on a computer. He glanced at her briefly, then refocused his attention.

When she asked to speak with Jack Livingston, Mick smiled pleasantly. "Jack's out with a student," he said and asked if he might help.

Glancing toward a row of chairs, Kelly shrugged. "I can wait."

"Might be a while," Mick said, probably figuring her for a saleswoman. Mick settled into some task at the counter, fiddling with a flat plastic device, something aeronautical, Kelly figured. She sat and mentally reviewed her little speech, culled from bits and pieces of speeches she'd created years before. She had a best-case scenario speech and a worst-case scenario speech. In her purse, she also had a picture of her daughter at age four months and an age-progressed picture of what Emily might look like this year.

The usual response after her spiel had been, **"I'll have to talk to my lawyer and get back with you."** Which was why she'd long ago settled on "stealing" the child's DNA, something rather easy to do if the child wasn't being protected by overzealous parents.

**This time, I'm keeping my promise to Chet**, she reminded herself, whispering yet another prayer for wisdom, for guidance, and frankly...for a miracle.

She heard a loud shout behind her, then the sudden eruption of an airplane engine fluttering into life. It startled her.

Mick offered her coffee, which she declined. "Too much already," she said, thanking him.

Another thirty minutes passed. "They're

late," Mick confirmed.

The older man in the office peeked around the doorframe, raising his eyebrows, and Mick made an apologetic expression. "Should be any moment."

The man nodded and went back to his tiny office. Apparently he was next in line—for Jack, or for the plane? Perhaps both.

Feeling antsy, Kelly stood and surveyed a wall of photos, pictures of students with their instructors, posed in front of various single propeller planes. Noticing her attention, Mick came out from behind the counter and proudly began reciting their pilot success rate.

**Now I'm a prospective student**, she realized, just then spotting a photo of Jack with Natalie in front of another single-engine plane, mugging for the camera. Below the photo, the caption read: **Jack and Natalie after a looooong flight.**

Kelly pointed to Nattie's **Higher Ground** T-shirt. "That's cute."

"Jack's sister designed them."

"How old is Nattie?"

Mick looked at her curiously. "How old do you think?"

"Around nine, maybe?"

"Bingo," Mick said.

**What did I just say?** Kelly cleared her throat, hoping her sudden screaming nerves weren't giving her away, because the entire world must have noticed she'd just identified Natalie by her nickname.

She had moments to cover her tracks, and although she couldn't be sure Mick had noticed her misstep, she threw it out there just in case. "I actually met Jack at church once. But I doubt he'd remember me."

"Ah," Mick said. "Of course."

**So he** had **noticed**, Kelly thought, trying to silence her blaring conscience at the outright lie. She forced herself to breathe easier, although she wondered if her attempted cover-up seemed a little too desperate.

**Game on**, she told herself, just as Jack walked in the door, followed by a young teenager in saggy jeans and a T-shirt, sporting an eager grin.

Jack called to the man in the office. "Sorry, Monty. It's all yours. Don's filling it up."

Monty grinned, grabbed something from the chair beside him, and headed out the door.

Jack glanced at Kelly, smiled warmly, and then shifted his attention to Mick. "Sign him up," Jack said, grinning at the teen. "Sean wants to start immediately."

"Excellent," Mick said.

Jack nodded to Sean. "This will be your instructor. Mick's the best in the business."

Mick beamed at Jack's compliment, and the two men shook hands, Mick's burly hand swallowing Sean's. Jack smiled over at Kelly again, as if to make her feel included.

Mick spoke once more, "Jack, this young lady would like a minute of your time."

Kelly registered Jack's height—about six-one—and his wavy blond hair, clean-shaven face, sturdy chin. Wearing jeans, boots, and a short-sleeved shirt, Jack extended his hand, and she shook it, introducing herself. A flutter of nerves coursed through her as she volunteered her real name, and she wished she'd gone more casual, instead of designer slacks, blouse, and blazer.

"You're selling something, aren't you?" Jack asked, but he said it with a twinkle, indicating that he probably wouldn't toss her out if she was.

"I am," she replied, aiming for a light touch. "But it won't cost you a cent."

Jack gave her a welcoming smile. "Mysterious. I like that." Jack gestured to his office beyond the counter. "It's rather messy."

"I don't mind," she said. She walked in after he did, pausing by the open door. Once Jack was seated behind a desk piled high with papers, books, and instruction materials, Kelly gently closed it. "If you don't mind, this is private."

He didn't object, but the curious expression in his eyes ratcheted up a notch. Now seated, Kelly noticed the entire wall behind Jack was filled with framed certificates and more photos of Natalie and Jack, and a young woman in

Amish clothing. **Laura**, she reminded herself, **Natalie's nanny**. There was another woman—**Sandra**, Jack's sister, Kelly recalled from Ernie's briefing. Mick had also referenced the rather tall woman, who was midtwenties, attractive, and scrupulously dressed in something straight out of **Vogue**.

"Beautiful child," she said.

Jack replied politely, "Do you have children, Kelly?"

"I'm not married," she replied, skirting the issue. Kelly noticed another photo of Natalie on the desk, and Jack picked it up, staring at it appreciatively. "I took this myself."

"May I see it?" Kelly asked, hoping her tone conveyed polite interest and nothing more. Jack extended it to her. As she gazed at it appreciatively, Jack got down to business. "How can I help you, Kelly?"

Kelly swallowed, poised to utter the first words of her elaborate speech, when she noticed a long scratch on Natalie's forehead.

She traced it with her fingers, and Jack

smiled knowingly. "Funny story behind that."

She was about to replace the photo without comment, but curiosity got the best of her. "Behind her injury?"

Jack cleared his throat and seemed to appraise her. She could imagine him debating, **"Why would I tell this to a perfect stranger?"**

But he did. "Nattie's quite confident, and her confidence sometimes attracts bullies who want to tear her down a notch."

She felt a catch in her throat. "Your daughter was bullied?"

"Yes, but…" Jack seemed to reconsider.

"I was bullied in school," Kelly said suddenly, searching for common ground. "I remember my mother basically telling me to chill out and toughen up."

Jack's eyes dimmed. "How did that work for you?"

"I walked to school in terror," she admitted.

Jack began adamantly shaking his head. "No offense to your mother, but I refused to let the same thing happen to Natalie."

Once again, he waved the story off, but she pressed, pushing the line of credulity. As far as Jack was concerned, she was there to sell him something, and therefore her questions about Nattie were transparent at best, manipulative at worst.

Despite this, he leaned forward somewhat reluctantly and began to tell her how, unbeknownst to Natalie, he'd gone to the little boy's house to talk to the parents and explain how Joey had pushed seven-year-old Nattie on the playground, and how the kid had apparently been following her around for weeks, taunting her.

Joey's father only laughed and said, "Kids will be kids…"

So Jack went to the school to file a formal complaint. Thinking it was merely Joey's word against Natalie's, they promised to monitor the situation. In the meantime, Joey continued to torment Nattie.

Jack now leaned forward in his seat, his eyes focused. "But here's where it gets interesting."

Kelly nodded, intrigued.

"I was about to contact my lawyer when Nattie figured out what I was doing and hit the ceiling."

Kelly frowned. "She was mad at **you**?"

Jack smiled. "Very. She said, 'I got this.'"

**I got this.** "What happened?"

Jack leaned back. "Well, apparently Nattie finally let him have it. She…uh… walked up to him, was going to kick him in the leg, I guess, but missed…."

Kelly cringed, and a small smile escaped her lips.

Jack shook his head. "Laura, our nanny, told me what Nattie told her, that she sat on Joey while he was writhing in pain and screamed, 'You could have had a friend like me!'"

Kelly laughed. "She **said** that?"

"Something out of one of her favorite movies, I think." Jack chuckled and reached behind him to grab another photo, extending it to her.

"A group of her closest friends," Jack said. "See the tall kid with the bangs to his nose standing next to her, his arm around her shoulders?"

Grinning, Kelly nodded.

"That's Joey," Jack said. "One-time tormenter, now all-purpose bodyguard, and one of her best friends...for a boy, that is. I guess he really did want to have a friend like her. Funny way to show it, eh?"

Kelly handed the photo back. "She's quite the girl."

Jack's story took less than two minutes to tell, but it told her everything she needed to know about him.

Suddenly, she now felt like a predator herself, having violated their privacy. **I'm the bully**, she thought. It was silly, sure, but for the moment, she was at a rare loss for words.

Jack cleared his throat. "Listen, I've taken too much of your time. How can we do business, Kelly?"

"Well..." she began, biting her lip. She took in Jack's innocent blue eyes, gazing at her attentively.

**A decent guy.**

This was the moment of truth. This is what she'd been preparing for, and she was this close to saying, **"I enjoyed your story, and boy do I have one for you! You see, I have reason to believe I'm your daughter's birth mother."** And then when Jack finally found his voice, she had planned to add, **"She was kidnapped from me nearly nine years ago."**

It could have been so easy. But instead of proceeding the way she'd planned, she said, "I've been told you're the best in the business." She felt her face growing hot with embarrassment. "I'm interested in an introductory ride in one of your flying tin cans."

Jack chuckled at her characterization but regarded her curiously again, obviously wondering why she hadn't mentioned this to Mick. She didn't need a private meeting in the owner's office to nab an introductory flight.

He nodded. "I can do that, but there's a slight problem...."

Kelly held her breath.

"All the planes are rented. We'd have to do it another day."

She signed inwardly, somewhat relieved.

"I'll be back, then."

Another moment passed as Jack continued to regard her with a puzzled expression. Finally she smiled and got up, and Jack walked her to the front door. "I'll look forward to seeing you again, Kelly."

"Me too," she said, still reeling from the way things had played out. **Why has telling the truth become so hard?**

Kelly had long since left, but Jack was still thinking about the strange woman who'd represented herself as a saleswoman and then switched gears, inquiring about flight instruction.

Mick came in a few minutes later. "What was that all about?"

Jack shrugged. "Apparently she wants flight lessons."

Mick seemed taken aback. "She didn't seem remotely interested in flying."

Jack grabbed a pen, testing it for ink. "No matter. I doubt we'll ever see her again." Jack wrote a quick note and began sorting the piles on top of his desk.

Mick hadn't budged. "Say, boss man?"

Jack lifted his eyes, noting the serious expression on his chief flying instructor's face.

"Just in case she comes back…"

"Yes?"

"She said she met you at her church."

Jack tossed his papers together. That **was** strange. She hadn't mentioned a previous meeting.

"And," Mick continued, obviously noting Jack's baffled reaction, "she already knew Nattie's name before she got here."

"Her name?"

"Looking at that picture out there." The CFI thumbed behind him. "I referred to your daughter as Natalie, but **she** referred to her as Nattie."

Jack considered this, questioning whether Mick was simply mistaken, but Mick nodded again. "Seriously, I know what I said. And I know what **she** said."

Jack shrugged, and then it came to him. **Of course.** "Now that you mention it, I think I know who she must be."

"Care to enlighten me?" Mick asked, and Jack did so, after which Mick breathed a sigh of relief. "Whew. I worried for nothing."

**Never a dull moment**, Jack thought, smiling.

The front door chimed again, and Mick went out to deal with another customer while Jack removed his notebook from the drawer, the one he'd been doodling in ever since Laura's revelation and his unwelcome confrontation with San.

He'd begun by jotting notes, ripping them up sometimes, and starting over. Eventually, it became a short little speech, and only recently had it transformed into a kind of rambling love letter. Well, not really a love letter. More like a proposal of sorts. He still wasn't sure whether he would say it or let her read it.

**We were growing closer, but something happened to us. I wish we could return to that. You belong with us, Laura. I'd like us to consider a more permanent future.**

Jack sighed, raking his fingers through his hair, and pondered tearing up the note and starting over again. Either way, it was time to fish or cut bait. He leaned back, taking a breather, and thought again of the woman who'd just left. **Kelly Maines.**

**Odd**, he thought, tossing his mechanical pencil on the desk. It was quitting time. He crammed a few papers into his top drawer and headed out of the office, eager to see his little girl and put Ms. Maines behind him.

Twenty minutes later, Kelly was driving home, baffled and chagrined with her own behavior. Jack's story had been the perfect opening. Nattie was the topic.

It was probably the most receptive she could have found him. He seemed like a reasonable man. But for some reason, she'd become tongue-tied.

And then there was that ridiculous faux pas in the waiting area.

**"Nattie,"** she'd said to Mick. **As in out loud.**

What had possessed her to say the girl's nickname? Mick was a smart man—a marine, after all—and surely he'd told super-parent Jack all about it.

**Of course he would**, she thought. **It's a dangerous world we live in, and bad people steal other people's kids.**

She'd half expected the cops to come squealing down the road, sirens blazing, at any minute. **"There she is, officer. That's the woman who knew my daughter's name."**

She smiled at her overwrought imagination, but she had no choice. If she wanted to check Nattie off her list, she had to go back, one way or another, either to extract Nattie's DNA on the sly, breaking her word to Chet, or by telling Jack the truth. Regardless, she had her work cut out for her.

Thirty minutes later, she got a call from Melody. "We still on for tonight?"

"And I'm bringing my appetite."

Melody cheered. "So you'll meet us there?"

Kelly confirmed this and hung up, sighing with relief. For the first time, she'd be included in Melody's group for a rare Friday night occurrence of girls' night out, and she couldn't wait. Sure, she'd be the only single girl in the bunch, but who cared? She needed this.

Fun, healthy diversions were on her "get a life" to-do list, and a solid group of Christian women seemed the perfect way to start.

Smiling, she tried to focus on her anticipation for tonight, but her mind wandered back to Jack. They'd shared a rather interesting private moment in his office.

**A nice guy**, she thought.

But she'd seen nice guys turn nasty in a hurry. She'd married one. Besides, nice guy or not, she had a more important task than to worry about Jack's feelings.

**I've got to fix this**, she thought. Before she could move on to another prospect, she needed to first discover the truth about Natalie Livingston. **Bully-thwarter extraordinaire.**

# Chapter 20

Jack left his car at home, then walked to the park, hoping to meet up with Laura and Nattie. He found them sitting on the bench, watching the action, a small group of kids unafraid of wet surfaces. It had rained last night, and the park was still damp. Nattie was refining her yo-yo skills, holding her mouth just right, and Laura was back to crocheting.

Laura spotted him first, shielding the sun with her hand, then waving. "We're taking a breather," she told him when he sat down. She pointed to the umbrella beside her. "Nattie wanted me to bring it so it wouldn't rain again."

**Good plan.** Jack smiled.

Nattie smirked and popped up, tossing her yo-yo into Laura's bag. "That's enough sittin' still for me."

Jack laughed, watching Nattie launch herself into the fray again, trying to remember if he'd ever had that much energy. Nattie's playground routine was reminiscent of how a bee flits from flower to flower. She'd practically sprint to the swings, and once she was high enough, she'd jump at exactly the correct moment, only to sprint back to the slide and begin again.

Moments later, she came prancing over, planting her hands on his knees. "Did you buy any pixie dust?"

It was a running joke between them—Nattie's desire to fly without wings. He grimaced as if he'd forgotten.

"Wanna teeter-totter with me instead?" Nattie asked. He readily agreed. It took them a moment to find the right leverage for a hundred-and-eighty-pound man to teeter with a sixty-pound nine-year-old, but they experimented until Jack was sitting halfway up on his side.

**A few years and she won't want to hang out with dear ol' Dad**, he thought.

**Strike while the iron is hot.**

Afterward, the three of them walked home together, and Nattie came upon a perfectly innocent puddle, a remnant from yesterday's downpour. Before Jack could protest, she beat it into submission, sending spikes of muddy water into the air, splattering her legs and arms and spotting her face. She stood there, paralyzed, shocked by the results, her face frozen with an oops expression. "I imagined that differently."

**I should hope so**, Jack thought. He could also imagine what San might have said: **"Now that you're nine, isn't it about time to put on your big-girl pants?"**—an expression that annoyed Nattie to no end.

He was encouraged, however, by Nattie's shame. Normally, she was unconcerned with seeming childish; she was that confident.

Laura, apron splattered and shoes speckled, was obviously chagrined, but she forced a helpless oh well smile. Jack pulled Nattie into a hug. "I'm all muddy,

Dad!" she said. But he kissed her mud-dotted hair anyway, wishing he could have pulled Laura into a group hug. "Now we're the three mudskateers."

Nattie giggled, and they walked the remaining block to their house. Nattie scampered up the stairs while Laura tossed her apron into the washer and tried to wipe off her tennis shoes with a rag. "You look lost in thought."

He shrugged.

Laura went to the sink, washing her hands, looking up to Nattie's room. "Nattie, shower time!"

Nattie shouted her answer, muffled behind her bedroom door.

Jack racked his brain, still thinking of the strange woman in his office. Would San have encouraged some potential date to traipse all the way to his shop, only to pose as a saleswoman? It would have been a perfect icebreaker. **"Hi, we met once, and I know your sister...."**

Laura went upstairs to assist Nattie, just in case she had forgotten her physical state of being a child covered in mud.

Moments later, he could hear them in the bedroom, giggling, followed by Laura's instructive voice, "Hold still, sweetie, this won't hurt a bit." Followed by "Ouch!" and a duet of laughter.

Jack sifted through the **Daily Record**, catching up on the local sports, enjoying the happy sound of Nattie singing at the top of her lungs from the bathroom upstairs while Laura busied herself filling a laundry basket with Nattie's dirty clothes. After a while he dialed San's number, and San answered, sounding less than thrilled to hear from him. "Have you called to apologize?"

Ignoring that, he started right in. "I think one of your potential blind dates showed up at my office." He described the incident, wondering if she'd admit to it.

"Oh dear," San said, more sarcastic than normal. "Can you blame me? I've been talkin' you up, dear brother, telling everyone how wonderful you are, lyin' through my pearly whites."

Jack bit his tongue. He heard a loud squeal and looked up to see Nattie, wrapped in a fluffy white towel, shaking her drenched head over the banister, little droplets falling to the lower level. Laura clutched Nattie's bare shoulders, making sure she didn't shake herself right over the balcony.

"Just a sec," Jack said to San, covering the receiver.

Humorously exasperated, Laura shook her head. "Getting this girl clean is a real job!"

Laura covered Nattie's head with a second towel, giving it a festive swirl. Nattie squealed again. "Hey, the lights went out!"

Jack got back on the phone. "Sorry—distracted."

"If you're finished, I'm a little busy," San said, her words clipped.

"Her name is Kelly," Jack said.

San went silent for a moment. "I know a **lot** of Kellys," she finally said, and before Jack could say **Maines**, San muttered good-bye and disconnected her end. Sighing, Jack hung up. **I should have apologized.**

When Nattie was among the dry, they ordered pizza and settled in for an hour of **Tangled**. While it was the first viewing for Laura, Jack had lost count of how many times he'd fallen asleep to this movie. He dozed a bit, then woke up to find Laura weeping softly at the ending, Nattie stroking her arm.

"Once you've seen **Tangled**," Nattie whispered to Jack, "you're never the same again."

**Of course**, Jack thought. A story about a young woman who finds her true parents.

"Can I grow my hair long?"

"How long is long?"

Nattie pointed to the floor. **Oh boy.**

In the days that followed, business at Higher Ground continued at an encouraging clip. In addition to the regular renters who came through, refining their skills and practicing crosswind landings, several folks walked in requesting instrument training. Along with a sudden slew of clients who were eager to earn ratings like Boy Scouts earn merit badges, the last half of summer was beginning to look very busy for Jack's team of flight instructors, most of whom were semiretired and enjoyed both the job and the extra money.

San texted him with the news that she was off to New York for some meetings. **Let me know when you are ready to apologize**, she signed off. Truly, he welcomed a break from his meddling sister and decided to wait for a face-to-face opportunity to clear the air. In the meantime, he polished his strange letter to Laura, working through phrases. But the more he worked on it, the less settled he felt.

Surprisingly, Kelly Maines, the mystery woman, showed up again on Wednesday while his ace-in-the-hole greeter, Mick, was still out on a flight.

Confined to his office, Jack was shuffling his paper work, wishing he could just burn the stuff, when the blue-eyed brunette strolled through the glass doors wearing dark jeans, a loose blue-and-white-checked blouse, and sunglasses.

Jack met her at the counter, and she

removed her shades. His antennae were up for sure, but he was surprised at how glad he was to see her again.

Kelly smiled. "So...what does a lady have to do to punch a hole in the sky?"

Jack laughed, dismissing any frustration he might have had with her unwillingness to actually schedule his time.

"I figured you'd never heard that before," she said, placing her hands on the counter as if she owned the joint, a glint of ironic humor in her expression.

"Sounds new, coming from you," he said. "Are you here for that intro flight?"

She shrugged, looking around casually. "Actually...now that I'm here, I'm having second thoughts." She gestured toward the runway. "I just saw a couple planes **barely** land."

"We could eliminate the usual end to these intro flights." She frowned. "Parachuting out of the plane?"

"No, where I let **you** land the plane."

"You're kidding," she said, her eyes narrowing. "After an hour lesson?"

"Hour and a half." Jack smiled. "The extra

half an hour makes all the difference."

He pulled out a questionnaire, plus some paper work required by their insurance, along with a pen. Kelly filled in the blanks, then reviewed the disclaimer. "It doesn't say anything about picking out a headstone, does it?"

Jack covered the bottom part of the document with his hand. "Not anymore."

Smiling, Kelly continued to read intently, as if worried she might miss a word. He found himself studying her mannerisms, the way she placed the tip of her tongue between her lips as she concentrated, and the way she frowned slightly at the end of each line.

At one point, she looked up and caught him staring at her. "Sorry, but I like to read the details."

"Feel free," he said, launching into a basic summary of what the paper work intended to accomplish.

"So the upshot is if anything tragic happens, too bad. It's on me."

Jack chuckled sheepishly. "Lawyer stuff. I couldn't get insurance if I didn't have the clients sign it."

"So am I safe, Jack?" she asked, her blue eyes unwavering.

"With me, yes," he replied.

"Alrighty, then," she said, and quickly, as if afraid of changing her mind, she grabbed the pen, signed, and dated the forms. "Let's do it."

Jack grabbed the document and placed it on his desk, but not without catching the address line. **Akron, Ohio?** She'd driven nearly an hour to take flight lessons in Wooster? When there were dozens of flight options in her own city?

He swallowed his list of growing questions about Ms. Maines, and for the next ten minutes, he went through the basic drill, explaining the fundamentals of flight, the basic terminology, and the rudiments of staying safe. "Never approach the propeller," he cautioned her.

"Count on it," she muttered.

From beneath the counter, he rustled up a spare headset with a protruding microphone and handed it to her. She grimaced affably at the accessory. "So much for that full hour in front of the mirror!"

Jack led her down the hallway to the doorway leading outside, where planes were lined up along the tarmac.

"Which one is ours?" she asked.

He pointed to the one on the end. "The Cessna 172."

They spent fifteen minutes preflighting the plane, checking the fluid levels, and examining the flight surfaces. When he was finished, he helped her inside, holding her hand, and couldn't help but chuckle. "Just as you'd feared. We're getting into an oversized sardine can."

Kelly laughed good-naturedly, and Jack climbed in on the other side, pulling the door firmly shut. He showed her how to fasten her seat belt, and for the second time, he saw a trace of fear flash across her face.

"Still good?"

She nodded. "It's different than I'd expected."

"That's normal," Jack replied, hoping she didn't feel uncomfortable with their close proximity.

Kelly moved slightly, her knees brushing against his. "Sorry," she whispered.

"Tight quarters," he murmured.

Jack plugged in his own headphone jack and reached over her lap to install hers, his face inches from hers. Settling back, he glanced at her expression again for any signs of terror. So far, so good.

Next, after following the checklist to the letter, Jack yelled out the window, "Clear!" and started the engine. It sputtered into life.

He turned on the avionics master switch and spoke into the mic, and Kelly smiled. "Yup. I can hear you."

Scanning the gauges and using his own controls, he taxied the plane to the edge of runway 28, prepared to head into the wind, as indicated by the wind sock and automated surface observation system, or ASOS.

After completing the run-up procedure, Jack looked both ways, searching the sky for signs of an incoming plane. Seeing nothing, he announced his impending departure over the radio, listening for sounds of life and hearing nothing but radio silence. He pulled out to the runway, straightening up the plane, still searching the skies for incoming.

He caught her eyes. "Ready?"

She nodded, giving him a brave smile mixed with a glint of **What have I done?** He slowly pushed the throttle to the metal, and the plane leaped forward, rumbling down the runway. Out of the corner of his eye, he saw Kelly gripping her controls with both hands, her face pale.

"We're fine," he said. "All routine. All according to plan. The air is perfect for a summer evening flight, unusually smooth and steady."

"Just tell me when," she said, practically gasping.

"Not yet," he said, hoping that once they achieved flight and left the bumpy runway, her fear would diminish.

Barreling down the runway, they reached fifty-five knots, and Jack directed her to begin pulling back on her controls. She did so, and just like that, they were slipping into the skies.

"We're climbing, Kelly."

She glanced out the window. "Oh my. It's...beautiful." Keeping an eye on the airspeed, Jack helped her position the nose on the horizon. Slowly they climbed to one thousand feet above ground, an accomplishment that seemed to marvel her.

She turned to him. "This is amazing."

He tried to put himself in her shoes, recalling his own first flight and the feeling of floating above a matchbox world of tiny houses and cars, all sparkling in the sun. Flying in a small plane held a magic all its own.

Once they were level, Jack summarized the basic details of controlling flight: the ailerons, the elevators, and the rudder. "But don't worry about the rudder," he told her. "I'll handle that for now."

"You won't let me...uh...do anything wrong, will you?"

Jack shook his head. "Just wait till we get a bit higher before you begin the aerobatics."

"Not funny."

Instructing her on the finer points of plane management, he said, "Slowly, and without moving the controls forward or back, turn to the left."

She turned and seemed to marvel at the reaction. "We're going left!"

"How 'bout that."

They buzzed around the landscape for nearly twenty minutes, turning every which way, and then he took her for a quick buzz over his neighborhood. It barely took a minute, and before long he pointed over the left side. "There we are. It's the one at the end of the block, by the trees."

Looking intently out the window, she finally nodded. "I see it!"

Heading back to the airport, he pointed out other landmarks and asked, "Wanna land it?"

"Huh?"

"We're going to join the pattern," he said, "just like I explained. Setting ourselves up for final approach."

Once they were in position, he pulled out the throttle a little, pushed the controls forward, and pointed to the altimeter, then the airspeed. "We're sinking and slowing down a bit, but we can't let the airspeed get below sixty knots."

As they descended, he told her to aim for the runway, and he led her step by step, at one point asking her to push the throttle in. "We're descending a little too fast."

"Should I pull back?"

"No," he replied. "That'll drop our airspeed."

Seconds later he pointed to the VSI—vertical speed indicator.

"Good. Our descent has stabilized."

"There's so much to keep track of."

"It gets easier."

The edge of the runway grew closer and closer. He could sense her tense up. Pointing to the runway lights, he encouraged her. "We're right on track."

Moments later, he pulled the throttle out, essentially cutting power. "We don't need this anymore."

"We don't need **power**?"

"We have altitude. Gravity power. Actually, if we're properly positioned on the base to begin with, we don't need the throttle at all, but the wind died down unexpectedly, leaving us a bit short."

"How did you know?"

He shrugged. "Experience, and—" he pointed to the wind sock in the distance —"the wind sock went nearly dead moments after we began our descent."

For the next few minutes they floated toward the runway, Kelly gripping the controls while Jack maintained a light touch on his own controls, just in case. When it appeared they were a few feet from the ground, he said, "Pull back slightly, a little bit, and keep doing it, a tiny bit at a time."

She did so. Then he said, "A little more, but gently."

An annoying high-pitched whistle reverberated through the tiny cockpit.

"Don't worry. That's the stall signal," he said. "This close to landing, that's a good sign."

When it seemed as if they were mere inches from the ground, he said, "Hold it back, don't let it down; hold steady, don't let it land—"

"Don't let it land?"

"Not yet. Pull back a little more."

She pulled back, and suddenly they felt a soft brush beneath them. A big smile broke on her face.

"Keep holding it back," he said, and she did, her arms shaking with the effort, until finally the front wheel slipped downward, gently touching the ground.

"**Now** you can relax."

She sighed loudly.

"That was nearly perfect," he said. "Good job."

She seemed amazed. "I actually **landed** the plane!"

"You did," Jack said, grinning. He gave the throttle some juice and taxied the plane back to the hangar. Once there, he went through the sequence of shutting down the power. Kelly took off her headset, her hair now a bit flat, and tried to finger brush it back to life.

"Did you like the flight?"

She nodded, frowning, as if startled by her own reaction. "More than I thought I would. I feel like…a super hero or something." Jack helped her out of the plane, holding tightly to her hand as she placed her foot on the step and then jumped down. Together, they walked back to the office quietly. She seemed to be processing what she'd just done.

"How much do I owe you?" she asked— a question he'd purposely avoided. Normally, he charged seventy bucks for an introductory flight.

"It's on me," he said, and she protested, though mildly, and stood there for a moment, hesitating, as if unsure of what to do or say next. He felt inexplicably drawn to her, and it wasn't just that she was attractive, or intelligent, or charming in that cute aw-shucks manner of hers. There was something else about her, something hidden beneath the surface.

Whatever secrets Kelly seemed to be harboring, he found her intriguing. And since she'd obviously come a long way simply to associate with him, for whatever reason, perhaps she might be willing to extend the afternoon.

"Say, I need to close up here," he began. "But…would you like to get some coffee? There's a place not far from here."

She met his eyes confidently. "I'd like that."

Kelly waited in one of his flimsy chairs while Jack sorted through some items on his desk and noticed his notebook, the one that contained his disjointed thoughts.

He sighed, thinking of its contents, and tried to justify his imminent date with Kelly. **It's just coffee**, he told himself. He placed the notebook in his drawer and shoved it closed.

# Chapter 21

It was four-thirty, nearly suppertime, late in the day for a coffee date, but Kelly welcomed this chance to come clean. **Finally.**

Waiting for Jack, she perused one of his aviation magazines, mentally preparing herself for the prospect of having an honest conversation with the man whose daughter might be her own.

When he was finished, Jack suggested she follow him in her car. "It's just down the street on the right," he said. "You can't miss it."

**Oh sure**, she thought, sliding into her Corolla. She'd missed **a lot** of can't-miss things in her life!

As she followed him, she wondered if his invite had anything to do with his suspicious nature, or if he simply found her interesting. Either way, it didn't matter. **It's time for the truth.**

Once there, Jack waited for her by the door. Carrying her purse, Kelly strolled up, acting casual, hoping her tension didn't show.

She settled in at a booth toward the back while Jack placed their orders.

She took a deep breath and studied the ambience of the place, letting it cool her nerves. The floor was a dark stained concrete, with wooden beams criss-crossing the ceiling and landscape prints on the wall. Tan leather couches and overstuffed chairs surrounded a stone fireplace. And the café was filled with folks—reading alone, talking in groups, typing away on their phones or computers. It felt welcoming, relaxing, and homey.

Sitting across from each other—her first date in a decade—they made pleasant small talk for a few minutes until she decided it was time. She twirled her mug in her fingers and said, "I have a confession to make...."

Jack seemed amused and beat her to the punch. "I know what you're going to say. We have more in common than I first thought."

Her heart nearly stopped. He'd probably Googled her, although that search wouldn't have yielded immediate results. As fate would have it, there was more than one Kelly Maines in Akron. Kelly Maines was also the name of a beloved, although sometimes controversial Democratic state senator, part of the wealthy Maines family, who'd succeeded her father, Marshall Maines, who'd succeeded his own father, Freddie Maines.

Yes, plug Kelly Maines into Google and you wouldn't find anything about **her** until page ten or eleven. And yet, it wasn't impossible for the persistent seeker, so perhaps Jack had found her after all. If so, it would make her job easier.

Seeing her hesitation, Jack continued, "I'm pretty sure San is behind our meeting."

**San?** She nodded, if only to buy herself time.

"She's been trying to set me up for

years."

She swallowed. A blind date? **Oh no!** Kelly's mind raced through possible responses, finally settling on **Just tell him the truth....**

"I'm really glad you came back," Jack said suddenly, hoping Kelly wouldn't think he was too forward. "I thought you might not."

She seemed startled by his compliment. He found her nervousness rather endearing, especially charmed by the anxious way she seemed to be studying him. And he wasn't surprised that she didn't deny the San connection.

"Speaking of sisters, do you have any siblings?" he asked.

An eternity passed before Kelly finally replied. "No. I'm an only..." And once again she gave him the longest stare, that calculating expression of hers, until she finally seemed to relax. She explained that her mother lived in Cleveland, having moved there after her father passed away. "I was close to my dad. My mom's rather close-vested. She lives for her church groups, society clubs, and music events."

He listened intently, enamored with her tentative manner. She had a rosy tan complexion, blue eyes, and her dark hair was styled casually.

Overall, she reminded him of what Nattie might look like when she grew up. But her anxiety seemed to be increasing again. **It must be me**, he thought. **I make her nervous.**

"We had an older brother," Jack said. "He died five years ago."

"I'm sorry," Kelly said.

"Car accident," Jack replied. "San and I weren't close growing up; she was the annoying baby sister, and it was only after I acquired Nattie that we actually became friendly."

He took a breath, hesitating, wondering if he'd just overshared.

But Kelly only smiled. "How **did** you acquire Nattie?"

She didn't have to ask twice. He told her the whole story, beginning to end.

"At first, I did it for my brother," he

finished. "And for Nattie. To not only keep her safe, but **feeling** safe. I wanted Nattie to have the kind of childhood I never had, free of stress and full of unconditional love."

Kelly's eyes dimmed. "You had a bad childhood?"

Jack shrugged. "Let's just say my mother should never have had kids."

"Oh," Kelly said. "I know the type."

Jack leaned back, studying this fascinating woman, who seemed so secretive. **Why did you come all the way to Wooster just to take an introductory flight?** "Did you know your brown hair gets slightly reddish when the sun shines on it? Nattie's does the same thing."

Kelly was holding her mug, staring at the creamy golden-brown tea. She smiled politely as her eyes slowly rose to meet his, and he could almost see the wheels turning behind her worried expression.

"Jack..." she began, her face suddenly anxious again. "You really love her, don't you?"

He nodded. "Nattie's my life. I look into

her future and sometimes it frightens me. I see her turning ten, like…**tomorrow**. And then eleven…and then twelve. And it's like…I've missed it. And where has the time gone? It feels as if I've already lost her."

"Are you really afraid of losing her?"

Jack chuckled uneasily. "Well, I know I'll lose her to adolescence, for a while at least. I'm prepared for that, but sometimes I feel like she doesn't really belong to me. She was adopted by my brother, and before that…someone else gave birth to her. I just happened to be standing in the right place at the wrong time. I'm more worried about not doing the right thing, being the best father, keeping her from real harm." He sighed, realizing he'd been rambling on.

"Do you take her to church?" she asked.

"Yes, I do." He told her his story, coming back to faith after his brother died, determined to teach Nattie those same beliefs.

"I was raised a Christian, too," she admitted, and he felt enormously relieved.

It opened an easy segue into a discussion of their mutual beliefs, and they began by talking about their respective churches, and before long, they were sharing their favorite Scriptures. Kelly's favorites all had to do with faith and answered prayer.

Jack told her George Mueller's empty-table story, and she nodded.

"I've been a Mueller fan for years and love that one."

Thrilled that she shared his faith, Jack glanced at his watch, stunned by the passage of time.

"I should let you go," she said.

Jack tried to hide his disappointment but agreed. He placed their tray in a rack by the garbage can while Kelly waited at the door. Exiting the shop, they stood in the afternoon light. Her blue eyes were softer now, but she still seemed troubled, and he almost asked, **"Is everything okay?"**

Instead, Kelly looped her purse over her shoulder. "Well...thanks for the tea."

Suddenly, Jack forged ahead. "I'd like to see you again, Kelly."

She seemed to hesitate. He was prepared for the worst: **"I really can't,"** or **"I'm too busy,"** or **"I'm not feeling very romantic,"** or even **"You seem nice, but I'm not looking for a relationship right now"**—all the things people say to keep a potential suitor at bay. He could hardly blame her; he'd probably come on too strong.

She surprised him. "You have my number."

"Of course," he said, thinking of the paper work she'd signed.

"Good night," Kelly said, meeting his eyes. "I hope we do see each other again."

He watched her walk to her car, an older model Toyota, the kind rarely seen on the road anymore because most of them had been relegated to junkyards. **She's driving back to Akron in that?**

Kelly tossed her bag in the passenger seat, slipped in, and backed out of the parking lot. After a moment's pause, the car hustled down the street, brake lights flickering.

Kelly drove home in a fog with the window down, the sun setting behind her, and the image of Jack across the table from her, asking question after question. And that deer-in-the-headlights feeling in her brain. **What was I thinking?**

She'd lied by commission and omission. Not only that, she'd had her chance, the **perfect** chance, and she'd let it slip through her fingers.

Jack hadn't been completely forthright, either. He **was** afraid of losing Nattie. While caring for Nattie had simply fallen into his lap, he'd been given an awesome responsibility, and he thrived on it. And he was terrified she'd suddenly disappear from his life.

So what would happen if Nattie was Kelly's? It would destroy him. She could picture the look of horror as his worst fears came to life.

She felt sick to her stomach. Jack was decent, kind, and honest. He didn't deserve this. **"I'd like to see you again,"** he'd said, and the sincerity in his eyes had made her shudder. And what had she said in return? **"I hope we do."**

She groaned. It could have been so easy. And just exactly why hadn't she come clean? That was the million-dollar question, wasn't it? Because she was rattled by how he looked at her, startled by her own emotions, haunted by that little voice that said, **what if?**

What if **what**?

**Ridiculous.**

So where did she go from here? She had only a few options. She could call him and confess everything. Or she could show up at his office again, tell him the truth. Or she could wait until he called. Assuming he **would** call. He might not—not if he talked to his sister, this San, who was sure to declare her ignorance of any such Kelly Maines from Akron.

But if Jack **did** call, hopefully it would be a date that involved Nattie, because if she still couldn't come clean, then she needed to break her promise to Chet. She didn't have to swab Nattie's cheek, although that would be preferable. She could also swipe some hair, grab a glass that Nattie had used, or scavenge the bathroom for fingernail clippings or a used toothbrush. Stealing the toothbrush wasn't the optimum approach, but it could work.

She imagined the other option, the possibility of a long, drawn-out confession. She could show him the newspaper article from nine years ago, explain, and apologize. **"I really liked you and I got caught up. I should have said this earlier, but all I want is a little DNA."**

He just might say, **"Why didn't you say so? Sure, I hand out Nattie's genetic code all the time. No big deal!"**

She scoffed. Yes, Jack might have been reasonable before, but it was highly unlikely he'd be reasonable now. The ship of cooperation had long since sailed. Jack would be furious with what he'd perceive as her deception.

No. She **couldn't** come clean, at least not before she knew the truth. And to get the truth, she had to steal Nattie's DNA.

She shuddered at the unintended consequences of losing her nerve.

Kelly heard a series of tones and

recognized Melody's signature calling card. She pulled onto the shoulder and read the text: **Hey girlfriend, how'd it go?**

Kelly texted back: **I blew it. I couldn't go through with it.**

Her phone rang immediately.

"Tell me what happened," Melody said, and Kelly was reminded again of how much she needed her dear friend. She described the coffee date, and Melody whistled.

"What?" Kelly asked.

"You said he was staring at you like he knew you."

"I've been in the local papers and on TV, you know. He just can't place me yet."

"Maybe," Melody replied. "Or maybe not. This might be really good news, Kel."

"How do you figure?"

Melody paused and lowered her voice. "Maybe he sees Natalie in you, Kel."

Kelly hadn't even considered that.

Jack arrived home to find Laura on the back porch, sitting on the swing, lost in the pages of a book.

"Sorry," he said, referring to his tardy return.

"No problem," she said, placing the book beside her.

Jack asked if Nattie was still around.

"She's at Katelyn's," Laura said. "I didn't want to leave until she got back. Late flight?"

"Later than usual," he said, reluctant to admit that he'd spent the last two hours at a coffee shop with a strange woman. Despite his odd attraction to Kelly, and in spite of what he'd said—**"I'd like to see you again,"** he was already leaning against pursuing her.

She seemed a little **too** mysterious. And besides, he'd already been down this road before. He couldn't risk losing Laura, and he'd all but promised Nattie. She was doing so well he couldn't bear to threaten her recent settled behavior.

"Well, I should be going," Laura said, grabbing her shawl. "It's cooler tonight, ain't?"

"What?" Jack said, lost in his strange

reverie.

Laura repeated her statement, and he agreed, walking her to the door. She wrapped the shawl around her shoulders and removed her keys from her bag.

They stood there for a moment longer, and she seemed to be studying him, noting his distraction, and for a moment he thought she might say something like **"You seem different,"** but she didn't.

"G'night," she said instead, giving Jack a quick wave before heading to her car.

Nattie came home minutes later, finding Jack in his office, and she wasn't happy. "What happened to you?"

Jack turned in his chair and was treated to the sight of his fire-eyed girl. "Lost track of time."

Nattie crossed her arms. "You **never** lose track of time. And besides, you never let me use that excuse. "

She was right. "Sorry, honey." Jack leaned back casually, clasping his hands on his stomach, calculating exactly how much he could risk telling her, but before he could answer her, Nattie deciphered his hesitation, her face growing cloudy. "You were with that woman, weren't you?"

**That woman?** "Excuse me?"

Nattie frowned. "Did Laura take that box?"

"What box?"

Nattie explained that she'd made Laura a special clay sculpture and put it in a box. Jack remembered seeing it on the counter when Laura had left, and Nattie rushed around the corner to see, coming back disappointed.

"She just forgot, honey," Jack said. "She'll be back tomorrow."

"So...tell me about her," Nattie said with a worried look. "Tell you about **who**?"

"Auntie San called tonight," Nattie said. "I told her you were late, and she said you were probably with someone named Kelly."

Jack struggled to hide his frustration with San. Just his luck, she'd remembered the name from their phone call.

"Why are you trying to keep it secret?"

"It's not a secret."

"So you **were** with her."

"Nattie—"

"What does she look like?"

Jack stood up and gestured toward her room. "You need to get ready for bed, young lady."

"You went on another date without telling me? After you said you wouldn't?"

"Nattie—"

"I thought you and Laura were dating now. You're always together on the swing. She bought you that...that...signature thing."

"Laura is **Amish**, Nattie. And she'll always be Amish."

Nattie frowned. "She'll leave if you marry someone else."

"I'm **not** marrying anyone else." Jack felt his own voice rising, his frustration pushed to the breaking point.

Nattie burst into tears. She clumsily wiped at her face and stared at him.

"Honey..." Jack knelt in front of her, hands on her shoulders, and she sniffed loudly.

"I'm thirsty," she muttered. "I played too hard."

"I'll get you a glass of water." Jack kissed the top of her head and headed out to the kitchen. Just before turning on the light, he glanced toward the entryway, and there Laura was, holding Nattie's box. Laura had come back for it after all, and the look in her tortured eyes broke his heart.

Laura gestured with the box. "I figured I'd just slip in quietly."

He could have swept the obvious under the rug, pretended she hadn't heard, but they all knew how well sound carried in this open monstrosity.

"Can we talk—"

"I shouldn't have walked in." Laura tucked the box under her right arm. "Please forgive me."

"Laura, don't go—"

She practically fled. Jack turned to see Nattie still standing in the doorway to his office, her own face a mixture of horror and misery.

"Nattie..." he started. He went to her and grabbed her, holding her close. She sobbed into his shoulder.

**What have I done?**

# Chapter 22

After Laura had rushed out the door, Nattie wept in Jack's arms. They sat huddled together on the couch as Jack tried to reassure her. "She's not going anywhere, honey."

"You don't know her like I do."

Eventually, Nattie seemed to calm a bit. He suggested a movie, something to get her mind off it, but she gave him a beseeching look. "Call her," she begged.

"Honey…"

"She's crying. I know she is."

So he dialed, but Laura didn't pick up.

They prayed together, **Jesus, please soothe Laura's feelings. Help her know how much we love her.**

But Nattie didn't hand him a furry friend for the night. Later that evening, around eleven, he went to Nattie's room, hoping to see her asleep. She was lying awake, staring at the ceiling, brooding and fuming. "I thought you liked her."

Jack planted a kiss on her forehead and settled into a chair in the corner of her bedroom, letting her fret out loud—and fret she did, for another half hour, until she finally fell asleep. Jack did his own brooding in the form of distracted prayer, watching the minutes whisk past midnight. "I could use a little advice," he whispered. "Actually, I wouldn't mind an outright miracle, but in lieu of that, how about a nudge in the right direction?"

He felt guilty, of course, as if he'd been caught cheating. As if he'd broken his promise to Nattie, and really...hadn't he?

And just exactly where did he and Laura stand? On his birthday, he would have said they were almost a couple. Laura had gone fancy, even giving him that extraordinary gift. But over the following days, everything had begun to crumble. She'd received the letter and had told him the story of her shunning, and of Jonathan.

And then, when San had come for a visit, Laura had told San she wouldn't stand in his way.

He cringed at the memory. **And now this.** He took a deep breath, letting it out slowly.

**I have to fix it**, he realized.

Finally creeping out of Nattie's bedroom and into his own, he considered his only option. When Laura came in tomorrow, he had to tell her Kelly Maines meant nothing to him, that it was simply a coffee break.

**Wasn't it?** He slid beneath the bedspread, laced hands behind his head, and stared into the giant white inkblot of his ceiling.

Frankly, he wasn't so sure it **was** just a simple coffee break. He and this woman had made some kind of connection, hadn't they? Had she felt it, too?

Something about Kelly seemed familiar, as if he'd known her for years, and not just a few hours. And wasn't **that** a cliché!

A shudder of guilt knocked on the door to his fantasy world. It was now one-thirty in the morning, and Laura had to be at home, crying her eyes out, afraid she was about to lose her place in their lives, and here he lay, imagining Kelly's face over and over, like a love-struck teenager.

Even so, he had to keep his priorities straight. He had to make sure their nanny didn't quit, because Nattie would never recover from it. He wasn't sure he would, either.

The next morning, Jack woke up groggy from his toss-and-turn night. He heard sounds from the kitchen: organized, methodical, gentle, un-Nattie-like. Laura was there already, and it came to him in a flash, everything that had happened yesterday. He lay there, ruminating, until he heard Nattie join her, followed by Nattie's chattering, as if she hadn't sulked herself to sleep.

Jack had a midmorning flight. Considering his tight schedule, he wouldn't be able to address last night's misunderstanding until later. He showered quickly, pulled on khakis and a short-sleeved button-down shirt, and headed downstairs. He could hear the thumping of the dryer—Laura had already put in a load.

She greeted him with a smile, and for a moment he allowed himself to hope. He sat at the bar, and Nattie barely acknowledged him until Laura turned her back, at which point Nattie turned to him, her eyes imploring: **"Do something, Dad."**

He shrugged and mouthed, **"Later."**

Nattie shook her head and spooned up another sugary mini-wheat. There was no fruit on her plate, one of the house rules when eating nutritionally challenged boxed cereal.

But he wisely let it go.

When he got home after work, Laura had already taken Nattie to the park. He decided to leave them be, waiting for a more private opportunity to talk when Laura returned.

Late in the afternoon, Jack was fiddling around in his office when he heard the front door open and shut, and then **nothing**—no whispers, no giggles. Highly irregular. Nattie did little without fostering a small cacophony of noise. Jack felt a sinking feeling. Moments later, he heard a soft knock at the door.

"Come in," he called, turning to face the door, expecting the worst.

Nattie stood there, her face sullen, her eyes red. "I was right."

Before he could respond, Nattie ran upstairs. He got up to follow, only to come face-to-face with Laura, who was standing with her hand on the counter, her eyes as red as Nattie's. "I wanted to tell Natalie first," she said, staring at him uneasily yet moving closer.

"Can we talk about this?"

Laura was already gesturing toward the backyard. **She's planned this** was his next thought. He glanced upstairs as he followed Laura out, saw Nattie gripping the banister, looking down at him with hopeful eyes.

Outside, Laura wandered past the swing without sitting, facing the trees on the forest-lined side of their house. Jack shut the door, letting the screen door creep slowly closed, wanting to delay the inevitable. He didn't sit, either, taking his position on the other side.

Turning around, Laura pursed her lips, her movements gentle and soft, her eyes apologetic. "Jack...Natalie and I had a long talk...and she's going to be fine with this."

Jack stood there, waiting for Laura to confirm what exactly **"fine with this"** meant. But he already knew, didn't he?

"I'm standing in your way, Jack."

Jack observed the seriousness of her expression. Rarely had she looked so determined.

"And Nattie really doesn't need a nanny anymore," she continued. "Once school starts in September, Diane can watch Nattie after school. She's already said so, even mentioned that Livy could help—she'd love to earn a little pocket money. It would be good for Livy, having the responsibility..."

Laura's voice trailed off, and Jack had this surreal sense, as if he were falling out of a tree but hitting the ground was taking forever. "I don't understand. I had coffee with someone…a new client, really. A woman I likely won't see again. And now… you're quitting?"

Laura swallowed hard, and tears began to form in her eyes. She wiped them with her sleeve, then her hand, finally pulling a crumpled tissue out of her apron pocket. "This has been a long time coming, Jack. And besides, you should be able to have coffee with whomever you wish."

He was confused. "But that's why you're leaving, isn't it?"

She stared at the sky, leaving the question unanswered. "It's not like we're dating, you know."

He winced at her reply. **Yes, it is.** "Are you going home? Is that it?"

Laura shook her head, still unable to meet his eyes. "No. I told you. That's closed to me forever."

He went for broke. "What aren't you telling me, Laura?"

She flinched, meeting his eyes suddenly, boring a hole, then looking away when he refused to look away first.

**There is something**, he realized. **She's**

**hiding something.**

"You've always told us the truth, Laura."

She wiped her eyes again. "**Jah**, I've never told you a lie."

He paused a moment. **Not the same thing.**

"San is right, Jack. As long as I'm here, you'll never find a mommy for Nattie."

"We aren't shopping for a mommy. We want **you**."

Laura wiped at her eyes furiously. She moved toward him, but he knew she intended to pass. He was tempted to grab her, **should** have grabbed her, but he didn't.

She placed her hand on the knob, turning back, and the tears were now streaking down her face. In that moment he wanted nothing more than to envelop her in his arms and soothe away the pain they both felt.

But the wall remained, that unyielding Amish wall that separated their cultures, keeping them apart.

In spite of this, he took a step toward her, but she leaned back, her eyes warning,

**Please don't.** "We've underestimated Nattie, Jack. She's more resilient than you think. She'll be fine," Laura said, as if saying it made it true. "I'll give you two weeks, and then we'll schedule times together all the way into the fall, **jah**? I love your daughter, and that'll never change. I won't just disappear, Jack."

She slipped through the door and did just that.

Jack collapsed in the swing, taking a moment to compose himself, then went upstairs to find Nattie hugging Bear Bear with all her might. He settled on the side of her bed.

"What happened?"

"Laura's not moving away, honey."

She stared at him, disbelieving, fresh tears beginning.

He hugged her close, doing his best to console her, and after the initial thunderstorm, Nattie recovered enough to relate the conversation on the park bench, where Laura had hugged the stuffing out of Nattie and given her a kid-version of what she'd told Jack.

"What are we going to do?" Nattie asked.

He kissed her cheek. "We're going to pray about it, and we're going to get through this together."

She nodded, sniffed again, but said nothing. She curled on her side and sighed heavily. She closed her eyes, and he stroked her back until she fell asleep, exhausted from her rough night and today's emotional firestorm.

Back in his office, he picked up the phone and dialed Laura's cell number. No answer. He dialed again, and this time left a message: "I'd like to talk about this further."

He hung up, his spirits sinking, feeling suddenly lonely, and thought of Kelly. He'd spent a mere few hours with this woman, was about to lose his daughter's nanny, and already he was toying with the idea of hearing Kelly's voice again. **What is the matter with me?**

He turned his fractured attention to something inert, like reconciling his bank account. He turned on the Internet radio, something folk or even country, or... whatever.

But try as he might, he couldn't drop the notion. **This is really dumb**, he thought, pulling out a piece of scrap paper with her number scribbled on it, copied from the paper work filed at the office. Before he could change his mind, he punched the numbers on his phone. It rang five times and went to her automated service.

Instead of leaving a message, like he had with Laura, he hung up.

When his phone rang, his heart nearly stopped. He checked the number, expecting to see Laura's, but it was Kelly, returning his call. Heart pounding, feeling exceedingly foolish, he answered it. "Hi."

"Hi," she answered, "I'm not sure if it's proper phone etiquette to call someone back when they didn't leave a message, but...well...here I am."

Expelling a sigh, Jack felt a sudden weight lift from his shoulders. "I just wanted to tell you..." He stopped, his words already bungled. In light of everything that had just happened, what could he say? **"Our nanny just quit, and I just wanted to hear your voice."**

"I had a good time yesterday." He'd just set a record for the lamest thing to say, but Kelly graciously gave him a pass.

"Well, I had a **great** time, Jack. And I'm not a big tea drinker." She chuckled at her own joke, and he clutched the phone tighter.

She spoke again. "We should do it again." Then she laughed. "I'm rather forward tonight."

He laughed with her, and then his phone beeped.

He checked the ID: It was Laura. He couldn't risk losing her again, so he apologized, claiming he had to get this call. He asked Kelly to stay on the line—"I don't mind, Jack"—and excused himself. He clicked over. "Laura?"

"I got your message," she said softly. "I'm fine. Really."

"I can't accept this, Laura."

She paused. "Jack, no offense, okay? But you don't have a choice.

And I told you—you're not losing me, just my employment. I'm not going anywhere."

"But can we still talk about it?"

"I've got to go, Jack."

It felt like they were breaking up. **Take it like a man**, he thought. And he could have, if not for Nattie. "Laura—"

She'd already clicked off. She'd never done that before, hanging up before hearing him say good-bye first.

Jack clicked back to Kelly. "I'm back."

"Are you okay?" she asked.

He must have sounded out of breath. He made some kind of explanation, and she let it go.

"I have to say," she began, "I'm a little embarrassed about why I missed your call."

"Were you outside, or—?"

She groaned. "Watching TV. I got sucked in by this Discovery Channel story about a dog who found his way home after getting stranded three hundred miles away. Here I was, wiping soppy tears away, when lo and behold, I missed your call!"

The story made him smile. Just hearing her voice had a calming effect on him. Easygoing, friendly, that familiar quality about it. Grateful for the distraction, Jack tripped along behind mundane talk for another twenty minutes.

"You seem a little sad," she said suddenly.

He used the age-old dodge, "Just a little tired," debating whether or not to mention what had happened tonight, then took the chance, explaining that their beloved nanny had just handed in her resignation.

Kelly expressed her sympathy. "Tell me about her."

He did, and she seemed to listen intently, occasionally probing for further, but not inappropriate, details. "We can't lose her," he finally said. "It's unthinkable."

"She sounds like a wonderful person," Kelly said.

Jack sighed. "She is."

Their conversation meandered until he realized they'd been talking for an hour. "I'm keeping you," he protested.

Kelly chuckled wryly. "You don't know me well enough to figure out whether you **want** to keep me."

He smiled, intrigued by her self-deprecating humor. He could tell Kelly really liked kids, from the way she kept asking about Nattie. It didn't bother him that she'd been married before, a marriage that, as she'd put it, **"was practically arranged by my mother."**

"I'm alone right now," she volunteered now, her tone sounding wistful, "but I'd love to be a mother someday."

"I bet you'd make a great one," he said.

"I'd like to think I would, Jack," she whispered.

"What do you think of diapers?" Jack asked, thinking of Angela, and Kelly laughed.

"Diapers are par for the course. Sometimes I visit the diaper aisle and just the **smell** stokes my maternal instinct!"

**Did she really say that?** "Please tell me you're kidding," he replied with a laugh.

"Oops, did I say that out loud?" she quipped, and they both laughed at her joke.

He looked at the clock again and went for broke. It didn't seem all that risky, not with their obvious camaraderie. And shoot, he'd already lost his nanny over Kelly. "I'd really like to take you out for dinner."

"Do you cook, Jack?"

He replied to the affirmative.

"Why don't I come to your place?" she asked. "You could introduce me to Nattie at the same time. From the way you've described her, I can't wait to meet her."

He thought for a moment. Nattie wasn't ready for this. No way. In fact, Nattie might **never** be ready for it again. "If you don't mind, I think I'd like to do dinner first, just the two of us," he said. "I'd be happy to pick you up. Take you somewhere in your neck of the woods."

She demurred. "Tell you what. There's that nice-looking restaurant on the outskirts of Wooster. You know, the one with the lake? I could meet you there."

**Wooster Country Club.** Finding her determination to drive down somewhat curious, Jack suggested a time, and she accepted.

"Afterward, if we have time, it might work out for you to meet Nattie. From the restaurant, our house is actually on the way back to Akron."

She seemed highly enthused with his plan. He hung up the phone, grinning like a kid.

Replaying every inch of their conversation, he now looked up at the clock. It was only nine-thirty. His new world, one without Laura, came blaring back.

He got ready for bed, covered his sleeping cherub with Laura's quilt, and whispered a prayer for the means to soothe her sorrow. In his own room, he went to sleep hearing the sound of Kelly's voice, but it was Laura who haunted his dreams.

# Chapter 23

Friday morning Laura arrived early again. Jack showered quickly, dressed in his usual jeans and short-sleeved shirt, and leaned over the railing. Surrounded by her stuffed-animal family, Nattie sat, gloomy and hunched over, munching her cereal. At least today he noted apple slices on a saucer.

Nattie and Laura talked in hushed whispers. Laura, her manner professional, almost detached, hadn't even turned on the radio. But he was encouraged when Laura slipped in beside Nattie and gave her a long hug, then whispered something in her ear. Nattie nodded.

Laura looked up and saw him. "Good morning, Jack."

He caught Nattie's sorrowful expression

as she turned in her stool.

After Nattie was done, he ate alone at the bar, chugging Laura's swamp smoothie drink first, followed by granola, while Laura gathered up laundry. I **won't miss the green drinks**, he thought, but it was little consolation.

When it was time for him to leave for the airfield, Laura was in the laundry room, and Nattie had already sequestered herself in her bedroom with the door closed.

He went to say good-bye to Laura, and she responded pleasantly, unlike yesterday, meeting his eyes. The whole thing seemed settled for her, as if now she'd made the decision, she was ready to move on.

Lounging in her pajamas, Kelly went online and looked up Higher Ground, Jack's aviation site. She scrolled through the tabs, found **Our team**, and clicked on it. A rather large group of pilots fanned out behind Jack in the center, wearing what seemed to be standard-issue jackets and shades. She recognized Mick to Jack's immediate left.

She clicked on a second tab and found another picture of Jack, this one alone, then one with Jack hugging Nattie in front of his plane. She read the caption below: **Jack's family**.

She groaned to herself. All that time waiting for Ernie, and she could have simply looked up Jack's site and found Nattie's picture.

**But I needed the break**, she thought.

She pictured the upcoming dinner date, thinking back on their previous long phone conversation, including Jack's obvious despair over losing Laura, and felt a small flutter in her heart. Nattie's nanny of over eight years had suddenly quit. **Without warning, it seems**, she thought. **Why?**

She dialed Ernie's number.

"What's the good word?" Ernie answered.

Kelly filled him in on the latest, and as she expected, he wasn't pleased. "Tell me again what happened at the airfield."

"I lost my nerve, Ernie."

He whistled. "I'm tempted to cheat on

this one, kiddo."

She didn't respond.

Ernie muttered, "It's your call. But I guess we can't forget that Chet's paying the bill."

Yes, she thought, feeling chastised. Against her better judgment, she told Ernie about last night's conversation, the coming date, and he seemed surprised. "So you guys are getting chummy? Is that just to get the DNA?"

**Good question**, she thought. "No," she said. "Come again?"

"It's...complicated, I think."

"No kidding," Ernie replied. "And dangerous."

She sighed. "I think Jack likes me."

Ernie cleared his throat, and just the gravelly sound of it was like an admonishment. "Kelly, you need to put your cards on the table and tell him you couldn't be honest before because you were distracted by his ocean blue eyes and Viking chin."

Kelly gave a nervous laugh. "I think I might modify that approach somewhat."

"So come up with your own variation."

"Fair enough," she bantered.

"Listen, you're one Google search from looking really, really bad, and with nothing to show for it," Ernie grumbled. "You didn't tell him your real last name, did you?"

Kelly cringed, closing her eyes, her silence telling him what he didn't want to hear.

"Wonderful," Ernie muttered.

**Point taken**, Kelly thought.

Considering the way Nattie moped around, it was as if Laura had disowned them and was moving to Alaska. Then again, Jack was impressed that Nattie wasn't taking it harder than she was. No tantrums, just tears. Learning that Laura wasn't going home to Pennsylvania, after all, and marking dates on the calendar for special girl time at least cut some of the pain.

**"We've underestimated Natalie,"** Laura had told him. As it stood, he questioned whether he was taking Laura's resignation harder than Nattie was.

Then there was Kelly. Since their late-night phone call, they had already texted a number of times, not unlike his early days with Angela.

In the meantime, as Laura began fulfilling her two-week notice, the closeness they'd shared during the early weeks of summer had all but disappeared, including their time spent on the back swing.

He missed it and was relieved when Laura suggested that she come tomorrow, on a Saturday, just for fun, "For Nattie's sake."

The three of them spent the day shopping, something he normally tried to avoid. They went to Walmart on the outskirts of town to shop for Nattie's school supplies, and for all their laughter, it would have seemed to the casual observer that Laura was a fixture. And yet, despite the occasional lightness and the sunny skies, a cloudy pallor hung over the quiet moments. When they finished shopping, they stopped for ice cream, and Jack tried to ignore the growing sense of unease.

"Are you going to visit home?" Nattie asked between licks, pretending it was a casual question.

"Probably not, honey."

"Will you text me?" Nattie asked. "I mean...when I get a phone?" She glanced at Jack, and he ignored the not-so-subtle jab.

Laura nodded, and Nattie seemed satisfied. After ice cream, they took a short drive in the country, just to feel the wind in their hair. Sitting by the window for a change, Nattie flew her hand out, her hair flapping around. Laura, too, seemed to enjoy the breeze in her face, closing her eyes and smiling wistfully.

It was impossible to overestimate just how much he'd come to rely on his Amish nanny, and Jack worried again how they could possibly make half a life without her. There were other nannies, other house-keepers, other gardeners, other counsel-ors, but only one Laura.

Nattie was still "flying her hand" out the window, but now tears were streaking her face. His heart broke at the sight of his little girl in such pain, trying to be brave.

**One loss after another**, he thought.

It was just after four o'clock when they got back, and Laura didn't enter the house like she might have. She said good-bye on the sidewalk and went to her car, parked on the street. He and Nattie watched her go, arms slumped at their sides, both of them barely holding it in.

Jack had bigger problems—tonight's date with Kelly. He'd already procrastinated as long as possible. He sat Nattie down on the couch and leveled with her, starting with the news that San was coming over. Nattie was already ahead of him. "If Auntie San is coming over, then you must have a date."

Jack nodded, bracing himself.

"With that girl," added Nattie.

He nodded again, sighing softly.

Kelly stared in the mirror, applying her lipstick. She mashed her lips together, taking in her reflection, noticing again the lines around her eyes. With the passage of years, she'd nearly forgotten the finer art of makeup application, getting by on the minimum.

Melody was in the next room, lounging on Kelly's couch with Kelly's laptop, checking out the website for Higher Ground.

She whistled. "Really cute, Kel."

Kelly leaned out, lip gloss in hand. "You think?"

"Jack's not bad, either."

Kelly laughed, leaning into the mirror again, rubbing the gloss over her lower lip. Stepping back, she stared at her blouse and turned to the side, examining her figure. She'd put on a few more pounds, and what a difference it had made.

**Okay, you can stop now**, she thought, smiling at what she saw. She wasn't nineteen, sure, but she didn't look forty.

That afternoon, she and Melody had spent an hour at the mall, harboring an unrealistic hope she might find something inexpensive yet worth wearing, something to make her feel feminine. She'd settled on a summery sleeveless blouse and a white skirt, something that showed off—kinda—what had recently come back.

"Are you trying to impress this guy?" Melody had asked. "I mean...what's the end game here?"

Melody was right, of course. **It's only a mission**, Kelly told herself. **Get in, smooth talk this guy, and get out with the DNA.**

She'd packed her DNA trick in the trunk—just in case, for when Jack decided to introduce her to his little princess.

**I'd like Nattie to meet you**, he'd texted.

**I can't wait**, she'd replied.

She should've been terrified, but in all truth, she was genuinely looking forward to tonight.

**Get in and get out**, she reminded herself.

Sure, she was intrigued by this guy. But this isn't about romance, she told herself, going to her bedroom and sitting on the edge of the bed. She extended her hand, palm down, and waited. No tremors, no nerves. Cool as a cucumber.

She walked out, twirled around, and

Melody whistled. "Miss Kelly Maines, you are lookin' **good**. Jack Livingston won't know what hit him!" Melody leaned closer and took a whiff. "That scent should require a license."

Laughing, Kelly put her hand on Melody's shoulder. "I'm so glad you're in my life again."

"Ditto. Just don't fall for some guy who's going to make you move to some dive called Rooster. I just got you back!"

Kelly laughed.

Melody got up, slinging her purse over her shoulder, and led the way out the door before Kelly caught herself. She'd almost forgotten her secret weapon, guaranteed to win Nattie's heart, just in case the opportunity arose. It was merely a back-up plan, of course. The lollipop trick came first. Kelly grabbed the magic purse from the counter, the one with the infinite bottom, and headed out again, pleased with her creativity.

At the end of the sidewalk, Melody threw a kiss to Kelly. "

"Go get 'em, girl."

Waving to Melody and heading down the street in her bucket of spare parts, Kelly realized she couldn't wait for the evening to begin. **Tonight I'll be wined and dined by a nice guy, and afterward, I'll meet Nattie...who just might be mine.**

## Chaper 24

Like the whirlwind she was, San arrived in time to order Nattie into the shower. Clearly all was **not** forgotten, and San wasn't back to her cheerfully annoying self. On the other hand, she wasn't firing eye missiles at him, either, so Jack walked out for inspection, wearing gray pants, a striped button-down, and what he hoped was a coordinating tie.

Absently, San shrugged. "At least you have a winning smile."

"Thanks, I think."

"So who's this Kelly?" she asked, scouring through his fridge.

"By the way, I brought a couple DVDs." She pointed to the end of the counter. Jack picked them up and examined the titles. "Uh…a little too scary."

"What?" San glanced at the titles. "They're supposed to be good for eight and up—"

"She'll cry, San. She can't handle anything remotely sinister. We still fast-forward through parts of **Aladdin**."

San waved her hand dismissively. "Fine, then."

"I met her at the airfield," Jack said, playing along with her game, as if San weren't fully aware of Kelly.

San picked up the DVDs with a look of dejection. "She's really too young for these?"

Jack shrugged. "You can try, but you won't get past the opening credits."

San made a face. "What did you say her name was?" He repeated it.

"Where'd you meet her again?"

"Funny, sis," Jack said.

San gave him a strange look, her eyes darting toward the ceiling, thinking hard. "I don't know a Kelly Maines."

Jack put his hands on the counter. "Well...she knows **you**."

San opened the refrigerator again.

"Dearest brother. I know nearly everyone in the world, and I know who I know."

"Maybe you forgot."

San gave him the "eye" and removed a small Tupperware container. "Chinese?"

Jack shook his head. "Something I whipped up."

Sniffing the contents, San made a face and tossed the remains into the garbage. Jack grimaced, his thoughts shifting to the devastating news about Laura. Reluctant to tell San, he dreaded the glee she'd bring to such a revelation. Then again, it wasn't right to make Nattie the bearer of the news, so he told her anyway, and just as he expected, San could barely contain herself. "This will mean a new start for you, Jack. And it'll be good for Nattie," she called after him as he marched upstairs to say good-bye to Nattie, peeling off his mismatched tie as he went.

He kissed Nattie on the cheek. "Be good for Auntie San Fran."

Nattie frowned. "I thought you didn't like that nickname."

"It's growing on me."

The night air was cool and breezy, but Kelly drove with the windows up, unwilling to let the wind undo her primping. The image of Nattie flickered through her mind—her shoulder-length hair, impish brown eyes, and the way her smile enveloped her entire face.

Kelly dismissed the image. It was too soon to get caught up in what-ifs. She'd already done that to her detriment.

Unwilling to rely solely on her memory, she followed Jack's directions with an eye and an ear to her GPS, arriving with a few minutes to spare.

**Well, I'm not wearing designer clothes, but at least I won't be under-dressed**, she thought, pausing at the sign, taking in the well-manicured area, a golf course that swirled about the grounds, and the lake behind the restaurant.

**"They have walking paths,"** he'd told her.

She took in a deep breath and drove through the parking lot. Jack was standing outside, more casually dressed than she'd expected, putting her mind at ease. He pointed toward the outer edge of the parking lot, to a single parking spot. She gave him a **got-it** smile and parked her increasingly embarrassing fifteen-year-old rust bucket.

Jack met her halfway to the door. She felt nervous, wondering how to greet him, but he made it easy for her, kissing her cheek.

He smiled. "You look great."

She thanked him, blushing and slipping a strand of hair behind her ear. She thought of Violet's line in the classic movie, **It's a Wonderful Life**, and repeated it verbatim, flipping her hair back with a flourish. And then she felt stupid, because it was only funny if Jack had seen the movie.

To her relief he had and played along. He grabbed her arm playfully, and in a passable version of Jimmy Stewart, said, "Whadd'ya say, Violet? L-l-let's dance till the sun comes up!"

Kelly laughed. "You are a multitalented man, Jack Livingston."

"It's lost on Nattie, I'm afraid. She doesn't appreciate seventy-year-old films."

"She doesn't like all things Bedford Falls?"

"Potter scares her." Jack grinned.

"Potter scares **me**!" Kelly exclaimed, allowing Jack to escort her as they ascended the front steps. They were off to the races, she realized.

**I'm one meal away from meeting her!**

Jack put his hand on the small of her back, holding the door for her as they walked into the dimly lit entryway and were greeted by the spirited laughter of a full house. Jack made his way to the smiling hostess behind the wooden lectern and gave his name, confirming their reservation.

While they waited for their table, they sat on country-style benches and made small talk.

Eventually, they were called and seated toward the back, where it was somewhat quieter. Jack pulled out her chair, and she felt like a princess. So far there'd been nothing in his manner to indicate anything amiss.

**Living on the edge**, she thought, smiling

wryly to herself.

"What?" Jack asked, noticing her smile.

She leaned over, covering the side of her mouth, as if to whisper a secret. "This is really **nice**!"

"You like?"

"I love!"

They were joined by the maître d', who asked for their wine requests. Jack met Kelly's eyes, noting her quick headshake, and declined. "Nothing for us, please."

The man nodded respectfully. "Your waiter will be with you shortly. I hope you enjoy your meal."

After they received their menus and studied them, the waiter came back and announced the specials. Kelly hadn't known the prices and now felt sheepish for suggesting this place. To her, lunching at a fast-food joint was decadent. A lot had changed in ten years, when Bobby would drop a hundred on a meal without batting an eye.

"I'm not sure yet," she said uneasily, encouraging Jack to order first. So he ordered the filet mignon. She gulped, still tempted to order the salad, if only to lower the bill.

Jack seemed to sense her hesitation. "Try the salmon," he offered, and the waiter seconded Jack's recommendation. "Or the roasted chicken."

"Salmon sounds delicious," she said with a tentative smile, closing her menu.

Jack ordered raspberry iced tea, and she, lemonade, and after the waiter left, they surveyed the room, mostly older couples in suits, ties, evening gowns, pearls and earrings, sharing stories, drinking champagne, laughing at their jokes.

Jack leaned forward on the table and gave her a curious look.

"I know that expression," she said, taking a drink of water, her nerves rising suddenly.

"Tell me about your work, Kelly."

She cleared her throat in what she hoped was a ladylike manner. She'd been prepared for the profession question, and she was relieved to answer it honestly.

"I have a degree in marketing, with a minor in accounting," she told him, reminding him she worked for an investment manager. "Just as an assistant, mind you, but I do hope to move up." She paused, worrying that she'd sounded too assertive. "I wish I'd been a finance major, since I've always enjoyed the world of stocks, bonds, and futures."

Jack seemed intrigued as Kelly talked about the business, hoping to give the impression she'd worked at her present employment for more than a month, knowing it was unlikely he'd check her employment references.

It wasn't lying, not really. She just wasn't telling him everything, like the real reason she'd showed up at his office, and the fact that a sociopathic monster, her former husband, had kidnapped her daughter.

**Things like that**, she thought wryly.

Overall, she was doing her best to appear forthcoming, and yet she couldn't help holding her breath, waiting for him to burst her balloon with, **"By the way, my sister doesn't know who you are,"** but it never came, and that in itself raised a red flag. Surely he wasn't **that** naïve.

At what she hoped was the appropriate time, she asked about Nattie, and it was like she'd offered him a million dollars. His eyes brightened, and it was again clear that Jack adored his daughter.

Jack transitioned from one story to the next, and she couldn't help thinking these were all the memories she'd missed out on. And yet she found herself studying Jack as he talked, observing his firm jawline, his cheekbones, the lazy way he styled his fine blond hair, casual and relaxed, and—Ernie had nailed it—those ocean blue eyes.

She was curious about his past, how long he'd been single, if he dated much—she doubted it!—and if he'd ever been married, although surely he would have told her earlier.

She decided to be direct and asked him outright.

Jack leaned back a bit, considering the question. "Marriage just kinda slipped through my fingers," he said, his eyes serious. "I wasn't exactly marriage material when I was younger, and then when

Nattie came along, I was too busy being a father."

A **good** father, she thought, hoping her expression was more whimsical then questioning.

He smiled, narrowing his eyes playfully. "What about you?"

"What?" she asked with a giggle.

"Why aren't **you** married?" he asked, covering her hand with his, making the question intimate.

She felt her breath leave and tried not to stare at their hands.

"Like I said…I was married once."

He nodded, waiting for her to continue.

"He was a larger-than-life kind of guy. A real charmer…and a drug addict," she said.

Looking sorry, he nodded again.

"Bobby died of an overdose." **After he kidnapped my daughter and sold her for drug money.**

"It was a difficult time," she continued. "I was clueless at first, not aware of his addiction until…much later."

"Perhaps it's a good thing you didn't

have children together."

She felt her insides collapse. This one would require a **black** lie.

She sighed. Or she **could** just tell him the truth, something along the lines of, **"Speaking of children, I should have said this earlier, but we did have a daughter...."**

"Jack..."

## Chapter 25

"Will you have time to meet Nattie?" Jack interrupted. His eyes practically sparkled with anticipation.

Kelly paused, trying not to seem too eager. "She'd be in bed, wouldn't she?"

Jack checked his watch. "She'll be waiting up, I'm pretty sure, but even if she's in bed, she won't be asleep." He smiled knowingly. "Trust me. Nattie and sleep don't mix."

"I remember those years."

Jack gave her an apologetic look. "I interrupted you. You were going to say something about...children?"

She shrugged as if she'd forgotten, and Jack apologized for causing her to lose her train of thought, but she hadn't, not really. The prospect of meeting Nattie had completely derailed her objective.

"Didn't you say you were once a magician's assistant?"

They heard an eruption of laughter from a large table across the room, a party of a dozen or so. By now, their entrées had been delivered, and Kelly quickly took a second bite of the salmon, trying to buy herself a little time before answering.

She swallowed, reluctant to deepen her deceit but not sure how to dig herself out. Fortunately, their waiter passed by, inquiring about their dining state of affairs, and Jack murmured their satisfaction. He turned back to her. "Well...Nattie loves magic."

"Magic brings out the kid in all of us," Kelly said with a bright smile, spooning up the rice pilaf.

**If I tell him the truth now**, she reminded herself, **I might never** meet **Nattie**.

It was a feeble excuse, but lately she'd been doing a lot of rationalizing. **Stick to the plan.**

After dinner, Jack ordered one raspberry cheesecake, two spoons, and an extra plate. A king-sized wedge of cheesecake, with a dollop of whipped cream and raspberries on top, sat in a chocolate sunburst that swirled about the plate. The presentation alone was exquisite. Kelly took a tiny bite, reluctant to ruin the artwork.

"Someday," Jack said, "I'll take you to Nattie's favorite dessert place."

Slicing off a piece from her side, she didn't miss the implication of future dates. Was he just being polite? And if so, did it matter, anyway? Whatever they were doing, whatever they were beginning, this whole dating thing wasn't sustainable.

She forced herself to meet his eyes and saw only kindness, and she had to look away. She felt dreadful. And if she hadn't believed it before, she believed it now—he was clearly taken with her. And she, in the name of her so-called righteous cause, was about to break his heart. **If so**, she thought, **the sooner the better.**

She reached in her purse, looking for a Kleenex.

"Everything okay?"

**No**, she thought. Removing a tissue, she dabbed at her eyes carefully, wondering if she'd smudged her eyeliner. She forced a smile, sneaking a quick look in her mirrored compact.

Jack was staring at her, worried.

It was the extensive lying that was starting to take its toll. She was accustomed to telling lies for a few minutes at a time, anything to find her daughter, but lying for hours?

**I have to tell him**, roared back at her. **Now. While we're in a public place.** She could turn it around, make it a joke. **We have more in common than you might think.**

But it struck her, as if for the first time... what if Nattie wasn't Emily? What then? Then something could happen here, something real for the first time in a very long time.

**I could date a nice guy for once** came the strangest thought.

They heard the tinkling of glass from the table across the aisle, an older couple dressed to the nines. They seemed gloriously happy. They noticed her staring and returned gracious smiles. The older lady, with white pearls and a dark blue gown, her white hair done up in a bun, raised her glass to her husband and winked at Kelly. "Fifty years, honey! It doesn't get better than this!"

Jack turned and wished them congratulations, then turned back to Kelly, his eyes hopeful. After a few more laughs, and a few more anecdotes about Nattie, Jack suggested a stroll around the lake.

Kelly agreed and Jack paid the check and escorted her out the back door, down the walnut steps bordered by luscious-smelling flowers. They broke out into the freshness of the summer evening, imbued with the scent of newly mown grass and the mossy, sulfur smell of the pond. Birds fluttered about the trees, crickets chirped, and there was an early evening peacefulness that contrasted with her anxious heart.

"I've got to stop talking about Nattie," Jack announced, taking her hand.

"Please don't," she said, hoping he

hadn't noticed how her back had shivered the moment his hand touched hers. Although he'd just promised not to, he continued to talk about Nattie incessantly. She found it charming.

Hand in hand, they walked around the entire lake, reaching the beginning point, and by now time was slipping from them. She didn't want to miss the opportunity to meet Nattie. "It's getting late, isn't it?"

Jack agreed and gave her the directions, and she pretended to be informed.

Moments later, she began following Jack's truck through the heart of Wooster. It was in her own car, contemplating the date and the way her hand fit in his, that she realized she'd not only been lying to Jack but lying to herself, as well.

Jack wasn't just a nice guy. She actually liked him. And with that admission, little what-ifs began streaming through her mind again. **Maybe I could love this guy. I could actually give this a chance.**

Up ahead, Jack's brake lights flashed, then his turn signal began blinking. She slowed down as he did, following him around the corner.

This was the perfect setup. Jack was asking her for magic. In a matter of an hour, she could have Nattie's samples, and no one would be the wiser. In a matter of days, she'd have her answers, and she could breathe easier.

But Chet's "royal way" nudged at her again, her promise to him and Eloise. Despite her determination to keep that tidbit confined in her dark little box of things not to think about, it kept leaking out.

Turning into Jack's neighborhood, she parked on the street, and Jack met her at her car. She rolled down her window. "Are you sure this is a good idea?"

Jack's optimism shone in his eyes. "Are you kidding? She's gonna love you, but she'll be shy at first, so don't feel bad if she doesn't warm up to you right away."

Kelly's next words came out without hesitation. "I just realized...I left most of my tricks...at home."

Jack shrugged. "Well, maybe next time."

"But I'd like to meet Nattie. I feel like I

know her." And then she remembered the purse trick in the backseat, the one she'd thrown in **just in case**. "Wait…I do have one magic trick she might like." Twisting in her seat, Kelly reached behind her, grasping her tan leather handbag.

"Wonderful," Jack exclaimed.

She returned his enthusiasm, but it quickly disappeared when Jack followed up with, "She's inside with San. Remember her?"

"Oh…of course," she lied, her throat suddenly in her stomach, nerves hitting a high pitch. And as they headed up the sidewalk, her mind raced for a way to respond when San would most certainly reply, **"I don't remember you, Kelly."**

But nothing came to her. She'd probably stand there and stammer away. **Yep, that's my grand plan**, she thought. **Stammer. And stutter.**

Jack opened the front door and gestured for Kelly to go first, her stomach in knots. She did, and Jack called loudly behind her, "Nattie-bug!"

The home smelled of vanilla and pine,

the inside resembling a grand-scale A-frame, open and sprawling, very contemporary, with hardwood floors, a long open kitchen to the left, the dining room to the right, and the family room up ahead. The wide wooden staircase leading to the second floor was topped by a balcony overlooking the main floor.

To the right, beyond the dining room area, she saw a couple of wooden shelves filled to the brink with board games and an upright piano nestled between.

Jack opened his arms wide as Nattie came bounding down the steps. Poor kid, when she spotted Kelly, couldn't hide her disappointment. Her expression clouded moments before she forced a polite guest face.

Kelly was neither surprised nor disheartened. If Nattie was like any red-blooded young daughter, she didn't want to share her daddy, but it didn't matter. Kelly was good at this part. Kids naturally gravitated to her.

It was San who terrified her, whom she kept expecting to pop out of the woodwork, and as Nattie came running up to Jack, Kelly glanced around. **Where is she?** Out loud, Jack asked the same question, "Where's Auntie San?" and Nattie gestured upstairs.

Feeling a trickle of perspiration, Kelly ignored it and leaned over. "Hi, sweetie."

"Hi" came a soft voice from the wide-eyed child. Adorable haircut, dark brunette, and those eyes. **Beautiful brown eyes.**

Kelly crouched to her level, hoping it didn't seem patronizing, then figured out Nattie was already too tall for this.

"I have something for you," Kelly said, holding the handbag with both hands.

Nattie's curiosity got the best of her. She positioned herself directly in front of Kelly to get a better view.

"It's something your dad said you don't have, but at the same time, it's something he said you have **a lot** of."

Nattie's eyebrows rose even higher, and then she squinted. You could read her expression: **What could it be?**

Slowly, dramatically, Kelly began to open her purse, and then stopped. Nattie took her eyes off the purse and met Kelly's gaze.

"Can you guess?" Kelly asked.

"What do you think it is?" Jack asked, now joining Kelly.

Nattie shook her head, biting her lip.

"Something you already have," her father prompted.

"Well, lookee here," a woman's voice declared.

Kelly glanced up to see San descending the steps, wearing leggings, a long paisley shirt, and black leather sandals.

"Hi," Kelly said, feeling the perspiration increase tenfold.

San wandered over. San, the overbearing sister, who, according to Jack, often said the first thing that came to her.

**This could go downhill fast**, Kelly thought, but then saw something that struck her as hopeful—the unmistakable passing of a warning glance from Jack to San: **Be nice!**

With a moist and clammy hand, Kelly stood and shook San's hand.

"Hi," Kelly said, trying to put an inflection

of **nice to see you again** in her tone of voice, which seemed rather feeble to Kelly, but her options were limited. Better to say as little as possible.

Fortunately, San said nothing, and her handshake was warm and encouraging. When San looked down at Nattie, Kelly stooped again.

"Magic trick," Jack said for San's benefit, nodding toward Nattie, who was still puzzling over the contents of Kelly's purse.

Nattie looked up at Jack. "Do **you** know?"

"I have no idea." Jack looked at Kelly. "I didn't realize Kelly was paying such close attention."

Kelly smiled mischievously. "I miss nothing." She extended the purse to Nattie. "Do you want to look through the purse and see if you can find it?"

Natalie seemed bewildered and looked up at Jack, her eyes questioning.

Jack nodded. "Go ahead."

San was in the kitchen now, wiping the counters, watching them intently, her expression engaged, as if enjoying the mystery.

Nattie took the purse and slowly wiggled the clasp, then pried the purse open, peering inside. She frowned, meeting Kelly's eyes again, holding it open for Kelly to see. "It's empty."

"What? That can't be." Kelly took the purse from Nattie and peered in. "Oh, you didn't look in the corner. Look closer."

Nattie grabbed the purse and looked inside, and again, her look of anticipation melted into frustration. Looking up, she met Kelly's gaze, then turned the purse upside down and shook it. Nothing came out.

Once more, Kelly pretended to be confused. "Now wait a minute. Let me see it one last time."

A small smile erupted in the corner of her mouth as Nattie extended the purse. Kelly reached in, wiggling about with dramatic effort, her expression confused at first, then turning smug, and finally without further machinations, pulled out a mini penguin and handed it to Nattie.

Natalie's expression did a one-eighty.

"How did you do that?" Staring at it closely, she exclaimed, "Hey, I don't have that one!" She squished the penguin to her cheek. "How did you know?"

Kelly smiled, threw up her hands, and made a face as if to say, **"I have no idea."**

"So **cool**," Natalie giggled, running into the kitchen to give her aunt a closer look before running back again to offer the stuffed animal back to Kelly. "Do it again!"

Kelly put the penguin into the purse and did it again.

"Are you a magician?" Nattie asked.

"You've seen the movie **Beauty and the Beast**, right?"

Nattie nodded.

"Do you remember the part where Beast turns into the handsome prince?"

"I love that part."

"I was ten when I saw that movie."

"I'm nine," Nattie announced.

Kelly widened her eyes. "Really? I figured you were closer to eleven."

Nattie beamed. Kelly expounded upon the magic scene, and how it had made her feel, and how she wished she could do the same kind of stuff. Some of it was true, but most of it was a fabrication designed to create a rapport, and from the looks of Natalie's enthusiastic response, it was working.

"Can you do other stuff?"

"Lots," Kelly replied. "I'll show you sometime."

**"Cool!"**

In a matter of minutes, Nattie was putty in her hands. But it was out by her car, after Jack had walked her out, that she realized she might have dodged the San bullet.

And then he kissed her, which took her by surprise, so much so that she barely realized what he had done until it was over. She wanted him to kiss her again, when she was actually paying attention, but he suddenly seemed shy.

Kelly put her hand on the door latch. It was cold to the touch, but Jack's warm hand was on her arm, and he was telling her something appreciative, but she was still lost in thought, her head spinning. And not just with the kiss, but with Nattie.

What a sweetheart!

**I should have tested her.** It would have been so easy: lollipop in, lollipop out—**presto!** But she hadn't, and yet she still hadn't been able to turn off the act, the manipulative strategies she employed to get children to warm up to her.

"I knew Nattie would like you," Jack said as she got into her car. He pushed the door shut, and she rolled down the window.

They said good-bye for another five minutes, and before long Kelly was driving down the street, heading for home.

A lone tear ran down her cheek, and she wiped it away, worried that "normal" was lost to her, wondering if she'd forgotten how to let relationships evolve naturally without employing manipulative strategies and techniques.

She did a quick calculation. In the past two years alone, she'd probably interacted with about fifty children, any one of whom could have turned out to be Emily. Fifty didn't seem like a lot, but for each one, she'd prepared meticulously.

Somewhere along the line, in the process of tricking little children, she'd tricked herself.

**How do I get it back?** she thought, wondering again why she'd decided not to get Natalie's sample. **It was in the bag.**

Another three miles down the road, it came to her. A simple answer, yet mystifying: She was genuinely fascinated with Jack, and not just Jack, but Jack and Natalie together, as a family. They had something special. They were connected to each other by something greater than mere DNA. Jack had told her story after story of their lives as a family, something that couldn't be revealed by a test, or granted by a court decree. It was forged by the caring and sharing of life experiences.

She smiled. Sharing of kisses, too. The kiss, the best promise of a possible life together, got to the heart of the matter. And she'd practically missed it, but what she remembered of it was **good**.

Her entire world had tilted in the simple act of Jack's lips pressing against hers.

Kelly took a breath, lost in the strange fantasy brewing within her, and a new hope—one she'd never even allowed herself to imagine. And it was perfect.

Because it occurred to her that, even if, or when, she finally found Emily, she still might not find what she'd been looking for. In fact, it was quite likely that what she'd been searching for, what she'd given up eight years of her life to find, was lost to her forever.

**I want this**, she realized. **A real family.**

# Chapter 26

I told you. I have no idea who that woman is," San replied, standing behind the island, removing the dishes from the dishwasher, drying them carefully, putting them into the cupboard above the oven.

Jack leaned on the counter, puzzled.

"I have a knack for faces, Jack, but I've never seen her, definitely not at church."

Jack heard scampering upstairs. Nattie had disappeared to put on her jammies and was probably desperate to get back down for fear she might miss something.

**So where did Kelly come from?** he mused, thinking back to that first day at the office. San removed her purse from the stool. "You're overthinking this. You met a nice girl at the airport who happened to hear Mick use Nattie's nickname." She tapped her temple. "She's probably like me, with a steel trap for names."

Jack nodded absently.

"What? You think she's a kidnapper or something?"

"No, of course not," Jack replied. "Wait... you actually liked her?"

"She's fantastic," San said, grabbing her clutch from the counter.

She snapped it open, removed her keys, snapped it shut again. "I wish I could take credit." She took a deep breath and let it out slowly, their lingering disagreement still in the air. Normally San would have leaned over and pecked Jack on the cheek, but not tonight.

After San had left, Nattie and Jack huddled in front of **Brave**, sharing a blanket. Clumsily, Nattie grabbed a handful of popcorn, spilling more on Jack than in her mouth, giggling at a story line that held zero surprises.

"Are you still mad at me?" he asked.

She shrugged. "I wasn't mad at you. I was sad at you."

"Okay," Jack answered, and a few

minutes passed.

"She's really pretty, Dad."

"Pretty what?"

Nattie gave him a look. "Puh-lease."

"You like her?"

She shrugged and pulled up the blanket to her chin, scrunching into Jack like the cuddle-bug she was. "I already miss Laura."

So did Jack, but he was growing extremely fond of Kelly. And yet, he had to admit, she seemed even more secretive than he had originally thought, whether in a good way or a bad way, he couldn't tell. **Mysterious.** Calculating in what she revealed. Choosing her words carefully, when carefully chosen words didn't seem necessary.

San would have said, **"All women are unfathomable, Jack. We're mysterious by design. Get over it! Enjoy it!"**

He also had to admit, kissing her was the highlight of the year, the taste of her like honey, her lips soft. And her scent—spicy flowers and sea breezes. But he had to admit, to his chagrin, she'd seemed rather distracted at the time.

"Watch the movie, Dad."

"I am."

"No you're not. You're thinking about stuff."

"Sorry."

The next day, Sunday morning, after texting Kelly and finding her up early, Jack called. Kelly greeted him enthusiastically, commenting on how she'd just been thinking about him, and they had a post-date kind of conversation.

"And I **loved** getting to meet Nattie," she added, commenting on how delightful his daughter was and how she hoped to get to know her better. After Jack hung up, he realized he should have requested another date. But something was nagging at him again. Was the connection to San really that important...or was it something else?

He and Nattie attended their own church, after which they took a drive, both lost in their own worlds—Nattie surely thinking of Laura, while he tried to get a grip on his conflicted feelings for Kelly.

On Monday, normally a slow day at the office, Jack decided to leave things to Mick. Nattie slept in till nine, and when she finally got to the kitchen, there were scrambled eggs waiting for her, plus two Pop-Tarts, one blueberry, the other chocolate fudge.

"**Chocolate fudge?**" She whistled. "I've been living right!"

Laura would have given him the look. "**Two Pop-Tarts?**"

After lunch, Jack mowed the lawn and cleared the rain gutters, in case the weather hit the skids like the weatherman had predicted. He also fixed the front-door lock as Nattie made tea for her dolls and served it on the front step. Jack joined her when he was done, and Nattie reminded him that the last tea party she'd thrown, both he **and** Laura had attended.

"We had cupcakes," she added, and just as the clouds finally rolled in, Nattie pushed the tiny table away and made a face. "Can't you try again?"

"I've practically begged Laura not to go."

Nattie looked horrified. "You mean you haven't **actually** begged?"

Sitting on the cement slab, watching the storm clouds grow darker and darker, he enfolded her into his arms, and she leaned hard against him.

"Are you going to ask Kelly to go with you?"

"Go where?"

"Stop," she said, playfully slapping his arm.

"Besides, grown-ups don't do that."

"What do you do?"

Jack shrugged. "After you've spent enough time with someone, it's just assumed you're together."

Nattie leaned her chin into her hands and stared straight ahead. He could imagine what she was thinking, that Laura left because of Kelly. So if Kelly wasn't in the picture, wouldn't Laura come back?

"Whatever happens, we'll get through this," Jack said. "You 'n' me, kiddo. Together, we're golden." He winced at how glib he sounded and added, "I miss her, too, honey."

Nattie wiped her eyes on Jack's shirt. "At least I get to see her on the weekends."

**Like child custody**, he thought, hoping Nattie's association with Laura would continue far, far into the future.

When Laura showed up on Tuesday she was fighting a cold or something, but despite her sickness, she buzzed around the house like the old days, and it broke his heart. So far, Jack hadn't even attempted to find a part-time house-keeper, still hoping against hope that she'd change her mind.

**Miracles happen**, he tried to tell himself.

And he still hadn't asked Kelly for another date.

Yesterday, San had texted him: **When do you need me next?**

**I don't know**, he'd texted back.

**Oh for Pete's sake! What kind of knuckle-dragger are you? Don't let this one go, Jack. I have a good feeling about her.**

She had a point. What **was** keeping him?

On Wednesday, he mustered up some courage and dialed Kelly's number, and as he listened to the rings, he was more nervous than he'd expected. When she answered, she seemed surprised to hear from him, as if they hadn't been keeping in touch all along.

In fact, they'd been texting throughout the day ever since their first date, and her texts were always bright, cheery, and encouraging. But the more they talked, the more nervous he became, putting off the inevitable question until nearly thirty minutes had passed, and he began saying things that would terminate their conversation.

He was about to hang up, feeling absolutely bewildered at his own feelings, when Kelly whispered softly, sounding lost, "Aren't you going to ask me out again, Jack?"

He felt a release in his stomach. Her question struck him as surprisingly vulnerable for someone as confident as Kelly seemed to be, but he liked feeling pulled into her life, into her heart. In a single moment, it was as if her secrecy had melted away, and wasn't that what had been bothering him?

He could imagine San, sitting on his shoulder with her trident and red tail, rolling her eyes: **"Men and their ridiculous egos!"**

He immediately suggested another date: Friday night.

"I feel...stupid," she said instead. "I shouldn't have pushed. We don't have to—"

"But I **want** to."

She sighed into the phone.

"Kelly?"

"What I'd really like to do is cook you dinner," she said. "You and Nattie, but my place isn't nearly as nice as yours. I just moved in, and I haven't had a chance—"

"I'd rather cook **you** dinner," Jack insisted.

Another hesitation. "Are you sure?" She sounded worried. "I mean...are you sure you want to pursue this? I'd like to, but I feel as if I'm guilting you into it. You really know nothing about me. I have a sordid past, Jack."

Jack laughed. "I doubt that—"

"I'm not very good at this dating stuff, either. It's been so long."

"Me either. Let's just see where it leads."

They talked for another half hour, cautiously sharing their uncertainty about romance and love, and reaching a kind of heartfelt honesty he'd never imagined was possible with another human being.

When he hung up, his nagging sense of concern had dissipated. **I'm falling**, he thought, and it felt wonderful.

That Friday, Nattie and Jack worked for nearly an hour, preparing their standard date fare: spaghetti and meatballs. Together they got the water boiling for the noodles, mixed the sauce using Laura's recipe, grated the cheese, and prepared the salad for tossing—Nattie's job.

Kelly arrived just after five o'clock, wearing a pair of jeans and a white blouse and carrying a package wrapped in colorful polka-dot paper. Jack met her at the door. "Welcome again to our humble abode!"

He kissed her on her cheek, and she brushed his arm.

Nattie came up behind him. "Do you have any other tricks?"

"Nattie, she just got here," Jack reprimanded, tousling her hair. Kelly extended the package. "Will this do?"

Nattie took it, her head barely containing her eyes. "That'll do just fine!" She was heading for the dining room table when Jack cleared his throat. Nattie caught the hint. "Oh yeah, thank you. Thank you!"

"And…you can open it later, young lady."

From the look on Nattie's face, you would have thought Jack had asked her to sample a green bean.

"What?"

"You heard me."

"Oh **ma-an**," Nattie whined, scampering away to her room, carrying the package like it was a treasured doll.

Jack turned to Kelly. "Bribery will get you everywhere with that girl. I think 'getting' is her love language."

"All girls love gifts," Kelly replied, smiling.

Jack led her to the family room, adding, "She's not as shy as you thought, is she?"

Kelly laughed, and then her expression turned pensive. "Thank you for inviting me, Jack."

She was about to sit on his sofa when Jack reached for her hand. "I never gave you the tour. It'll take all of fifteen seconds."

"I'd love a tour." Kelly squeezed his hand and followed him upstairs to Nattie's room. The door was already closed.

He knocked softly, and Nattie barked from within, "Hark! Who goes there!"

Jack grinned back at Kelly. "She has this ridiculous notion of privacy."

Kelly laughed. "Like she thinks this is **her** room."

Nattie opened the door and curtsied, gesturing forward. "Welcome to my palace."

"Thank you for allowing us entrance, m'lady," Kelly replied.

Nattie giggled, and she grabbed Kelly's hand. "Please come, your royal highness, I want to show you something!" she said, thrilled to engage her own British accent.

The official tour became an extended journey into Nattie's world, but Jack was pleased. Things couldn't have gone better if he'd tried engineering them, and he was fascinated with how easily Kelly interacted with Nattie.

Minutes later, he excused himself to check the stove, where the sauce was simmering. Eventually, Kelly and Nattie came down, Nattie's mouth running on automatic, carrying her Pop-Tarts Favorites list.

"I was just showing Kelly all twenty-nine flavors, in order of the best to the worst."

"My, my, and she's still awake."

"Don't start, Dad," Nattie said, helping set the table while Kelly offered to assist.

"We got this," Nattie said. "You relax."

At one point, Nattie moseyed up to Kelly. "By the way, do you eat tomatoes?"

"Cooked in spaghetti sauce? Absolutely," Kelly said, then wrinkled her nose. "But raw? Only if someone threatens me with utter and complete destruction."

Nattie pumped her right fist. "Yes!"

Carrying the sauce to the table, Jack

caught her eye. "You have no idea what kind of bond you just created."

Kelly made a **what can you say?** gesture with her hands.

Once everything had been transported to the dining room, Nattie and Jack stood back from the table, surveying their display. "Perfect," Nattie announced.

Kelly took the same place as Jack's other dates, to his left, with Nattie to his right, across from Kelly, and dinner progressed without much assistance from him. Nattie and Kelly carried on as if they were long-lost friends.

But there were times during the meal when he would catch Kelly looking at him, and she'd actually twinkle. It was unsettling how little control he had over his feelings.

"Do you like salad?" Nattie asked Kelly.

"I do," Kelly said between bites, "but only if drenched in ranch dressing."

"That's what I'm talking about!" Nattie exclaimed, and then took a deep breath, forming her next question.

**Oh boy**, Jack thought. **Here comes the big test.**

Nattie's tone was hushed and momentous. "Also…what do you think of green beans?"

Kelly dropped her fork. "Seriously? Why do they even **grow** those things!"

"I **know**!"

Jack had to chuckle. Green beans and tomatoes. What was next? Dessert didn't go badly, either. Nattie led the charge. "We have peach pie, ice cream, or…"

"You pick," Kelly said. "I have a feeling I'll like whatever you like."

Nattie looked as pleased as punch. She picked the pie, and Kelly reveled in it. Afterward, Nattie told Kelly, "Sit tight while Dad and I clean up."

In the kitchen, however, once the table had been cleared off, Nattie pushed Jack back into the dining room. "I got this. Don't let her get lonely," Nattie warned. "She might wander off or something."

Later, they gathered in the family room. Nattie finally opened her gift from Kelly, an anniversary edition DVD of **Babe**, and Nattie squealed with delight. "I don't have this one!"

But when Kelly asked to see one of their famous photo albums, Nattie declined. "Sit and talk to my dad," she said. "I'll leave you two alone." She scampered upstairs to play.

Kelly laughed. "Does she always play matchmaker?"

"Only with people she really likes," Jack replied.

Kelly bit her lip. "I like her, too."

At the end of the evening, Jack escorted Kelly out to her car.

Lingering for a moment, he kissed her for the second time in their lives, and this time she paid attention.

"I could get used to this," Kelly whispered dreamily.

He kissed her again, and she said good-bye.

The evening had been a resounding success. Kelly and Nattie had gotten along famously, and yet after Kelly had left, and during the tuck-in, Nattie seemed strangely subdued.

"Did you have a good time?" Jack asked her, pulling the covers up to her chin.

She shrugged.

"It seemed like you did."

Another shrug, more regretful.

"Did something go wrong?"

Nattie made a face and shook her head. "I wish it had."

Jack considered this. "You'll see Laura tomorrow."

"Can I tell her about Kelly?"

"It might be too soon."

Nattie nodded. "Yeah."

"And..." he began, gingerly. "We don't know for sure if Kelly is going to stick around."

Nattie's expression dimmed. "Are you kidding me?"

"I mean...I hope she does, but she might decide she doesn't like me as much as she thought, or hoped...or..."

Nattie looked at him skeptically. "I see how she looks at you."

"You do, eh?"

"It's in the bag, Daddykins."

"Daddy**kins**?"

"That's new," she informed him. "I can't exactly say Dad-a-Lantern, you know. Or

Dad in the Beanstalk. I have to think up new stuff."

"I'm sure Auntie San will help."

After praying, mostly about Laura and a little about Kelly, Jack kissed Nattie good-night and traded stuffed animals, acquiring Nattie's gray monkey with the long, skinny striped limbs.

Jack shut out the lights. In the master bath, he was brushing his teeth when the phone rang. It was Kelly.

"I forgot something," she said apologetically.

Jack was already heading downstairs to find whatever it was that Kelly had left behind, thinking **purse...keys...earrings...** when she clarified. "Nattie asked me to take her to the park next Wednesday."

"I'm taking the day off, actually—I have to since I'm working tomorrow—and I happened to mention this to Nattie—"

"And she invited you down," Jack finished.

Kelly chuckled sweetly. "Is she still up? I'll just let her know that it's too soon, you know, to nudge myself into your lives. I shouldn't have said yes, but she caught me by surprise."

"Can't you make it?"

Kelly hesitated. "Well sure, but—"

"Then no problem."

"But still..."

"We could grab fast food afterward," Jack offered.

Kelly went silent.

"Kelly, I think things are going well between us."

"Yes, I think so, too."

"Then, if you want to take Nattie to the park, it's fine with me. Just the two of you."

Kelly paused again. "I guess I'm nervous."

"Why?"

"Because she's the most important person in your life, Jack. And I don't want to blow it."

Jack sat down on the couch, and she sighed. "I was just thinking maybe things went too well tonight."

"Nattie won't raise the bar," he replied, "if that's what you're worried about."

"Maybe I am."

Jack opened his mouth to make some kind of promise, give her some kind of assurance, but it didn't seem right. Everything was still too new, too uncertain.

"I know **I'd** like to see you," Jack suggested. "Well, then. That settles it."

# Chapter 27

Nattie sat on the dryer the following Tuesday, thoroughly entertained by her father's confusion as he tried to decipher the detergent requirements for a half load of washing.

"Cold is for colors," she reminded him.

Moments later, the phone rang and Laura called in sick with the flu. She must have felt pretty bad, as Jack couldn't remember the last time she'd canceled for illness. The small farewell cake, decorated with a photographic image of the three of them in the booth at the Mexican restaurant, taken by San on Jack's birthday, would have to languish in the freezer until Laura was well.

"We **could** deliver it to her," Jack offered.

Glumly, Nattie shrugged. She trudged

to the kitchen, poured milk on her cereal, propped her elbows on the counter, and hovered over the bowl, dejected.

Jack came up behind her and kissed her cheek. She sniffed softly; then the dam burst. Jack hugged her, and a few minutes later, when Jack reminded her Kelly was coming tomorrow, she stopped crying. She stared up at Jack through damp eyes. "Does she swim?"

Jack figured she probably did. Nattie asked him if he had to fly today, a not-so-subtle **"Please stay home with me,"** and he offered to skip the morning. While Nattie went upstairs to wash up, Jack called in, much to Mick's glee. "Fair disclosure: We gotta couple of live ones."

"They're yours," Jack said before hanging up. **I'm missing way too much work**, he thought. **But hey, I own the place.**

They went swimming at the local neighborhood club, and Nattie's mood improved dramatically. They dove for coins, had underwater breath-holding contests, and when a couple of Nattie's friends arrived, they played Marco Polo and Keep Away with an orange ball.

Finally exhausted, Jack lazed out on a lawn chair in his old good-enough swim trunks and sunglasses, slathering on sun block and watching them play, now and then admiring the hazy rainbow that appeared whenever someone dived into the pool.

Nattie, of course, knew the best way to get his attention: "Hey, Dad, watch this!" Because in his experience, nothing good happened after **"Watch this!"**

The next day, after dropping Nattie off next door with Livy and Diane, Jack headed to the airfield, if only to check in. Diane was tickled to spend a little time with her "two favorite girls," and Jack could tell Livy was excited to prove herself a capable sitter.

"Wow, aren't you getting tan!" Livy chimed, holding out her own sun-browned arm for comparison.

A little after three o'clock, Jack was confirming the latest FAA compliance issue for his 182 with Neil, his mechanic, when Nattie buzzed him. Kelly had arrived.

"We're going to the park now!"

He could hear Kelly in the background. "Hello, Jack." Nattie giggled. "When are you coming by?"

"A little later, munchkin."

"Not too soon, okay? We have some serious girl talk to do." Jack chuckled. "Don't scare her away."

"We'll probably talk about you."

"Just wonderful."

Nattie grabbed Kelly's hand as if they'd been walking to the park for years, and she jabbered away, telling Kelly about her friends, her favorite movies, and her favorite music, all of which, she informed Kelly, were catalogued on meticulous lists safely stacked in her bottom drawer.

As they walked, Nattie pointed out each neighbor's house, providing a tiny tidbit about each one, such as Mrs. Guilfoyle, "who is twice my dad's age and still mows her own lawn with a push mower, which is a lot harder than a gas mower, according to Dad."

In turn, Kelly asked her questions about school, and Nattie responded by telling Kelly about her dad's dinner date with Karen Jones. "It didn't go too well."

"By the way my real name's Natalie," she continued. "But when I was a kid I couldn't pronounce it, so Nattie stuck."

Kelly had to smile. **When I was a kid.**

"Do you like Nattie better than Natalie?"

Nattie shrugged. "I like 'em both. But Laura prefers Natalie."

Eventually, Nattie divulged a few family secrets. "My dad isn't very good at dating." She lowered her voice conspiratorially. "He only started because he thought I needed a mother." She grimaced. "He doesn't know I know that, so I probably shouldn't have said anything."

Kelly touched Nattie's hair. "It'll be our secret. Okay?"

"Okay," Nattie agreed. "My dad says I talk too much. I think he's right."

"Talking's fun, though."

When they reached the playground, Kelly offered to swing with Nattie, but Nattie seemed pensive at first.

"What, honey?"

"I was just thinking about Laura again."

Kelly took her hand and motioned to the bench. "I heard she's really special to you. I'd love to hear more about her, if you have time."

Nattie shook her head. "I think we'd better play first."

"Okay, then that's what we'll do."

"Wanna see who can get the highest?" Nattie asked, pulling Kelly over to the swings without waiting for an answer. Before long, they were both pumping their legs furiously, hair flying behind them, laughter filling the park. "I'm nine, but I still **love** swinging!" Nattie shouted to the sky.

Things played out naturally after that, with Nattie showing Kelly the ropes around "the biggest playground in the world," which it certainly seemed to be. Kelly had never seen such an extravaganza of playground delights, and when a couple of Nattie's friends showed up, Nattie politely scampered off, but not without checking with Kelly first to make sure she wasn't lonely.

Kelly assured her otherwise and continued to watch from the bench, as Nattie flickered from one place to the next. Kelly felt her heartstrings drawn tighter and tighter. No wonder Jack loved this girl. At such a young age, Nattie had an unusual regard for others' feelings.

Kelly had a love-hate relationship with parks. Over the years, she'd gone to stare at the children, noting the ones who would now be Emily's age, and imagine she was watching her child play.

Some people used to tell her, in effect, to get over it. **"Just trust God that she's safe and move on. Meet another nice man, have another child! Time to heal, Kelly!"**

But she couldn't, of course, and today, this park, watching Nattie, made Kelly wistful. **This could have been my life**, she thought. **This is what I've missed out on.**

**Not anymore**, she thought. **I'm here now.**

But what if Nattie wasn't hers? The next thought surprised her. **It doesn't matter.**

And yet the question nagged at her like a festering thorn in her finger. **I can put this all to rest**, she thought. **One little test.**

She fidgeted nervously at the bench, suddenly feeling uneasy, if not a little nauseous. **But then where will we be?**

**"Dad thought I needed a mother,"** Nattie had just told her.

Kelly smiled wryly, uncertain Jack would see her entrance as a brilliant answer to prayer. She was still lost in her world of wistful what-ifs when Nattie came running over with a friend. They pulled up in front of Kelly and stood there like statues, grinning. "This is Katelyn. She's my best friend."

Katelyn was also a brunette, wearing an adorable denim outfit and sequined sneakers.

Nattie leaned close and whispered in Kelly's ear. "Do you have any magic tricks?"

Kelly nodded. Nattie stepped back and crossed her arms dramatically. The two girls looked at Kelly as if she could hang the moon. "I have a couple, in fact."

Katelyn's eyes lit up.

"Told you," Nattie replied, elbowing Katelyn.

Kelly dug in her bag, her heart thumping wildly, and removed the magical lollipop.

Nattie's eyes widened. "That's a new one."

**This is different**, Kelly told herself. **Nattie's not a stranger anymore.**

She unwrapped the lollipop, and Nattie popped it into her mouth while Katelyn observed. The trick went off without a hitch.

An hour later, Jack stopped by and saw the two of them, Nattie and Kelly, digging in the sandbox. Nattie squealed when she spotted him and went running over. "Guess what? Guess what?"

She sprang into his arms. "Kelly has a scar just like me!"

"Amazing," Jack replied, grinning at Kelly, who was holding a plastic shovel, digging between her splayed legs, her jeans covered in moist sand.

"We're digging to China," Nattie exclaimed,

giggling at the notion, although a couple years earlier she might not have found it so humorous.

"Whoa," Jack exclaimed. "Then I'd better come back later. You're gonna need another hour. At least."

Nattie pulled on his shirt. "But we're hungry, too. China can wait."

Kelly wiped her dirty forehead, though little good it did. "I second that notion. Can't dig to China without nourishment."

Jack knelt beside her and brushed her forehead free of offending particles while Kelly smiled up at him.

"Am I decent now?" She laughed.

The three climbed into Billy Bob with Nattie in the middle and Kelly on the outside in Laura's old spot. Along the way to the nearest burger establishment, Nattie updated Jack on their activities and close calls.

"And Kelly did a trick for Katelyn!"

"Really?"

"A **new** trick."

"Well, Kelly will have to show me that later."

Kelly grinned at Nattie, putting her arm around her and pulling her close. Nattie beamed.

They chortled their way to downtown, changing their mind halfway, discarding the fast-food idea in favor of a locally owned, retro-fifties café, its floors covered with black-and-white-checkered tiles, the walls filled with posters of Elvis and James Dean and President Eisenhower.

Once there, Nattie led the way while Jack held the door for Kelly. Nattie found a red booth along the front windows, and then she and Kelly slipped into the ladies' restroom to make themselves presentable.

When they came out, Nattie bit her lip expectantly. "Can I sit with Kelly?"

Jack pretended to be disturbed. "Where am I going to sit?"

"Over there," Nattie said, pointing to the other side and sliding in next to Kelly. "Girls stick together."

They ordered burgers and shared more park stories, and Nattie recounted every moment of her "splendicious" time with Kelly.

"So tell me about that magic trick," Jack asked.

Kelly leaned forward. "I've got a better idea."

Nattie squealed. "**Another** one?"

Kelly nodded, pulling out a deck of cards from her purse.

"Cool!" Nattie exclaimed, and for the next few minutes Kelly entertained them with one card trick after another, pausing after each one to let them figure it out. They rarely could.

Time flew quickly. Later, at the truck, Kelly kissed the top of Nattie's head and winked at Jack, and in turn, Nattie hugged Kelly tightly, burying her face into Kelly's blouse. When Kelly climbed in, Nattie cuddled close to her while Jack drove them back to the house, where Kelly's car was parked.

Kelly got out, and Nattie followed her to the car. "When are you coming back?" Nattie asked.

Kelly pressed Nattie's face in her hands, smiling brightly with reassurance, rubbing Nattie's nose with her own. "Very soon."

"Promise?"

Jack touched Nattie's back. "Can we get a moment of privacy, please?"

Grudgingly, Nattie agreed and headed up the sidewalk to the house.

Jack folded his arms awkwardly. "We have a tradition in the Livingston household..."

Kelly looked at him with anticipation as Jack described their usual Friday nights, which included a movie and popcorn, junk food, and late hours. "Of course, dinner is first."

"Wow, you're going to spoil me."

Jack considered giving Kelly a kiss until he heard the clearing of a preteen voice. "We're in public, Dad. The neighbors are looking."

Kelly laughed, putting her hands on his chest as if to forestall any further attempt. He let her go unkissed but with intentions for many attempts to follow.

From the front stoop, he and Nattie hugged each other and watched Kelly drive down the block, welcoming her into their lives.

# Chapter 28

Kelly awakened to the scent of eucalyptus, and for a moment it was as if she hadn't moved. She heard a furry sound, followed by a soft **meow**, and looked over her bed. Sleepy-eyed Felix was looking up at her. **"Hey, boss lady, I'm hungry. How 'bout you?"**

Wearing her oversized T-shirt, Kelly pulled back the covers and stumbled to the bathroom, took a peek at the mirror, her hair scattered in every direction, and winced.

When she returned, Felix was in the middle of the room, cleaning his paw, his green eyes narrowed to lazy slits.

She sat at the bedside again, and Felix made a beeline for her legs, practically diving into her ankle, dropping to his side, and pawing at the carpet.

The morning sun twinkled off the brass handles of her distressed white dresser. And the answer to her question, the answer she'd been seeking for years, now lay in a plastic bag on top—the sucker-disguised swab she'd used on Nattie at the park. Kelly picked up the bag and stared at it, then sat back on the bed. She turned the plastic bag over, the sucker sliding about, and tears formed in her eyes. Getting to know Nattie had severely complicated things.

She wasn't just a prospect. She was a darling girl. Kelly hugged herself in the stillness of a bright morning. **Are you my daughter?** More than anything, she wanted the answer to be yes. In fact, she was **way** overinvested in the answer.

Already she'd vacillated, changing her mind a dozen times. She could throw the sample away, or she could send it in. Here it was, three days later, and she still hadn't made up her mind.

Her cell phone chirped. She picked it up and read the text from Melody. **You're**

**gone tonight, right?**

She texted back: **Meeting Jack again. Sorry!**

Melody: **Yikes. Does he know yet?**

Kelly: **Sigh**

Melody: **I'm here for you.**

Kelly drove the familiar route and met Jack at a little French eatery called Chantal. Kelly noted that the café was the perfect combination of upscale and homey—white tablecloths and votive candles, fresh flowers, and not too exotic for small-town Wooster. He met her at the door dressed in new jeans and a blue-striped button-down shirt, in keeping with the recent cool weather.

"Well, my day has certainly picked up."

She patted his chest playfully. "You say the nicest things."

The hostess led them to a window table, and after placing their orders, they fell into comfortable conversation. Jack talked about his work and about Nattie, of course, and she waxed on about her own work.

In the spotlight of Jack's enamored

focus, it was becoming easier for Kelly to compartmentalize, to conduct herself without feeling as if she were lying about nearly everything she talked about. And really, she wasn't. She was merely keeping the **Emily** part of her life cordoned off— simply withholding the truth about how, and why, they'd met.

Sure, she'd suspected Nattie was hers, and yes, she'd tested Nattie, just in case, but she'd all but decided not to submit it to the lab, because knowing the truth would change everything for her…and for them.

What mattered most was that she'd been invited into their family and wel- comed with the full red-carpet treatment. Nattie regarded her as if she were the designated future mommy. And so did Jack, for that matter.

**I'll tell him the truth when the time is right**, Kelly thought, and she meant it, though there was always the chance that she was overestimating his willingness to forgive. **"Why didn't you tell me before?"** he would joke, but then he'd enfold her into his arms. **"This is even better than I could have imagined! I've been dating Nattie's birth mother!"**

She sighed at her hoped-for scenario. Truth was, it was a big risk, telling Jack.

**Don't think about that now**, she told herself, dipping the crusty bread into her bisque and smiling over at Jack.

After dinner, Kelly followed Jack home. Nattie came running across the yard from Diane's. They shared some salted caramel ice cream together before Kelly needed to head back to Akron.

At one point, after Nattie had administered another dose of hot fudge and whipped cream to Kelly's ice cream, Kelly teared up.

Nattie looked stricken. "Are you okay?"

Kelly wiped her eyes. "I'm fine. I'm just… so happy."

Jack pulled her close and kissed her cheek. "So are we, honey. You have no idea."

Kelly swiped another tear off her cheek. **I'm already "honey."**

Nattie kept watching her, as if worried

she might break in two. Kelly gave her an **I'm really okay** smile, but Nattie didn't seem to buy it. Nattie was already hovering like a daughter. **The daughter I was never allowed to raise.**

Later, Nattie walked her to her car and hugged her so tightly she almost lost her breath. When Nattie let go, she looked up at her. "Call us when you get home. My dad worries."

Jack kissed her, and she had to smile because Nattie didn't protest about his public display of affection.

Kelly drove home in dead silence, barely aware of the passing miles, and opened the door to her quiet apartment, the only place she wasn't living a lie.

**I'm so unbelievably, incomprehensibly happy**, she realized, hugging herself on her couch, letting the tears fall again.

**And so miserable.**

In the days that followed, Jack and Kelly continued with their flirtatious texting, their routine nightly calls, lasting minutes to hours, until their relationship became a given.

During one of their phone conversations, Kelly made a reference to what her boss had asked, "So tell me about your boyfriend…"

She explained how she had described Jack's profession and his lovely daughter, but Jack could tell she was actually waiting for him to either confirm or correct her assumption.

He swooped in and did just that. "Boyfriend, eh?"

She went silent.

"I like the sound of that," he added. "Are you my girlfriend?"

"I think three dinner dates equals commitment," Kelly replied.

"We're practically married, you know."

"Yup," Jack said. "I read that somewhere."

"Does that mean I have a standing date for Saturday night?"

"It does," he said.

"Do I have to buy new clothes?"

"Heavens, no," Jack said.

"How does Nattie feel about everything?"

He was about to say, **"She's already**

**asking if she can be the flower girl,"** but decided against it.

Fridays became "family time," hanging out with Nattie at the house, watching movies, most of which, for some inexplicable reason, Kelly hadn't seen. Nattie thrilled to the joy of introducing her personal favorites to Kelly for the first time, and Kelly enjoyed playing Nattie's rating game. In fact, Nattie began placing the DVDs on the shelves in order according to Kelly's favorites, starting with **Finding Nemo**.

Jack's favorites, **Chicken Run** and **Shrek**, didn't even come close to hers, and Nattie made sure they all knew it.

"Poor guy," Kelly whispered back, loudly enough for Jack to hear, winking at him.

Nattie turned and grinned. "You're outnumbered."

"What else is new?"

"It's a girl's world, you know," Nattie added. "You're just living in it."

Jack laughed at the accurate assessment.

On Saturday nights, Jack and Kelly went out for dinner, leaving Nattie with Livy—supervised by Diane, of course. Dinner was usually followed by something relaxing, like miniature golf, walks around various lakes and parks, or a stroll through the College of Wooster Art Museum. They even tried line dancing once, which went well but not well enough to repeat.

"Maybe square dancing," Jack suggested.

"Or ballroom dancing?"

"Hmm," Jack muttered.

Kelly laughed. "Or maybe not!"

Eventually, Kelly even came down for Wednesday night church,which Jack and Nattie had rarely attended but now resumed if only to find another excuse to spend time with Kelly. Jack admitted as much to Kelly, and she only chuckled. "I feel special."

Nattie heard this. "You left **special** in the dust."

One night, sitting alone on the sofa, while Nattie gave them space, Jack mentioned Laura's gardening touches, and with her elbow on the top cushion, Kelly asked casually, "Do you miss her?"

"Nattie does, of course..." Jack began. **And so do I.** "But there haven't been as many tears as I'd expected."

Kelly nodded, her eyes sympathetic. "I can't imagine how Nattie must feel, losing her nanny after so long."

Kelly had no idea of the events that had led to Laura's quitting, and he certainly wasn't going to tell her. Without Kelly in their life, of course, losing Laura would have seemed unbearable.

Kelly's path finally crossed Laura's one day when Laura dropped off Nattie after a visit to the farm, and Kelly happened to show up a little early. Jack heard about it from Kelly and later that night from Nattie.

Apparently Kelly and Laura went overboard to make nice, and according to Nattie, there wasn't anything fakey about it. Laura even led Kelly to the back porch swing while Nattie ran inside to grab some iced tea for everyone.

Nattie said that Kelly asked Laura about her gardening, commenting on what a wonderful job she'd done, and Laura thanked Kelly for her kindness.

Upon hearing Nattie's account, Jack felt strangely conflicted. He still missed Laura, and not just as his nanny, but as someone with whom he'd shared his life. And now, with Laura physically gone, he couldn't help feeling that he'd been going through a weird kind of rebound with Laura's departure. He didn't want to tell Kelly this, of course, but as it turned out, he'd underestimated Kelly's powers of observation.

After dinner one evening, while Nattie was playing upstairs, he asked Kelly how she might have felt if Laura were still working for them. Kelly gave a thoughtful reply. "It would have been fine for me. But…it might have been tricky for Laura."

She touched his arm. "Is that too honest?"

He took this in, absorbing the tender look in her eyes. "Does it bother you?"

Kelly shrugged. "I'm not worried about Laura, if that's what you mean. I don't play the jealous game, Jack. If we are meant to be, we'll be together."

He gave this more thought. She squeezed his hand again with reassurance. "I knew from the beginning that you might have had feelings for her."

Jack winced. But she was right. Forgetting Laura hadn't been easy. By now, he'd even expected his feelings for Laura to have vanished. But they hadn't.

He sighed softly. "So…why did you take a chance on me, Kelly?"

She bit her lip and gave him a humorous smile. "What can I say? I like blue-eyed blonds."

Jack laughed and squeezed her hand. "I don't want to lose you over this."

"You won't."


One hot summer day, Kelly drove down after work, meeting Jack at home. Nattie was gone to a friend's, no doubt commiserating about the upcoming start of school.

Jack met her at the door. "I'm almost finished with something." She followed him into his office and waited, reviewing his aviation wall, marveling again at the signature by Wilbur Wright. She also noticed the picture of Jack with his father, taken in front of an older 172. Jack joined her at the wall.

"You're right," Kelly said, leaning in closer. "San looks like your father."

Jack touched her arm and sighed. "Maybe...but she still reminds me of my mother."

"You two seem close."

Jack shrugged. "I don't know if anyone really gets that close to San."

"How did your father die?" Kelly asked.

"Coroner's report says cardiac arrest. But as far as I'm concerned, he died of a broken heart."

Kelly seemed to consider this. "You have no pictures of your mother?"

"Only one I keep in a drawer." **In the dark**, he thought. Kelly leaned closer to him, slipping her arm around his waist, still staring at the picture of his father.

"Do you have any **good** memories of her, Jack?"

Jack shook his head. "If I do, they're

buried beneath the bad ones."

Kelly went silent.

"I don't hate her," Jack said, as if trying to convince himself. "I just don't want to be reminded of her."

He could tell she was holding her tongue. Actually, most of the time, he probably did despise his mother, although he'd been fighting it for a lifetime. Lately, considering the dustups with San, encountering her razor-sharp tongue, he seemed to be losing the war.

"I'm trying, Kelly. Some days are better than others. That's the hardest part. For the longest time I drowned my anger in the same thing that had made her so hateful. Alcohol."

"She must have been in a lot of pain."

Jack scoffed. "The only pain I remember is the pain she caused my father. As far as I'm concerned, she took my father from me." And then he sighed with embarrassment. "Like I said, I **am** trying."

Kelly hugged him. "I don't think we ever feel like forgiving until we do. I think the feeling comes after the choice. We have to step out in faith. Besides, forgiveness isn't for her, you know. It's for you."

She looked up at him apologetically. "I guess my short marriage taught me a thing or two about the subject. Was that too preachy?"

He shook his head. Coming from San, it would have felt like a lecture. Coming from Kelly, it felt like hope, but he was taken aback. She rarely talked about her husband.

"Someday it'll just click into place," she said. "You're almost there, you know. I mean...that's what I like about you, Jack. You always see the best in everyone."

**Obviously not**, he thought.

"We all want to be remembered for our better moments," she said softly. And then she chuckled. "I know **I** do!"

Jack kissed her cheek, unable to remember a single "better" moment with his mother, much less a good one. "Here's a good thing," he said wryly. "Mom reminds me of what I don't want to be."

They headed out the door to the airfield, and thirty minutes later, they were in the air again—only the second time they'd flown together. This time, Kelly was noticeably less nervous. They flew over the lake they'd walked around after that first dinner date, and Kelly marveled at the sight. "It's sooo tiny!"

"We're two thousand feet above-ground." He laughed. "It **should** look tiny."

He turned to the north and asked her, "Wanna land it again?"

Her eyes widened. "I don't think so, Jack. No. But thanks for asking."

He smiled, continuing their short tour, pointing out further Wooster landmarks. An hour later, he landed the plane, and they headed to the off-ramp. When he pulled up, he set the brake and shut it down. Kelly grabbed his shirt, pulled him closer, and kissed him.

"What was that for?"

"For taking me into the clouds, Jack. In every way."

Jack laughed and kissed her back.

Later, they stopped at the coffee shop and sat at "their booth" for another hour as Kelly described the thrill she felt in the air. He was only remotely aware of the sounds around him, the explosive guffaw of the table of men, the whoosh of the coffee machine, the whine of a small child. He was too busy thinking about the thrill he felt knowing this incredible woman. **What if she'd never come back?** he thought, remembering that first day when he'd told her Nattie's bully story.

He must have been staring at her too intently, because she blushed. Holding her mug, she turned away. "You're cute, Jack."

He took a breath and took a chance. "You and I have something else in common."

Smiling, Kelly waited expectantly.

"We both lost our favorite parent."

Kelly grinned, agreeing. "I look like my mother, but I have my father's temperament."

"Me too," Jack replied. They shared a laugh.

"I was my daddy's girl," Kelly continued. "I think Mom always felt a bit like she was on the outside looking in, not that it bothered her. She was always so busy. Motherhood never really defined her life. She's the type who feels like now that she's done raising her daughter, it's time to move on." Kelly sighed softly, holding her mug. "I love her dearly, and she loves me, but…we're not close. We have so little in common. It's like we struggle to find a reason to talk to each other."

Jack reached for her hand. "You mentioned your husband earlier."

Kelly shrugged, but he could sense a sudden tension.

"Have you forgiven **him**?" Jack asked. It was a leading question, but he was curious about a part of her life she rarely addressed.

"I have," Kelly said simply. "But it took years, you know, so I understand the difficulty you might have."

"But…**how** did you do it?"

She cleared her throat. "I think I finally realized…" She took a breath, pausing, then met his eyes. "He was driven by his addiction and didn't grasp the conse-quences of what he was doing. He was trapped within his own skin."

Jack squeezed her hand, feeling the intensity of the moment, sensing she wanted to talk about this but also guessing the topic was uncomfortable. "What was so difficult to forgive?" Then he shook his head, regretting the question. "No... sorry...that's too personal."

But she was shaking her head. "No, it's not. Not for **us**." Tears welled up. "Jack, there is something I need to tell you...."

He waited, overwhelmed by her emotion. She opened her mouth, and then seemed to reconsider, as if steeling herself from the pain of something she could barely address. "But...I'm not ready."

She seemed to shrink before his eyes, suddenly deflated. Jack tried to encourage her, smiling, and it confirmed his deeper perspective that there was way more to Kelly than met the eye. "Of course. I'm here when you're ready. I can wait."

"I believe you, Jack."

At her car, he reached for the handle, and her door creaked open. He made a mental note to oil it the next time she came. "I wish you never had to go home."

She shrugged, getting in. "I don't mind the drive." He closed the door, and Kelly leaned through the open window.

"That's not what I meant."

"I **know** what you meant," she said, smiling coyly. "I can't exactly pitch a tent in your backyard."

Jack laughed at her humorous dodge, and Kelly reached out and took his hand. "You don't know me that well, Mr. Livingston. I have many more surprises for you."

"I can't wait," he said, releasing her hand reluctantly.

Jack watched her roll down the street, thinking he should maybe forget oiling the hinges and just help her find another set of wheels.

He recalled their conversation about his mother. Kelly was right. He was losing the battle of forgiveness, and he needed to try harder and pray more. Lingering arguments with San only exacerbated his angry memories. But really, the last thing Jack needed was a picture of his mother on his wall. He swallowed and made yet another promise to do better.

Thinking of Kelly and the influence she was having over the smallest details in his life, he wondered how on earth a naïve, marriage-phobic man like himself was so blessed to find someone like her. He was tempted to pinch himself.

**Thank you**, he whispered.

# Chapter 29

San called on Thursday morning, just after seven. They hadn't spoken much in weeks, and sadly, Jack hadn't minded the silence. Having spent the night with a friend, Nattie was gone and wouldn't be back until early afternoon.

Glancing at the ID first, Jack answered the phone, rubbing the bleariness from his eyes.

"Are you sitting down?" San asked.

"Actually, I'm still lying down." Jack stretched himself into a pretzel configuration, yawning loudly. "What's up, sis?"

"I got to thinking about this Kelly of yours, how much I liked her, and how she looked so familiar, like I'd seen her on TV or something."

Jack cleared his throat, fighting a sudden

sinking feeling.

"And so I Googled her," San continued. "I did a little search on her name and Akron, Ohio, and I came up with the Maines family. No big surprise, right? So I muddled through a dozen pages and was about to give up, when I found this website…and lo and behold, it appears to be Kelly's website."

Jack could feel his stomach tighten. Kelly had never mentioned a website. "Don't you mean Kelly's Facebook page?"

"Nope," San said. She cleared her throat again. "It's called: Finding My Emily."

Jack considered this. "Who's Emily?"

"Who do you think it is?"

Exasperated with San's dramatic flair, Jack rubbed his eyelids.

"I don't know—her sister?"

"Try again."

Jack exhaled with frustration. "Okay. Her daughter?"

"Bingo."

Jack took this in. "So…she needs help finding her daughter?" He leaned over the bed, elbows on his knees, adding

**daughter** to the list of things she hadn't mentioned. "Are you sure you have the right person?"

"Click on the info and you'll get her picture, brother dearest," San said, laying it out in glaring detail. "Plus, there are pictures of what Emily would look like today. And who do you think Emily would look like?"

Along with his growing stomachache, Jack felt the beginning of a headache in the corner of his temple.

"I'll tell you," she said. "Emily looks like Natalie, Jack. She looks **exactly** like Natalie."

Jack took a long, deep breath.

"How did you meet her again?" San asked.

"The office," he whispered softly.

"You okay, Jack?"

"No."

"Me either," San muttered.

**So that's why we met. She's been looking for her child.** He tried to wrap his brain around the whole thing, but the most obvious implication came crashing through: **She lied.**

"I haven't told you everything," San continued. "She didn't give her child up for adoption, Jack. Her child was **kidnapped**…by Emily's father."

New shivers started in his gut and spread throughout his body.

"Apparently Kelly's husband stole Emily and ran off to New York City. He sold her."

**Sold her?** Jack whistled softly.

"Some kind of black-market adoption web, and he must have received a ton of money. At least that's what Kelly asserts on her website."

"This can't be true, sis," Jack insisted. "What kind of father would sell his own daughter?"

"Maybe a stoner?"

Jack scratched his head, wishing he could start the day all over.

"Apparently this dude was really whacked out. But there's more, Jack."

**It gets worse?**

"This Bobby Maines OD'd in a hotel, and with his death, any solid link to Emily was gone forever." San sighed into the phone.

"But I **still** haven't told you the worst part."

San, the master of dragging it out.

"The police hardly looked for the kid. Because they suspected Kelly and her husband were working together."

"Was she charged?"

"No," San responded. "And personally? I find it hard to believe that she had anything to do with it. Why spend eight years looking for your kid if you're responsible?"

"But still…"

They were silent as the mind-boggling implications set in.

He felt as if his entire life were falling away, as if he'd been living in a house of cards and it was now all crashing down around him.

They'd been dating for over a month, and he didn't have a clue as to Kelly's real identity. Suddenly, she was a stranger. Finally Jack broke the silence. "If Natalie is her biological daughter, why hasn't she said something? Why this dating ruse? Why not just say, **'Hey, I think your kid is mine'?**"

"That's what I don't understand," San

admitted. "But I have a couple options for us to consider."

"Shoot."

"Thinking she's found Emily, Kelly now wants to be fully involved in her life, knowing that she wouldn't be if she came clean and took you to court. Because at this point, the courts probably wouldn't give her full custody. So Kelly wants to marry you in order to have Nattie in her life."

Jack cringed as San continued. "Here's another option. What if Kelly simply can't bring herself to tell you the truth, and she's been trying to work up the courage?"

"Truth about what? That Nattie is hers?"

"Or...that Nattie **isn't** hers. Maybe when she found out that Nattie wasn't hers, she couldn't break free. Maybe she's truly in love with you, Jack."

"There's another option," he suggested. "Maybe she doesn't even know one way or another...yet."

San scoffed. "I really doubt that."

So did he. Jack blew out an exasperated breath. "So you think she's tested Nattie?"

"Don't **you**?"

**Of course**, he thought.

Jack stood up and headed for the bathroom. Mercilessly, San wasn't finished yet. "Like I said, I think she already knows Nattie isn't her daughter, which is why she hasn't said anything, and that's also why I think she's for real."

"For real?"

"She loves you."

Looking in the mirror, Jack studied the anger in his eyes. "Maybe we're missing the most obvious: She intends to kidnap Nattie."

San snorted. "I **really, really** doubt that, Jack. I mean, yes, she's lied through her teeth, but she'd have to be a sociopath or something, and I just don't see it."

Jack continued staring at his reflection, a strange image of him holding the phone, his hair spurting out in Einstein fashion.

"We can't assume anything, San."

"No, I understand that—"

"I need to protect Nattie."

"It's too soon to lawyer up," she argued. "Just tell her you know the truth and see what she says. You might be surprised and find she has a perfectly rational excuse for why she hasn't told you. She's probably sick about the whole thing."

Jack shook his head, still trying to come to grips with the situation. "How can you be so relaxed about this?"

"Jack, I'm not—"

"One way or another," he continued, "I need to find out for myself if Nattie is her daughter."

"And how are you going to do that without asking Kelly for her DNA?"

Jack jogged his memory. "I have a couple of ideas."

"If you're going to do this, you have to do it right, Jack. You have to get a sample from her. **Directly.**"

**No, I don't**, he thought. And he wasn't ready to confront her, not until he knew the truth for himself. In fact, that was the last thing he wanted to do—confront her **before** he knew what he was talking about.

"Jack, what are you thinking?"

"I'll call you back, San."

# Chapter 30

Sliding his laptop out from beneath the bed frame, Jack located several local companies that specialized in DNA testing and reviewed the general information offered. Apparently, if he didn't employ the standard DNA testing method of using a cotton swab on the inside of Kelly's cheek, he was left with nonstandard and less accurate options: hairs, toothbrush, chewing gum, etc. In short, swabbing was best, but other sources could work if collected properly.

Next, Jack called a local testing lab and asked about testing hair samples. According to Jennifer, who answered the phone, they needed at least three hairs, and preferably more, to produce a confident result.

"We need the roots," the woman emphasized. "And be sure not to **touch** the roots as you collect them."

**Our house is full of hair**, he thought, but knowing whose hair was whose would be difficult. Fortunately, obtaining Nattie's sample, the starting point to his own test, would be as easy as swabbing the inside of her cheek.

Jack went to the kitchen and found a pair of thin disposable plastic gloves. He put them on and went through the house, examining every chair, every cushion. Without Laura meticulously vacuuming the house, he was sure to find a couple of hairs, especially since his own house-keeping skills were sorely lacking.

He found plenty, nearly two dozen on and around the couch, but none of them had roots, and besides, determining which were whose was another matter. They could have been Nattie's, Laura's, Kelly's, or even San's, for that matter.

**Wait a minute.** Jack went to the upstairs bathroom and located several hairs from Nattie's hairbrush and compared them to his samples. **Bingo.** Nattie's hairs were thinner and a different shade of brown, enabling him to eliminate hers from the others.

But he needed samples with roots, and he still needed to distinguish between the women who'd been in his house. He considered the porch swing out back. Kelly had spent hours there, but so had Laura. On the other hand, overly restless San rarely graced the swing, if ever. Good place to start.

He was immediately rewarded. The swing cushions were like hair magnets. He found ten right off the bat, eliminating Nattie's. But the remaining could have been either Laura's or Kelly's, and upon closer examination, he realized they also lacked the necessary hair root.

Jack sat on the swing, frustrated, racking his brain for a solution. Finding a hair with a root just might be impossible. They had to be plucked to retain the follicle. Then he noticed the chain holding the swing. He smiled. Nestled within the links...there they were...**three hairs**, snarled and tangled...roots and all.

Extracting them carefully, he compared them to the hair from Nattie's brush. These strands were thicker and darker in color. No match. But that still left the inevitable question: Were they Laura's or Kelly's?

He would have guessed Kelly's, but he couldn't be 100 percent sure. Putting them into a plastic bag, Jack suddenly remembered his personal plane, the 182 that was never flown by anyone but him. He and Kelly had just taken it into the skies, and she'd worn the extra headset that never left the plane. Almost certainly, he'd find more samples of her hair, easily distinguishable from his own.

But would he find the roots? **Doubtful.**

He paused at the bar, stared at his bagged collection of hairs, and began to reconsider the entire strategy. Maybe San was right, and he should confront Kelly directly. Let her explain herself. And if she had evidence that linked herself to Nattie, she'd be more than willing to provide her own DNA for confirmation testing.

Jack sat on a stool and rested his

forehead on his hands. **But I have to protect Nattie**, he thought, reconsidering. And he didn't want to provoke a confrontation before he knew the truth for himself. **She's a magician**, he reminded himself. Who knew what kind of tricks she had up her sleeve?

His anger hardening into something solid, he grabbed his laptop again and surfed to her website. Sure enough, there it was: a picture of Kelly, her name, and a picture of Emily. He thought of the 182 again and made the decision.

He showered and shaved and grabbed the keys off the kitchen counter. Heading out to the airfield, he drove quickly, his mind twirling around the implications.

Once there, he went to the hangar, unlocked the plane, and slipped on another pair of gloves. Gingerly, he extracted the headset from beneath the backseat, studied it carefully, and caught a break. Five unsuspecting brunette hairs dangled from the plastic foam. They had to be hers. More importantly, three of them still had the roots attached. Carefully, he put them in a separate plastic bag and headed back.

On the way, he drove by the local coffee hut, ordered an espresso to go, and made a beeline to the testing center for their swabbing kit. Before he submitted the hair samples, he needed to extract Nattie's sample, then submit them all together.

While his heart was breaking, and his temper was struggling for dominance, he couldn't deny that a spark of hope flared. Maybe, just maybe, there was a simple explanation for the whole thing.

Later that night after Nattie brushed her teeth, Jack called her into his office.

"What's up?"

Jack showed her the swab. "I need to do a little...uh...medical testing."

"Oh," Nattie said, frowning at the little white stick he held. "Is this gonna hurt?"

"Not a bit," Jack replied, forcing a cheeriness he didn't feel. Dutifully, Nattie opened her mouth, and he swabbed the inside of her cheek.

"Done?"

"Got it."

Without a care in the world, Nattie ran off, oblivious to the storm swirling about them.

San came by in the morning while Nattie and Jack were having some cold cereal. She gave her niece a big smooch on the cheek.

Nattie grinned. "What are you doing here?"

"Do I need an excuse to see my number-one girl?"

Nattie played coy, putting her finger to her cheek, twisting her mouth as if thinking it over.

San mussed her hair. "Don't hurt my feelings, kid."

With Nattie busy pouring a second bowl, Jack caught San's eye and gestured toward the office. In the shadow of his wall of airplane memorabilia, San closed the door for what Jack hoped wasn't another endless strategy session. San sat in Laura's chair; Jack at the desk.

San began their discussion by repeating everything they'd already discussed, coming back to her conclusion that Kelly hadn't come clean yet because she was truly invested in their lives, and that Nattie was **not** her daughter.

"She would have told you by now," San argued. "And I still don't believe that she's a danger for Nattie."

Jack frowned. "Maybe **you** can rule that out—"

"I just can't imagine it, Jack," she quickly added. "She's not a criminal." She sighed. "Why don't you just call her? Get it over with?"

Jack shook his head.

"Nattie doesn't even look like Kelly," San repeated.

Jack frowned. "Yes, she does."

San pursed her lips. "Seriously. Call it a hunch, Jackenheimer, but I still think she's already abandoned the idea that Nattie is hers."

"How can you be so sure?"

"I told you already...because she would have said so."

Jack leaned back, thinking it over. His cell phone buzzed. It was Kelly texting him: **Good morning.**

Last night, they'd traded a dozen texts, with Kelly's last: **You sound really tired, mister. I'm signing off, but I plan on dreaming of you....**

**G'night** was all he'd texted back.

"Don't let on yet," San now whispered. "You're not ready for this."

**No kidding**, Jack thought. He texted Kelly back: **Good morning**. He pulled his sandwich bag out of his desk drawer, along with the swab, and San's eyes widened. "What's that?"

He explained, and San freaked out. "How do you even know those are Kelly's?"

"Three hairs from the airplane. She was the last to wear the headset."

San narrowed her eyes skeptically, then shook her head as if dealing with a surly child. She pulled out her cell phone, thumbed a little, and peered down at it. "I need to be somewhere in an hour. I hope you know what you're doing."

After San left, Jack took off for the lab, his mind in overdrive. Their last flight together was ever before him—the way Kelly kept touching his arm, her implicit trust in his ten thousand plus hours of experience.

He'd been showing off, pure and simple, acting like a he-man, trying to impress his woman, and all along she'd been harboring a secret.

Mentally, he regurgitated every alternative he and San had already discussed. But considering the missing pieces, his conclusions kept changing. And he still couldn't buy San's optimistic assumption.

No, as far as he was concerned, the reason Kelly hadn't told him the truth was surely because she was trying to fraudulently insinuate herself into their lives.

And if so, when was she going to tell him the truth? On their wedding day? During their honeymoon? Five years down the line?

Could she even keep it a secret that long? **Maybe**, he thought, and that only added to the mystery. A more sinister explanation suggested she might have hoped to win Nattie's heart before enacting a legal filing for custody.

**I never, ever, had reason to trust her**, he realized, and that was

what hurt the most. But it didn't matter how he felt. What mattered—what **always** mattered—was Nattie.

The lab was located in downtown Akron, on a side street near the hospital. Jack parallel parked out front, fed the meter, and went inside. Sitting in an orange plastic chair and thumbing through out-dated **Car and Driver** magazines, he waited for a couple of worse-for-the-wear men to complete their tests. Finally, he approached the lady he'd spoken to on the phone.

Jennifer took his samples and meticulously placed them in new packets. She clarified the process as she went, examining the hairs from the swing and the plane that he attributed to Kelly.

Holding them up to a bright lamp, she smiled. "Looks good."

Relieved, Jack ponied up the money, filled out the appropriate forms, and headed back home. After parking in the garage, he jogged next door to Craig and Diane's to get Nattie, giving Livy an extra tip for the last-minute baby-sitting.

They traipsed into the house, and he grabbed some juice out of the refrigerator and leaned against the sink. Nattie went into the garage to attach a new blinged-out nameplate to her bike, something she'd received from San.

Taking another swig of juice, Jack considered the immediate future. He had a couple days till the results came in. From here on out, it was a waiting game, and that was all it was: a game. There was no Jack and Kelly. Not anymore. There was no romance, and there was no future.

Nattie came waltzing in. "Come and see, Dad!"

"Just a minute," Jack said, lost in thought. He shuddered: What if San hadn't found out?

And then the irony struck him between the eyes. If the test was positive, Nattie would have what she'd been searching for: her **real** mother, her **birth** mother. The thought unnerved him.

Until yesterday, he had been so eager to add Kelly to their little family, but in the space of a few hours, she'd become the enemy. He thought back to their first date again and remembered Kelly's first meeting with Nattie.

**She could have extracted the DNA then.** He also remembered how Kelly had mentioned Nattie's name **before** she'd been introduced.

Of course. It all fit together, especially her strange behavior that first day. Yes, without a doubt, she'd known of Nattie long before she'd ever arrived at his office. She'd been stalking her, and she'd pretended to know San when San clearly didn't know her, trying to cover her tracks, making it up as she went along. So many pieces were finally making sense, but there were still a few pieces that didn't fit.

Jack sat in the kitchen, sipping his orange juice, trying to analyze the last month.

"Dad?!" Nattie whined from outside. "C'mon!"

Jack drained the last of his juice and headed to the garage.

**How can I help Nattie survive this?**

Pretending interest in the latest stripes on her ride, half listening as Nattie explained her bike fashion strategy, Jack suddenly remembered. It was Friday night. He groaned.

"I want Kelly to see this," Nattie said, smoothing the stripes with her hand, wiping the residual dust on her jeans.

"She will, honey."

Jack met Nattie's eyes, and they twinkled back at him. And once more, his spirits sank. "I love you, sweetie."

Nattie raised her eyebrows, a soft glint in her eyes, challenging him. "I love you more."

Kelly was due to arrive in one hour.

In the short time they'd been dating, a cute routine had already developed. They heard Kelly's knock first, then Kelly stuck her head shyly around the door, followed by a clear voice, "Hel-lo!"

Nattie would go running to greet her,

and they would tumble through their playful contortions.

Same thing happened tonight. Once inside, Kelly held out her arms. "What's a girl gotta do to get a hug?"

Nattie extended her arms: "I thought you'd **never** ask!"

They collapsed into each other's arms, giggling as if they'd just unwrapped the funniest joke. Kelly pulled back, holding Nattie. "How's my favorite girl?"

"Now that you're here, things are definitely looking up!"

Another hug. Another round of giggles.

Observing them, Jack felt like snatching Nattie and making a run for it. When Nattie finally pulled Kelly into the living room, Kelly sat at the edge of the couch, leaned over, and planted a big one on Jack's lips. She pulled back, narrowing her eyes flirtatiously. "You okay, Jack?"

He forced a smile. "Long day."

Kelly studied him, considering his answer. "Wanna talk about it?" she asked. Her face broke into a grin, and she leaned over and elbowed Nattie, whispering conspiratorially in her ear. "As if guys want to talk about **anything**."

Nattie giggled. "Ain't that the truth?"

Kelly stopped suddenly, sniffing the air.

Nattie acted worried. "What?"

Kelly nodded, convinced. "Call it a hunch, but I detect a severe lack of Pop-Tarts."

"That's what **I'm** talkin' 'bout."

Kelly stood straight, and both she and Nattie turned to give Jack the stink-eye. His heart was breaking, and he certainly didn't care about Nattie's Pop-Tart quota.

"What if we just ate popcorn for movie night?" Jack suggested, and both Nattie and Kelly laughed as if he'd just said the funniest thing.

Nattie suddenly squealed and scrambled up the stairs. "I wanna show you something."

Kelly stood there watching Nattie disappear and then turned her gaze upon Jack, still smiling but less humorously. "Seriously, boyfriend. Something I said?"

Jack shook his head. "No, just...got bad news today."

Nattie came down with some pencil

sketches, new art accessories he hadn't seen yet, probably from San or Laura. Nattie was already bypassing him, not that it had bothered him in the least, but it only confirmed for him that losing Kelly would ultimately devastate his daughter.

Kelly's gaze hadn't left his eyes. "Are you hungry?"

"Not really," Jack said, "but I could eat."

"Wanna go out instead?" Nattie asked, sorting her colored pencils.

"We could," he said, trying to act the happy boyfriend, but he could tell Kelly wasn't buying it.

Nattie sat on the couch, and Kelly oohed and aahed over Nattie's art, examining it. He stared at her.

**Is she Nattie's mother?** he wondered.

**And what if she isn't?** That meant her test result—the one he and San were convinced she would have done on Nattie—was negative, and yet she'd stuck around anyway. And the big question to that would be...**why?**

Because she's for real, San had said. **Because she loves me...or Nattie.** But could he possibly believe anything Kelly had to say at this point?

She held up a drawing for Jack to see. "Did you notice Nattie's shading?"

He had. Nattie rubbed her hands together. "Dad says I should take art lessons."

"You should," Kelly said, glancing at him again, a concerned frown edging the corners. "But only if you really want to try it." She held his gaze, as if checking whether her response to Nattie met with Jack's approval.

He smiled agreeably. "Yes, if you'd like to, sweetie, but we've already got piano."

"I can do **everything**," Nattie announced, arranging her pencils in a row.

Kelly mussed Nattie's hair, looking at Jack. "Yeah, Dad. We can do **everything**!"

They decided on Chinese takeout, one of Nattie's new favorites, and ate in the backyard. It was a hot evening, but a soft breeze trickled through the leaves, perfect for outdoor dining. Nattie and Kelly bantered throughout the meal while Jack observed, feeling thoroughly sidelined. Every so often Kelly met his eyes, giving him another friendly frown.

The wisecracks that normally came so easily to him during happier occasions didn't come at all. Despite his determination to play along, his efforts fell flat.

"I think we've left Dad behind," Nattie quipped.

After eating, Kelly and Nattie kneeled before Nattie's tower of DVDs to select a movie. Nattie was eager to introduce Kelly to something she hadn't seen before, so they settled on **The Lion King**.

"It's got my favorite song of all time," Nattie declared.

Nattie was reluctant to sit between them, but after Kelly's urging, she agreed. "Jack and I have our date tomorrow," Kelly said, encouraging her.

Afterward, Jack walked Kelly to her car, and Kelly effused appreciation for the good time. She touched his arm. "You're sure you're not feeling a little under the weather?"

He assured her. "We've had a good time, haven't we?"

Kelly held his eyes. "Yes, I've really

enjoyed these Friday nights. Getting to know you and Nattie has been a blessing."

Jack bit his tongue. Normally he would have kissed her goodbye, but he didn't tonight, reaching for a hug instead.

"Drive safe," he told her, and she flashed him her winning smile, the smile that had stolen his heart the first day he'd met her.

He forced another of his own, but it felt all wrong.

Once in the car, but still in sight, Kelly struggled to keep her emotions in check. She waved at Jack again, hoping he couldn't see her watering eyes. And although she'd had plenty of time to prepare—weeks, in fact—nothing could have prepared her for how she felt now.

**He knows**, she realized.

She put her car into gear, so frustrated with herself she was tempted to peel out, although her Toyota wasn't exactly peeling material.

Halfway down the street, out of eyeshot, the first tears slipped down her cheek. **I've lost Jack.**

The lollipop was still sitting in the top drawer of her bedroom dresser, within a sealed plastic bag, untested. She'd almost thrown it out, in an attempt to achieve some kind of pathetic redemption.

**I should have been honest from day one**, she thought for the hundredth time. Of course, there was no way Jack would have asked her out if she had been honest. She still believed that. The last month would never have happened.

The urge to tell the truth boiled up within her. Even now, she was tempted to turn the car around, march up to his door, and come clean. Even now, she had the crazy notion that she could fix things.

**But what if I'm wrong?** she thought. What if Jack was merely having a bad night?

Yet, in the long run, did it matter? Either way, she had to come clean eventually. She'd always known this, hadn't she?

She thought again of the lollipop that held the truth to her question. **Is Nattie my daughter?**

**I have to test it now**, she realized. **I**

**have no choice.**

All the way back home, she kicked herself. For being so deceitful. And for falling in love.

Once back inside, Nattie came up to Jack and tugged on his shirt. "Hey, grump. Something **I** can do?"

Dropping to his haunches, Jack reached for a hug. She complied, whispering in his ear, "You're freakin' us out, Daddykins."

"Tired, is all."

"You keep saying that." She shook her head against his shoulder. "Are you mad at Kelly?"

"No."

Her eyes locked with his. "I **like** Kelly."

Here was where he was supposed to assure Nattie that he, too, liked Kelly. "Well, I know for a fact she likes you back."

With crafty eyes, Nattie pursed her lips, catching his slippery slide. "Don't **you** like her anymore?"

"Kelly's wonderful, honey."

Nattie sniffed, unsatisfied and annoyed. "I'm going to bed, Dad."

"I'll be up in a sec."

In his office, Jack sat in his chair and took a long breath. He wasn't up for tomorrow. Not after tonight, and before he considered it further, he picked up his cell and texted Kelly: **I need to cancel our date tomorrow.**

Moments later, his phone rang, and he read the ID. It was Kelly. He cringed. She wasn't one to text and drive.

"Hi, Jack," she said when he answered. "That's fine. I'll miss you, but I'm here if you want to talk."

Jack said good-bye and hung up.

Holding the phone in his lap, he tried justifying his terse behavior, recalling the information he'd read on Kelly, how she'd been held in a cloud of suspicion regarding the disappearance of her daughter. According to one article, the police still believed she'd been involved, even to this day.

The idea was laughable. San was right, and the police were wrong. There was no way Kelly was involved in the kidnapping and sale of her own daughter. But still...

that didn't change her lies.

When he tucked her in, Nattie talked about Kelly at first, and then after a few minutes, she transitioned to Laura, whom she hadn't seen in over a week. "Do you think she was just saying she wasn't going home?"

Jack kissed her cheek. "No, honey. Laura always tells the truth."

"Yeah," Nattie said thoughtfully.

"You wanna talk to her?"

Nattie leaned up. "Actually...I wanna **see** her again."

Jack pulled out his phone and dialed Laura's number. Nattie pulled herself to a rigid sitting position, crossing her legs.

Laura answered on the first ring, and when he apologized for calling so late, she demurred. "I was just reading."

"Nattie misses you," he said, asking if Laura had time for a quick visit in the next couple of days. Sounding amenable to the idea, Laura suggested that Jack drop Nattie off at the farm tomorrow.

"Tomorrow?" he said for Nattie's benefit, who was enthusiastically nodding her head.

"How's she doing?" Laura asked. "Fine," he replied.

Laura must have detected the hesitation in his tone. "Is everything okay?" she asked, sounding worried. "I mean...with you and Kelly?"

"Not at all," Jack said simply. "Oh dear," Laura said.

# Chapter 31

Laura was waiting for them on the porch of the farmhouse. She waved, and Nattie fidgeted like a jumping bean.

When Jack stopped the truck, Nattie scampered out, calling, **"Ich habb dich oahrich gmissed!"**

Laura laughed melodiously. **"Guck emol du!"**

Jack sighed with a smile. The best he could make out, they'd said something about missing each other. Nattie ran to Laura as though she hadn't seen her for months. Staying inside, Jack rolled the window down, and following yet another tender moment, Laura came over to the truck, holding Nattie's hand.

"We're going to visit the ponies again," Laura said brightly.

Nattie grabbed Laura's arm, and Laura surrendered to Nattie's tugging.

Jack said good-bye and decided to take a short drive to collect his thoughts, then stopped at the airfield for a few hours.

Just after lunchtime, Laura called him. "Nattie is hoping you could take us to the park."

"I'll be on my way in five minutes," Jack responded, eager to ditch the paper work at the office.

When he arrived back at the farm, Nattie and Laura hopped into the passenger side of the truck, slamming the door shut. "Howdy, stranger." Nattie laughed.

Jack leaned over, taking an exaggerated sniff of Nattie's hair as she located her seat belt. "Don't start, Dad. I can always take a shower later."

Closest to the window, Laura reached behind her, trying to fasten her own seat belt. Jack couldn't help looking at her after she'd clicked it into place, still recalling the day she'd tried "fancy" on for size.

Nattie swished at her face with both hands, sweeping clear the offending strands. The gravel sputtered as he backed up, creating a cloud of dust particles, spattering the underside of his truck.

In the distance, Jack noticed the Troyers' nineteen-year-old son, Samuel, their youngest, going to the stable, completing the afternoon chores. He recalled from their previous conversations that Samuel was engaged to be married to his sweetheart.

"When is the wedding?" Jack asked, nodding in Samuel's direction.

"October." Laura chuckled softly. "He's ready to grow a beard, that's for sure. Ready to be a man, as he puts it."

**Soon enough**, thought Jack.

At the park, it was like old times. Laura teeter-tottered with Nattie for a while as Jack watched. Later, he joined them for a fierce game of tag, with Nattie's friends eagerly joining the fun.

Worn out, Laura and Jack let Nattie enjoy time with her friends, and they made their way to a nearby bench, which he pretended to dust off. "Your throne awaits, m'lady."

Laura laughed and sat down, demurely crossing her legs. They sat in silence for a moment.

He'd been mulling it over all day, and now with her sitting there, he finally decided. "I need to talk to you about something."

Laura turned to him. And swallowing hard, Jack spelled out the story, describing San's phone call and her discovery of Kelly's true identity, ending with his accumulation of DNA evidence.

Stunned, Laura's face fell, her eyes narrowing in dismay.

Jack removed an Internet article from his pocket, the one with an early picture of Kelly, and passed it to her. Laura read it, her face growing pale when she came to the end: **Kelly Maines remains under a cloud of suspicion after years of running her nonprofit organization, which many detractors suspect is merely a front for personal gain.**

Her eyes fixed on the page, Laura sighed loudly. "They really put her through the shredder, ain't so?"

He agreed.

"So...Kelly must think Nattie is hers? Is that why she found you?"

Jack shrugged. "What other explanation is there?"

Her eyebrows arched. "You mentioned hairs."

He told her what he'd found, and she frowned. "But, Jack, I'm sure my hair is all over the place."

"I know I've got at least three of Kelly's hairs," Jack explained, staring at the kids running around, playing an impromptu game of kick the can.

He sighed, the noise of the park mingling with a swirling sense of unreality. "No matter what I think, or hope, I have to admit that Kelly looks like Nattie."

Laura seemed to consider this and shook her head. "Kelly's not Nattie's mother."

Jack was taken aback, surprised by Laura's adamant tone. "But what if she is?" he pressed, unwilling to let it go. "I have to be ready for that."

"No you don't," she said, her voice

lowered to a hush. "She's **not** Nattie's mother." Her continued conviction stunned him.

"But—"

"She would know by now, right?"

Nodding, Jack conceded this. After all, he and San had already taken this argument to the same conclusion.

"Is it such a stretch to believe she actually likes you?" Laura said gently.

Jack shrugged and let it go.

Hugging herself, as if suddenly cold, Laura sniffed softly. "I'm more worried about Nattie. She doesn't need this." She stood up and wandered back to the playground, where Nattie greeted her with unbridled enthusiasm.

Jack took a few shots with his ever-present camera, then made a little video of his munchkin. After a few minutes, Laura returned. Nattie wasn't remotely ready to leave, and he wasn't surprised. He felt the same way. Being here with Laura reminded him of the old days and the old hopes.

"Nattie really likes Kelly," Laura said, continuing the topic. "This will break her heart."

"She still talks about you every day," Jack replied.

Laura looked away.

**Come back**, Jack thought. With the looming test results, their

future was up in the air. Everything hinged on whether Kelly was or was not Nattie's mother.

**What if Kelly had never come into our lives?** he thought. Laura wouldn't have quit, and he could have spared Nattie another heartache, and in time...maybe, just maybe he and Laura might even have married. Was that so impossible to believe?

"I don't see how Kelly and I can survive this," he now whispered. "No matter what the test says."

Laura nodded, lost in thought. She chewed her lip, clearly anxious.

Eventually they headed toward Laura's home. Nattie sat in the middle but said little, tuckered out. In front of the house, Jack could see someone pull back the curtains and then let them fall into place again. Laura must have noticed, as well. She got out of the truck, stood on the gravel for a moment, then looked at Jack, her words confident, her meaning unmistakable. "You have nothing to fear. Okay?"

Jack nodded, and Nattie turned to Jack, questioning. He patted her back, and wondered again how Laura could be so convinced. But he didn't push it. "I'll call you to let you know how things turn out."

"I'll be praying," she said, gave them a final wave, then was gone.

On the way home, Nattie buzzed with curiosity. "What was **that** about?"

"Grown-up stuff."

"You mean, Nattie-can't-know stuff." "Sorry, sweetie."

# Chapter 32

By midweek, Jack was still waiting on the DNA results. Jennifer at the lab apologized for the delay. "Usually it takes only three days. I'm so sorry. Let me track this one down, and I'll get right back to you."

In the meantime, Jack decided to sneak away from the office and make an attempt at dusting and vacuuming the house, rallying Nattie to help clean up the kitchen. Late afternoon, he received a call from one of his corporate jet clients, Stonebridge Capital Investments, requesting a flight to San Diego on Friday. The top brass hoped to treat its elite clients to a California vacation, free of the stress of flying commercial.

It couldn't have come at a worse time, of course, but due to his contract, Jack couldn't decline. They paid him well to jump through their last-minute hoops.

Wishing he could have called Laura to stay over with Nattie, Jack dialed San instead, who was eager for some extra time with her niece. Since her own place was in such disarray, due to packing and preparation for storage, San suggested she simply stay at his house. Nattie, of course, was thrilled.

Jack texted Kelly to cancel both standing dates, Friday and Saturday evenings, relieved to have an excuse. **I'm flying the corporate jet to San Diego.**

A few minutes later, she texted back: **I'll miss you. Have a great flight!**

An hour later, Jennifer from the DNA lab called to explain the reason for the delay. "They've discovered two different hair samples and weren't sure which ones you wanted tested."

Jack had been afraid of this. "Can't you test both samples?" he asked. "I mean, do two tests?"

Jennifer hesitated. "Well, sure. It will cost an additional fee. But do you know which is which?"

"No," Jack replied, "but I'll figure it out."

So they settled upon a strategy. Jennifer agreed to ask the lab to label one set as Sample A, and the other set as Sample B. Although Jack didn't know which sample belonged to whom, he guessed one sample had to be Laura's—from the swing—and the other had to be Kelly's—from the headset.

Jack swallowed his frustration and thanked Jennifer.

That Friday at the airfield, Jack preflighted the minijet, eager to take it up again. It was a fine specimen, with room for six passengers. He had just completed the flight planning when he received another call from the lab. The results were in. Jennifer agreed to email the document.

**Perfect timing**, he thought wryly, deciding to wait till he got to his room to look at it, postponing the final reckoning.

The flight itself went smoothly, although his raucous passengers were thoroughly sloshed by touchdown. Once there, a large Mercedes sedan, undoubtedly featuring top-of-the-line amenities, was already waiting. **Good thing, too**, Jack thought.

Once settled into his hotel, a sparse loft-style high-rise with wood floors and brick walls, Jack leaned back in the king-size bed, propped his tablet on his lap, found the email, and tapped Download. Seconds later, he had the document, two pages in all.

He closed his eyes and whispered a quick prayer before scanning the top lines for immediate information. The moment of truth was highlighted in bold: **Sample A cannot be excluded as being the mother of the child, Natalie Livingston**, followed by the next line: **Based on these data, the probability of maternity is 99.9999% as compared to an untested randomly chosen woman.**

He closed his eyes and took a long, laborious breath, exhaling deeply. He could hear a siren in the distance, kids bustling down the hallway, the slamming of doors.

**And there we have it**, he thought. The worst-case scenario. Not only was San wrong, but Laura was wrong, as well. Jennifer had explained that nonexclusion was lab-speak for "positive match," which meant only one thing: Kelly was Nattie's birth mother.

He set the tablet to the side of the bed, leaned back, and briefly covered his eyes with his arm. Surely Kelly knew this, as well—that Nattie was her daughter. She'd probably known for weeks.

Did she hope to simply join their family and then spring this news? Or even worse, battle him in court over Nattie?

**I need to contact my lawyer**, he thought grimly, doing a quick Internet search for custody cases, if only to confirm what he'd already suspected. It was unlikely that any court in the land would award Kelly custody of Nattie, not after all these years. But a judge **might** award her some kind of visitation.

He sighed. It was too soon to surmise the legal aspects. His phone beeped with Kelly's texts, but he ignored them, growing more angry with each passing moment. It was time to put his measly cards on the table. He picked up the phone and did something last century. He dialed Kelly's number.

Kelly answered on the third ring, her voice bright. "Hi! It's great to actually hear your voice! How are you?"

He told her about the flight and the posh hotel they'd arranged for him, and she, in turn, told him about her day at work. "And first thing, I spilled coffee on my blouse, and I didn't have another, so I had this big splotch for hours." She laughed. "And then the market dropped two hundred and fifty points!"

"That can't be good for client relations," Jack replied.

"Which part? The market drop or the slummy-looking assistant?" Jack felt a catch in his throat—everything sounded the same, as if San had never called him with the revelation.

**What if I just pretended nothing happened?** He shook his head at the notion.

"Bill doesn't think it's a true correction yet," Kelly continued.

"As it is, I had to field calls from nervous clients all day. They kept asking, 'Are we in the market? Are we out?'"

Jack forced a chuckle. "But you can't change positions on a dime, can you."

"Not as fast as they would like," she agreed, and as a long pause set in, it struck him again. He was talking to Nattie's **birth mother**, the woman who'd brought his girl into the world. Despite his resentment over how she'd handled everything, he felt sorry for her.

Really, how could he be angry with a woman whose child had been **kidnapped**?

"I'll be home this Sunday," Jack said. "I was hoping you could come down on Monday, or..."

"Sure," she said immediately. "Special plans?"

"I just thought we could talk."

Another pause, then, "Hey, I'm a girl," Kelly said humorously. "I **love** to talk!"

Minutes later, they hung up, but the mixed bag of anger and sadness and sympathy continued to hang over him.

The fact remained: Kelly had found her child. After spending years of looking, years of heartache and suffering, she'd finally found the daughter who had been taken from her. If anything, it was cause for celebration.

In fact, when she'd answered, he should have said, **"Kelly, I have great news for you!"**

Still holding the phone, he actually considered punching in her number again and redoing the conversation. They could finally rejoice together. He could forgive her on the spot, no questions asked.

But he didn't. He couldn't. Not until he knew for certain why she had deceived him, and not until he determined her plans—for Nattie's sake, and for his own.

Jack placed the phone on the lamp table and prayed for the strength to endure his own foolish ego.

Kelly hung up and sat at the edge of her bed, fear and panic setting in. **I'm about to lose everything**, she thought. **Again.**

She was tempted to text him back: **What is this about?** Maybe get a conversation started. But she resisted the temptation. She needed to see his face when he confronted her.

Her own test results had come back, but she hadn't opened the document yet. The envelope containing the truth about Nattie still languished in her dresser drawer, because if she didn't open the envelope, then maybe she hadn't actually broken her promise. Yet another brilliant rationalization.

Kelly leaned back on her bed and closed her eyes, whispering a prayer for guidance. **I'm sorry**, she prayed. **Forgive me. I really blew it.** Felix jumped up and rubbed against her side, rumbling softly, concerned by his owner's tears.

**How could I ever think that deceit was okay?** She took the cat into her arms. She was tempted to call Melody. **Not even Melody can dig me out of this.**

The next day, Jack decided to clear his head with a walk around Balboa Park.

While there, he called San, getting an update on things at home.

"Nattie's been eating about ten Pop-Tarts a day," she informed him. "Hope you're okay with that."

He could hear Nattie's voice in the background. "Good one!"

Jack laughed but threatened her with broccoli. San relayed the message, and Nattie squealed with agony. "I'll be good! I promise!"

By Sunday morning, his passengers were ready to return home. They arrived at the airport looking scraggly and disheveled, confirming Jack's long-ago decision to abandon alcohol.

Once in flight and with the plane in auto, he began to anticipate tomorrow's meeting with Kelly, thinking ahead to how Nattie would respond to the discovery that Kelly was her mother.

Nattie would probably associate the news with their earnest prayers, and who was to say she was wrong? Maybe this was how God answered a little girl, and if so, who was Jack to stand in the way?

He could imagine the conversation: **"Kelly's my birth mom? How did that happen?"**

Regardless, it didn't set well with him.

**Get over yourself**, he reminded himself again. **Kelly has found her daughter.**

Nattie greeted him at the door with all-out intensity. "I bet my weekend was better'n **your** weekend!" she exclaimed.

Jack couldn't help laughing. "I bet you're right."

San was her usual overly cool self. "Hi there, jet-setter." She socked Jack in the arm, then leaned over for a kiss from Nattie.

"Gotta go," she said, and made a **call me** gesture to Nattie. "One more special night, 'kay?"

Nattie looked up at Jack, her eyes pleading, **"Please?"**

Jack chuckled. "Do you really think I'd say no?"

Nattie jumped up and did a quick high-five with her auntie.

San took off in her candy-apple-red Corvette, and Nattie led him into the dining room to inspect their artistic activities since he'd left, which included clay sculptures and two watercolor paintings.

Jack examined each piece closely, asking questions to show his interest. Later, he unpacked upstairs, reminding himself to tackle the laundry tomorrow morning. He sat on the bed and ran his fingers through his hair, sighing nervously.

Nattie peeked in. "You look tired. Are you going to work tomorrow?"

Jack considered that. "Kelly's coming down," he said simply.

Wide-eyed, Nattie's eyebrows arched. "Tomorrow?"

He nodded. "We need some time together," he said, then added, "it's going to be adult time, though."

She scampered off. "Fine. I'll settle for the scraps."

On Monday afternoon, Jack leaned back in his office chair and studied his aviation trinkets on the far wall, trying to imagine how the conversation would go, unsure if they could actually talk here, in this big open house—with Nattie lurking about. While the thought of Nattie's penchant for eavesdropping put the clamps on that idea, he didn't want to be in a restaurant for this kind of discussion. **Maybe a drive in the truck?**

**No,** he thought. He picked up the landline and made yet another request of Diane, who was more than willing to have Livy watch Nattie for an hour. She asked about Laura, and Jack filled her in.

"I miss seeing her out in your garden."

**So do I**, Jack thought.

Just after four-thirty, the doorbell rang, but silence followed—no hello, no opening of the door. Instead of walking in as she'd been doing for the past few weeks, Kelly had chosen to wait outside.

## Chapter 33

The next thing he heard was the pounding of footsteps as Nattie raced from her room to the door. Jack sat in his office, his heart hammering in his chest.

He could hear Nattie's exuberant greeting, "What's a girl gotta do to get a hug?"

Finally, he could put it off no longer and walked out to meet them both in the entryway. Kelly brightened, her smile filling the room, but the intensity of her enthusiasm only added to his gloom. She came to him, and he kissed her on the cheek, noting her flowery scent and the long black lacy top over jeans.

Nattie was dismayed. "A cheek kiss?"

"You're going to Diane's for a bit," Jack told her.

Nattie's face fell. She squished closer to

Kelly, linking their arms together. "But Kelly just got here."

"Sweetie…"

Nattie must have seen the seriousness in Jack's eyes, because she stopped fussing. Mournfully, she headed for the door.

"Head right there," he cautioned her, immediately regretting his bossy tone.

The door slammed behind Nattie, and Kelly's own expression, despite her best efforts to appear pleasant, had turned into a mixture of happy dread. She looked at him pensively, stepping back a bit. "Is everything okay, Jack?"

He'd rehearsed his little speech, but now that the moment had arrived, nothing he'd prepared seemed appropriate.

He gestured toward the sofa, and she slipped around the edge, then sat down in the middle. She put her hands on her lap and smiled expectantly.

Jack sat down across from her, and without any kind of preamble, just came out with it: "I wish you had told me the truth, Kelly."

Holding his gaze, Kelly said softly, "Can

you be more specific?"

"You've been looking for your daughter."

She pursed her lips and resituated herself on his couch. "I wanted to tell you, Jack. I had planned to tell you everything the day I met you, but—" Kelly stopped, moisture filling her eyes. She looked away, then forced a smile through her tears. She was clearly miserable, and he felt torn between anger and fear. Was he simply being manipulated…again?

He steeled himself and asked her the question, the one to which he already had an answer. "Do you think Nattie is yours?"

She cleared her throat and slowly shook her head. "I don't know, Jack."

He frowned.

"I really don't," she repeated.

"How do you expect me to believe that?"

Kelly wiped her eyes again, her throat bobbing as she swallowed.

"I didn't **want** to know."

**Impossible**, he thought. "So you're telling me you **didn't** test her?"

Kelly made a face. "Actually…I did, Jack." She shrugged and wiped her eyes, fishing a tissue out of her purse. "I have the envelope in the car. I never opened it. I **couldn't**."

Jack leaned back, his heart pounding through his chest, unsure what to believe.

Kelly scooted forward on the couch, close enough that their knees touched. "I was waiting for, I don't know…permission, I guess."

"Kelly—"

"I know, I **know**, Jack. I can't expect you to trust me. And I don't blame you."

She locked eyes with him again but just sat there, her hands still in her lap, waiting for him to continue. He repeated it, more a statement than a question. "You have the information, but you still don't know whether she is yours."

She made to answer, then simply shook her head instead. The distrust must have shown on his face, because her eyes welled up with tears again, slipping down her cheeks.

He crossed his arms, turning off his own emotion. "Let's open it together," he said flatly, although he already knew what her results would say. Kelly's eyes were suddenly fierce and hopeful. She leaned forward again. "What if we **didn't** open it?"

He frowned at her.

"What if we just threw it away?" she said, her eyes alight with the possibility. "What if...we just continued on like before?"

He was stunned. "As if you hadn't deliberately deceived me?"

Kelly recoiled at his words but reached for his hand. "I don't care anymore, Jack. I think we are good together, and it doesn't matter...."

Jack was shaking his head, pulling his hand away.

"I love you, Jack," Kelly pressed. "And I know you love me."

"But this isn't about us," he said softly. "This is about Nattie."

Kelly went silent, the light in her eyes diminishing. After an awkward moment, she finally spoke. "Of course, Jack. It was...a silly idea. I'll get it."

She pushed herself up and proceeded to go around him.

Once she'd left, Jack realized he was

now carrying on his own charade. He had his own test, and his own results, after all. And her results would surely confirm his.

**Now who's lying?**

Kelly came back in, padding softly, and gently laid the envelope on his lap, sitting back on the couch, several feet from him. She stared at him, her eyes red.

Quickly he opened the envelope, removed the page, and scanned to the bottom. The definitive phrase hit like a blow. He nearly dropped the envelope.

Kelly didn't say anything. She simply sat there, hugging herself, staring at the floor, waiting for him to say it out loud, as if doing the best she could to manage her emotions with dignity.

Without speaking, he handed her the report. She took it and read it aloud. "This means it's negative." And then she smiled. "I'm relieved, Jack..."

But she also seemed disappointed. Of course she was. On the other hand, he was confused. The result couldn't be negative. Negative meant she wasn't Nattie's mother. But his test said the opposite.

Kelly touched him again. The room swirled, and her words seemed to come out in a haze. "Can you forgive me, Jack?"

Jack shook his head, the only response he could manage as his mind raced through the ramifications.

She flinched but soon a kind of surrender finally settled over her. She practically crumpled in her seat.

He should have come clean, right then and there. **"I completed my own test,"** he should have said, but right now, he just needed to think. Maybe her test was wrong. And maybe his was right. Hadn't he already learned that DNA tests could be prone to error? Maybe Nattie was her daughter, after all.

After a few moments of painful silence, Kelly stood up. She adjusted her purse and forced a pathetic smile.

She was halfway to the door when she turned back. "I should have told you the truth. I realize that…but if I had, would you and I ever have had a chance?"

"I guess we'll never know," he said.

She hesitated, considering his answer. "May I say good-bye to Nattie?"

Jack shook his head. "She'll know. She'll see it in your eyes. And I can't do that to her."

Kelly nodded. "I truly wish you the best, Jack. I think you're a special person, and I admire you. I did from the first day I met you. Please know, too, that I have grown to love Nattie, whether she's mine or not. What I feel for you, and for her, has always been genuine."

With that she walked down the hall and out the door, shutting the door with a click that reverberated through him.

Moments later, Jack heard her car buzz down the street while he sat at the couch, justifying his actions and shoving his guilt away. **She was only trying to find her child.**

He was tempted to text her. **I just need some time.**

But he was too confused to know what to do next. And he still couldn't wrap his brain around what had just happened. Her test was negative, but **his** was positive.

Determined to find an answer, he went to the office, removed the printout of his own report, and stared at it. There it was in bold letters: **Sample A cannot be excluded.** Which was the same thing as positive.

He turned the page, to the second report, and found the opposite phrase, **Sample B is excluded.** Just as he had expected, which meant **negative**.

And then it finally hit him. Sample B had to be Kelly's hair. But Sample A...

"Oh no," he whispered.

His heart thumping wildly, Jack placed the report back into the desk drawer and headed out to retrieve Nattie as the memory of his conversation with Laura flooded back, including her adamant response to his suggestion that Kelly might be Nattie's mother. **"No, Jack, she's not."**

And just exactly how could Laura have been so sure?

Well, now he knew why.

Holding the screen door open, Diane smiled graciously. "That was quick."

Jack thanked her, and Nattie came running, Livy strolling out after. Both girls now had matching French braids dangling down their backs, and Jack was grateful the teen had taken such an interest in his daughter.

Nattie pulled on his sleeve. "Where does Kelly want to eat?"

Livy laughed and tugged on Nattie's braid. "That's all I heard. Kelly this, and Kelly that."

Waving their good-byes, Jack led Nattie out the door to the truck. Keeping in step, Nattie noticed Kelly's missing car and frowned. "Is she meeting us somewhere?"

"It's just us, sweetie."

Nattie stopped in her tracks. "Say what?"

"She had to go home, honey." He winced at his own exaggeration.

Nattie didn't move. "You have some 'splainin' to do, Dad."

"Over dinner, okay?"

She rolled her eyes. Jack waved toward the pickup. "On board, princess."

In the corner of McDonald's, Nattie ate slowly, dipping her nuggets in barbecue sauce, her eyes smoldering. "Are you guys having a fight or something? I mean, you guys **never** fight."

Jack barely heard her.

His cell phone was in his front pocket. He was tempted to text Kelly, ask for more time to get his head together. Sure, he still could be wrong, but he doubted it. The owner of Sample A—the hairs retrieved from the porch swing—had to be Nattie's mother. And there was no doubt whom she could be.

In the meantime Nattie was staring at him, waiting for a reply to a question he hadn't heard.

"What, honey?"

"Can I call her?" Nattie asked.

Jack shook his head, and Nattie took another bite of her chicken.

"Aren't you going to keep her?"

His phone began buzzing. He saw the name and breathed a sigh

of relief at the irony. **Laura.**

"Who is it?" Nattie asked.

He told her and offered her the phone. "I'll bet she wants to talk to you."

Quickly Nattie chewed the food in her mouth and wiped her fingers on her napkin. Jack made a face of mock impatience.

"What?" Nattie protested. "I want to be presentable." She took the phone and talked for a few minutes, then gave it back to Jack.

He spoke into the receiver. "You should have seen Nattie perk up."

"She's sounding good, **jah**?" Laura said.

He gazed at Nattie. "She's eating, and that's always a good thing."

Nattie gave him a humorous frown and popped a chicken piece into her mouth, listening intently to Jack's side of the conversation.

"So...have you heard yet?" Laura asked, lowering her voice.

Jack held out his index finger to Nattie—**give me a minute**—and wandered to the windows, outside the range of Nattie's ears. "Yes, I did...." He paused, not sure how to continue. "Actually, I need to see you."

She went silent, then her words came

out hushed, as if she didn't want anyone to hear her. "Is this about the lab results?"

He ignored the question, considering his options. Jack didn't want her to be able to walk away. And he didn't want others listening in. So that left out public restaurants, parks, his house, or hers. He wanted to get her into his truck and keep her there until she revealed the truth and heard him out.

"How about I pick you up tomorrow? I already checked with Diane—anything works for her."

He could hear Laura breathing and could imagine her twisting it over and over. "Okay, Jack. How 'bout three o'clock?"

He hung up and sighed.

Back at the table, Nattie flattened her nugget box with a fist, clearly frustrated. "You had to walk all the way over there to talk to Laura?"

"Grown-up stuff."

"Someday I'll be a grown-up, too, you know."

Jack pushed the remainder of his nuggets across the table to her. Nattie eyed them for a moment, appraising Jack's Cheshire twinkle. She narrowed her eyes, weighing their value, giving him the business end of her glare. Finally she shrugged, giving in. She began squirreling them away, nibble by nibble, then said casually, midchomp, "Nuggets won't always work, you know."

Jack crumpled his paper bag for his small fries into a tiny ball. "It's not like I can bribe you with broccoli."

"True," she said. "But you've never really discovered the power of Pop-Tarts. Tarts could open up an entirely new world for you."

"Thanks for the tip," Jack said.

Nattie gave him a lopsided grin, and it soothed his soul. At least they were okay. Even when the whole world seemed to be falling apart, he still had his little girl.

# Chapter 34

Kelly was fiddling with her keys, blinded by tears, when Melody opened Kelly's front door from the inside and gave her friend a long hug.

"Got your text," Melody whispered, "and thought you needed some company, so I let myself in."

Kelly crumpled in her arms. "It's my own fault, you know."

They moved into the kitchen, where Kelly tossed her keys on the counter, and Felix nudged up against her, meowing loudly. She couldn't believe the way things had turned out. Not until Jack opened the envelope had she come to grips with what she'd suspected. Nattie wasn't hers. And because of her lies, now she'd lost both Jack and Nattie.

"I pushed Jack to this," she said.

"If this is meant to be, he'll come around, Kelly."

Kelly hugged her arms, rubbing life into her body. "I'm exhausted, Mel."

Melody grabbed her hand. "C'mon, girlfriend. Let's go out."

"I can't," Kelly muttered. "And I'm keeping you from your family."

"They went to the movies," Melody replied. "When did you last eat?"

Kelly groaned. "This morning."

Melody scowled. "We're going out for comfort food. My treat. You're not losing weight again, not on my watch. I have a reputation to uphold."

Kelly smiled for the first time in hours but couldn't help checking her cell phone as she climbed into the passenger side of Melody's minivan. No texts. **Of course not.**

"Seat belt, Kelly," Melody whispered, turning a corner.

Feeling like a child, Kelly slipped it on, clicking it into place, remembering the surprised look on Jack's face when he read her report, as if he'd been expecting something different. **He was anticipating the worst**, she realized.

At the restaurant, talking loudly enough to be heard over the music, she recounted the entire scene, beginning to end. Melody listened carefully but with prejudice. She could tell Melody was growing frustrated with this Jack Livingston, despite Kelly's objections. "It's not his fault."

"It just seems to me he's not giving you a chance," Melody muttered.

When Melody slipped to the restroom, Kelly texted Jack a couple times, then felt stupid. She could imagine Melody's reaction—**"He should be pursuing you, Kel!"**

Kelly set her phone down, deeply grateful Melody hadn't left her alone tonight, despite her initial objections.

After an hour or so of pointless commiseration, Melody dropped her off at home, but not until they'd made plans for tomorrow morning.

"Text me!" was the last thing Melody said before spinning out of Kelly's apartment parking lot.

Alone again, Kelly headed inside, where Felix met her at the door, meowing miserably.

Gently setting Felix on the couch and tossing her purse on the counter, she decided not to turn on the lights. She didn't turn on the radio or the TV, either. She needed silence. And darkness.

It resonated with her soul. She needed to talk to the only Friend who'd ever stuck with her through thick and thin. And she needed a good cry.

Later, she wiped her eyes and tried to figure out if there was a way to repair the damage she'd done. If things between her and Jack were truly over, she could write Nattie a letter, tell her how much she'd enjoyed getting to know her, and how she wished things could have worked out differently. **Tell her I miss her.**

Fresh tears began to flow, and she snatched a few more tissues, blowing her nose and wiping her eyes. **No, leave her alone. I've caused enough trouble.**

She checked the front-door deadbolt

and made her way to the bedroom in the dark. It was only nine o'clock, but she went to bed and stared at the ceiling, realizing the only path forward was honesty. She was done with her tricks, done stealing DNA from unsuspecting suspects. And she couldn't let Ernie invade other folks' privacy for the sake of finding her daughter.

The end did not justify the means. **But where do I go from here?**

She had no idea. But God would direct. She knew that for sure. One step at a time.

An hour later, unable to sleep, Kelly dialed her private investigator. Normally, Ernie was a night owl. Through the years, he'd often called her late.

Penny answered. "Kelly dear, Ernie's having a bowl of oatmeal. I'll get him."

Ernie was surprised to hear from her. They made small talk at first, and then Kelly got him up to speed on the latest, embarrassed by the tears she couldn't hold back. Ernie didn't seem surprised by how things had turned out and expressed his condolences.

"I'm pulling the plug, Ernie," Kelly said. "I can't do this anymore." What she **meant** to say was, **"We're doing the wrong thing,"** but she didn't want her dear friend to feel judged.

"You sure? I've got one last name..." he began.

Kelly shook her head. "No more names, okay?"

"But—"

"I can't."

Ernie paused. "Fair enough, kiddo."

They made arrangements for the return of Chet's unspent money, and Kelly thanked Ernie for sticking by her.

Next, she called Chet, apologized for the late hour, and did what she hadn't been able to do for months. She told the truth, the full truth. "I wasn't completely honest with you."

A few moments later, in his Texan drawl, Chet said the words she needed to hear. "God forgives, my dear. And so do I."

She told him about her call to Ernie, and once again, Chet merely listened. She sniffed softly and felt her cat snuggle near.

"He'll return what he hasn't spent."

"Have you had enough?" Chet asked her.

She thought of what Chet had been telling her for years. **"The darkest moment is the greatest opportunity to shine the light of faith."**

"I'm regrouping," she told Chet, and he seemed pleased, sparing her further advice.

Nothing had changed. She was still the importunate widow knocking on the judge's door in the dark of night, waiting for the door to open, begging for justice. Despite her own mistakes and failures, she believed God was bigger than her foolish sins.

When she hung up the phone, it occurred to her that both Chet and Ernie had seemed strangely subdued. In fact, she was surprised that Ernie hadn't fought to stay in the game. Even Chet had let things go a little too easily.

**They are relieved I'm throwing in the towel**, she realized.

In the bedroom, lit only by the light of

the moon peering in through the window, she pulled the covers back and climbed into bed.

Truth was, she felt strangely rejuvenated by the sense of losing everything again. She had nothing left but empty faith, nothing to offer God in return for answers to her prayers, nothing but a small candle of faith to light in the darkness.

Kelly felt tears slip down her cheek. **It's better to believe than to receive.** She smiled through her tears, and it felt good. "Thank You for providing," she whispered into the darkness. "Thank You for taking care of my daughter when I can't. I trust You."

She pulled her phone from the lamp table. One last chance. She wasn't going to let go of Jack and Nattie without a fight.

After tucking Nattie in and fielding more of her attempts to "get to the bottom of this," Jack was able to get Nattie distracted long enough to pray and fall asleep.

He wandered downstairs to his office. Closing the door, he called San and gave her the news about Kelly and her test results, but held back the biggest part, the part about his own test and new suspicions.

"Wait a minute," San interrupted. "You broke up with her?"

"You have to ask?"

"Oh, Jack. We talked about this. And besides, you need someone in your life. Someone besides a nanny, I mean."

Jack leaned back in his swivel chair, the springs squeaking softly, trying to bottle his sudden anger. "San, what is your deal with Laura? Really."

"We've been through this before, Jack. Old news. **Old.**"

"You got what you wanted. She's gone. Just tell me the truth." San blew out a breath, and it sound raspy in his receiver. "There is no 'truth,' Jack. I've just never liked the idea of Nattie learning about the world from someone stuck in the nineteenth century."

"You mean someone who'll teach her about manners, and kindness, and hard work?"

San scoffed. "Sarcasm doesn't wear well on you, Jack."

He bit his tongue. San was hiding something. He was sure of it.

Usually, he'd let it go, but not tonight. "What do you know that I don't?" Jack demanded, trying to back her into a corner, but San did not like corners. Usually she came out swinging.

"Jack...please."

"If you didn't like Laura so much, why didn't you just tell Danny not to hire her?"

Silence for a moment. "I did," San finally said.

"So then...why did he?"

San cleared her throat, and when she began, her words came more softly. "You weren't there, Jack. You were in Kansas somewhere licking your wounds, trying to forget you had a family."

Jack rubbed his eyes, his frustration growing. "Don't turn this back on me."

"Fine." San sighed. "She just showed up on Danny's doorstep, this Amish-woman, answering Danny's church ad in person, of all things."

Jack waited.

"Laura was a stranger from nowhere. Nattie was a newborn, and Laura had zero references. And you know how Danny was. Too trusting by a mile, and so was Darla. Seriously, how did we know that Laura was even Amish? She could have taken off with Nattie, and we would have never seen her again."

"San—"

"I'm not finished, Jack. So there we were, with a strange woman standing on Danny's doorstep."

Jack remembered that San had been staying with them at the time of Nattie's birth, the summer before San went off to college. She was practically still a child herself.

San continued. "No references. No family. No work history. Just a shawl, a **Kapp**, and a prayer." She cleared her throat again. "So I suggested a background check."

Jack leaned forward, stunned.

"Of course Danny objected, but Darla certainly didn't oppose the idea. She had a mother's cautious worry, so Danny gave in, and we hired a PI, and he, in turn, hired someone in Lancaster County for the legwork, to check out her story."

She paused for a minute, then said defensively, "You would have known all this, Jack, if you'd ever visited when Nattie was first born."

Jack remained silent, determined not to let San verge off track.

"Anyway, what we discovered was that Laura came from terrible family circumstances, which is rather strange considering her religious upbringing. This Amish clan, they were doozies, Jack, let me tell you. According to the investigator, they seemed meanspirited and suspicious of outsiders."

"Who did you talk to?" Jack asked, his heart beating through his chest. Had San known the truth about Laura all these years? Is that why she despised her?

"No one would talk about her. That's what we found at first."

"That's not surprising, is it?" Jack countered. "She was a shunned woman. They were following their cultural protocol."

"Well, that in itself was a big red flag," San said. "You'd think we could have found **someone** to vouch for her, but no one would. In fact, no one who knew her who would give her a positive reference."

Jack considered this. "So that's your big deal. No one would talk about a shunned woman?"

San sighed. "Still…"

Jack felt his face redden. "I mean, no criminal record, no history of abuse, no **unborn** children—just a shunning." He'd strongly emphasized **unborn**, thinking she'd bite, but she didn't.

"The Amish don't shun for nothing, Jack."

"To **us** they do," he argued.

"Like I said. **No one** would talk to us, except…well…her ex-boyfriend."

Jack paused. "Jonathan."

"Yes, Jonathan." By now, San was thoroughly defensive. "Listen, I gotta go, Jack. It's late."

"So you found nothing on her. A big fat zero."

"Yes, Jack. You win. We never had a

reason to doubt her. But I wanted to be sure. I wanted my niece to be safe."

"You should have appreciated Laura for what she did for us, for me, and for Nattie."

"Oh, for pete's sake, Jack. I did. I just never cozied up to her. That's all."

The phone went silent. Finally San spoke softly, a defeated tone in her voice. "It's all in the background report, Jack. There's nothing worrisome, obviously. But you asked, so I told you. Actually, I told you this years ago. Don't you remember?"

"No."

San sighed. "Will you let me go now?"

Frustrated, Jack said good-bye and hung up, sweating profusely, and to top things off, his own cell phone pinged.

A text from Kelly: **Can we talk?**

He wanted to talk to her, to fix things, but what he was uncovering now was a game changer.

He replied: **I'm sorry.**

**So am I.**

He sat there waiting, contemplating what else to say. His phone beeped again, and he glanced at the message. **I miss**

**you.**

Kelly had only been gone for a few hours. He almost texted the exact same words back. His anger toward her had long since subsided, leaving only confusion.

He thought of Laura and how drastically things were about to change. Change how, he wasn't sure, but he had an idea.

He shut off his phone, leaning back in his chair, body trembling. He wiped his hands on his jeans and set about the task at hand, finding the truth.

**"It's in the background report,"** San had said. **"I told you this years ago,"** she'd added, and bits and pieces of that conversation were starting to come back to him. The report had contained nothing to implicate Laura of devious motives, but maybe there was something else, something hidden they hadn't seen.

As for the report itself, there was only one place it could be—that is, if it still existed.

Danny had been freakishly organized, but after his passing, Jack never bothered to actually review any of the files that used to be stored in the bottom drawer of the desk where he now sat—old financial records he'd intended to throw out... eventually. Grieving over his brother's death, he couldn't bring himself to do it. What was the point?

Jack now racked his brain, trying to remember where he would have stored them. **Garage attic?**

He trudged out to the garage and spotted the pulldown ladder leading to the attic above. If the files still existed, they would be up there. Grabbing a flashlight, he pulled down the makeshift ladder and climbed to the top, looking into the compartment smelling of fiberglass and dust.

A couple yards away, illuminated by his flashlight, Jack spotted an assortment of file boxes. **Jackpot**, he thought grimly. After retrieving a musty carton, he went back to his office and began digging through Danny's stuff.

At the time of Danny's funeral, San's phrase **"background report"** had barely registered, and he'd quickly drawn an assumption: Of course. **Something to do**

**with Nattie's adoption records**, he'd thought. Or a background report on the accident, neither of which interested him in the slightest.

Leaving the stacks of papers, Jack wandered upstairs to check on Nattie, only to find her sawing logs. **Poor kid.** No one seemed more innocent and harmless than an unconscious Nattie.

After tucking Laura's quilt around her, he slipped back downstairs quietly, and once in his office, he commenced rummaging through Danny's file.

There were indeed the adoption records, which he opened first, not expecting to find anything. He'd seen them before during the formal proceeding for his own guardianship of Nattie.

He thumbed through dozens of papers and receipts and was about to put everything away when he noticed a few stapled pages in the back. Removing them, he glanced at the top of the first paper, caught a stray word, and knew he'd found the fated background report, including a duplicate check attached to the back. Darla had signed the check drawn on their account.

In short, the background check on Laura produced the grand result of three single-spaced pages, a somewhat rambling account of the investigator's limited findings.

Toward the end of the third page, one paragraph popped out at him, including a reference to a hasty and somewhat contentious conversation with a Jonathan Glick, Laura's childhood sweetheart.

There was a photo attached, a picture of a rather unhappy young Amishman, raising his hands to object, clearly displeased by the violation. Jack wondered why they'd taken the photo in the first place. Perhaps to prove the conversation had taken place?

Don Fielder, licensed PI and Lancaster resident, had done the fieldwork in Pennsylvania for a local PI and had typed it up, typos and all:

Typical Amish bowl cut, Jonathan Glick answered the door. He works at the Lancaster Central Market for

Huber Farms. At first, he declined to be interviewed, but after we mentioned the topic, Laura Mast, he changed his mind. In response to our questions regarding her suitability as a nanny, his manner became belligerent, and he replied, "You obviously don't know Laura, or you wouldn't have to ask me this."

According to the last pages of the report, "Jonathan declined all further questions, and basically shut the door in our faces."

**I'm not surprised**, Jack thought, noting that Jonathan's contentious retort could have been taken two ways.

Jack flipped back to the front page to recheck the date of the conversation, a full two years after Laura's departure and her subsequent shunning.

He thought about this for a moment. They'd conducted this investigation **two** years after Laura's departure. He stared at the photo. Something didn't seem right, but he couldn't put his finger on it.

He closed the report and scanned the

top line again. **John Gibbon, Licensed Private Investigator.** His address was listed as an office suite downtown.

Jack sat there a moment, mulling it over, but the conclusions remained the same. While the background report had yielded little in the way of corroborating information, the DNA was inescapable. San's skepticism was justified.

**Laura is Nattie's mother.**

In the morning, Nattie was still in bed when Jack got up and started the coffee machine. Thumbing through his phone, he noticed another text from Kelly, sent about twenty minutes earlier: **Hope your day goes well. Give Nattie a hug from me.**

He felt another sickening thud in his stomach. He texted something back that must have seemed terribly cold to her, and couldn't help but remember what she'd asked him yesterday evening. **"If I had told you the truth, would you and I have had a chance?"**

The answer was no. He would have

shown her to the door, hired legal counsel, and dug in his heels. Even if he had allowed Nattie to be tested, it would have been conducted through his lawyer.

**We never had a chance.**

As if he hadn't tortured himself enough, he went to his office and opened the background report again. The more he thought about it, the gap in time made sense, the time between when Laura had left her community, according to her, and when she'd showed up answering Danny's posted advertisement for a nanny.

Only she'd omitted the part about why she'd left her community, pregnant with Jonathan's child and abandoned by her family. At eight, Jack set the file down, closed his office door, and called the lab.

"Do you have a moment to discuss my lab results?" Jack asked, when Jennifer answered. "I'm having a problem deciphering them."

She said she was more than willing to provide assistance, pulling up Jack's report on her computer.

"Is it possible," he asked, "that I

accidentally included hair strands from my daughter and tested **them** against her own swab sample?" In his view, this was unlikely, but he wanted her opinion.

"The lab would have detected an exact match and determined immediately that it was a collection error," Jennifer said, going on to explain her answer in more technical terms.

Jack asked her a few more questions, which she answered cheerfully. He thanked her again and hung up. He sat in his chair and chewed on it for another half hour. The conclusion was obvious. And the timeline fit. San's suspicions fit. The DNA fit. **Everything** fit.

All that remained was **why**? He considered this. Obviously, after giving Nattie up for adoption, Laura must have had second thoughts. Somehow, with information as to her child's whereabouts, Laura had then followed Nattie to her city and was miraculously able to get a job as a nanny for her very own child.

But one part didn't fit. How was it possible that Nattie just happened to be placed in the same town as Laura's cousin?

Highly improbable.

Unless…

He sat up as another possibility struck like lightning. What if Laura had engineered Nattie's placement? What if she had selected Danny and Darla because they lived in the vicinity of her cousin? What if she had always planned to watch over her child?

In that case, however, if she was so worried about her child, wouldn't she have opted for an open-adoption arrangement?

Jack returned to the kitchen and poured his third cup of coffee. He leaned against the counter. Nattie still hadn't stirred.

Jack took a sip. Maybe Laura didn't want anyone to know she'd had a child. That was possible, because an open adoption would have revealed her sin to the Plain community.

Jack sat there, his mind swirling around, trying to make sense of not only the information, but what he would do with it.

Ultimately, it came down to what was best for Nattie.

# Chapter 35

Early in the morning, Kelly opened the office doors, took the phone off night mode, and quickly checked emails.

Just before this, while sitting in her car, she'd texted Jack. **Hope your day goes well.** It sounded hopelessly out of touch, as if nothing had happened last night. Jack had texted back: **You too.**

**Give him space**, she thought. **And while you're at it: Get over him.**

In the meantime, she had a job to do, a job she still loved. During the past weeks a few clients had already contacted her boss, Melody's father, to compliment him on her hire.

**"I look like a genius!"** Bill had told her, and she'd laughed, appreciating the compliment. But there was little doubt she was good at this. If anything, work would give her time to heal, time to figure out the future.

Melody's father came out with the company newsletter for her to edit, plumbing another of her talents. Smoothing out the sentences for clarity, Kelly also looked for ways to add a shine of professionalism and savvy to otherwise dry information. Interspersed with this, she poured a cup of coffee for a client and made friendly conversation until her boss was ready to see him.

During her lunch break, she rechecked her phone. There was a happy, chatty text from Melody. But nothing more from Jack.

**Let it go**, Kelly told herself again, opting for the distraction of a quick trip to the deli down the street, where she sat in the corner, eating her turkey and Swiss sandwich while catching up on world news. When she was finished, she called Ernie and apologized for sounding so abrupt last night.

Ernie laughed it off.

"I'll stop by the office for a hug." Kelly

laughed.

"I'll hold you to it, kiddo."

She thought of Chet and Eloise, wanting to do something special to thank them. She couldn't possibly repay them, but she **could** thank them with a special gift, and she could be the best "daughter" she could possibly be.

Despite last night's decisions and tumultuous ending, she felt a strange peace. No matter what happened, things were going to be fine. She knew this, even though she couldn't explain it. She recalled the story of George Mueller's faith, thanking God for food while the orphans sat waiting. **The table only looks empty**, she decided.

Sure, she might find another way to search for Emily. Or she might simply move on. She didn't really know yet. But she had the utmost confidence that God would give her wisdom, despite her many mistakes.

**All things work together for good...**

Nattie wandered down about nine o'clock that morning, holding Bear Bear. She peeked in Jack's office, her hair in disheveled braids, still wearing her cartoon pajamas, her perturb having carried over from last night. "How come you didn't wake me?"

Jack tossed his pencil on the desk, leaning back in his squeaky chair. "Thought you needed sleep."

"When will I see Kelly again?" she asked sharply. Her gaze threatened to bore a hole in his face.

"Do you want to text her?"

She made a face. "Texting is for scaredy cats."

The phone rang. Mick at the office. Paper work questions. Nattie harrumphed at Jack's sudden preoccupation and headed out to the kitchen, presumably to dig up some Pop-Tarts.

When Jack hung up the phone, Nattie whimpered from around the corner at the bar. "I'm all alone out here..."

Jack hustled out to the kitchen, kissed Nattie's cheek, and offered to cook an omelet for both of them, an event that Nattie greeted with polite skepticism.

He opened the cupboard, noticing how

empty it seemed. He went to the dish-washer to retrieve a clean plate and realized they hadn't been washed. **We really miss Laura**, he thought. He poured in the detergent, glancing at the glasses along the top row. He removed one and spotted the telltale sign of smudged lipstick— Kelly's. Feeling wistful, he set it aside on the counter.

He started the dishwasher and asked, "Where were we?"

"Omelets," Nattie interjected. "Laura uses coconut oil instead of butter."

"Got it. Coconut oil." He went to the cupboard but didn't see anything. He turned to see Nattie pointing to the other cupboard.

"Of course," Jack said. "I knew that."

He grabbed a bottle of oil and headed for the stove.

"That's olive oil, Dad," Nattie muttered.

"I knew that, too." Jack chuckled, returning to the cupboard.

Next he went to the fridge and looked inside. **No eggs.**

He turned around. "So...how 'bout

toaster waffles for breakfast?"

Nattie sighed and put her face in her hands.

Later, Jack sat at his desk again and reviewed the background report, searching for something he'd missed, as if he hadn't already read it repeatedly. Nattie had begged to swim this afternoon, and he'd agreed to take her. It was the least he could do.

He noticed the Lancaster Central Market again and accessed the website, curious about this nostalgic world of Laura's where the English and Amish cultures collided. There was a market directory and a miniweb page for each vendor. He found Huber Farms, where Jonathan had worked, and clicked on it. On the right, there was further vendor information, including their personal website, independent of the market.

Waiting for Nattie to come down, he clicked on it. The farm's official website appeared. He stared at it. Nine years ago, Jonathan had worked here—no doubt he'd long since moved on.

He heard a soft rustling outside his office and looked over to see something slide under his door. He got out of his chair to investigate. It was a piece of notebook paper, the heading: **My favorite things about Kelly.**

Taking a deep breath, he began to read: **She's prettier than Angela. She plays with me. She makes me laugh. She likes my drawings. She listens to me... like Laura. She can do magic! She already acts like a mother, even though she's not. She likes YOU!**

Jack had his work cut out for him. Sighing, he placed the list in his drawer and sat down to surf again. He poked at a couple links for Huber, and a large photo of the farm's location at the market popped up, treating him to an unexpected sight: a photo of an Amishman, his arm around an Amishwoman, standing beside an English couple. The caption read **Jonathan and Becca Lynn Glick, and owners, Bill and Jane Huber.**

The same bowl cut, the Amish hat with

the required brim width, the black vest, a smile for the camera, the camera flash glistening off his pale clean-shaven cheeks.

He stared at the picture. It was the same man he'd seen in the PI photograph, definitely older, but undeniable: Jonathan Glick, now married to Becca Lynn.

Jack's heart broke for Laura and for what might have been, and it made him even more determined to care for her. **"We're her family,"** Nattie once told him. **"She belongs with us."**

Thoughts of her disastrous meeting with Jack, still fresh and raw, brought waves of regret the next morning, and to top it off, Kelly was running late—according to her own standards, that is. Even if traffic was rough, she'd easily arrive on time, but she liked to leave early—beat the rush.

Kelly dropped a piece of bread into the toaster, still hearing Melody's exhortations in her ear, and grabbed some almond butter and a knife. From the cupboard, she grabbed a couple of granola bars for her afternoon break.

She clicked on her calendar for the day and smiled, a sudden wave of relief flooding through her. She had a dental appointment at eight. She'd forgotten she'd moved it up. She wasn't expected at the office until ten o'clock.

She took a deep breath. **Too much on my plate**, she thought. She even had time for a leisurely breakfast with English muffins and a bowl of cereal.

Felix wandered out, meowing softly, nose-bombing into her ankles and flopping onto his side. She laid out the Meow Mix and rubbed his neck. The purring increased with intensity.

"You're rather high maintenance, you know that?"

Felix meowed that he was worth the effort.

Thirty minutes later, Kelly tossed her ever-present cell phone into her bag and headed out the door, dreading yet another drive in the Toyota. Maybe it was time for another car. She could afford it, couldn't she?

**As if**, she chuckled to herself. Although she'd put on weight, her bank account was still astonishingly thin, despite the good pay.

She was driving to the dentist appointment when Ernie called. She was surprised to hear from her old pal, considering their recent commiserations.

Ernie sounded out of breath. "Are you sitting down, kiddo?"

"I'm driving, Ernie. What's up?"

"Listen, Kelly. I've kept something from you, and you should know the truth. It's about that other prospect."

**The other name?** "Ernie—"

"I didn't want to say anything the other day, not until I knew for sure. Well, now I do. We know for sure."

She was confused. "I don't understand."

"I contacted the parents myself...well, actually **Chet** did. He's better at that."

**The parents?** "Wait a minute. Whose parents?"

"Okay. Now that I've got your attention, hear me out. You are **not** going to believe this..."

While Ernie talked, Kelly took an immediate turn for a shopping center and parked in an empty slot in front of a drugstore. "This one came through the website, Kelly. An attorney contacted us. I wanted to make sure it was legit before I said anything...."

She could feel her arms tremble as Ernie described what he'd been doing during the past month. All with Chet's blessing, of course, and that was the best part. No deceit had taken place. No one's privacy had been invaded or compromised.

When Ernie finally got to the point, Kelly nearly dropped her phone.

They were at the pool. Despite the cloudy day, the temperatures hovered in the eighties. This morning, Nattie had announced a change in her list of favorite summertime things. She was now too old for the park. The pool was where it was at.

Jack lay on his back, wearing sunglasses, catching his breath following a spirited underwater contest, which Nattie had easily won. Jack looked out toward the pool. Catching his eye, Nattie was about to leap into the water, frowning at his distraction.

**What now?** she mouthed.

**I'm watching**, he mouthed back.

Nattie leaped into the pool, then surfaced, climbing halfway out of the water, holding herself up on trembling arms, half in, half out of the pool, a water-drenched little girl. "Aren't you coming in?"

"I just got out."

Nattie gave him the face, a powerful mixture of pity and love that could nearly always get her what she wanted.

Jack nodded wearily, and Nattie squealed with delight, checking behind her and then flailing backward, splashing into the water.

Jack picked up his phone and, without thinking, ran through Kelly's old texts. **It doesn't feel right...I miss you...can I call you?**

"Da-ad!"

He got to a sitting position. He could

feel Nattie's eyes on him. He could hear the frantic splashing of water, the squealing of a dozen kids.

He pulled up his email. Something in the report didn't make sense, and something about the Huber website was bothering him, as well. And yet there was no mistaking the picture of Jonathan and his wife, Becca Lynn Glick. Laura had pined for her first love for nearly a decade, but apparently no grass had grown under Jonathan's feet. He'd wasted little time finding another love.

He thought about Laura last June, sitting on the bench, reviewing their day, enjoying their mutual love for Nattie.

Jack thought back to that first date with Kelly. At the coffee shop, and then at the fancy steak restaurant. And their first kiss.

"Da-ad!"

Their hours of conversation, the feeling that his heart had found its home. And wasn't that why he'd been so angry? She'd led him to hope and to believe. Only to jerk the rug out from beneath him.

**It doesn't matter**, he told himself again.

Laura was Nattie's mother, and that changed everything. It changed the past, the present, and the future.

Ernie had already purchased the plane ticket for Kelly, a one-way ticket to Chicago, scheduled for departure on Friday morning.

Kelly's Emily was now Megan, and she lived with her family in an upscale suburb of Chicago. She'd been adopted at the ripe old age of four months by parents who were fully capable of paying the exorbitant prices demanded by a no-strings adoption agency, the kind of agency that provided results in days rather than years.

Ernie had submitted Kelly's DNA, already on file, and Megan's family had submitted hers. The test came back positive, and indisputable: Megan was Kelly's child.

According to Ernie, Megan's parents were sickened by the news of their unintentional involvement, and they wanted to make things right, but with their daughter's best interests at heart. Although they'd raised Megan with full knowledge of her adoption, they were worried about Megan's capacity to emotionally deal with the truth at such a young age.

A slow transition, ultimately leading to shared custody, would be worked out by lawyers, Megan's parents, and Kelly. All she had to do was move to Chicago, preferably within a few miles of her daughter, and begin the process.

**I found her**, Kelly thought, her body shivering with the realization that her search was over.

Despite her own mixture of feelings, she would agree to their requests, saddened to lose her new job, but excited by her future.

**It's worth it!** she told herself.

In the meantime, she had to find a new job and a place to live.

"Done," Ernie said. "And forget giving notice. I talked to your friend Melody, and she talked to her dad. They've already arranged a leave of absence for you. And Chet's got a buddy in Chicago who needs some office temp work. Start with that until we know what we're dealing with. You can always make a quick trip back to pack up your things."

"But I still need a place—"

"That too. Done."

Determined to remember this moment forever, Kelly cued up a favorite song and stared at the storefronts nearby until she couldn't see for the tears.

Happy tears.

Emily had been safe all along.

**I knew that, didn't I?** But no, she hadn't known that, not for sure. But she'd believed it. She'd **believed**.

# Chapter 36

Jack pulled up to Laura's country home at three o'clock that afternoon, as they'd agreed. Rolling down the truck window, he sat for a moment, taking in the farm air, steeling himself for what would come next and praying for the right words.

Along her cousin's porch, a mixture of flowers displayed Laura's handiwork—only sparser. He felt a twinge of guilt. She'd worked so hard at his home, bringing color into their lives, only to leave little time to enrich her own.

In the distance he saw a mangy cat scramble for the barn, tracking its prey. The trill of a hummingbird came from the honeysuckle bushes, and Jack smiled, reliving those early weeks of summer, the three of them sitting on the back porch, watching their own hummers, learning their species because Nattie had been so determined to categorize her favorites.

**How I miss those days!** Jack remembered Laura's strange behavior the day he'd driven her home and sprung his dating plans on her, and then their awkward conversation that day in the laundry room. It all made sense now. She must have been dying to tell him the truth.

Jack took a breath and let it out slowly. They had a lot to talk about, and a lot to decide. Yet even now, sitting there, waiting for Laura, he couldn't help remembering Kelly, haunted by the pain in her eyes when she'd been confronted with her lies.

**Her lies**—how ironic! After all, Kelly wasn't the only one who had lied to him. Laura would have kept her own deceit for these many years.

He sighed. His head was spinning. **Forget how you feel**, he thought. **Do the right thing.** The future was clear. Jack whispered it out loud, "Do the right thing. For Nattie. For Laura."

Crunching across the gravel and

crossing the creaky porch, badly in need of fresh paint, he knocked on Laura's door, feeling like a suitor, wishing he'd brought flowers. Suddenly the door burst open, and there she stood, her expression bright but apologetic. Her face seemed rosy, as if she'd just washed up, and her hair shone in the sunlight, her **Kapp** neatly pinned on top. "Jack! I didn't hear ya pull up."

He felt out of breath, as well, but for a different reason—nerves. She wiped her hands on her apron and stood there, primly, now looking as anxious as he felt. "Are we goin' somewhere?"

"A short drive, maybe? We won't be long. I promise."

She studied him for a moment.

"I want to discuss the test results," he said, noting her reluctance. Without saying anything further, she removed her apron, tossed it just inside the door, and followed him out.

It was like old times, the way she climbed into his pickup and settled in, smoothing her dress with suntanned hands. Clicking the seat belt, she took a deep breath, her shoulders rising and falling quickly, as if to say, **"Okay, here we go!"**

She regarded him with bemusement as he got himself situated, that charming way she had of watching him out of the corner of her eye.

Jack put the truck into gear and turned around, kicking up dust, heading back the way he'd come. He paused at the blacktop, noting the scent of new asphalt, and once he'd pulled out, Laura asked about Nattie.

He told her the latest, and Laura grinned at the details. They were never more comfortable with each other than when talking about Nattie, discussing her issues, her moods, and her recent shenanigans.

Eight miles back to Wooster, he finally said, "We miss you, Laura."

"Well, I miss you, too," she said politely, before pointing to the right. "There's a park just down the street."

"Got it," Jack said, turning.

It was an older neighborhood dominated by dogwoods, maples, and ashes. He rolled the truck to a stop.

Getting out into the breezy sun-dappled

side street, they walked along a pathway leading to a secluded and shaded park bench. He could smell fall in the air, sunshine flickering through the branches, the topmost leaves just beginning to show their rich colors.

Laura sat down, demurely placing her hands in her lap. Jack plopped down on the bench beside her, feeling the wood planks give under their weight. They sat for a moment, taking in the sounds of a riding mower, driven by a young long-haired landscaper in jeans, and the energetic squeals of elementary school girls jumping along the sidewalk across the street.

Earlier, he'd been nervous, but now her openness, her cheerfulness, gave him courage.

"I'm not here to harass you into coming back," he said kindly, although that wasn't exactly true.

Her smile turned into a grin. When he couldn't avoid it any longer, he said, "Kelly's not Nattie's mother."

Laura nodded, adding a soft **hmm** as if

to say, **"I told you that."**

And instead of scaring her with what might seem like an ambush, he began to relay his DNA testing process, finding the strands of hair and submitting them against Nattie's DNA, all the while gently backing her into a corner, where she **had** to admit to the truth.

She listened intently, keeping up with his explanation, her expression receptive, but there was a glint of confusion, as well, as if wondering if he'd taken her all this way just to tell her what she already knew.

He plunged ahead. "My test was different from Kelly's."

He studied her response but saw nothing—no glint of surprise, not even a whisper of guilt.

"**My** test was positive," he added for clarity.

Her eyes narrowed. "I still don't understand."

He tried again. "One of the hair samples I submitted matched Nattie's DNA."

Now Laura leaned back, as if considering this. And then he saw what seemed to be a tiny chink in the armor: a look of acceptance. She wasn't puzzled anymore. In fact, she wasn't surprised at all.

"Jack—"

"Laura, don't say anything yet." He didn't want her to begin denying it before he had a chance to make his little speech.

He put his hand on the back of the bench, his arm practically around her shoulders. "Do you remember earlier this summer, sitting on the swing, talking about anything that came to mind, sipping iced tea at the end of the day and laughing at Nattie's latest antics?"

She smiled but seemed to steel herself.

"And you gave me that gift I will treasure forever, not just because of what it is, but because it came from you."

Her gaze was steady, unyielding.

"We were growing closer, Laura."

She nodded, sniffing softly.

"But something happened," he said. "After my birthday."

Her expression dimmed suddenly, but he continued. "We were on the brink of something, Laura."

"**Jah**, we **were** growing closer," she said. "But after your birthday, I had to make a decision."

She reached over and patted his arm, as if to ease the blow of what she was about to say. "You'd never really seen me before that day, Jack. I mean truly seen me. And it was nice, you know, to have you look at me that way, but the truth is, I'm not fancy, Jack, and I never will be." She looked away for a moment before continuing quietly, "And I don't think you've ever accepted that."

"Give me another chance," he protested.

"**Ach**, Jack—"

"For Nattie's sake, if not for mine."

She shook her head slightly, but her eyes softened at the mention of Nattie.

"You took care of us for years, Laura. I want to take care of you now." His voice cracked with emotion, and he had to look away for a moment before whispering, "Come back to us."

Her eyes grew misty, and for the first time, she seemed receptive to him. He swallowed and edged closer, leaning in, not sure if she'd let him kiss her, wondering if he was about to break a profound taboo, an Englisher kissing an Amishwoman. But then he was struck, suddenly, by the realization that never once, in all of their years together, had he ever imagined kissing her.

**And why was that?** He was inches from her face—she had already closed her eyes—when he stopped, as if frozen in his tracks.

Laura opened her eyes, and a look of bemusement fell over her. She leaned back, and her words came out playfully. "You couldn't do it, could ya, Jack?"

He stared at her, trying to make sense of his conflicted emotions. "I'm sorry...I mean...I thought..."

Laura's eyes danced with humor, and she laughed, shaking her head. "Do ya understand now?"

"It doesn't change anything," he replied, feeling defensive and sheepish all at once.

She laughed again. "Oh, Jack! It changes **everything**."

"Laura—" He stopped, tempted to

simply blurt out what he knew, that **she** was Nattie's mother, but sighed with frustration.

"We were good friends, partners even," she continued. "And I will always miss that."

"Then let's make this work," Jack said, still trying to fix the mess he'd made.

Laura's eyes twinkled again, but she shook her head. "Jack, you are handsome and kind, a **gut** man, and you've always looked out for me. But I want something more. I want a love like I had with Jonathan. And you should seek that, too."

She looked down for a moment, and when she met his gaze again, a flicker of recognition crossed her features. Her eyes widened in surprise. "You think I'm Nattie's mother, don't you? Isn't that what this is all about?"

He nodded. "You can tell me, Laura."

She pursed her lips, and her words came out with strong determination. "Jack, as much as I love Nattie, she is not my child. Jonathan and I..." Her voice trailed off, and a rosy blush crept across her face. "There was **no** baby, Jack. If you believe nothing else, believe that."

Laura looked away, leaving Jack dumbstruck by her fervent denial. He took another breath and let it out slowly, nodding slightly before staring straight ahead. He considered the test again. Hadn't he read that sometimes these DNA tests were simply wrong? Contaminated? Maybe he'd made a mistake. Either way, it didn't matter anymore.

A breeze brushed against them. The sun had disappeared behind a cloud, lowering the temperature suddenly. She seemed out of breath again. He sighed and slumped in the bench, staring straight ahead, toward the street. **"If you believe nothing else, believe that."**

He did believe her. He wished he didn't. Truth was, he'd wanted Laura to be Nattie's mother.

"I'm sorry," she said, seeing his obvious dejection.

"No," he whispered. "I'm sorry for dragging you out here."

"It's okay, Jack." She touched his arm.

"Are **you** okay?"

He nodded, too embarrassed to speak, and really, there was nothing more to say. He got up, and she followed suit. Silently, they walked across the park, Laura hugging herself tightly, stepping carefully through the freshly mown grass, her tennis shoes padding as she navigated around the small clumps.

They got in the truck and he drove down the street. On the way to the farm, Laura said nothing, enduring the silence. He was back to square one. Worse than square one. What began as a foolish attempt to bring someone into Nattie's life had only made matters worse. Laura was gone, and she wasn't coming back.

He turned into her cousin's driveway again and traveled the gravel road to her house. Coming to a stop, he shifted into Park, and they sat there as the truck idled for a moment.

Laura put her hand on the latch. "Well…"

"I'm sorry I didn't kiss you."

She smiled. "Did you want to try again?"

Her reply broke through the gloominess,

and Jack couldn't help but laugh. Laura joined in, the earlier tension slipping away. Another wave of silence engulfed them, but Laura didn't get out. She bit her lip and finally spoke. "There's something else," she said. "This isn't my place, but I think ya have a right to know, Jack."

He nodded, if only to encourage her to continue. He had no idea where she was going with this.

"The lab results," she added, lowering her voice to a whisper, as if telling a grave secret. "Ya didn't make a mistake, okay? I suspected it for years, but I never lied to you, Jack. It just wasn't my truth to tell."

He frowned. "Laura, I don't under—"

"Be gentle, okay? Sometimes we keep secrets for a reason."

Before he could ask her to explain, she grabbed the handle, pulled it down, and stepped out of his truck.

Jack sat there, bewildered, as Laura climbed the porch steps, opened the screen door, and disappeared inside.

**What on earth does she mean?**

He shook his head. The sun was setting,

and Nattie would be anxious. He needed to get back, to try to salvage what remained of their lives.

He put the truck into gear and turned around in front of the barn, pausing just as Samuel Troyer rounded the corner. He waved, and Jack returned the gesture, thinking that if he ever saw the young man again, Samuel would be married and sprouting a full beard. Jack smiled at the thought, took another breath, and headed down the drive, stopping at the edge of the highway.

Something wasn't right.

He squinted through the dust particles his tires had kicked up. In the rearview mirror, a hundred feet behind him, he could see Samuel crossing the road, heading to the house. Something nagged at Jack, but it had nothing to do with Laura's strange riddle.

**Then what is it?** He racked his brain. He glanced at Samuel again, clean and shiny-faced Samuel, soon to grow a full beard because that's what Amish boys do when they marry their sweet-hearts.

And then it hit him.

Heart beating against his chest, Jack put the truck into reverse and backed up the long driveway, stopping in front of the house again. Scrambling up the porch, Jack pounded on the screen door. It rattled against the old frame.

"Laura?"

No response, so he pounded again. Laura appeared in the doorway, wiping her hands on a kitchen towel, her brow furrowed in concern. "Jack? What—"

He pulled her onto the porch, then yanked out his phone, typing **Lancaster County Market** into the search bar. Laura waited for him to speak, her eyes narrowing. "Jack, what is it?"

"Jonathan," he said simply.

Laura looked at him, confused. "What about him?"

The site came up, and Jack clicked on the adjacent link, the company website. And then he navigated to the photo, the one with the caption: **Jonathan and Becca Lynn Glick.**

Jack handed the phone to Laura. She

took it curiously. She stared at it for a moment, her eyes softening. "Sure, that's him."

"And the woman?" Jack asked.

"**Jah**, that's Becca Lynn, his sister," she said. "Remember I told you about her?"

He hadn't remembered, not until now. The younger sister with special needs.

Laura's face went pale. "Wait a minute. When was this taken?"

Jack told her it must be recent and pointed to the copyright on the newly created website. She frowned. "No. That can't be." She stared at it, shaking her head. "There must be some mistake."

**They lied to her**, he realized. **To punish her.**

Laura gripped his phone tighter, but her hands were shaking. Finally she handed it back, tears slipping down her cheeks. She wiped them away brusquely, almost angrily, and looked off into the distance, folding her arms and breathing heavily now, hope and sadness mingling in equal measure on her face.

Jack could only imagine what was going

through her mind: her first love, still unmarried, and her family, keeping the truth from her all these years.

"My Jonathan..." She turned to him, wonder shining in her eyes. "Could it be he's waited for me?" She brushed another tear away, then whispered, "And here, all this time, I've stubbornly refused to go home." Her expression changed then, and she smiled tenuously.

"You'll go back, then?" Jack asked.

She nodded, adding quickly, "I'll stay in touch with you and Nattie...let you know how it goes for me, okay?"

"We'll worry," he said. "Until we hear something."

She smiled, but already her thoughts seemed a thousand miles away. Laura stood there for a moment longer, her eyes shining in the lowering sun. She took in a deep breath, as if sensing the world for the first time, and when she turned to him, he'd never seen her so happy.

But it worried him sick. Laura hadn't been home in years. **What will she find?**

"'Bye," Jack whispered, but Laura was

already gone, letting the screen door slap behind her and rushing up the stairs as if she couldn't wait another minute for her new life to begin.

Back in the truck cab, Jack paused, struggling with his own mixture of emotions. **Protect her, Lord**, he thought before putting the truck into gear and heading back down the driveway. At the intersection, he pulled out onto the highway, focusing on the road, accelerating to sixty. The truck rattled a bit, showing its age, but the engine was strong.

**Good ol' Billy Bob**, he thought, thinking of Nattie waiting for him at Diane's.

His head continued to spin, but he smiled suddenly, remembering Laura's comeback: **"Would you like to try again?"**

He sighed. **I couldn't even kiss her.**

Minutes later, he pulled up to the house, and Nattie came careering out of the Farleys' door. It warmed his heart, and tears filled his eyes. No matter what, Nattie always seemed so happy to see him, even on those occasions when she wasn't all that happy **with** him.

He didn't bother getting out of the truck. Nattie pulled open the door and, without due process, hopped inside. "Where are we off to, Dad-ee-o? Just so you know, there's **nothing** in the fridge."

He smiled. "Nothing?"

"Nothing edible." She slapped the seat. "Oh! I forgot something. I want to show you my picture."

"I'll wait."

She hopped out and ran to the house, using her own key to open the door.

From the door of her own home, Diane caught his attention and waved, and he waved back.

Jack closed his eyes and tried to calm his racing mind. **What a day.** He gripped the steering wheel, wishing he could turn his brain off, but Laura's words, buried in the momentous discovery that Jonathan was still single, came back to him. **"I suspected it for years."**

He blew out a frustrated breath. **Suspected what?**

Another moment passed; and then a

shiver crawled up his spine. It felt like a key slipping into a lock, the tumblers clicking into place. **"I never lied to you,"** Laura had said. **"It just wasn't my truth to tell."**

He groaned inwardly. Nattie was pulling open the truck door again, holding her latest masterpiece, when the final realization struck him hard.

Nattie's mother had been with them all along.

## Chapter 37

Not surprisingly, no one met Kelly at Chicago O'Hare, a sprawling warehouse of giant tunnel-like halls and endless gates, all leading somewhere, but serving only to magnify her growing nerves.

Kelly was about to meet her daughter for the first time in nine years, and after the initial excitement, she'd slowly grown terrified. Of course, Megan wouldn't remember her, but what if Megan didn't **like** her?

At the rental-car agency, which seemed miles from her arrival gate, Kelly produced her license and credit card for the woman behind the counter.

"For now, I'd like it just through the weekend," Kelly said as she signed the contract. "But can I add on days if necessary?"

The woman nodded, putting on her glasses before circling a phone number on Kelly's copy of the paper work. "Just call us before it's due back, and we'll quote you a new price."

Since she was friendly enough, Kelly dug her notes out of her purse. "Any idea how far it is to 900 North Michigan?" she ventured, her heart pounding again.

"In this traffic?" the woman said with a frown. "Might be a good forty minutes, honey."

Kelly groaned and headed out of the building, squinting at the blazing sun reflecting off the hundreds of windshields. Grabbing her sunglasses, she followed the numbers until she found 204, dropped her roller bag into the trunk of a very compact tan Chevy, and buckled into the driver's seat.

After following the signs out of the parking lot, ambiguous arrows that seemed to point everywhere, she managed her way onto I-90. According to her GPS, she was now twenty-eight minutes from her destination, cutting it rather close, considering traffic and parking.

**Very tight**, she thought, her nerves heightening.

From the moment Ernie had told her the news, she'd brooded over this meeting, obsessing about it, praying over it. How would she feel when she saw Megan's adoptive parents? Already, she'd alternated between relief, joy, despair, and rage.

**They bought my baby**, she thought. And since she'd agreed not to press charges, the parents had agreed to introduce Kelly into Megan's life. How dare they place conditions?

**"Forgive,"** Chet and Eloise had counseled her. She'd stayed overnight in the couple's home, in the beautifully appointed spare bedroom suite. They'd fed her a gourmet breakfast in the morning, and then Chet had driven her to the airport.

"I do forgive," she'd told them, **"but it's easier said than done."**

**"They didn't know,"** Chet reminded her.

**But they should have**, Kelly thought. They didn't **want** to know.

They wanted their beautiful brown-eyed beauty, their little trophy child. My child.

She drove in mind-numbing traffic for as long as the GPS had promised, then found her destination. The office itself was on the twelfth floor of a limestone and glass high-rise in the middle of downtown Chicago, anchored by upscale shops at the street level, and thankfully, underground parking.

She located a spot for her car and gathered her things in the dingy darkness, making her way quickly to the bank of elevators leading up to the offices. She wrinkled her nose at the dank, oily smell of the parking lot and breathed a sigh of relief when the elevator doors finally opened with a muted **ping**.

A tranquil environment greeted her—lush carpet, etched glass, dark wood, and modern art.

The blond woman at the front desk greeted her with a guarded but professional smile.

"Kelly Maines," Kelly said softly. "For Michael Stedman."

"Maines," the woman said out loud, clicking the keys on her keyboard, the artificial smile still in place. Finally she asked her to have a seat and spoke into her phone. Kelly could imagine the conversation: **"We have an unfortunate interruption, a poorly dressed woman who goes by the tedious name of Maines."**

Kelly clutched her own phone and texted Chet to soothe his worries. Earlier, he'd fretted, **"Downtown Chicago is no picnic."** He'd planned to accompany her to the meeting, but a family illness had kept him away.

**I'm here**, she texted.

**Wonderful**, he responded. **I was praying.**

She smiled. Sometimes Chet treated her as if she were barely out of middle school, and yet it was comforting.

**How can I ever thank you?**

He texted back: **The smile on your face is all the thanks we'll ever need.**

**I'm so happy**, she replied, perhaps the worst lie she'd told in years.

Truth was, she was scared to death. Yes, she wanted desperately to see her daughter, but her own emotions, tangled and contradictory like a twisting tornado switching directions at a whim, threatened to tear her apart. She had no idea what she was going to say to her daughter's parents. She had no planned speech. No kind words: **"Thank you for watching over her all these years."** Not at the moment. Maybe later. Maybe never.

She bowed her head subtly, lest the receptionist roll her eyes, and prayed. **Again.** She'd prayed constantly since that phone call from Ernie, but nothing seemed to resolve the turmoil of emotions.

From what Chet said, these people were rich. As in yachts and jets, vacation homes in Aspen and Paris, and whatever else people purchased when they had enough money to buy other people's children.

She closed her eyes. **Help me be kind, Lord.**

Suddenly the door burst open and a

friendly faced man—**isn't he too young to be an attorney?**—wearing an immaculate blue-gray suit greeted her warmly. "So! You must be Kelly Maines!"

He had wavy brown shoulder-length hair, parted in the middle, about an inch from requiring restraint of some sort. Fortunately, the suit compensated for his Bohemian appearance.

Kelly forced a smile as he took her hands in his.

"I'm Michael." He pushed open the door and gestured for her to go first. "It's an honor to meet you. I have to say, you look just like Megan."

Kelly felt as if she'd been punched. Her head was fuzzy again, and she feared she might actually faint.

Oblivious to the effect of his insensitive remark, Michael led the way down the hall, past a dozen cubicles. Halfway to where he seemed to be leading her, she stopped, frozen. Paralyzed.

**I can't**, she thought, feeling dizzy.

Michael was several yards beyond her before he realized she wasn't with him anymore. He turned around. "Kelly? Are you okay?"

**No**, she thought, looking down, leaning over, hands on her knees.

"Ellen!" she heard him call.

Someone answered from the cubicle next to her, and suddenly there was a young brunette woman holding her arm and telling her, "Breathe, honey. Do you want to sit down? Do you need something to drink?"

Kelly swallowed and righted herself.

**No**, she thought forcefully. **I can do this. I will. I have to.**

She cleared her throat, swallowed, and now Michael was on the other side of her, also holding her arm, and not in a comfortable way.

"I'm okay," she protested.

"You don't look it," Ellen replied gently, pushing up the frames of her thick dark glasses with one hand, the other still firmly planted on Kelly.

Kelly stopped again and politely pried herself loose.

"I know this must be hard for you,"

Michael said, and she thought, **You have no idea.**

"They're very nice people," Michael added, hands outstretched as if she might tumble at any moment. She looked forward, her blurred vision refocusing.

"Do you need some time?" Michael asked.

"No," she said sharply.

Just then, farther down the hall, another door opened on the right, and a thirty-something woman with highlighted blond hair, a casual dress, and black patent flats, stepped out. She looked to her right, then to her left, and spotted them. Spotted **her**.

It was her gaze that struck Kelly first, the way her eyes melted with concern. Kelly remained bolted in place. **What am I going to say?**

The woman was rushing, practically running toward them. Kelly looked away. **Oh God, please. Don't let me hit her.**

"Kelly?"

She looked up.

"Kelly Maines?"

"Yes," she said.

"You **are** her mother," the woman exclaimed but with a truthful smile. "You are as beautiful as I had imagined, the spitting image of your daughter."

Kelly blinked back tears.

She reached for Kelly. "May I?"

Kelly nodded, reluctantly at first, and then she was embracing this woman whom she'd wanted to tear limb from limb. The woman—**Michelle is her name**, Kelly thought—wouldn't let go, refused to let go.

"I can't tell you how sorry we are," Michelle whispered in her ear. "We will do whatever we can to fix this. We have so much to tell you, so many pictures to show you. I can't **wait** for you to meet Megan."

**Megan.** At that moment, Kelly tightened her grip on Michelle. She wasn't angry anymore.

**It's going to be okay**, she realized.

# Chapter 38

"Too bad you're not into cars, brother dear," San chirped, elbowing him in the arm. They stood in the doorway to the garage, admiring the sleek curves of her Corvette, distinguishable beneath the canvas. "Or I'd leave the keys, too."

Nattie frowned. "We don't get to drive it?"

Jack leaned over. "Don't worry. I've got a spare set."

Nattie giggled, and San scowled good-naturedly.

After his final visit with Laura, Jack had called San, apologizing for his part in their rift and offering an unexpected invitation. Their summer spat forgotten, San sounded thrilled. "I thought you'd abandoned me, brother dearest."

Until she left for New York, San would inhabit Laura's room, sleeping where Laura had slept when Jack was flying his clients. During the day, in preparation for her new job, San would Skype her training program.

Nattie helped him redd up the guest room, making the bed with another of Laura's quilts, and both of them got a little nostalgic. Nattie sniffed, and Jack hugged her close. It never really was a guest room. It was Laura's room. And now it felt as if someone had died, and they couldn't bear to change anything, determined to keep the memories of Laura alive.

Surprisingly, Nattie took the news of Laura's return to Lancaster with undiluted joy and hope, excited for Laura, saying, **"True love is worth going back for."** It was like the ending to one of her movies.

The arrival of Nattie's favorite aunt helped soothe whatever sorrow she felt, and San's time with them turned out to be one long pajama party for his daughter, the perfect conclusion to a turbulent summer. During the day, San worked from home, clicking away at the dining room table, and every night, they sampled a new flavor of ice cream, and not the generic stuff, either.

When they weren't eating ice cream, San and Nattie worked through her school-supply list, making sure she was ready for the start of fourth grade, new outfits and backpack included. And sometimes, late at night, after letting Nattie stay up longer, the three of them would reminisce, often about Laura.

The time Laura had shown up at the market wearing a dress and high heels was already a legendary moment; or when she'd thrown herself into the task of cleaning the fish Jack and Nattie had caught at the lake, a task she knew nothing about; or when she'd tried to tell a joke about the farmer who crossed the road but couldn't remember the punch line, and how her exasperated expression turned out to be funnier than the joke itself.

There were dozens of memories like these. Even San joined in, her attitude softened now that Laura was gone. It rankled Jack a little, but he let it go. **Water under the bridge.**

**"I never lied to you,"** Laura had told him. **"It just wasn't my truth to tell."**

Now, late at night, the house quiet and Jack unable to sleep, he thought back to Danny and Darla, lovebirds, married for three blissful years, but with no imminent patter of tiny feet.

Jack was in Kansas when Danny had called with the news. **"We're thinking of adopting."**

At the time, he was sitting in his dingy apartment, living his dingy life, feeling sorry for himself. But he loved Danny. After all, Danny was the optimist in the family, always encouraging Jack, always prodding him to think higher.

**"Come see us sometime,"** Danny had said.

He'd only met Darla once, and she'd seemed like a nice young woman, full of cheer, the daughter of a prominent family.

**"With Mom not doing so well,"** Danny began, **"San is staying with us this summer. You should call her some-**

**time, Jack."**

Jack had grunted. He didn't care where his seventeen-year-old sister was living. San was the proverbial bull, and he was the china shop. San said what came to mind with little filter, just like their mother, and he'd long since reached his limit with the Livingston women.

When the adoption was final, Danny had called him again.

**"Come meet our little girl!"**

**"I can't afford the time off,"** Jack lied.

**"San's still here, too,"** Danny argued. **"She'd like to see you before she heads off to college."**

Jack had mumbled something about commitments, promising to work it out, but he never did.

It was during San's extended visit with Danny and Darla that Laura must have shown up to answer their ad.

Another four years passed. Jack stayed in Kansas, sleep-walking through his life, flying by day, drinking by night, observing the FAA eight-hour rule of "bottle to throttle," but just barely, sometimes by minutes.

Teaching others to fly, sharing his passion, was the sole bright light in his life, providing others with his own patented means of getting away from it all.

More calls from Danny followed, then one day: **"Hey, Jack, I miss you. I hardly remember what you look like."**

**Look at my picture**, Jack thought. **"Gotta go,"** he'd said and hung up.

That was their last phone call before Laura phoned with the tragic news, leaving a message while he was airborne, flying between the clouds, still trying to leave it all behind. And with his brother's death, **"Gotta go"** became his last words to the only person who'd loved him unconditionally.

Jack could have descended into a pit of remorse and regret for how he'd treated his brother. And he could have refused the guardianship—**should** have refused it, in fact. But he'd decided to raise his brother's daughter, determined to keep Danny's memory alive in her heart, determined to raise her like Danny would have.

Three days after the funeral, he'd moved back to his hometown, into Danny's house, where there was a little girl to get to know, to raise as his own. Soon after that, San returned to Wooster, following through on her promise to help him out for one year.

The rest, as they say, was history. Slowly, Jack and San had forged a workable bond, albeit shaky at times. San stuck around and became the favorite aunt, the go-to person when Nattie needed cheering up or some full-on spoiling. Laura became Jack's comrade-in-arms. And Nattie became the reason he got up in the morning, and the reason he prayed before dropping off to sleep at night.

With each passing year, the past was becoming more distant and fuzzy, and although Jack loved San—loved her dearly, in fact—he still held a grudge against her, if only for reminding him of their mother.

Even though the Bible didn't mince words on this topic, he still couldn't look at his mother's picture without remorseful anger.

**"Forgiveness isn't for her,"** Kelly had said. **"It's for you."**

This coming from a woman who'd learned to forgive the man who'd taken her child. If Kelly could do it, so could he.

Jack slid back the comforter and reached for his robe. Turning on the bedside lamp, he retrieved his mother's photo, hidden in the bottom drawer, seeing for the first time what he couldn't before.

Jack no longer saw heartache. Instead, he saw Nattie's eyes.

The next day, Jack proposed a radical new idea. Nattie was excited. And when San came out of her room, **Laura's room**, Jack made the same proposal. San was surprised but amenable.

"It's about time," Nattie chirped.

So they piled into Billy Bob and drove to Wooster Cemetery, just south of town. Parking at the side of the road, off the beaten path, Jack stood there and stared at the hundreds of markers. He hadn't been there since Danny's death and had only a vague idea where the family grave site was located.

"Follow me," San said simply, leading the way to the northern edge, down the last row of markers, pausing to place a hand on Danny and Darla's shared gravestone, then her father's, until she stopped, finally, and stared down at the simple gray granite marking their mother's burial place. They stood there for a few minutes, lost in thought. Jack put his arm around her, and she leaned in toward him, slightly at first, almost reluctantly, and then fully. Although she'd often kissed his cheek, he couldn't remember the last time he'd hugged his sister.

He fixed his gaze on his father's stone first. **Walter Livingston.** Feeling his heart clench, he looked again at his mother's grave. **Helen Livingston**, the stone read, and it gave the dates for her birth and demise. No Scripture verse. No platitude. Just: **Wife and Mother.** A week earlier, Jack would have said, **"Barely either."**

He glanced over at Nattie, who was crouched down, tracing the names of Danny and Darla, in awe of the truth again, that his little girl was his mother's granddaughter. His niece. In fact, the Nattie he adored had his mother's eyes, his mother's nose, and in many ways, his mother's temperament. All these years, he'd been raising his mother's flesh and blood.

After a few minutes, they held hands and prayed; then Jack knelt at her grave and felt San's hand on his shoulder and Nattie nudging against him. **I forgive you, Mom**, he thought, and then he said it out loud.

Nattie hugged his neck and said to the grave, "Hi, Grandma. I miss you." Leave it to Nattie to miss someone she'd never met, and when Jack stood up again, San had tears in her eyes, even though San wasn't a big one for emotion.

Afterward they headed to Nattie's favorite dive for greasy burgers and fries.

Their moods lightened a bit, despite the imminence of San's departure. Nattie sat on San's side of the booth, squished in so close San had to eat with her left hand. Normally San would have said, **"Give me some space, kid."** But not today.

Jack smiled as he watched them interact: Nattie's appreciation for San's clever retorts, Nattie's admiration of San's fashion sense, Nattie's own slick and often unfiltered tongue. **All this time**, he thought. **I should have known.**

On Friday, Jack called Laura's cell and got a disconnected message.

"She's gone home," he whispered to himself. And although he admired her courage, it didn't set his mind at ease. If anything, he worried more, if that was possible. He called her cousin's number next, who confirmed his suspicions.

"Would you tell her I called?" Jack asked. "When you hear from her?"

Laura's cousin agreed. "She's taking a big risk, you know. Her family is a little extreme."

**No kidding**, Jack thought. He said good-bye and hung up.

That evening, after supper, San came into his office and sat down in Laura's chair, the one she'd sat in for years as they'd planned the day and the week, discussing

Nattie's struggles and triumphs.

He missed her terribly. And so did Nattie. And yet, Laura was right. They were doing okay without her. Not flourishing, maybe, but they hadn't fallen apart.

Jack put his hands behind his head and leaned back in his squeaky chair.

San made a face. "You should oil that."

"And stifle the chair's only voice? Never," Jack retorted, chuckling.

San rolled her eyes, then turned uncharacteristically pensive. She asked about Laura, and Jack told her what he'd just heard.

She nodded. "I hope it works out."

They sat in silence. He'd already decided not to broach the subject, taking Laura's advice. **"Be gentle. We keep secrets for a reason."**

San had obviously long ago decided she didn't want anyone to know the truth. As a seventeen-year-old with her life ahead of her, already dreaming of college and a career in fashion, San wasn't ready for motherhood and wouldn't have let one mistake alter that track. Her reasons were her reasons. And with Danny and Darla eager to become parents, the solution would have seemed clear. Besides, San wasn't the kind to contemplate deeper meanings or shoulder regrets.

Wisely, Jack was weary of confronting women about their supposed maternity. He'd already done that twice, with disastrous results.

Strangely enough, it was San who broached the subject. "You never told me what your test said," she mentioned, referring to the hair samples.

He told her, and she frowned. "So...your test result was different from Kelly's?"

Jack nodded.

"She did **her** test by swabbing Nattie's cheek?"

He nodded again. Nattie had told him as much, a few days after Kelly had walked out. **"The lollipop trick,"** Nattie had called it, and he'd put two and two together.

San made another face. "Well...that's why your test was wrong. Hair samples are notoriously unreliable, you know. Subject to contamination."

Jack felt a sinking feeling. San wasn't ready, and that was fine. Maybe none of them were ready.

San got up from her chair, and he turned toward his desk. He felt her hand on his shoulder. "G'night, bro. And by the way, you're a great father."

He swallowed, his throat tight. And then she was gone.

Moments later, Nattie came in and kissed him on the cheek. "I'm sad," she told him, leaning against his shoulder, putting her arm around her dad.

"Me too."

She scampered upstairs, but not without making sure they were on for a story later. And while waiting in his office, he considered San's response to the DNA, but it didn't bother him.

Days ago, he'd asked Nattie if San ever sat in the swing, where he'd gathered the hair samples. Nattie had cocked her head like a puppy. "Are you kidding? Auntie San **loves** the swing!"

He'd only chuckled. Of course, for his own peace of mind, he already had redone the test. He'd submitted no less than ten strands of San's hair, root and all, extracted from her hairbrush, and had it tested against Nattie's DNA. He'd received the results in a few days. There was no doubt. Laura was right. San was Nattie's mother.

In the end, it seemed to Jack that San simply loved Nattie too much to raise her. And someday, when Nattie revisited the subject of her birth mother, as she probably would in a few years, he might call his sister and finally have it out. "It's time," he might tell her, and she might agree.

Or she might not. Besides, how would Nattie respond when she learned that her aunt was actually her mother, and that her aunt had deliberately deceived her? At nine, not so well. At thirteen, not much better. At eighteen, maybe?

Would she feel betrayed? **Of course.** It could destroy their relationship. But he doubted it. Knowing her as he did, Nattie would come to grips with it eventually, but it wouldn't be pretty. Nattie approached changes with great drama. **We all do**, he thought. But when it came to forgiving others, Nattie was a natural. She'd probably learned that from Laura.

In the meantime, he would withhold the truth until the moment was right, until he thought Nattie ready. And he suddenly thought of Kelly. **Kelly withheld the truth.** And here he was, doing the same thing.

**Were we ready for Kelly?** he thought, sighing with regret.

He had little recourse but to continue praying for the best, asking God for direction, knowing the storm was coming, yet believing that somehow they would get through it.

He thought of something else Kelly had said. **"Without the darkness, we would all be deprived of the candle of faith."**

# Chapter 39

Saturday, the three musketeers packed up the truck, stowed San's suitcase and carry-on bag in Jack's grungy truck bed, and headed out for the big airport, forty minutes to the north. Akron-Canton was San's preference for a direct flight to New York's LaGuardia.

For most of the way, they traveled in solemn silence, watching the landscape pass, until finally San broke the quiet, repeating to Nattie what she must have said a dozen times that week. "We'll video chat every Saturday morning. Until you tire of me."

"I won't," Nattie objected, her lower lip drooping, her head leaning against San's shoulder. San draped her arm around Nattie. Jack dropped them off near the departure sign for U.S. Airways, then drove around again, taking the exit to park the truck.

He met them at the self-service ticketing kiosks, where San checked one bag, pleased about dodging the extra bag fee. "First class, baby!" Nothing made his sister happier than the prospect of luxury service.

After the clerk took her bag, San crept close and whispered in his ear, "Don't look now, but someone's here."

"Who?" Nattie asked, displaying her keen sense of hearing.

Although Jack didn't catch San's meaning, he ignored Nattie's question and kissed the top of her head.

"Okay, don't tell me," Nattie muttered.

San gave him another furtive look, and he glanced around, trying to appear casual, and finally spotted her. Kelly was there, conducting business at the Delta counter, accompanied by an older gentleman with bright white hair and Texan attire, complete with necktie.

**Her father?** Jack speculated, then remembered her father had passed.

He shrugged toward San, who mouthed, **"You sure missed the boat!"** He almost laughed at her final dig. Pure San.

Jack picked up her carry-on bag, and they walked across the hall, joining the end of the security line, a line which looked to be longer than usual, leaving them a good twenty-five minutes before San would enter the heart of TSA.

Jack wondered if Kelly would end up joining them in the same line, if only a few feet behind, and he worried how Nattie would respond. She'd probably pull on his shirt. **"Kelly's here! Can I say hi?"**

Jack whispered his intentions in San's ear and mussed Nattie's hair. He noted she was busy with her spiral notebook. He traced his way back to the ticket counter, keeping an eye peeled for Kelly.

He found her just outside the coffee shop, standing with the gentleman he'd seen earlier. Her eyes lit up when she saw him, greeting him without reservation.

"Kelly," he said simply, smiling and hugging her as the tall Texan looked on, taking in her scent, remembering the way he felt when she was near. Regret swirled within him like a sickness, and he wished he'd never let her walk out of the house.

Kelly gestured toward the Texan and introduced him as Chet. "He's like a second father to me."

Chet shook his hand, giving him a close scrutiny, his bushy eyebrows furrowing.

As if in answer to Jack's unspoken question, Kelly patted Chet's arm. "Jack knows everything."

Chet's eyebrows climbed his forehead. "Everything?"

Kelly smiled at Jack. "Well…not the latest." She seemed absolutely radiant, and he guessed her news immediately.

"May I?" Chet asked like a southern gentleman, slightly tipping his head toward her in a kind of deference.

"Please."

Chet fixed him with a dignified expression. "We found Emily."

Jack wasn't surprised, but he was taken aback by his own emotions. He felt terribly relieved for her. "Congratulations," he said, looking at Kelly.

"I've just come back to box up the rest of my things. I'm moving to Chicago," she announced, a wistful sadness now mingled with her obvious joy. "I get to meet her next week." She looked away, and Jack felt another twinge of regret for how she must feel in his presence. This was her big moment, what she'd waited years for, and here he was, raining on her parade.

"I'm so happy for you," Jack said, politely backing away. He glanced up the hallway and realized that San and Nattie had barely moved.

Kelly touched Chet's arm. "Jack's a pilot." The admission appeared to raise his estimation in Chet's eyes, thus preventing Jack's quick escape. He chatted with them a few minutes longer as Chet peppered him with aviation questions. All the while, Kelly studied him. Apparently Chet had flown years ago and had always wanted to rediscover flight, now that he had the time for it. Their conversation ended when Jack offered his business card.

Chet pulled out his readers, studying the scant information.

"So…you **teach** flying?"

Jack nodded.

"Excellent, young man."

Jack finally managed a good-bye, which he and Kelly did without sharing another hug, although Chet clutched his hand like a good Texan should. "Expect my call."

"I'll look forward to it," Jack replied, backing away, giving Kelly a final nod.

He rejoined San and Nattie in line, glancing back to see Kelly and Chet heading into the coffee shop. With any luck, they wouldn't be in line when he and Nattie walked out of the airport.

San glanced at him, obviously curious about the conversation, and mouthed the words, **"You see her?"**

He nodded. "It's all good."

Nattie whipped around. "**What's** all good?"

"Noo Yawk, baby!" San said, and she tapped Nattie's head.

Nattie gave Jack a suspicious look. **I know that's not what you meant.**

There were only three people ahead of them. They had seconds to go when San turned and locked eyes with him. He gave her a tender smile, and another flicker of knowing seemed to pass between them.

Jack touched her arm. "I love you, sis."

San sighed miserably and reached for him.

Hugging her, Jack patted her back. "I can't wait to visit you in the Big Apple. Nattie's already stoked."

"Thank you for being my brother," she whispered, and he was about to let her go when she added, "And thank you...for the cemetery. It meant a lot to me. What you said, you know?"

He shrugged and was about to release her again, but she still wouldn't let go.

"I know you forgive Mom, but...do you forgive me, too?"

"Of course," he murmured back.

"It wasn't a mistake," she whispered. "Picking you. We always knew you were the best choice."

Jack patted her back and felt her squeeze him even tighter, and before she broke away, she said, "Take care of our little girl, okay?"

He promised, and she finally let him go, turning to Nattie, who had been eyeing them curiously. San engulfed Nattie in her arms, and Nattie's eyes watered. Her lip quivered, and San popped her chin gently. "Hey, hey, none of that crying stuff. I'll see you in two weeks!"

Nattie sniffed and nodded. "Two weeks. Promise?"

"Hope to die."

Nattie laughed through her tears. "Don't say that."

San grinned and Nattie stuck out her hand. "Deal."

San shook on it. It was official. And by now, she was next in line. San wiped her eyes and extended her ID to the security agent, who examined it with a blue light, peered at the boarding pass, then handed everything back to San, officially clearing her through to the next phase of examination.

Jack and Nattie ducked out of line and watched San as she headed for the conveyor belt. Jack glanced to the right, his eyes sweeping the crowd. Kelly still hadn't entered the queue.

San placed her shoulder bag in a tray, removing her shoes, and putting them beside the bag. She turned one last time, mouthed **"I love you,"** and patted her heart.

Jack did the same. And so did Nattie. They watched as San walked through the metal detector, facing the front for a moment before walking out the other side.

Holding Nattie's hand, Jack steered her toward the escalators, worrying all the while whether Nattie might look back and spot Kelly.

They walked to the truck in silence, and on the way home, Nattie stared out the window, her expression glum but thoughtful, too.

"I saw her, you know," she finally said, her voice matter-of-fact.

Jack sighed, feeling stupid. "I'm sorry."

"It's okay."

"I didn't know what to do," he offered feebly. "I was afraid you'd be upset."

"I would have cried."

Jack swallowed his own remorse.

"She's moving away, isn't she?"

"Yes."

"I didn't want to say good-bye twice in one day."

"I understand."

For the rest of the way home, the miles rushed by, a blur of memories and brown grass. Jack thought of Kelly and how often she'd traveled that exact route down to see them. He'd never once traveled up to see her. He'd offered a couple times, but she'd always found a way to demur.

Nattie remained subdued but not depressed, not by the sound of her tone, and if anyone could decipher Nattie's mood, he could.

When they turned off the highway, Nattie whispered softly, "We're home."

"We are."

"It's just you and me now," she said.

"Is that okay?"

She looked out the window. "I guess some kids just don't have mothers, you know."

Jack nodded.

"It's okay," she whispered softly. "Especially when they have cool dads to make up for it."

# Chapter 40

Kelly's high-rise apartment was located a mere three miles from Megan's family and only two miles from Kelly's temporary job with Westin and Westin, a financial management firm—an envelope-stuffing job and a step down, but she didn't mind.

The day following her initial arrival, when she'd met Michelle Sparks in the hallway of the legal firm, Kelly had also been introduced to Michelle's husband, Harold, CEO of a pharmaceutical company.

During that particular meeting, Kelly became persuaded that Megan's parents were innocent of any complicity. At the time of the adoption, they'd had no idea Megan was channeled through a black-market network, although as the years went by and they learned of the adoption agency's indictment for fraud, their fears had developed. Horrified at the possibility that their daughter might have been stolen, they became determined to uncover the truth. In fact, their attorney had been the one to contact Ernie, having learned of his name through Kelly's website.

Kelly and Megan's adoptive parents met a second time to hammer out a slow transition to what would ultimately become something akin to shared custody. Kelly had made a quick return trip to Akron for more of her things, and after a few days to settle into her new place in Chicago, she was quite eager to meet Megan, albeit under pretense.

As far as Megan would know, Kelly was her new baby-sitter.

Their young, ultra-hip chauffeur picked her up and drove her to the Sparkses' home, where he parked in the circular driveway while Kelly headed for the front door to meet face-to-face the little girl she'd so longed to see.

The home's exterior was similar to a Tudor-style mansion. When she was ushered inside by a housekeeper, she felt as if she'd stepped into a British castle. The surroundings were more intimidating than she had imagined, and it gradually dawned on her why they were willing to allow her such liberal access to Megan. **They're highly exposed to a potentially expensive wrongful adoption suit.**

In a few moments, her daughter wandered down the long staircase, wearing jeans and a frilly pink shirt. With one hand on the banister, she gazed at Kelly somewhat shyly, brown eyes intent.

"This is Kelly," Michelle Sparks announced awkwardly, standing back a bit.

**My Emily.** It was hard to keep her breathing steady, but Kelly was determined to make this the best possible moment for the two of them.

Michelle had been quite correct. Megan was the spitting image of Kelly, and if she didn't mind thinking so, the young brunette was truly beautiful.

"Kelly's going to spend some time with you, honey, while we go into the city," Michelle told Megan.

"It's a pleasure to meet you, Miss Kelly." The well-mannered child stepped forward to offer her slight hand, responding as a charm-school student might.

Kelly shook her small hand. **Remember me?** She wished she might wrap the darling girl in her arms, holding her for all the moments—years—she'd been deprived of her. **Oh, the pain...and, at last, the joy.**

Some time later, before Megan's adoptive mom left the house, Kelly asked if she might bake some cookies with Megan and was surprised that this would be a first for the girl. It took no time for Megan to get into cookie-making mode, there in the high-ceilinged kitchen, surrounded by hardwood cabinets and marble-topped counters. Especially after Megan had her first taste of raw cookie dough. "Yummy," she said, licking her fingers. "This tastes better than cookies!"

So the ice was broken, and a friendship forged. And while the cookies baked, Kelly produced a few magic tricks for her spellbound daughter.

"Will you please show me how, Miss

Kelly?"

Kelly agreed as they laughed together, and soon Megan was sharing stories about her private school, her friends, and even a couple of nerdy boys—**Yuck!**

The second visit, the following week, went equally well. Kelly once again arrived in the guise of a sitter, and this time Michelle met Kelly at the door instead of the housekeeper.

"She hasn't stopped talking about you," Michelle exclaimed. "You made quite an impression." Michelle's voice was upbeat, even optimistic, but Kelly could hear a pensive tone, a tightness to her voice.

This time while Megan's parents "went into the city," Kelly and Megan played computer games on a sixty-four-inch screen, in a luxurious space filled with overstuffed couches and chairs, floor to ceiling paneled wood walls, and covered with plush carpeting.

When Megan's parents returned, Megan hugged Kelly for the first time. "When are you coming back?"

Her parents smiled sweetly at this and the progress Kelly had made so far, but their eyes betrayed them.

For the next visit, a third Saturday, Kelly determined to tone it down further, unwilling to alienate the dear people who had invited her into their lives, although Michelle pulled her aside before Megan came down, and praised Kelly. "You've made Megan so happy."

Kelly wasn't sure how to respond. "I want you to know, Mrs. Sparks—"

"Michelle," she corrected, gently.

"I'm not trying to win her over or anything...or compete with your affections," Kelly said, touching Michelle's arm. "I just want to make a good impression."

Michelle shook her head. "It's all good, Kelly. We **want** Megan to like you. We want her to **love** you."

Michelle pulled her into Megan's playroom. The walls were lined with shelves, well-loved picture books competing for space among chapter books and posters of current Christian bands. "You're free to spend time in here with Megan," she said.

"I think I've read a few of these books hundreds of times." Michelle gestured to the childhood classics that lined the lower shelves.

Kelly looked around at the expanse of educational reading material.

"I taught her to read at three," Michelle added. "You have a very smart daughter. And I can't say how glad we were to hear that you are a believer."

Kelly nodded.

"Megan is learning about the Lord from all of us," Michelle said, but her throat caught, and her eyes teared up.

Kelly agreed. **Another gift from God.**

When Megan appeared in the doorway, she ran to Kelly and hugged her. "I heard we are going to the mall!"

Kelly confirmed this, and Megan cheered, pulling on her vest and tan boots.

Once there, they spent most of their time in an apparel store, trying on jeans. After an hour of this and a dozen discarded pairs, Megan finally found something she thought would get her mother's approval.

"Did you know my mom's birthday is

coming up?"

"Have you bought anything?"

Megan shook her head. "Dad usually buys something to give her."

Kelly suggested they change it up and pick something out together. While they walked the mall trying to decide, Kelly secretly called Harold Sparks. He answered in a worried tone. "Is everything okay?"

Kelly meekly presented her suggestion, not wanting to step on his plans, but he was pleased. "I haven't purchased anything yet, so it's perfect."

In the end, Megan picked out a card at Hallmark and a glass plaque, which included the words **To the Best Mom in the World.**

In the food court, they ate tacos for lunch, sitting across from Baskin-Robbins, eyeing their next plunder.

"Let's get cookie dough!" Megan announced.

Later, while Megan experienced cookie dough ice cream for the first time, she fixed Kelly with a curious expression.

"You're not a normal sitter, are you?"

"Why do you think that?"

She licked her cone. "Because my parents are at home." Kelly made some kind of excuse, following the rules they'd set, a timeline that wouldn't give Megan the full truth for another month.

"I really like you," Megan announced.

"I like you, too."

Having finished their cones, Kelly took Megan to a gift-wrapping kiosk, and they surrounded Michelle's gift in festive flourish. Thirty minutes later, Kelly dropped Megan off at the stone steps that led to the massive arched oak front door.

Megan turned in her seat. "I can't wait to see you next week."

"Me either," Kelly admitted.

"Can I text you?"

"Let's ask your parents, and if they agree, I'll give you my number." Kelly mussed Megan's adorable brunette hair.

The fourth week, Kelly took Megan to a movie.

"My mom is sad," Megan said before the theater went dark.

"Why?"

"I don't know, but she doesn't think I know."

They munched on popcorn and watched the latest Disney release, and Kelly thought of Nattie the entire time. How far toward the top of her favorite list would this movie climb?

They went to a photo booth and had goofy pictures taken together, giggling at the results. Kelly gave them to Megan.

"Do you have another job?" Megan asked suddenly.

Kelly nodded.

"My mom never worked," Megan announced. "She told me all she ever wanted was to be a mommy, and she said that when she saw me for the first time, her life was finally perfect."

"I can see why."

"I'm adopted, you know."

"Yeah," Kelly said. "How do you feel about that?"

"Lucky," Megan said. "My mom picked me out. All the other moms are stuck with what they get."

Kelly had to smile, but her heart was breaking.

"I grew in my mom's heart," Megan added. "That's **better** than her belly, you know."

"It is," Kelly said. "Although you can have both, you know."

"I know," Megan said, sipping on her Coke and looking thoughtful. "You and Mom could be friends."

"I think we are."

"She likes you," Megan said. "I can tell by the way she says nice things about you."

"I like her, too."

When they pulled up to the Sparkses' lakeside mansion, Megan asked Kelly to wait while she ran inside to ask permission. She came out minutes later. "My mom says it's okay!"

Kelly gave Megan her cell number.

"See you later!" Megan announced, skipping back up the stairs and bounding inside, and Kelly's heart constricted at the bond they'd forged in such a short time. **My daughter.**

The following weeks were hectic, as usual, as Nattie dove back into school—"Fourth grade is so much harder, Dad!" At home, Nattie did her homework on the table while Jack read, surfed on his tablet, or gave her assistance. In spite of the tumultuous summer, the tears and fears of last year had all but dissipated. **"Nattie's more resilient than we think,"** Laura had told him.

They still ate popcorn on Friday nights during their movie date, continuing their tradition, no matter how many school friends vied for Nattie's attention, but it felt bittersweet. Kelly's absence was keenly felt, and Laura's presence seemed to linger in the atmosphere.

For a while after Kelly's departure, Jack had been given Bear Bear to sleep with, until Nattie decided he didn't need him anymore. These days, he'd been sleeping with Jeffrey the Giraffe because, according to Nattie, Jack "needed to lighten up."

But one night, Nattie turned a corner.

"You know, Dad. You're too old to sleep with stuffed animals."

"Hmm."

"You should go cold turkey."

"I'm willing to try."

"They're not real, you know."

Jack shrugged, and Nattie gave a giggle.

Things were settling for Jack, as well, sifting to a final realization, as if everything had been tossed in the air and was only now landing in some semblance of order.

He still worried for Laura and wondered how things were turning out. And as they waited for a letter, they prayed for her nightly.

Truth be told, he missed her, and yes, he loved her dearly. He doubted he'd ever forget the day when Laura had gone fancy. For a moment in time, she'd joined their world. But Laura had been right: He'd never truly joined hers, and theirs wasn't the kind of love to build a marriage.

In time, it was Kelly and those sparkling blue eyes who haunted his sleep. How many times had he been tempted to text her, only to resist?

**Give her more time**, he thought.

Once a week, Nattie commandeered Jack's tablet to video chat with San, and boy, if San wasn't excited. "New York is treating me very well!" she exclaimed. "But I miss you guys to death. And...uh... Jack?"

"Yes, sis?"

"That shirt does **not** go with those pants."

"I told him," Nattie whined, "but he doesn't listen."

Chet called Jack a few weeks after their serendipitous meeting at the airport, and they discussed aviation for nearly an hour. Eventually, Chet answered his unspoken question. "She's doing fine, Jack, in case you were wondering. She and her daughter are getting on famously."

"I **was** curious," he replied. "Thank you."

In the end, Jack referred Chet to another capable CFI a mere five minutes from his home, filing Chet's number in case he might need it again. Jack even followed up with Chet after making his recommendation, just to make sure Chet was being treated well. Having flown twice since their last conversation, Chet was thrilled, if that was a proper way to describe a very enthusiastic Texan.

"This is better'n golf," he told Jack, and Jack agreed.

A month after he'd said good-bye to Kelly in that Akron airport, he and Nattie finally received a letter from Laura.

He'd placed it, unopened, on the dining room table, waiting for Nattie to get home from school. When she finally spotted it, her squeal nearly shattered the windows.

**Dear Nattie and Jack**, they read together, and Nattie smirked. "Notice she put my name first."

"She always did like you best," Jack agreed.

"Are we going to read it or not?"

"**You** read it to me."

Nattie did, and when she was finished, she broke into tears.

Jack put his arm around her. They could barely speak.

They read the letter again, from the very beginning, and it read like a fairy tale. **An Amish fairy tale.**

Once upon a time, a brokenhearted young Amishman by the name of Jonathan Glick, who had never married, couldn't believe his good fortune when the love of his life—a woman he thought he'd lost forever—just happened to show up at the market where he worked....

"I wish I could have seen that," Nattie said.

"She's happy," Jack whispered.

"Of course she's happy," Nattie said, holding the letter. "She's in love."

## Chapter 41

With Megan safely back inside her parents' home, Kelly put the car into drive and headed down the long tree-lined path that led out of their ten-acre estate.

It was only three days later when Megan's text turned into a phone call. And Kelly could tell she'd been crying.

"What's the matter, sweetie?"

"Can I ask you a question?"

Kelly held her breath. "Sure."

"Remember those pictures we took?"

"I do." Kelly cringed.

"Well…you look like me, you know?"

"I know." They were ahead of the plan, but there was nothing she could do about it.

Silence.

She heard a sniff. "So…are you my mom?" came Megan's voice finally, sounding tiny and unsteady.

Kelly wasn't sure how to continue. They'd already agreed that if Megan should ask, Kelly was permitted to be honest. "I gave birth to you, honey."

Once again, Megan didn't say anything.

Kelly broke the silence. "How does that make you feel?"

Another sniff. "Scared."

"I don't blame you. And...I understand, honey."

"Are you going to take me away?"

"No, Megan." Kelly brushed at her own tears. "You know what? I'm so happy that you have two wonderful parents who love you very, very much."

"Sorry, but I have to go now."

She'd hung up before Kelly could say good-bye. Kelly wept off and on for the rest of the night, not just for what she'd lost, but for what she was about to do, for what she'd been contemplating for several days now.

From the very beginning, she had compared Megan to Nattie, and while any comparison was unfair, she couldn't help it. They were two delightfully different girls, both big-hearted and kind, but she couldn't forget what Megan had said: **"I grew in my mom's heart."**

Just as Nattie had grown in her own.

God had answered Kelly's prayers, helping her find her daughter, but also by keeping Megan safe, providing her with a wonderful home, with doting parents. It didn't matter that Megan was rich, but it did matter that her mother and father both loved her beyond measure.

And it came down to a simple fact: Kelly was about to irrevocably alter a family, unwittingly perhaps, innocently, yes, but all good intentions aside, the result would be the same. Tearing lives apart, changing things in a way that might not make it better for the girl they all loved.

On the night Kelly had decided, she'd almost called Jack, yearning to hear his voice, desperate to share her feelings and get his opinion. She missed their talks. He'd always been a good listener, skillful at reading her heart. Until the end…

But she couldn't blame him, and she

would never forget that sendoff at the airport, the providential meeting, like God was telling her to bid farewell to her past.

She called Chet instead, and surprisingly, he fully supported her decision. "I understand," he told her. "Are you sure about this?"

She was, and he agreed to call the attorney to begin the process.

The following Saturday, Megan came running out to greet her. "Mom says you're going away?"

Kelly got out of her car and hugged her little girl. "I have to go home for a while."

"Are you coming back?"

Kelly nodded. "I'll come to see you, yes."

Megan seemed a little relieved. And Kelly guessed they might work their way toward each other in the years to come. Someday, Megan might even ask Kelly, **"Why did you give me up?"** Or Megan's parents might tell her the truth, or she might even discover it for herself, on the Internet.

And how would Megan handle that?

688 DAVID AND BEVERLY LEWIS

Kelly didn't know; no one could know. But whatever happened, she'd be available to Megan. Kelly leaned over, eye to eye with her daughter. "I've loved getting to know you, honey. I'm going to miss you."

Megan smiled. "My mom **loved** her birthday gift. And um…thanks for coming to meet me…for finding me, you know." She looked up shyly. "Can I still text you?"

"Absolutely." Kelly paused, thrilled that they would keep that connection and trying to hold her tears in check. "And, Megan? What you have here…is really wonderful."

Megan nodded, then held out her arms as Kelly hugged her again.

Megan stepped back. "Well…good-bye."

Her daughter ran up the steps to where her mother would be waiting. Kelly had expected to be devastated today, but she wasn't. She was sad, sure, but there was peace in her heart. Perhaps later it would hurt terribly, but for the moment she was thankful. Megan seemed relieved, and for that, Kelly was glad.

Kelly was rounding the corner of her car

when the front door opened again. She figured it was Megan running out for another hug, but it was Michelle.

"Wait, Kelly." Michelle descended the steps and extended her hands, warmly holding Kelly's in hers. There were tears in her eyes. "You didn't have to do this."

Kelly nodded, smiling. "Yes, I did."

"We'll take good care of her."

"You already have," Kelly said.

Michelle promised to send Kelly updates as often as possible.

"And come visit us anytime, really."

Kelly hugged her again. "Megan loves you, Michelle."

Michelle burst into tears. "And I love her so much, you just don't know...."

**I do**, Kelly thought.

She got into her car, said good-bye, and as she made the curve, waved. Michelle was still standing there, waving back.

Megan was right—in another time, under different circumstances, she and Michelle could have been friends. And perhaps there would be a time for that down the road.

Kelly had no idea how the future would play out, but she had no doubt she'd done the right thing for her little girl.

Kelly drove back to the long-term rental agency, then took a shuttle to the airport, arriving three hours before her flight. She sat in a lounge, watching as others drowned their anxieties and boredom in alcohol while she tried to come to grips with what she'd just done. To anyone else, it would have seemed as if she'd just thrown away everything she had been trying to find for the past eight years.

But to her, it felt right.

Besides, what if Bobby hadn't kidnapped Emily? What if Bobby hadn't killed himself? What would their life have been like?

**Dreadful**, Kelly thought. Parents fighting. A mother living in fear. A father incapable of love. A likely divorce. Joint custody. A little girl torn between two families.

Shaking her head in wonder, Kelly was overcome with gratitude to a God who had made something good out of something so horrific. He hadn't just kept her baby safe, but He'd rescued Emily, placing her with two loving parents who could give her even more than Kelly had offered. Any good mother would sacrifice her own life for her daughter...and really, wasn't that what she had done today? In a way, she'd sacrificed her own motherhood to give Emily—now Megan—a bright future ahead.

Chet texted her in the middle of her iced tea: **How you doing, kiddo? You okay?**

**I'm actually doing pretty good**, she texted back.

**You're not trying to con a con man?**

**Nope**, she replied, adding a smiley face.

Chet let her know he wouldn't be able to meet her at the airport, but he'd made special arrangements for her transportation back to her apartment.

Kelly texted back: **I can always take a cab.**

**Nonsense**, he texted back.

**Thank you, Chet.**

She tried texting Melody but didn't get a response. No matter. Kelly smiled through her happy tears and thought of Jack and

Nattie again. Although her sadness had lessened considerably, and she still regretted how things turned out, her mistakes couldn't haunt her anymore. She had the rest of her life, and she knew she could trust God to lead the way. He had something marvelous planned for the second act of her life. And she couldn't wait.

Kelly's flight landed just after six. When the wheels touched the tarmac, she breathed a sigh of relief. On Monday, she would begin her old job again, and Melody's father was thrilled to have her back after her month-long hiatus. Kelly walked down the jet bridge, heading to baggage claim to pick up her bags, passing a dozen gates as she did so, lost in thought and feeling a little adrift but glad to be back. She'd flown out of this airport a hundred times before. In a way, this airport meant home to her and represented hope, as well. She smiled at that, because her airport days were definitely over.

Checking her cell for the time, she decided to grab a sandwich at the deli.

She was no more than a few yards away when she felt a tug on her blouse. She turned and nearly gasped.

It was Nattie, mischievous eyes looking up at her.

Kelly broke into a wide smile. "What are **you** doing here?"

Nattie gave her the sweetest yet coy smile in return, and without saying more, Kelly enveloped Nattie, hugging her tightly, and then held her at arm's length. "You are **such** a sight for sore eyes, kiddo."

"How was your trip?" Nattie asked.

Kelly paused for a heartbeat. "It was good," she said sincerely. And then she saw Jack, standing behind Nattie, watching them with a look of bemusement.

"I hope you don't mind," he said. "Chet called."

Until that moment she hadn't fully put it together. Jack and Nattie didn't just happen to be here—they were here for **her**.

Jack stepped closer. "I must have called Chet a dozen times wondering when—if—you were coming back."

She bit her lip. "You did?"

"At **least** a dozen times." Nattie giggled. "Probably closer to a thousand."

Jack's eyes softened. "I was an idiot, Kelly…."

Kelly moved closer and put her fingers to his lips. "Shh. So was I."

Nattie tugged on her dad's shirt. "Dad, this is where you're supposed to kiss the girl. Like now."

And he did. Right there in the middle of the same airport Kelly had flown out of for years, surrounded by strangers, he took her into his arms and kissed her not once, but twice.

"So…we washed Billy Bob," Jack said, touching her elbow.

"And **waxed** her," Nattie chimed in, linking her arm through Kelly's. "Just for you."

Kelly laughed. "So where are you two taking me?"

"Where do you think?" Nattie asked. "**Home**, of course."

Home, Kelly thought, trying not to cry. "Do I ever love the sound of that."

# Epilogue

There were times over the next few months when Jack found himself staring at Kelly across the room—fixing burritos in the kitchen for the three of them while she listened to Nattie, who had a never-ending cache of stories from school; tucking a strand of hair behind her ear, though the hair rarely stayed where she'd put it; humorously wrinkling her nose at something Nattie said and catching his gaze before she erupted into laughter—and he shuddered at how close he'd come to losing her forever.

In February, he took Kelly to the setting of their first date, the Wooster Country Club, and to commemorate they ordered the same things they'd ordered the first time: Jack, the filet mignon, and Kelly, the salmon. After the entrée, Jack went down on one knee, removed the diamond ring from his pocket, and proposed.

Putting her hand to her chest, a tearful Kelly said yes and was thrilled to discover Nattie peeking around the corner, Chet and Eloise arm in arm just behind her. Kelly squealed with delight, Nattie rushed in to hug her mother-to-be, and Jack watched his two girls with glowing pride.

Nattie oohed and aahed over the sparkling engagement ring, then joined them at their table, with Chet and Eloise settling down nearby. They celebrated with—what else?—ice cream, the only change to their original orders. With matching dabs of whipped cream on their noses, Kelly asked Nattie to be her flower girl, and Nattie giggled her yes. "I thought you'd never ask!"

In June, San made a special trip for the wedding to fulfill her role as one of Kelly's bridesmaids, as did Melody, Kelly's matron of honor. Chet and Eloise, who'd become regular visitors to Wooster, made the trip, as well. A small group of friends, family, and coworkers witnessed the ceremony at Jack's church. Afterwards Melody hugged Jack. "You have no idea how lucky you are!"

Megan's parents sent a gift—a silver tea set, along with a silk-covered memory book. Inside, Michelle had written, **"Marriage and motherhood, both miracles to be cherished,"** and Megan had also signed her name in her little-girl handwriting. Kelly hoped that one day when the time was right, **both** of her daughters could meet.

The next week, while San caught up on girl time with Nattie, Jack and Kelly flew his Cessna 182 to a cottage on the water in Mystic, Connecticut, where they strolled the beach at midnight and dreamed of their future together.

Soon after they'd settled in to family life, Kelly asked Jack what he would have done if she'd stayed in Chicago. He'd smiled sheepishly, taking her by the hand and leading her to his office. He pulled out his drawer and reached in, removing an envelope. Inside was an expensive plane ticket to Chicago.

"I already knew where to find you," Jack said, smiling. "Chet was a very helpful man."

Kelly laughed. "And when you found me, what then?"

Jack shrugged. "I hadn't gotten that far."

Kelly's eyes sparkled with amusement. "You spent a lot of money on a ticket you didn't use."

"Worth every penny."

Kelly waved the ticket. "Can I have this?"

"What for?"

"Our memory book."

In August, Jack flew Nattie and Kelly to Lancaster, Pennsylvania, and they stayed in Bird-in-Hand, close to the restaurant where Laura now worked.

They'd arranged, along with a little conspiratorial help from the management staff, to be seated at her table when she came over to wait on them. Laura was yards away, in fact, when she spotted them. Nattie sprang from her seat and flew into Laura's arms, and together the two of them stood in the middle of the restaurant talking in Pennsylvania Dutch, hugging and weeping for joy.

Management gave Laura an hour off, and she joined them for dinner. They talked about the past, and the present. Laura and Jonathan had married and were living in his home, taking care of Becca Lynn, and the way Laura told the tender story gave Jack shivers.

"If you hadn't seen Jonathan's market picture, who knows what might've happened," Laura said softly, amazement in her voice. She still hadn't taken the church vow, however, and although her mother and father had warmed up to them, things were still strained. After all, they were still under the Bann, and in fact, Laura confided, "I guess I'm fancier than I thought. I couldn't part with my car or electricity."

Nattie was all over that. "I told you!"

"**Ach**, you did," Laura said and blushed.

"Come back to us!" Nattie pleaded.

Laura glanced toward Kelly and smiled demurely. "That might not be a good idea."

Nattie spoke up. "Why not?"

Laura shrugged, embarrassed, and Kelly put a hand on her arm.

"Laura, you're always welcome in our home. You were part of Nattie's life for many years, and she misses you."

Tears glistened in Laura's eyes, and she brushed them away. "I'm forever grateful, to all of ya, for everything." She smiled and then blushed. "While we'd love to come visit, I'll soon have my own family to care for." When realization dawned, congratulations echoed all around the table, and Nattie's eyes grew saucer sized with excitement.

Later in the meal, Kelly and Nattie left the table for the restroom, leaving Jack alone with Laura.

"So what is it like to be back in Lancaster?"

She looked out the window at the parking lot and the farmland beyond. "I missed this place, but you know...sometimes you really can't go home again."

"Are you happy, Laura?"

A humorous glint shone in her face. "I am, Jack. I have my dear Jonathan, and you to thank for it."

Jack chuckled. "It was Kelly who got the whole thing started."

"**Jah**," Laura whispered. "Thank God for Kelly."

Nattie was ten when she started fifth grade and—as San might have said—ready to put childish things behind her. Her DVD tower of favorites had long since fallen into disuse. "I've **seen** them all," she complained.

**Finding Nemo** was now for babies, and Nattie rarely created favorites lists anymore. Pop-Tarts wouldn't have even made the top ten, and she preferred swimming to swinging, but she wasn't too old to be tucked in by her favorite dad and her favorite mom—although she hadn't handed Jack a stuffed animal in over a year.

"You have a **real** person now," she informed Jack, pointing at Kelly. "You don't need a stuffed animal." And at that, he agreed.

Jack heard a soft meowing behind him, and Nattie leaned up, tapping her mattress. "Come on, Felix!"

Felix sprang up onto Nattie's bed, and Nattie swallowed Kelly's cat into a giant hug. Felix soaked it up, purring magnificently.

They prayed together, thanking God for His many blessings and submitting new requests, usually for Laura's family situation and for Nattie's teachers to be nicer, and sometimes for God to convince Dad that she **really** needed a cell phone.

"We'd lose you for sure," Jack said one night, after they'd finished their prayers.

Nattie turned her pleading eyes to Kelly. "What do **you** think, Mom?"

Amused, Kelly glanced at Jack. "I think she's getting the knack of having two parents!"

"Didn't take long," Jack agreed.

Kelly leaned over and kissed Nattie on the cheek and whispered, "I'll work on him."

"Thank you!"

Jack laughed. "I heard that."

Standing, Kelly tugged at Jack's shirt collar. "C'mon, my love.

Time for bed."

"Eww!" Nattie whined, putting her hands on her ears but grinning all the same.

Kelly and Jack retired to their room, now fully feminized, with new drapes at the windows, soft lighting, and a picture of both his father and his mother framed on the wall.

One cool fall evening, while holding each other and recounting their day, Kelly casually asked Jack when he thought Nattie might be ready for the truth.

Jack considered this and asked for her opinion.

"Well…" Kelly began tentatively. "Maybe when Nattie starts asking again, but only after San gives permission."

That made sense to Jack, and after another minute or two, he whispered, "San gave up a lot for Nattie's sake."

"She did," Kelly agreed. "But that's what mothers do."

Jack nodded in the darkness. "I love

you, Mrs. Livingston." Kelly snuggled into his arm contentedly. "I love you more, Mr. Livingston."

Jack kissed her nose. "Care to wager on that?"

"How much are you prepared to lose?"

Jack paused. "Hmm. Perhaps I might reconsider."

Kelly laughed softly. "Perhaps you should."

He kissed her, and she kissed him back. Jack snuggled her in closer, and she murmured approvingly. They listened to the night sounds for a while before Jack broke the stillness. "What do you think is in our future?"

"Hmm," Kelly considered. "I think our future is like an empty table...about to be filled with the most delectable of foods."

Moments later, they heard a knocking against the door. Jack called, but Nattie didn't come in.

"Is it safe?" she asked cautiously.

Kelly laughed. "It's safe, honey."

Nattie peeked her head in. "I can't sleep. I'm going downstairs for ice cream. You guys want some?"

Jack shook his head in disbelief. "Excuse me?"

"It's Saturday night."

"So?"

"Actually…" Kelly began, pulling off the covers. "I have a hankering for something chocolatey."

Nattie jumped on the bed, springing up and down. "That's what **I'm** talking about!"

Kelly was already up, putting on her robe. She looked over at her husband. "C'mon, sleepyhead."

Nattie and Kelly were already gone by the time Jack put on his robe. He could hear giggling downstairs, the opening and shutting of the freezer, the clinking of silverware.

"Da-ad! C'mon!"

He turned on the dresser lamp and gazed at his mother's picture on the wall, tracing the outline of her face, recognizing Nattie's eyes shining back at him.

Jack smiled, warmth filling his heart. He turned off the light and headed downstairs to fill up on ice cream with his girls.

# Authors' Note

We are thrilled to co-write **Child of Mine**, our second novel together, remembering all the fun of developing multiple story lines for our first co-authored novel, **Sanctuary**, deciding who would write which character's viewpoint, and so on. Yes, the long wait is over, and thanks to the many devoted readers who have pleaded for more from our fiction-writing partnership. It would be only half the joy without you!

Our heartfelt thanks go to the readers of the earliest stages of the manuscript, as well as to Amish consultants and research assistants in various Plain communities, including Lancaster, Holmes, and Wayne counties.

Special gratitude to Hank and Ruth Herschberger; Sherri Sturgeon; Fay Landis;

Alice Henderson; Donna De For; Julie Garcia; Roswell and Sandra Flower; Dave and Janet Buchwalter; Dale and Barbara Birch; Beth M. Sparks, Esq.; Keene & Sparks, LLP; Ben Sparks of Sparks Willson Borges Brandt & Johnson of Colorado Springs, Colorado; and Michael Phillips, CFI.

We are privileged to work with the brilliant editorial team at Bethany House Publishers and offer sincerest gratitude to David Horton, our acquisitions editor, who immediately caught the vision for this story; Barbara Lilland and Rochelle Glöege, wonderfully talented development and line editors; Ann Parrish and Sharon Asmus, insightful reviewers; Jolene Steffer, Cheri Hanson, and Sabrina Rood, eagle-eyed proofreaders.

It is also a blessing to work with Paul Higdon, art director, and Dan Thornberg of Design Source Creative Services for such stellar cover art.

Finally, this story was covered with prayer by numerous people, including Beverly's dear father, Rev. Herb Jones, who devoted his daily prayer time during his two-year battle with cancer to the inspiration and far-reaching impetus of **Child of Mine**. Dad joined the Church Triumphant on January 9, 2014, prior to our book's publication.

> **"Since we have such a huge crowd of men of faith watching us from the grandstands, let us strip off anything that slows us down or holds us back, and especially those sins that wrap themselves so tightly around our feet and trip us up; and let us run with patience the particular race that God has set before us."**

Hebrews 12:1 TLB

—Dave and Beverly Lewis

**David Lewis** is the bestselling author of **Coming Home**, his first solo novel, as well as a keyboard artist and pilot. He is the first editor for his wife, Beverly Lewis, as well as research partner and manager. David was born in Minnesota, grew up in the Midwest, and met Beverly in Colorado, where they currently make their home.

**Beverly Lewis**, born in the heart of Pennsylvania Dutch country, is the **New York Times** bestselling author of more than ninety books. Her stories have been published in eleven languages worldwide. A keen interest in her mother's Plain heritage has inspired Beverly to write many Amish-related novels, beginning with **The Shunning**, which has sold more than one million copies and was recently made into an Original Hallmark Channel movie. In 2007 **The Brethren** was honored with a Christy Award.

Beverly has been interviewed by both national and international media, including **Time** magazine, the **Associated Press**, and the BBC. She lives with her husband, David, in Colorado. Visit her website at www.beverlylewis.com for more information.